I MARRIED A MOTHMAN

Prime Mating Agency

REGINE ABEL

CONTENTS

I MARRIED A MOTHMAN

He's everything she never knew she wanted.

When Venus embarked on a luxury cruise, she never expected to rescue a young Promethean demi-god—or that he'd bind her as his guardian. Now stranded on his primitive planet, she agrees to a temporary marriage of convenience to Atlas, the Commander of the Black Guard, in exchange for protection against those hellbent on seizing control of the youngling in her care. Against all odds, she finds herself falling for the sweet and honorable Atlas—antennae, scales, wings and all.

She is his light, his impossible dream.

As an Achromatic Promethean, Atlas has accepted that his society considers him lower than dirt, until the arrival of a fascinating human turns his life upside down. When forced to pick a husband, Venus not only chooses him over the elite, but treats him with a kindness and respect he's never experienced. As they join forces to thwart a threat to his people, her intelligence, beauty, and fierceness soon stir in him desires forbidden to his kind.

In their dire race against the clock, will Venus and Atlas solve the mystery of the impending cataclysm, or will it destroy everything, including the impossible happiness blossoming between them?

DEDICATION

To those who judge others based on their character, words, and deeds instead of arbitrary nonsense such as appearance, status, or wealth. To those who refuse to be crushed by the people who treat you as lesser in order to elevate themselves. Ignorance, especially when influenced by bigotry, greed, or fear can drive even usually kind people to commit the most atrocious actions.

You are not defined by how others perceive you or by what society deems desirable.

You are beautiful and worthy, just the way you are.

CHAPTER 1
VENUS

Serena and I exchanged a long, bone-crushing hug, although she did most of the crushing. While we were of the same height, Serena had always been the stronger and more muscular one. I released her with much reluctance, saddened by the fact that I wouldn't see her again for many weeks, if not for many months.

As much as I hated that her new life had taken her away from us even more than her previous hunting career, I couldn't resent the sincere happiness she found here on Trangor. Had anyone told me my baby sister would end up marrying a snakeman, I would have strongly suggested they urgently seek therapy. And yet, here we were.

I caressed her hair, my fingers lingering on the softness of her locks. Serena immediately narrowed her eyes at me. I snorted and made a face at her.

"Don't give me that look," I said mockingly. "I was merely thinking that your hair looks really healthy and smells incredibly good."

My sister puffed out her chest before giving me a smug

smile. "Of course it is. And guess what? It's all thanks to a hundred percent natural products."

I waved a dismissive hand. "Obviously. It's not like there are any spas or salons here," I replied, the disapproval highly audible in my voice. "But you know, I have a few acquaintances who would love to commercialize—"

"No!" Serena interrupted in a tone that brooked no argument while she leveled a stern stare at me.

I rolled my eyes and shrugged in concession. "You're hopeless. You've never learned to seize the countless opportunities that keep strutting their stuff in front of you."

"Venus, you're even more hopeless than I am. I don't need those *opportunities*. I have everything I need and want right here," Serena added, gesturing at her sons flanking her husband next to us, in the docking bay where I was readying to board my vessel.

It was Szaro's turn to puff out his chest and give me a taunting smile. I had never been particularly attracted to other species. While it freaked me out the first time I saw what species Serena had been forced to marry, I had to admit that my brother-in-law had grown on me. I no longer saw a being who was half cobra, half man, but a very muscular, fine-looking male, with a heart of gold, and who treated my sister like a goddess. I couldn't have hoped for a better partner for her.

"Fine, fine. Be that way," I retorted with pretend discouragement. "But you could use a manicure. And so do I for that matter."

Serena burst out laughing and shook her head at me like I was beyond redemption—which I was, in this instance.

"You're so high maintenance!" Serena chastised affectionately.

"I am, and shamelessly so," I deadpanned in an unrepentant tone before giving her one last hug.

"By the way, Mother is planning another exposition for

Belle. Both of them would be thrilled if you could make it," I said in a slightly more serious tone, my palms resting on the gorgeous golden scales she had developed on her shoulders and arms since bonding with her husband.

"We'll see," she said in her usual noncommittal fashion.

Ordosians never left their planet. Not only had they not bothered to develop space travel technology, but they also held zero interest in traipsing around the galaxy. In the six years since marrying her husband, Serena only left the planet five times. Each trip had been a very brief visit. The fact that it was her choice not to travel more often didn't make it any easier or lessen how much I missed her.

I turned to my nephews, Sethe and Gallen, the perfect miniature replicas of their father, with their snake tail instead of legs, human torso, and a face that was the loveliest mix of human and reptilian framed by a large hood. The boys each gave me the most tender embrace before stepping aside so that Szaro could do the same.

After one final wave, I headed towards the shuttle that would take me from the surface to the space station. With Trangor not allowing off-worlder tourism, this place was always empty. As the planet was still classified as primitive, the Prime Directive continued to severely restrict its access. Therefore, it cost a hefty sum to appoint a luxury cruise ship to make a detour here, pick me up, and take me home.

Needless to say, as soon as I checked into my cabin and dropped my luggage, I made a beeline for the spa. While enjoying a mani-pedi, and getting a facial, my thoughts kept going back to Serena. It shamed me that I should feel any envy towards her.

Obviously, her life wasn't for me. I was genuinely far too high maintenance and addicted to my creature comforts to rough it out in the outdoors looking after wild beasts or culling their numbers when they threatened their ecosystem like she did. But I couldn't deny longing for the type of obvious love she shared with her husband and children.

I resented my loneliness.

Sure, I loved my job. As a lobbyist—mostly in the medical engineering and sustainability fields—I got to put my finger on the scales that would have lasting impacts on cities, countries, and even entire planets or solar systems. I enjoyed a good mind game, spanking narcissists and assholes that wielded their power, wealth, and influence to crush others, and being the voice for those who had none. Unfortunately, that also meant I was constantly surrounded by superficial, greedy, and self-serving people. None of them qualified as mate material. The handful of decent potential partners had been snagged off the market a long time ago.

The fact that I was particularly picky and a strong, independent woman, didn't make things easier.

I headed back to my room, looking through what clothes I had brought with me. As Ordosians held few social gatherings, and since their people didn't wear clothes, I hadn't brought too many fancy outfits. After ten days straight of casualwear, I was way overdue to strut my stuff fully decked out. While boarding, I spotted a few members of the elite on their way to the bar. Shame still burned my gut that they glimpsed me so basically dressed and with my nails looking like they belonged to a harpy.

Prepare to be impressed!

A sudden pressure at the back of my head pulled me out of my superficial musings. I wasn't prone to headaches, but this one was quickly building. I stopped walking in the middle of the hallway and rubbed my temple then my nape. The discomfort didn't lessen, but it also didn't increase. Feeling both baffled and annoyed, I resumed walking towards my cabin, hoping I had some painkillers that would nip this in the bud as I had no intentions of remaining cooped up in my room.

To my dismay, the pressure increased with each step, going

from unpleasant to downright painful. I stopped again. Like the previous time, the pain remained at the same level, neither increasing nor dampening. Another step forward caused it to crank up a notch.

That's not possible!

Refusing to accept the horrible thought crossing my mind, I turned around and walked in the opposite direction. To my shock, the pain immediately decreased, each step further lessening it. Wanting to confirm my suspicions, I turned around again to head back towards my room. The pain came back with a vengeance.

Feeling on the verge of panic, I debated what to do. I doubted I could reach my cabin without the pain reaching a debilitating level. A million thoughts raced through my mind as I tried to make sense of what was happening.

I retraced my steps, the pressure-pain steadily waning. It completely vanished when I arrived directly in front of cabin 16A.

What the fuck is going on?

As soon as I walked past it, the pressure came back. I couldn't decide if whatever was causing this was trying to lure me to that cabin, or if that area was the only safe zone. Not wanting to be caught loitering in front of that room in case someone came out—or worse tried to drag me inside—I moved as far away as I could without the discomfort entering painful territory. As I began tapping a few instructions on my com—an advanced prototype I designed myself—a couple I didn't know entered the hallway.

My heart leapt with a mix of hope and worry. I shifted closer to the wall so as not to stand in their way and gave them a polite smile as they walked past me. They returned the smile before continuing on their way, seeming totally unfazed by whatever was affecting me.

More baffled than ever, I launched the short-range scanner

from my com. It immediately picked up the sonic signal emanating from cabin 16A. When I first realized something was happening, I feared we were under some form of sonic attack. In such instances, the aggressors used directed pulsed radio frequency energy to discreetly harm their targets. The effects would be gradual, from dizziness, to headaches, nausea, sensory defects, and flat-out brain damage.

But this was different.

Beyond the fact that sonic attacks normally had an area of effect, thereby impacting all the people within the targeted radius —not just a single person—the symptoms didn't manifest themselves this quickly, and certainly didn't fluctuate in real time the way mine were. But the dead giveaway was the fact that the signal emitted from that room did more than just specifically target me. Its frequency matched that of a telepathic communication. The scanner also clearly indicated it wasn't coming from a device but from some type of life form it couldn't identify, who shared the room with a human male.

That freaked me out even more.

Despite reorienting my career to mainly work as a lobbyist, I held a PhD in mechanical engineering, and still worked from time to time as a biomedical engineer. For years, I specialized in designing medical equipment meant to diagnose and heal foreign species using the most extensive database available in the known galaxy. What the hell kind of species was unknown to my device?

I immediately sent a message to the security team of the ship before using my high security clearance to send another message directly to the Enforcers. Having connections certainly came in handy. It didn't hurt that both my parents were also involved with the highest spheres of intergalactic politics, which opened many doors for me.

Although it felt like an eternity, the ship's security team arrived promptly. To my surprise, Captain Simmons himself was leading the three armed guards following him. He was a big, burly man in his late fifties. His muscular body testified to his previous career as a Space Marine before joining the largest commercial fleet to spend time with his new wife.

In a hushed tone, I swiftly explained what was happening and showed him my scan. His guards frowned at seeing my device, but Simmons didn't blink. He knew of my diplomatic security clearance, which allowed me to have and use technology forbidden to most common passengers. Obviously, this type of scanning could be deemed intrusive and a violation of people's privacy.

"Is there any way you can go wait in the safety of your cabin?" Captain Simmons asked.

I shook my head. "Believe me, I wanted nothing more than to call you guys from my cabin. But the pain was getting too debilitating to let me reach it."

"Very well. Stay here. Hopefully, we can get this swiftly resolved," he replied grimly.

Heart pounding, I watched the four men march resolutely towards the cabin. One of them kept walking past it, as another passenger entered the hallway. He gestured for her to stay put. Captain Simmons first pressed on the door chime before firmly knocking.

"Captain Simmons," he announced in a booming voice. "Please open the door."

It took about twenty endless seconds before the human male my scanner had detected opened the door. I couldn't see him from where I stood, and his voice was too hushed by the distance for me to clearly hear the conversation that ensued. However, judging by the increasingly stern way the captain was talking, I could guess the man was not being very cooperative. My stomach dropped when the two guards still flanking Simmons put their hands on the blasters hanging on their weapons belt.

"Mr. Tobin, we can do this the easy way, or the hard way,"

Simmons suddenly exclaimed. "Whether you like it or not, we're coming in to inspect your cabin. We have undeniable evidence that you smuggled an unauthorized life form on board. So you can step aside and let us investigate, or we can arrest you and still investigate. Any way you cut it, we're coming in."

"FUCK YOU!" the man named Tobin suddenly yelled.

I gasped and instinctively flattened myself against the wall when Captain Simmons lunged forward. The muffled sound of a blaster going off resonated in the distance, followed by the typical noises of physical battle. The two guards also charged forward. At the other end of the hallway, the passenger stopped by the third guard took cover behind the wall of the connecting corridor she had come from. Still, she poked her head forward, her wretched human curiosity taking over her sense of self-preservation.

The ruckus in cabin 16A quickly died down, indicating the captain and his men had managed to restrain Tobin.

"You can't do this! I have rights!" Tobin shouted.

For the next few minutes, he continued raging and shouting, the guards apparently completely ignoring him as they searched the cabin. According to my scanner, it was a three-room suite—deemed luxurious by most interstellar cruise ship standards but basic for our ship, the Radiant Star. While it didn't display detailed images of that location, it showed me the guards securing the first two rooms before heading to the back one where the unidentified being was located.

To my shock, the orange line indicating the sonic wave targeting me shifted to a blue color. This meant the frequency no longer had potential to be harmful. Only then did I realize that the pressure squishing my head had faded away. Instead, a lovely sound filled my ears. That wasn't quite the proper description as I wasn't actually hearing it through my ears. It felt more like telepathically hearing a hauntingly beautiful melody.

Flashes of color started appearing before my eyes as the

music grew into a crescendo. Mesmerized, I marveled at the life-size kaleidoscope swirling before me, drawing me in. Distant voices attempted to pierce through the music. The more I tried to cast them out, the more urgent they sounded. A part of me told me I should heed them, but I didn't want to.

"Miss Bello, STOP!" Captain Simmons shouted.

The frightened sound of his voice snapped me out of my daze. I blinked. My jaw dropped, and my heart nearly leapt out of my chest when I realized I was now standing inside cabin 16A and right in front of some sort of heating cushion. On top of it, what I could only describe as a large cocoon appeared to be glowing from within. Shimmering colors, reminiscent of the kaleidoscope that had floated before my eyes, danced over the rippling yet smooth surface.

I attempted to step away from it. Not only did I fail to emit any sound when I tried to gasp, but I watched in horror as my hand reached for the cocoon with a will of its own. Captain Simmons' large hand grabbed my forearm in an effort to drag me away. No sooner did he make contact than he cried out and fell to his knees. The glazed look in his eyes hinted that, like I had when I was entranced to walk here, he was hallucinating. That thing had taken over his mind.

But my hand coming into contact with the cocoon squashed any thought of the captain or his guards. A tingling sensation spread from my palm through my arms and entire body. My knees wobbled, and I started feeling faint, seconds before a stabbing sensation brutally pricked the center of my palm. Only then did the thrall break. I yanked my hand away and stumbled a few steps back. The tingling sensation multiplied a thousand-fold, and my vision blurred. Seconds before a veil of darkness descended before my eyes, I saw a sharp thorn-like spike resorb inside the cocoon before the seam closed shut.

CHAPTER 2
VENUS

I woke up with a start, the slow and steady beeping sound of medical machinery playing in the background. Not bothering to look at my surroundings, I lifted my hand before my face to examine my palm. Aside from a slight lingering redness where the puncture had occurred, I detected no clear sign of a prior wound.

Still shaken, I glanced around the room, my stomach dropping at the sight of the cocoon resting on a large hover stretcher, a few meters away from me.

Why the fuck would they bring that near me?

I jerked into a sitting position in the medical bed I was lying in, tempted to jump out and run away. But the sound of approaching voices stopped me. Seconds later, the door opened on two uniformed Enforcers—a male and a female—and Andrea, the ship's medical officer.

"Miss Bello! Good, you're awake," the male Enforcer said in an enthusiastic tone.

"Why the hell did you bring that thing here?" I exclaimed in lieu of a greeting. "It attacked me!"

He raised his palms in an appeasing fashion. "He didn't mean to harm you," he replied in a soothing tone before waving at Andrea. "As Nurse Raskin can confirm, you are in perfect health and totally safe. We will try to answer as many of your questions as we can. Unfortunately, we only know the basics. The higher ups will be able to fill the gaps once they get here. By the way, my name is Jordan Fisk, and this is my partner, Jessie Allard. I am a unit leader with the Enforcers. We received your call and were the closest team patrolling in the area."

"Hello, Agent Fisk, Agent Allard," I said, forcing myself to speak in a controlled tone, although my eyes kept glancing at the cocoon. "Thanks for coming so swiftly. What is that? And what did it do to me? Is it like an Atreall?"

He chuckled and shook his head.

"He is not an Atreall, although what he does shares some similarities," the agent conceded, a sliver of amusement sparkling in his green eyes. "He did not leave a mark on you like the Atreall Queen did to the Zamorian. But he did select you as a form of protector."

Two years ago, my sister's former enemy, Bayron, had been stung by an Atreall Queen who he had just saved from certain death. Heavily pregnant, and helpless until she could lay her eggs, it had been her way of appointing him as her royal guard until enough of her soldiers hatched to protect her new hive. But Bayron was one of the most formidable Hunters in existence. That this giant insect would choose him as her protector totally made sense. But who the heck would choose me?

"That's completely illogical!" I exclaimed, flabbergasted. "Do I look like a protector to you? I'm a politician. My weapons are sarcasm, using the law efficiently, and giving idiots the type of tongue lashing that requires stitches. So unless whatever this is expects me to verbally chew up someone or legally spank them, he made the wrong pick. And what is he, anyway?"

"He's a Promethean," Agent Fisk said matter-of-factly.

My jaw dropped, and my eyes nearly popped out of my head as I gaped at the cocoon. No wonder my scanner had been unable to identify the species it belonged to. The Prometheans fell under the strictest Prime Directive guidelines. Most of the galaxy—myself included—only found out about their existence a few months ago after the biggest drug bust on Shimli.

A few of them had been abducted by a Nazhral female running experiments on young Edocits—a dryad-like species. Edocit teenagers naturally produced special leaves in the vines adorning their hair, which acted like a wonderful recreational drug. The Nazhral female had hoped to integrate specific genetic traits from a few other species into those teenagers to transform their harmless leaves into the most addictive drug in the universe.

The Prometheans rescued during that mission allowed the rest of us to discover their existence. From what limited footage had been shared about them, they were a rather fascinating bipedal species aptly named in that they shared many similarities with the Promethea silk moth.

"Another kidnapping?" I asked, although it was more of a statement.

"Yes, and one that could have destroyed an entire species," Agent Allard replied in Fisk's stead, a somber expression on her face.

"An entire species?" I echoed, intrigued.

She nodded. "He is the rarest type of Promethean in existence. His people call him a Prism. Only one is born every three or four generations and plays a pivotal role in the survival of their world. Had you not detected his presence and enabled his rescue, there is a good chance their homeworld would be destroyed. An entire species owes you a debt of gratitude."

Once more, I found myself gaping in disbelief at the huge cocoon, the size of two large pumpkins side by side.

"Okay. That's kind of cool," I said carefully. "But I still don't understand why he stabbed me since the rescue was already almost completed. And why did you bring him here in my room?"

A terrible sense of unease washed over me when the two agents exchanged a hesitant look.

"As I stated earlier, people in higher positions are better suited to answer those questions," Agent Fisk said in a non-committal fashion. "All I can say is that he stung you to create a physical bond. The psychic waves he used to draw you to him could have damaged you over time. But you must remain near him to avoid any discomfort to you."

"For how long? Am I bound to him until he hatches?" I exclaimed, ready to lose my shit.

"If all goes well, you will be able to resume your journey home no later than tomorrow, and pretend like none of this ever happened," Agent Fisk said reassuringly.

My gut was screaming bullshit.

Still, they answered a couple more logistics questions before leaving me with the promise that a senior agent would be in contact with me within the hour. The agents left me with Nurse Andrea who ran another quick series of tests to make sure everything was fine. To my dismay, the agents were camping outside the Infirmary, ready to escort me back to my quarters, the cocoon on a hover platform cart in tow.

Room service brought a fancy meal to my cabin as I couldn't expose the Prism to the general public, and my attempt to go to the dining hall without him had me feeling on the verge of choking after only a few meters outside the room.

Saying I was livid was the understatement of the century.

Thankfully, less than twenty minutes after I returned to my cabin, I received a highly secured encrypted vidcall from the United Planets Organization's Intergalactic Affairs office. Seeing the face of Linsea Voln appearing on screen instantly twisted my insides.

As beautiful and lovely as the Temern female was, Linsea was only ever assigned to the most high-profile and critical cases of the UPO and the Enforcers—the intergalactic peacekeeping force of the UPO. But more importantly, her husband ran the Prime Mating Agency. He specialized in finding mates for the most primitive aliens in the galaxy. After the unfortunate events that could have led to the execution of my sister on Trangor, he was the one who orchestrated her marriage to Szaro to save her life.

Thanks to his empathic abilities, Linsea's husband Kayog could say with perfect accuracy if two people were soulmates after only conversing with them for a few minutes. While their two careers were completely unrelated, I couldn't help the uneasy feeling that the wretched birdman would strike again.

Despite the stiffness of her beak, Linsea smiled with a warmth that immediately put people at ease. With her beautiful white feathers with a few dark specks on her chest, she reminded me of a snow owl, though her eyes weren't round like with those birds but oddly human in their shape.

"Hello, my dear Venus," Linsea said in her delightful voice. "We meet again."

"We do. As delightful as I find you, I wish our meetings would occur under more joyous circumstances. At least—and I mean no offense—I'm relieved to see your husband isn't around," I said only partially joking.

She burst out laughing, her blue eyes sparkling with amusement and mischief. "Ouch. I felt that for my poor beloved. But fear not, my friend. We're not trying to match you."

"I'm glad to hear it," I mumbled, genuine relief flooding through me.

Despite my earlier thoughts of how I wished I could find my happily ever after like Serena, I had no desire whatsoever of landing on some primitive, backwater planet, with a mate who had never seen a com system or heard of a holodeck.

Her smile broadened for a few seconds before she sobered. I didn't have to ask what she was looking at when she glimpsed over my shoulder.

"It seems like heroic rescues run in your family," Linsea said in a more serious tone.

"Serena is the hero. I just happened to get psychically manhandled by a chrysalis who randomly picked me. Then I called security to deal with it. Except, it seems he's not done with me yet," I said in a grumpy tone.

"You were not randomly chosen, Venus," she countered, the way in which she said it piquing my curiosity. "The fact that you know diplomacy better than anyone makes you the perfect candidate for this, in more ways than one. This child is a Promethean Prism. Only one is born every hundred years or so. To his people, he is like a god."

"Then how did that Tobin guy get his hands on him?" I asked, intrigued.

"Like Saydi—the Nazhral who kidnapped the adult Prometheans for her drug experiments—Tobin violated the Prime Directive. In his case, he got 'lucky' and stumbled on something far more valuable than anything else he could have hoped for. The fool didn't even know what he had."

"Why kidnap that specific child if he didn't know how unique he was?" I argued.

"Promethean children grow the same way humans do. There is a live birth, and then they learn how to walk, talk, and fly while interacting with the rest of the world. Only a Prism transforms into a chrysalis," Linsea explained. "He realized that child was unique for that reason."

"Okay. But why did the kid pick me? What does he want from me? There are countless people on board, especially the security guards and now the Enforcers, who could do a much better job of keeping him safe."

"Like I said, he is god-like. He sensed something in you that convinced him you were the one that would keep him safe until he could be reunited with his people," she replied calmly.

"That's insane! I can't fight. When things went crazy with Bayron and the Atreall Queen, it made sense. But what do I have to offer that anyone else couldn't?" I insisted.

Linsea smiled. "He doesn't need you that way. You're basically his legal guardian. You will be his voice for now and get to make the decisions on his behalf until someone else among his people takes on that role."

"Like hell! I don't get to make any decisions. I can't even go to the bathroom without him choking me!" I exclaimed.

She gave me a sheepish expression, her majestic white wings shifting behind her. "That's only because he can sense your reluctance. The range will increase as soon as he feels confident you won't abandon him."

"I have a life of my own! I can't be stuck babysitting a chrysalis forever. How far is his planet even located? How long before I can go back to my own life? The way I understand it, whatever he injected me with cannot be taken out. I'm forced to stay with him until he lets go," I argued.

"If all goes as planned, as soon as the Prism is back on his homeworld Sylvar, he will release you," Linsea said in a reassuring tone.

"Well that's a good start," I grumbled. "How long before we get there?"

She gave me a mysterious look that got me genuinely intrigued. "The UPO and the Enforcers now enjoy some very quick transportation methods. They're not normally shared with civilians. An exception has been made in this instance since not only do you have a high security clearance, but we also want to quickly resolve this situation. We know too little about their species and cannot risk the Prism coming to harm by being away from his people."

"Okay, but tangibly what does that mean?"

"My goal is to have you on your way back home before the night is over," Linsea said smugly.

"I knew I liked you," I said with a broad grin.

She burst out laughing.

CHAPTER 3
ATLAS

Grinding my teeth with aggravation, I forced myself to keep a neutral expression on my face as I observed Ajustus Agar grandstanding once again. As Chancellor of our homeworld's Capital City Japhyr, he pretty much ruled over our people. And did he ever love reminding everyone of his status. It boggled my mind that he kept getting reelected each time his mandate ended, considering how the majority of the citizens hated him.

Sadly, he always won fairly, making it impossible for us to depose him.

"After your previous egregious failure, I dare hope the Black Guard will do much better in protecting the Prism once he's returned to us. Allowing him to be kidnapped is nothing short of treason," Ajustus snarled, his yellow wings deployed to the maximum to make himself look bigger and more imposing.

By the Lights, how was any of that *our* fault? The Prism was taken in Thesia, another large city located a three-day flight from here. In theory, Thesia's Black Guards could be blamed for that failure. But in reality, their population had grown so complacent that no guards had been assigned to little Xarin. My tongue burned with the urge to point these facts out. By the looks on the faces of my unit, they also ached to set the record straight. As that would be pointless and only give Ajustus more motives to berate us in self-righteous indignation, I kept my peace. At least, my highly-trained warriors displayed their impeccable discipline and also remained stoic.

If he only knew how much my hands itched to tear off his antennae and shred his wings. However powerful his magic, he wouldn't stand a chance against me or any of my guards.

"Thankfully, and with my full collaboration, my high-ranking off-world contact's troops were able to find and rescue the Prism. Ambassador Linsea Voln will arrive any minute now to return our beloved Xarin. I expect you to keep the peace among the attendees and bring no further shame to your forces."

It took every shred of my willpower not to roll my eyes in disbelief. Of course, the pompous narcissist would try to take credit for the rescue of the young Prism. Before the off-worlder female named Linsea contacted him earlier today, the Chancellor had been just as panicked as the rest of us at the thought of what would befall our world should Xarin not be recovered in time, if ever.

"You will not find our performance lacking," I replied as diplomatically as I could.

"See that I don't, Razus Atlas," Ajustus said in that haughty tone that always got under my scales.

With this, the foul male turned around and headed out of the antechamber we were standing in and into the Great Hall. A good thing, too, because I doubted my warriors and I would manage to rein ourselves in much longer.

Although he wasn't actually our monarch, Ajustus strutted his way in, his chin high, chest puffed out to further display his lustrous golden fur, and his wings spread out to flaunt they're bright yellow color, orange gradients, and blue eyespots that marked him as a powerful polychromatic. Considering what a formidable fire mage those colors would have made him with proper training, it always surprised me he hadn't followed a Warrior or Hunter career. Then again, he wasn't selfless enough to put his life on the line in the defense of others.

Like in most governmental buildings and large social gathering places, the Great Hall would almost be deemed depressing by Promethean standards. While stunning in its design with four-meter-high vaulted ceilings, intricate carvings adorning the ceilings and walls, the dominance of white and gray everywhere clashed with the otherwise colorful pallets used elsewhere.

The Black Guard faced a lot of resistance when they demanded such changes a few generations ago. The Senate, Great Hall, courthouse and Grand Plaza all used to be awash with every possible color to meet the needs of the people. However, having such readily available sources to channel from enabled great tragedies when disgruntled criminals unleashed their lethal powers unto unsuspecting victims. As very few people could channel magic using white or gray, it significantly reduced the risk of unfortunate incidents.

With their usual discipline, my guards spread out in front of the colorful crowd that filled both sides of the rectangular hall. A single glance confirmed that, as usual, the vast majority of the nearly one hundred people allowed inside were Polychromatics, wealthy, or highly influential. Monochromatic Prometheans—or worse, Achromatic ones like my guards and I—were not deemed good enough for such an important event.

While we didn't expect any type of criminal activity, we needed to be ready to intervene at the first sign of trouble. We had no reason to expect any threat to the Prism. Our people quite literally worshiped him. But that same religious fervor sometimes prompted certain people to throw themselves at him. It only took one to get a mass movement of people rushing the Prism to receive his blessing or merely to touch him. In this instance, as he was still inside his chrysalis, a mob might damage the cocoon, forcing Xarin to expend energy to repel them that he should otherwise keep for his maturation.

Moments after we finished taking our positions, the foreign device Chancellor Ajustus had been given by the off-worlders started beeping.

"They're coming!" Ajustus exclaimed, his voice bubbling with excitement.

A hush descended over the crowd. Their palpable excitement reflected the one I felt. It wasn't just the fact that I would be in the presence of a Prism—which in itself was the blessing of a lifetime—but also the fact that we would see off-worlders again. They were the strangest beings we ever beheld.

The ripping sound of thunderclap resonated through the hall, and a giant dark portal opened in the wide space at the bottom of the elevated dais upon which Ajustus stood. To his left and right, six on each side, the members of the Senate looked on.

I stared in awe as a human first stepped out of the swirling dark circle that acted as a gateway between distant planets and ours. As powerful as Promethean magic was, none of us could perform something so incredible it defied logic.

I recognized the human male as Tedrick Wilson. He escorted the Shimli Survivors back home—our brethren who had previously been abducted by a feline-looking species to perform experiments on a hallucinogenic leaf. Seconds later, a bird-like female also came out of the portal. I had seen her as well that previous time. She acted as an ambassador for a coalition of planets. It still boggled my mind that those strangers had developed the technology to fly off their homeworld and visited each other so frequently they ended up forming an alliance. I couldn't even begin to fathom how they built something capable of such a feat.

Her appearance still threw me off. I struggled to come to terms with the fact that she was a bipedal, sentient, and talking bird. Granted, her body had much in common with ours, with two arms, two legs, and a pair of wings. But her face entirely belonged to a bird, including a beak. The three segments of her legs, complete with talons, further reinforced her avian appearance. And yet, there was no denying that she was a person, not an animal.

The most disturbing part though was the presence of a White Achromatic in our midst. Seeing her that first time sent the population into a panic. Whites were too dangerous to be allowed near populated areas. They weren't evil, far from it. But as they could channel every color, all it took was for them to lose control during an emotional peak to blast enough energy to raze a city to the ground. It was only once our Archmagus confirmed she didn't possess the ability to channel colors that people calmed down. And yet, their discomfort lingered as they watched her approach the dais.

"Greetings, Chancellor Ajustus," the female bird said in a melodic voice. I had forgotten just how pleasant and soothing it sounded. "Thank you for receiving us on such short notice."

"Ambassador Linsea, Officer Tedrick, it is a pleasure to see you again, especially under such circumstances. Of course, everything is secondary to seeing to the welfare of the Prism," he said in that pompous fashion he loved taking in public.

That the off-worlder addressed him by his given name further supported his claims of having a close relationship with them. Naturally, he addressed them the same way to make sure everyone knew of their special rapport.

By the Eternal Lights, how I despise that male.

To my shock, the large portal closed. The same confused—not to say worried—look settled on every face. Even Ajustus' boastful expression gave way to a frown.

"Speaking of which, where is he?" Ajustus asked, failing miserably to hide the suspicion seeping into his voice.

"He is coming," Linsea said in a reassuring tone. "He's currently with his chosen Prima, a lovely woman named Venus

Bello. As she is unfamiliar with your people, and you with her, we thought it would be preferable for Tedrick and I to be here to receive her and the Prism. She might be lost and confused, and we wouldn't want any unfortunate diplomatic incident to occur while returning young Xarin to his people."

The Chancellor's shoulders slightly relaxed, as did the tension that had begun to take root among the attendees.

"That is a sound approach," Ajustus conceded.

"We want things to go smoothly," Linsea continued. "Venus is also looking forward to returning to her own life once she has discharged this important duty."

I repressed a smile. That female was growing on me. I never considered myself much of a diplomat, but I could appreciate it when someone defused a situation with tact while also putting people in their place. Indeed, the female Xarin claimed as his Prima had no reason to feel particularly blessed by what would likely be a burden for her. A non-Promethean would undoubtedly resent being shackled against their will to someone they understood nothing about.

"Of course," Ajustus replied, his smile a little strained this time. "We appreciate the sacrifice the Prima made on behalf of Xarin. We look forward to setting her free."

As if in response to that comment, another thunderclap resonated in the room followed by the appearance of a new portal. This time again, another male walked out first. While he also had a pale skin like Tedrick, his hair was a coppery reddish hue instead of black. I caught myself involuntarily nodding in approval. Between his white skin and reddish hair, he could invoke decent combat magic as well. But as Ambassador Voln said the Prima was a female, I stretched my neck to see who else would come out.

To my dismay, the female in question turned out to be a brown-colored Monochromatic. Despite sharing their shock, my guards and I quickly silenced the disbelieving murmur that rose from the attendees by glaring sternly at them.

Such a choice for a guardian defied logic. Granted, brown Monochromatics—especially those with her specific shade—could display powerful earth magic. Her skin tone was found abundantly in nature, from the rich soil to ancestral trees. But didn't her black hair curse her with the same limited magic that Achromatic Prometheans like my guards and I possessed?

Or does it shield her like it shields us?

Only then did I notice the lovely shade of red on her plush lips and on her nails. Brown and red were a powerful combination. Had it been in her hair, she would have combined respectable earth and firepower, likely strong enough to hurl molten lava at an enemy. But was such a small amount of red on her enough to invoke that kind of magic?

On further inspection, it suddenly struck me that the red shading on her lips and nails wasn't integral to her, but aesthetic additions. Could she still use them to channel color magic? After all, Prometheans also wore accessories in the colors they could channel in case they were stuck in an environment where that color wasn't naturally present.

Despite the extensive amount of clothes covering her, Venus shared many of our females' traits. Her body was quite harmonious and perfectly drawn. Her nose, lips, and the oval shape of her face would be deemed very attractive among my people. But those strange eyes, too small and with irises and pupils like animals unsettled me. The absence of frontal scales, the lack of antennae, and especially the missing wings took away too much.

By the Lights, I had so many questions about that species. It saddened me that Venus Bello couldn't stay a little longer. I would love to pick her mind about her people and the worlds beyond.

As soon as the Prism came out of the portal, following the human on a cushioned floating platform, the entire crowd started clapping their wings, the soft humming hailing the return of our savior with the proper level of deference. My own wings joined in on the clapping with a will of their own. I felt humbled to be in his presence.

The human Prima seemed slightly taken aback by this greeting. The way her eyes, as dark as her hair, flicked this way and that, we probably looked just as strange to her as she did to us. However, I saw no fright or disgust on her surprisingly pleasant features. In truth, a hefty dose of awe superseded her understandable curiosity.

"My dear Venus, here you are," Linsea said in a warm tone as soon as the clapping stopped.

There was something incredibly welcoming and soothing in the way that female spoke. Even though the words had not been addressed to me, I instantly felt the desire to smile.

"Hello, again Linsea," Venus said.

Her polished, throaty voice felt like a warm summer breeze flowing over my skin at the moment of initiating a flight. Her accent made it even more enthralling. As I understood it, most off-worlders were implanted at a young age with a galactic translation device. While they also learned a common language called Universal, they used the device to be able to converse with species that either couldn't speak it due to anatomical limitations or struggled to master it because of too great a difference in thought or speech pattern.

In our case, we didn't speak Universal—although Chancellor Ajustus had hinted we would need to in the near future. Therefore, their leading organization called the UPO had included our language into their device. It then sent signals to their brains, allowing them to speak their thoughts in our tongue. As their muscles had not been trained to pronounce certain sounds—or maybe they lacked the ability to form them—it made for a delightful accent.

"Venus, this is Chancellor Ajustus Agar, leader of the

Promethean Capital City Japhyr," Linsea said, waving at Ajustus. "Chancellor, this is Venus Bello, the Prism's temporary Prima and rescuer."

"Greetings, Chancellor Agar," Venus said.

I instantly loved the polite way she responded, with the proper level of deference due to his rank but without the obsequiousness people far too often gave him. I always hated it when people fell all over themselves merely for being in the presence of some high-ranking personality.

"Greetings to you, Venus Bello," Ajustus said.

Although his tone couldn't be found lacking, I knew the wretch enough to read contempt and superiority in his demeanor. While it surprised me that Xarin chose a Monochromatic Prima, Ajustus likely found it offensive that she received such a tremendous honor. My hatred for the male cranked up another notch.

"Thank you for finding and returning our Prism. We are in your debt," Ajustus continued in an appropriate tone. "I will be happy to take over his care."

As he spoke those words to her, his gaze shifted greedily towards Xarin's shimmering chrysalis. That didn't go unnoticed, and Venus narrowed her eyes at him in a subtle fashion. That piqued my curiosity. Although nothing in her behavior betrayed that sentiment, at a visceral level, I sensed she was an excellent judge of character and instantly disliked Ajustus.

That made me like her.

"Are you his father?" Venus asked.

Under different circumstances, I might have burst out laughing at the offended expression that settled on the Chancellor's face and in response to the hushed gasps that rose from the crowd. Ajustus essentially imposed himself as Xarin's new Primus. Many mumbled about it, but no one voiced their objection. Although the human had asked the question in a totally innocent tone, I didn't miss the underlying challenge, and neither had Ajustus.

"I am not Xarin's sire," he replied stiffly. "His parents are dead, murdered by the off-worlders who abducted him. An unfortunate turn of events. But their survival wouldn't have made much of a difference, anyway."

Venus visibly recoiled, while Linsea flinched.

"Excuse me?" Venus asked, outrage seeping into her voice.

"Parents rarely keep the guardianship of the Prism," Ajustus said with a dismissive wave of his hand. "Therefore, even if they still lived today, the likelihood of Xarin remaining in their care would be slim. Each prismatic generation chooses the person best suited for such an honorific role until the Prism ascends."

He puffed out his chest as he spoke those last words, making it clear he was referring to himself. Although subtle, I didn't miss the way Venus's stare hardened. I shared her disgust. While his words were correct in that the birth parents rarely took on the Primus role, he didn't need to be so callous and dismissive of their deaths.

"I see," Venus replied in a noncommittal fashion.

"Well, thank you again for your service," Ajustus said, clearly impatient to put an end to this. "What compensation can we offer you for the inconvenience?"

This time, Venus made no effort to hide how contemptible she found his words. Even I bristled at such rudeness. If he wanted to reward her for her heroic actions, he should have merely presented her with the gift. By asking what compensation she required, he turned her act of altruism into a basic mercantile transaction if she listed anything.

"I require no *compensation*," Venus said in a clipped tone. "No one should be taken from their home without their consent. I'm glad I was able to make sure this innocent child—and one visibly important to your people—is now safely back where he belongs. But as I relinquish my duty, it is only natural that I should inquire who will now look after him."

"There is nothing for you to concern yourself about," Ajustus said in a haughty tone. "Your part is done. And we're grateful for it."

Venus pinched her lips. Although clearly displeased by this interaction, she kept her thoughts to herself. However, it was the troubled expression on Linsea's face that held my attention. She glanced in turn at Xarin then at Venus, a frown creasing her feathery brow.

"Goodbye then, Chancellor," Venus said in a polite voice devoid of any warmth before turning to the chrysalis. "And goodbye, little Xarin," she added in a much softer tone.

To our collective shock, she raised her palm as if to caress the cocoon only to catch herself at the last second. For a brief instant, I wondered if the Prism had stopped her, or if she reined herself in out of respect. But my antennae quivered as the haunting melody of the Prism's song soared in the room. A shiver ran down my spine, and I felt heated to my core, as if the heavenly Lights had wrapped around me in a warm embrace.

The song wasn't aimed at me or any of the other attendees, but at Venus. I knew beyond any doubt that the enticing melody prompted her to press her palm against the chrysalis after all. She gave it a couple of gentle caresses, and its surface shimmered like the dancing lights that sometimes lit up the northern skies.

A wistful smile stretched her lips before she pulled her hand away. The song ended, snapping her out of the trance-like state it had put her in. Stunned, she glanced at her palm as if expecting to see something in it. She blinked, finding it unchanged before peering inquisitively at Xarin. She shook her head as if some-thing didn't make sense then started heading towards the portal.

To my surprise, Ambassador Linsea didn't follow Venus. Instead, she tilted her head in that strange way birds often did when they observed something. Seconds later, Venus's steps faltered, and her hand flew to her throat, as if she was struggling to breathe.

"Impossible!" Ajustus hissed.

Venus turned around, shock and confusion visible on her features. She backtracked towards the chrysalis, and instantly appeared to be able to breathe more easily.

"What's going on? You're home!" Venus said to the cocoon, with obvious confusion.

Despite my own wish to bear witness to what was happening, I forced myself to focus on the crowd that was becoming agitated at this unexpected turn of event.

Unexpected for everyone but the Ambassador.

Among all those present, Ambassador Linsea was the only one who didn't look shocked. It then dawned on me that, as an empath, she felt Xarin's reluctance at letting Venus go just yet. That likely explained her disturbed expression earlier.

"Prism, you no longer need the human," Ajustus said in an imperious tone while descending the three steps of the dais to come stand next to the hovering platform upon which the chrysalis rested. "You are among your people. I will watch over you and protect you until the time of your ascension comes."

He reached a hand towards the chrysalis to touch it in an appeasing fashion similar to what Venus previously did.

He never made contact.

The cocoon's mesmerizing shimmering colors turned into a toxic green while a series of spikes spread all over its surface. The Chancellor recoiled, yanking his hand back seconds before he would have touched one of the most virulent toxins on Sylvar. Although I doubted the Prism would have given him a lethal dose, the toxin would have had Ajustus writhing on the floor in agony for hours if not days until he purged it out of his system.

His golden scales darkened over his beige skin, making them stand out even more in this public humiliation. The crowd erupted in shouts and gasps, quickly followed by increasingly loud arguments that their leader and presumed official Primus should be so soundly rejected.

"Calm!" I shouted, raising my palms and spreading my black

wings to draw the frantic crowd's attention. "Calm! Control yourselves!"

My guards also spread their wings and echoed my words. All of us prayed we wouldn't need to move to more coercive methods. Whenever the Black Guard had to discipline Polychromatics or the elite, the latter always made sure to retaliate in all manners of underhanded methods against every Monochromatics and Achromatics. They had the wealth and power to get away with it.

"Ajustus!" Senator Cassius called in a booming voice that instantly claimed everyone's curiosity. "It appears the Prism still wants the human as his Prima."

I didn't miss the mockery in his voice as he spoke those words. His indigo wings testified to his gentler disposition as he was on the calm spectrum. But their yellow eyespots also hinted at the searing nature that lurked behind that stoicism. As a high-ranking member of the Senate, he could have easily claimed the role of Chancellor, especially since he never hid his disapproval of Ajustus in that role. And yet, not once in the past three elections had he presented himself as a candidate for the position.

"That is not possible or acceptable!" Ajustus exclaimed. "By law, only a Promethean can be a Primus to the Prism. She is an off-worlder who knows nothing of our ways, and who is eager to go back to her own life."

"True though this may be, the fact remains that Xarin has chosen her and refuses to let her go. So, she will just have to become a Promethean."

CHAPTER 4
VENUS

Saying I was seething couldn't even begin to describe the anger raging inside of me. Aside from feeling blindsided, I hated being trapped and held against my will. At the same time, I couldn't even hate Xarin—whatever a being in his current state of development would be described as. In his shoes—or rather chrysalis—I also wouldn't have wanted that slimeball Ajustus having any kind of power or control over me. But surely there was one Promethean among the countless folks in the crowd that could become a suitable Primus?

When that other male suggested I became one of them, the crowd went berserk. While the black Prometheans—who acted like some sort of royal guards—tried to rein them in, one of them swiftly led us out of the Great Hall and into this meeting room.

Under different circumstances, I would marvel at the stunning beauty of our surroundings. Like the Great Hall, the walls had been intricately sculpted like the plaster carvings in a Marrakesh mansion. Here again, gray shades dominated. I could only presume it was to avoid any clashes with their colorful population. But I was too pissed to enjoy the architecture or decor.

My eyes threw daggers at Linsea, the burning suspicion which had taken root while we still stood in the Great Hall cranking up another notch.

"You knew this was going to happen, didn't you?" I snarled at the Temern.

She shifted her wings uneasily, her sheepish expression confirming her guilt.

"You trapped me!" I hissed.

"No, Venus. I promise you, I didn't," Linsea replied in a firm but gentle tone. "When I first heard about the Prism choosing you instead of one of your ship's security guards, I began to suspect he might have a greater purpose for you. After all, you possess unique talents that are extremely convenient for the situation here on Sylvar. But the moment you both exited the portal, the emotions Xarin broadcast in the presence of Ajustus made it clear to me things would not go smoothly."

"None of this makes sense! I won't argue with the kid's unwillingness to have the Chancellor as his guardian," I said as tactfully as I could, despite my anger.

Although the guard left us alone in the room with Xarin, he and Tedrick were standing right outside the door. However primitive their technology was, and even though I couldn't detect any spying device in the room, I knew better than to underestimate the possibility that Prometheans might possess extremely acute hearing. Talking trash about their leader—especially one that struck me as being a narcissist—wouldn't benefit me in any way.

"But why in the world is he latching on to me? I know nothing about their world. Surely he can sense by now that I want nothing to do with any of this," I argued.

"I cannot tell you what he specifically wants you to do and can only speculate," Linsea replied in a commiserating tone. "But until we find a replacement Primus who he will deem acceptable, you will have no choice but to remain by his side. None of us can do anything about it, even if we wanted to. He has created a psychic and biological bond with you. It's not like there's an implant that we could remove from you."

"So what the hell does that mean?" I asked with a mix of outrage and disbelief. "I'm not mommy material! I'm the type who only hugs a baby for thirty seconds while they're smiling or nodding off. I don't do diapers, and I especially don't do crying. I'm the worst type of person to take care of their Prism baby! And I sure as hell refuse to be stranded here for the next eighteen years!"

Linsea chuckled, her beautiful eyes sparkling with genuine amusement. "You will have absolutely no maternal duties to perform, and especially not for eighteen years. Xarin only needs you to be his eyes and voice. Before entering his cocoon, he consumed all the food he needs until he reaches maturity. He will emerge a full adult within the next four months. At which point, assuming he has not released you by then, you will be free."

"Unless something else goes awry, and he decides I should stick around a while longer," I countered, the same anger audible in my voice.

She shook her head firmly.

"No. There will be nothing beyond that. This, I can promise you."

While I was far from being mollified, hearing the conviction in her voice slightly appeased me. It still didn't resolve my problem, but four months already sounded much better than eighteen years.

"The Prism is like a prophet. According to the Promethean lore, Xarin is reborn once every century or so, right before a major cataclysm that occurs on a recurring cycle. He plays an important role in balancing the beacons upon which the very existence of this world and of its people rely. He's also the only one able to cleanse some of the scorched lands that are struck by Thaudras—the cataclysm in question."

"And then?" I asked, unable to hide my curiosity, although I had more questions about whatever the beacons were.

"And then he dies, only to return when he's needed again," Linsea said, matter-of-factly. "The Prism is ephemeral. Once he emerges from his chrysalis, his lifespan rarely exceeds a few weeks. The one known to have lived the longest walked their world for nearly six months. But their people had also faced the greatest tragedy of their history. It would be too long for me to go into details about it right now, but know that if he chose you, it is because you will play an important—if not vital—role that will define the future of all Prometheans until he next returns."

That struck me hard, my anger instantly fading to be replaced by sadness and compassion that he should have such a heavy burden to carry out in such a short time. The instinctive wave of protectiveness that surged through me left me reeling.

I opened my mouth only to have the Temern shake her head in response to the comment I had not even spoken yet.

"No, Venus. His fate cannot be changed. Nor does he want it to be. He has a purpose, and he is looking forward to it. Do not feel sad for him. But your reaction confirms you are the right choice. He perceived your compassion. I can feel his love for you and the great hope he lays at your feet," Linsea said in a gentle tone.

I didn't know how to handle this situation, or how I even felt right now.

"Your family has been involved in the highest spheres of intergalactic politics for generations," Linsea continued, this time tension seeping into her voice. "I believe this is the reason why Xarin chose you. This world needs you."

"What are you saying?" I asked, genuinely shocked. "This planet is under the highest restriction level of the Prime Directive. By rights, we shouldn't even be here. These people shouldn't know of our existence. I absolutely cannot meddle in their affairs, least of all in their politics. It would completely derail their evolution."

To my shock, instead of immediately concurring with me, Linsea hesitated.

"In theory, you are correct."

"In *theory*?!" I exclaimed.

"Ignorance, especially when influenced by religious beliefs, can drive even the kindest people to commit the most atrocious actions," Linsea said carefully. "We must let every culture make their own decisions. However, when faced with genocide, what is more important? Observing the rules or bending them a little?"

"Genocide?" I asked, my stomach dropping.

"We know very little about the Prometheans. Their entire culture relies on magic fueled by their ability to channel colors. The extent of their power isn't dependent on skill but on genetics. What colors they can channel are directly linked to those found in their wings. The more colors, the more powerful, and the more influential each individual is."

"The fewer colors and the further down the ladder you are," I said with sudden understanding.

She nodded with a grim expression. "The Monochromatic and Achromatic Prometheans live a pretty harsh life. And with the impending cataclysm, things will only get worse for them. You're a mechanical engineer. Your scientific knowledge and your political acumen give you all the tools needed to avert a disaster."

"How are their fate and the cataclysm related?" I asked, battling an uneasy suspicion.

"Like many primitive species, Prometheans believe that natural disasters are divine punishments. To them, the power surges in their beacons are a sign of the wrath of Kiaris, the Goddess of Light. To appease her, they sacrifice those considered as a stain among their people."

"No!" I breathed out, horrified.

"During your stay here, you might be able to understand the nature of the energy source that emanates from the power cores they call Sibris. That loosely translates as beacon or light well in Universal. And with that, you could provide the Prometheans with the scientific explanation—and maybe even solution—to put an end to those genocidal sacrifices."

I narrowed my eyes at her. While I didn't doubt she genuinely wanted to avert those senseless deaths, I suspected a different motivation explained why they assigned *her* to this matter instead of one of the lesser ranked ambassadors of the UPO.

"Why did they send *you* here?" I challenged. "What's in it for the UPO?"

She smiled, doing me the honor not to insult my intelligence with lies.

"There are many reasons. Averting the sacrifices I outlined is definitely the main one," Linsea said in a noncommittal fashion.

"The main one for *you*. But what about for the UPO?" I insisted. "My money says they're quite interested in finding out more about that energy source."

Her smile slightly broadened, and a glimmer of approval sparked in her eyes. "See? You are the perfect candidate for this situation. Obviously, the United Planets Organization is always interested in new energy sources, especially one as powerful as this one, which also happens to be extremely clean. Except when Thaudras occurs. It's a cataclysmic event similar to a solar flare erupting from those beacons. By the time it ends, it's like a nuclear bomb went off with all the radioactive fallout. We need to figure out why it's happening, and how to prevent it."

"And then hope that, in their infinite gratitude, the Prometheans will be open to trade talks with the UPO," I replied, my voice dripping with sarcasm. "I won't lie, Ambassador, I'm a little disappointed to see you play these games."

Instead of bristling or recoiling with indignation, Linsea gave me an indulgent, almost maternal look, like a parent would with a child that clearly still had a lot to learn.

"You, better than anyone, should know that, in politics, it's always a game of give and take. I have no interest in energy sources, any more than you do in enriching yourself whenever you lobby to push forward your agendas. How many shady deals have you consented to in order to make sure lesser planets had access to the biomedical resources they needed?" she asked, a hint of challenge in her voice.

I pursed my lips and bowed my head in concession.

"We all do what we must to achieve our goals. When I met my husband, I made it clear that my greatest aspirations were charity work with those who had no power, no voice, no leverage," she continued, a hard glimmer appearing in her eyes. "I soon realized that altruistic endeavors took you nowhere unless you were in a position of power. I do more good and have greater influence as a UPO ambassador than I did as a militant. If that means I have to trample some of my principles to make a difference, the price is well worth the reward."

"You really believe there is an impending genocide?" I asked in a much gentler tone, feeling duly chastised.

"I do. I think you can stop it—and I'm convinced he believes it as well," she added, glancing at the cocoon in the corner of the room. "Naturally, we will provide you with any equipment and scientific or technical assistance you may require to help solve this mystery and save these people."

"Fine. I'm willing to give this a go, though I'm not sure how much of a difference I can make. So what does becoming a Promethean entail?" I asked in a grumpy tone.

The mischievous glimmer that sparked in her eyes instantly had my spine stiffening with preemptive dread.

"Like with your sister's new people—the Ordosians—the only way to become a Promethean is through birth or marriage," Linsea deadpanned.

"Oh, hell no!" I exclaimed, jumping to my feet. "You guys are not pulling this shit on me!"

She chuckled and raised her palms in an appeasing fashion. "Peace, Venus. Peace. Please sit. The two situations are not the same *at all*. Technically, nobody can force you to marry, but I strongly suggest you do. Since the Prism chose you, whether Ajustus or anyone else disagrees, Xarin will remain under your care until he chooses someone else or hatches. If you do not marry, you will be no more than a guest—almost an employee— of whoever will be your host. And make no mistake, Ajustus will demand you reside in his house, if you remain a guest."

"Fuck that!" I hissed as I let myself drop back into my chair like a child throwing a tantrum.

My mother would spank me raw if she witnessed my behavior since this whole ordeal began. Usually, I was almost frighteningly cool in stoicism during tense debates and perfectly reined in my propensity to have a potty mouth. Cussing in a diplomatic setting was unbecoming. But this whole situation had me on edge.

"I figured you'd feel that way," Linsea said with a mocking smile. "With marriage, you become a free citizen and Xarin's true legal guardian. You make all the decisions regarding both yourself and Xarin. So long as your actions do not break their laws, Ajustus will have no say. Please note that it's purely a contractual union. You won't be expected to mate with your partner, and you will be able to dissolve the marriage the moment the Prism releases you. Naturally, the UPO will take care of relocating you back home as soon as you're free."

"How can you be so certain the Prometheans will go for that? This entire mess literally just happened," I challenged.

The Temern gave me a smug expression. "What do you think I was doing before contacting you? Every scenario was explored with the Promethean Senate before our arrival. They didn't believe this outcome was possible. But like I said, the moment the Prism chose *you* over a warrior, my gut told me he had greater plans for you. I like being prepared for all eventualities."

Once more, I glared at her with resentment, despite being grateful she was on top of things. The wretch only seemed amused by my annoyance.

"Assuming I even go through with this madness, they are a primitive species. How do they treat females?" I asked.

Linsea waved a dismissive hand. "While Prometheans are not advanced technologically, for them, dominance is defined by magic, not physical strength. Therefore, gender bears no importance in the power dynamics. Male and females are equal in all the ways that matter. So do not fear."

My shoulders relaxed as I shed the tension I had not realized was stiffening my back.

"At least, that's a positive," I grumbled. "But that's still a hell of a gamble. Do I get to choose my husband, or are they going to impose one on me? How would I even pick when I don't know any of them? What if the male I end up with is a total douchebag? And when does this whole thing have to go down?"

"All very valid questions," Linsea said in a friendly tone. "You certainly get to choose, and it doesn't have to be a male. You can marry a female if you prefer. But to make sure you are paired with someone that will be agreeable for you to cohabit with for the next few months, Kayog will assist you in making that choice."

"Oh, fuck that! I do *not* want your husband anywhere near this!" I exclaimed, panic immediately settling in the pit of my stomach.

To my surprise, instead of being offended by my instinctive outburst, Linsea laughed, genuinely amused by my distress.

"My dear, you are such a gem. My poor beloved will get a good laugh at seeing how terrified you are at the thought he might find your soulmate for you," she said with a chuckle. "But he's not coming here to match you. He's just going to help find someone that you can have pleasant and friendly interactions with. Wouldn't you prefer that than to find out the hard way that you made a terrible choice?"

"Yes, I get that. But you're a Temern, too! Why can't you help me assess who is a good candidate?" I argued.

She gave me a sympathetic smile. "I *am* a Temern, but my husband possesses an extremely rare trait amongst our people. He is what we call an Edal—an empath who can hear souls. The rest of us can feel emotions, but he goes beyond that. When I asked him to describe it, Kayog said it sounds almost like a melody to him. Each person has a unique song that can only be matched by their soulmate. The same way you recognize someone by their face or voice, my husband recognizes souls by their song. When you hear a popular song, even when interpreted by someone else, with different instruments, and even in a different style, you still know what song it is."

"So when he meets someone new and recognizes their song as one he heard before, he knows he found their perfect match," I said with sudden understanding. "But that's not what we want for me."

Linsea nodded. "Correct. But once he hears your song, he'll be able to assess which Promethean has a melody that harmonizes with yours. To compare with human music, if your song is classical, he will instantly know not to pair you with someone who is death metal."

"I bet Ajustus's song sounds like that annoying circus music," I muttered.

Linsea burst out laughing. "Oh, Venus, you truly are delightful! I promise, you will not regret this. And it needs to happen quickly. Tedrick already informed my husband, who should be here any minute now. He was finalizing a wedding for one of his recent matches."

I scrunched my face, still unable to believe this was happening. "My parents are going to lose it."

Unfazed in the least, Linsea cocked her head in that strange way birds often did, an amused expression on her beautiful face.

"They certainly will, and my office will not hear the end of it for the next few weeks until you return home. But you will be a heroine, just like Serena has been. As upset as they were by the situation, her heroic rescue and arranged marriage boosted their fame and status among the galactic community. And if my gut proves me right—yet again—you will be even more famous for how you will change the fate of an entire species."

"No pressure," I mumbled.

Fifteen minutes later, Tedrick knocked on the door before entering the room with the same guard who had escorted us here. Everything about that guard was black, but for his greige skin, and the silver eyespots in his wings. Based on what Linsea said, he likely fit in the Achromatic or Monochromatic category. Would he be sacrificed, too, when that Thaudras cataclysm occurred?

Despite my strong phobia when it came to bugs and any type of creepy crawlers, I couldn't deny Prometheans held a certain beauty. Their oversized eyes, fully black without sclera were a little unsettling, but their faces and bodies were otherwise mostly humanoid.

From where I stood, this male looked rather handsome, with wavy black hair, sinfully sexy lips, a cleft chin, and the type of body that would have many fitness models drooling with envy. The dark fur around his collar looked insanely soft and fluffy. The smattering of scales on his forehead and parts of his arms, chest, and legs had a lustrous sheen to them. Like the other Prometheans in the Great Hall, he was naked but for a fancy loincloth.

His antennae lightly flickered as he also appeared to be discreetly assessing me. I wondered what information they revealed to him about me. I never delved too deeply into the abilities of moths and butterflies. However, like Serena's husband who flicked his snake tongue to gather information about a target or his surroundings, moths could use their antennae to smell and interpret chemicals in their environment.

He was doing a great job of keeping an unreadable expression on his face, with that guarded look often displayed by seasoned members of the military. I didn't miss how he glanced at the Prism, as if to make sure he was still unscathed. I would pay a lot to know what thoughts were crossing his mind.

"Kayog is ready," Tedrick said, while tapping some instructions on his com.

Unlike when Jordan Fisk had opened a portal from the Radiant Star to bring me here, Tedrick didn't snap a black stone for it. He merely turned his back to us so that he would face the wall. Moments later, following a thunderclap, a giant black portal opened in front of him. I could only presume that when he typed on his com seconds ago, he sent the coordinates to whoever opened this magical doorway. This time, we were able to see through it. My jaw dropped at the sight of a golden dragonkin with shadowy horns standing next to Kayog.

Despite the awe filling me, my gaze flicked to the Promethean guard. Understandable tension stiffened his broad shoulders. Although he didn't touch the impressive blade hanging on his side, his hand hovered near it, ready to go on the offensive.

And yet, his features betrayed the wonder he failed to fully hide.

Seconds later, Kayog stepped out of the portal, reclaiming my attention. Seeing a hovercart with my luggage following him twisted my insides. It finally sank in that I was truly going to be stranded in this foreign place for the foreseeable future.

The tall dragon-like being on the other side flicked his wrist, and the portal instantly collapsed with a whooshing sound.

"Okay, how do I get myself a friend like that?" I said with

awe, still staring at the now vacant spot where the portal had been.

Tedrick snorted. "You don't. No one does. In the wrong hands, such power would be too dangerous. But in the right ones, he's undoubtedly useful…"

"Right," I said, giving him the 'You're no saint' look before turning my attention to Kayog. "Hello, Master Voln."

He chuckled, totally unbothered by my less-than-cordial tone. "Venus, such tender emotions emanating from you warm my old heart."

I scrunched my face at him, annoyed by how charming I always found him to be in spite of everything.

"You're hardly old. It's your habit of marrying off the Bello sisters that's getting old," I grumbled.

He pressed a palm to the golden down feathers of his muscular chest and bowed his head in an almost conceding fashion.

"I wish I could apologize, but I can never be sorry for helping Serena find true happiness. What better gift is there than for two soulmates to be reunited?"

I glared at him, further annoyed that he was indeed right. For all my whining, I also shared his sentiment about my sister's happiness.

"Yeah well, remember that you're not here to matchmake me, but only to find me a friendly partner until my duty is done," I said, feeling silly for being so grumpy.

His silver eyes sparkled with mischief.

"Rest assured, Venus, I will find you the ideal partner for however long your stay here will be."

Why do I not like the way he said that?

Before I could respond, the Temern turned to greet Tedrick, then the Promethean guard. While his nod was brief and courteous, something struck me as odd in the way Kayog looked at him. But seeing his face melt into a world of love and tenderness as he approached his wife messed me up. Linsea's entire expression also shifted, looking almost timid and awed as he closed the distance with her. He took both her hands in his, drawing her into his embrace. She melted against him, while flattening her pristine white wings against her body. He deployed his maroon wings, the same color as the rest of his body, wrapping them around his mate while they rubbed their beaks against each other's.

They made a striking tableau, him maroon and gold with a long white tail, and her like freshly fallen snow. But the infinite love radiating from them filled the room almost like a physical entity. My chest constricted, both with joy for them and shameful envy.

Yeah, there cannot be a better gift than for two soulmates to be reunited.

To my shock, while Tedrick was looking at them approvingly, the Promethean had lost his mask of stoicism, a look of sadness and longing settling over his features. He suddenly jerked his head towards me, having apparently sensed me staring at him. The speed with which he plastered a neutral expression on his face gave me whiplash.

His antennae flickered again, and I forced myself to avert my eyes, embarrassed to have been caught spying on him. Kayog releasing his mate with obvious reluctance saved me from further awkwardness.

"Well, if everyone is ready, let's go get you married, Venus," Kayog said with enthusiasm.

CHAPTER 5
ATLAS

I stared in disgust at Japhyr's so-called elite. They were strutting and flaunting their attributes, each male and female rivaling each other in their pursuit of power. Only a handful actually cared about protecting the Prism.

The poor human had already been discussing with potential candidates for the past forty minutes. Despite the maximum of five minutes awarded to each person to make their case about how they would be the right mate for her to choose, Xarin's Prima would still need another two to three hours to go through the line of hopefuls.

Thankfully, she seemed to be a good judge of character. The speed and firmness with which she kept dismissing the vultures one after the other gave me hope. Granted, they brought the Ambassador's mate who could apparently read souls in order to help Venus make her decision. But from what I observed so far, he offered very little input, content to nod his approval every time she cast a suitor aside—which was every single one of them.

On a few occasions, I caught him studying me. It was unnerving. Knowing he could sense what emotions coursed through people, it shamed me that he likely felt what uncharitable thoughts filled my mind about my own people. Did he think me unfit to lead the Black Guard or disloyal because of it?

"Look at Ajustus, huffing and puffing with anger," Pythus said mockingly. "At this rate, he will give himself a heart attack."

"Indeed," Leodros replied with a smile in his voice.

I slightly frowned as I glanced sideways at my guards. They spoke in a hushed tone, and we stood far enough from the crowd that none would hear us—not that they would even pay us any attention. But it was still inappropriate behavior.

"Truth be told, I wish the hunan would choose him. Can you imagine Ajustus being married to a Monochromatic?" Pythus said with a chuckle.

Leodros snorted. "Worse, by her looks, she would qualify as an Achromatic. Although I've never seen one of that brownish color."

Both males laughed. I squashed my own urge to snort at the thought of that self-aggrandizing narcissist in fact marrying one of those he regularly made sure to remind everyone were lower than dirt and beneath him.

"Enough!" I snapped at the two males.

They immediately wiped the amusement off their faces and stood at attention.

"Apologies, Razus," Pythus said sheepishly. "We didn't mean to gossip. But it's such a unique situation…"

"It is," I conceded in a softer tone.

I wanted nothing more than to join in on the gossiping, but as the Commander of our homeworld's Capital City Black Guard, I had to set the example. That didn't prevent me from sharing their petty thoughts.

"What do you think of the hunan?" Leodros carefully asked. "You spent more time in her presence."

"It is not hunan, but human," I absent-mindedly corrected.

"Apologies," Leodros replied.

I grunted while reflecting on an appropriate response. "She seems smart but also very weak. I conversed with the human enforcer Tedrick while Ambassador Voln explained to her what would happen next. He confirmed Venus Bello does not possess magic, just like the Temerns. Apparently, no other off-worlder species channels colors as magic the way we do."

"Then why would the Prism choose her as his Prima?" Pythus asked, echoing the question that plagued me since Xarin rejected the Chancellor.

"Your guess is as good as mine, Pythus. But depending on which house she chooses to join, we may need to provide added security for her and the Prism," I said pensively.

"For *her*?" Pythus exclaimed, taken aback.

"If she's taken out of the equation, the Prism will be forced to choose another," I said in a factual manner.

Leodros recoiled. "Surely you don't think someone would murder her over this?!" he exclaimed in a hushed tone.

With a will of its own, my gaze flicked to the Chancellor. "I never rule out any possibility. And right now, my gut tells me that foul play is afoot."

"It can't be that bad," Pythus weakly argued.

I faced him, making no effort to hide how troubled I felt. "You know what new laws they want to pass," I said in a somber tone. "Thaudras is looming over Japhyr. When other cities were threatened, we always stood back and merely sent them our thoughts and prayers. But now that the center of the Promethean world is in jeopardy, our leaders will go to any length to preserve their way of life. Ajustus will have no qualms blindly sacrificing us in a preemptive strike. The only person who could stand in the way of him getting what he wants is the Prism. Whoever speaks on Xarin's behalf holds our fate in their hands."

My companions nodded grimly, our collective gazes shifting to the slender female as she dismissed yet another candidate.

Despite her keeping a polite expression on her rather harmonious features, I knew at a visceral level that she was beyond fed up with the entire process. My eyes flicked to Xarin's chrysalis still sitting on the hovering platform. The soft pastel colors shimmering over its surface testified to his contentment.

He approved of his Prima's current decisions.

Movement at the edge of my vision drew my attention. I groaned inwardly as Aletros spread out his wings and bunched his muscles in a menacing fashion as he invaded Temnon's personal space. What in the world would possess the silly male to provoke a Green Polychromatic? With their affinity with toxins and poisons, Greens could make their opponents ill and even kill them with little effort. Thankfully, the Great Hall didn't have any green that Temnon could channel to launch an attack—not that he would be foolish enough to do so.

I hurried to their location while they started shoving at each other. Beyond my annoyance at this childish display, I felt embarrassed that our elite should make such a spectacle of themselves in front of off-worlders, and above all in front of the Prism.

"That's enough!" I shouted.

Aletros, with his red wings and light-green eyespots, reined himself in first, ready to stand down. But with his volatile temper, Temnon continued to grapple with him, forcing me to intervene. I grabbed his forearm and yanked him back forcefully. The idiot turned to face me with an angry growl, raising his palm in a threatening fashion.

My eyes widened in disbelief at the sight of the halo swirling around his hand. This magical energy could be used to destroy, sculpt, or transform whatever it entered in contact with. Its weak amount would barely bruise anyone he used it against. But it confirmed he was attempting to channel. The only source of green would be found in the clothes worn by the other guests. As there was a limited amount and all in varying shades of the spectrum, they didn't allow him to achieve a level that would be cause for alarm.

"You dare?" I hissed, spreading my own wings.

As a Black Achromatic, I was immune to magical attacks. My wings absorbed all light wavelengths and dispelled the halo energy. As I couldn't reflect light—and therefore colors—it also kept me from casting magic. The silver eyespots in my wings were the only thing that allowed me to perform a small amount of magic, but as silver wasn't a color commonly found in the environment, that already weak ability was further stunted.

Temnon paled as he snapped out of his anger. He immediately folded his wings and lowered his eyes, the green glow of his halo around his hand vanishing.

"I didn't cast," he mumbled.

"But you were going to," I replied in a harsh tone. "You invoked your halo in these hallowed halls, in the presence of the Prism, with the intent to harm another."

"He cut in front of me!" Temnon exclaimed in self-righteous indignation.

"And for *that* you violate our laws?" I retorted, flabbergasted.

The fool had the decency to look embarrassed, his scales darkening.

"You will leave this hall immediately," I commanded.

"You cannot do this!" he snapped.

"Be grateful I am giving you the opportunity to leave rather than jail you, as your trespass dictates," I said in a dangerously calm voice.

"He should be arrested," Aletros interjected, looking at the others for support.

Realizing the real possibility this could happen should he linger, Temnon turned on his heel with a furious growl, then marched angrily out of the room under the jeers of a few of the remaining candidates.

The contempt I felt for the lot of them cranked up another notch.

What a shameful display.

After a final warning look at the people still lining up, I glanced towards the human. Venus was sitting at a table with the Temern as her suitors took turns on the guest chair across the table from them in the hopes of swaying her in their favor. To my surprise, instead of talking to the male in front of her, she was looking at me with a grateful and approving smile. It did the strangest thing to me. I wasn't used to this kind of reaction, even when I did nice things for people. To them, they were entitled to it.

But the Temern's intense stare unnerved me the most. I'd caught him stealing glances my way on a few occasions since these speed interviews began. What did he want with me?

To my dismay, he whispered something to the Prima before rising to his bird's feet and following me as I headed back to the edge of the room where my unit stood watch. I tensed when he continued his approach.

"Calm," the Temern said, raising his feathery palms in an appeasing gesture. "I'm not a threat and would simply like to have a word with you."

"I'm afraid it will have to wait. As you can see, I'm on duty," I replied in a firm tone despite the curiosity that burned my gut.

"I'm well aware," the Temern said in a cheerful tone. "However, this is important. It concerns the Prism."

I stiffened, my senses going into full alert as I cast a worried glance towards the chrysalis.

"All is well," the Temern said quickly upon noticing—or was it sensing?—my reaction. "There's nothing wrong with him, but I want to discuss matters concerning him with you."

"Very well," I said reluctantly. "Speak."

He cast an apologetic look at Pythus and Leodros. "It is for your ears only," he said gently.

My frown deepened, but I gave him a stiff nod.

"Pythus, you're in charge," I said.

"Yes, Razus," he replied promptly.

I gestured for the Temern to follow me, and I led him to a nook in the back corner of the room, designed specifically to prevent sound from traveling. It also gave a commanding view of the room. We often used it to stand watch over official proceedings held here.

"My name is Kayog," he said with that same energetic tone. "I understand yours is Razus?"

I shook my head. "Razus is my title as Commander of the Black Guard. My name is Atlas. Atlas Zaos."

"Ah, I see! Well, it is a pleasure to formally make your acquaintance Razus Zaos. Would it be acceptable to address each other by our given names? I am very informal," the Temern said in a friendly tone.

That took me aback. Achromatics were rarely addressed with such consideration.

"I… uh… yes, if you wish," I replied clumsily.

"Excellent! I was curious about your thoughts on the ongoing situation," Kayog said, as one would speak of the weather.

"Ongoing situation?" I echoed carefully, uncertain which specific topic he was referring to.

"The Prism, of course. Finding a suitable mate—temporary though it will be—for Xarin's Prima. If I may be so bold, my empathic abilities tell me that, like Venus, you do not approve of the suitors who have approached her so far," he said in the same friendly and casual tone.

Nevertheless, my scales darkened with embarrassment to have my suspicions confirmed that he could read my uncharitable thoughts about my own people—or at least what emotions their actions stirred within me.

"My opinion is irrelevant. And anyway, I am in no position to pass judgment on—"

"Yes, you are," Kayog interrupted, his silver gaze slightly hardening, like when a parent caught his child lying. "You are the head of security of your capital city. Until he hatches, the Prism will also be your responsibility. Venus is tiring, but with the number of suitors remaining, this could go on for at least a couple more hours. Her choice is too important to have her settling out of exhaustion. Your insight could significantly help."

I tilted my head to the side, confused as to why he would approach me about this. Granted, I was the Razus, but I would have expected him to speak with one of the Senators—all of whom were already married, and therefore ineligible.

"Why me? How is my insight more valuable than the opinion of one of our high-ranking officials?" I asked with genuine curiosity.

"Because in the entire hour we've been going at this, you're the only one to have emitted no self-serving emotions. You truly worry for the Prism," the Temern said in a factual manner.

I shifted on my feet, flattered that those were the emotions from me that had retained his attention.

"I am the Razus. It is my duty to worry about the welfare of *all* my people, and especially of the blessed one," I said with a shrug.

It was silly of me to pretend like his words hadn't touched me. Judging by the slight amusement quirking the corner of his beak, Kayog was once again well aware of the emotions coursing through me.

"Excellent. In this case, in your opinion, who among these suitors would be a good or at least acceptable fit as a temporary mate for Venus?" he asked.

I hated being put on the spot like this. In my opinion, none of them were a good fit. However, if my words could truly have an impact on the outcome, then it would be foolish of me not to try to increase the chances the Prism would be surrounded by the one who cared at least somewhat for his welfare.

I scratched my chest fur in a gesture that betrayed my unease or embarrassment, depending on the situation.

"This is merely my opinion," I said cautiously. "But among all of these candidates, Lord Cassius or Lady Elana would make decent spouses for the human. They have fairly agreeable dispositions, and they would put the interest of the Prism before their own. Both their houses are a little weak, but with the Black Guard as added security, all should be fine."

I didn't add that neither constituted a great choice in my humble opinion, but they struck me as the best options.

Kayog nodded slowly, his silver eyes seeming to delve into the deepest parts of my soul, leaving me feeling exposed.

"Interesting. And what of the human? What do you think of her?"

I blinked, wondering how that was relevant. "I do not know her. I believe Xarin made a strange choice by selecting her. But who am I to question the wisdom of a Prism? He undoubtedly sees something in her that we don't."

"You did not answer," Kayog insisted. "What do you personally think of her, based on what you've observed so far?"

I shifted my wings and scratched my fur again, confused as to this pointless line of questioning. I almost called him out on it. Considering my actions could reflect on his opinion of our people as a whole—and in light of the less than impressive display the others made moments prior—I elected to show myself cooperative.

"In truth, I do not know what to make of her. Everything in me says she's a terrible choice. She doesn't know our world, can't fly, and according to Agent Tedrick, she possesses no magic. What's her purpose? On top of all those shortcomings—at least as far as living in Sylvar is concerned—she's Monochromatic. For that alone, I foresee much hardship for her, especially from her mate who will likely deem themselves superior. I'm genuinely confused."

My gaze flicked to the human who had just dismissed yet another suitor. To my shame, I couldn't help a mocking smirk at the disgruntled expression on Nereus's face. Like Ajustus, He tended to be full of himself and wasn't used to being refused anything he wanted.

"For all that, she seems smart, and so far displays good judgment. More importantly, in the brief interactions she's had with Xarin, she appeared to genuinely care about his welfare. That's extremely good."

"She does," Kayog said with conviction. "Venus would not have chosen this path for herself, but she understands the importance of the moment and has always been a strong defender of those in a position of weakness or unable to speak for themselves."

"That could explain why the Prism chose her," I mused out loud while studying her rather pleasant profile.

The texture of her skin and especially of her hair fascinated me. I had never seen such tightly curled locks. She had bound her hair into two thick and long elaborate braids. Venus absent-mindedly caressed the right braid while listening to yet another suitor make his pitch. I doubted he realized this was a telltale sign that he was already dismissed. She had a few tells that I had come to identify. Although I could be wrong, this one signified he was boring. When she twisted the tips, it meant she wanted to strangle the idiot babbling in front of her. And to hide an urge to laugh at some stupidity, she would chew on her bottom lip.

Suddenly realizing what heavy silence had settled between the Temern and me, I turned my head to look at him. The intense way he was staring at me had my skin darkening again. By the Lights, when had I ever acted so distracted while on duty?

"What of you, Atlas?" Kayog asked in a mysterious tone.

"Me?" I repeated, confused.

"Would you be a suitable husband for her?"

This time, I flat out recoiled at such an outrageous question.

"What?! Are you insane?" I asked, taking a step away from him as if he was contagious.

"Why do you ask that? You're a Promethean and unwed, are you not?" he asked, the pretend innocence of his question not fooling me in the least.

"Because I'm Achromatic! We cannot marry!" I said, anger seeping into my voice as a part of me suspected he already knew that.

"Really? Is it stated in your books of law?" he challenged.

I opened and closed my mouth a couple of times, my instinctive inclination to say yes dying on my tongue as I weighed the question.

"Well… no. Technically, it is not stated in the law, but it is common knowledge," I conceded uneasily.

"Therefore, you would be eligible. So would you be a good match?" Kayog insisted.

"No," I said firmly. "Such a pairing would be scandalous. If we had offspring—"

"It is not a real marriage," Kayog interjected, interrupting me. "This union only seeks to provide legal protection for Xarin for the remaining four months of his incubation. Can you think of a better protector than yourself for both him and her?"

I stared at him at a loss for words. No, I couldn't think of anyone in the Capital City who would be more devoted to both their protection. After all, I was the Razus for a reason.

"Whatever my opinion on the matter is irrelevant, Kayog," I said in a reasonable tone. "No one would ever accept this."

"It is not their call to make," Kayog challenged. "Venus is the only one who can decide who she will take as a mate."

I waved a dismissive hand. "She would never agree."

"Are you sure?" he asked with a hint of defiance.

"Yes. Who in their right mind would choose me?"

"Let's see!" Kayog retorted with a mischievous glimmer in his eyes.

To my dismay, he turned on his talon and headed straight back to the table where yet another candidate was approaching to settle in the guest chair. The Temern raised his palm to stop Ludus from taking a seat, apparently requesting a moment of privacy to speak with Venus.

A wave of panic surged through me, snapping me out of my horrified frozen state. I almost ran over there to stop him. But I couldn't make a spectacle of myself like that. Anyway, there was no need for me to get myself worked up. Although her imminent rejection would sting, I would be spared the public humiliation of everyone rallying against me should she make the impossible other choice.

Heart pounding, I stared at her face while Kayog whispered to her. Her eyes widened in shock, and her head jerked towards me. My scales burned with embarrassment. To my shock, instead of the look of horror I expected, Venus's surprised expression gave way to something akin to approval. My heart leapt when she nodded distractedly to Kayog, her eyes still locked on me as she gave me an assessing once over.

And then she smiled.

My stomach dropped when Kayog turned around with as wide a smile as his stiff beak allowed, and he waved for me to come over. Shocked murmurs rose from the crowd wondering what was going on. Seeing my hesitation, the Temern waved me over again with a bit more insistence. Mortified, I complied under the confused stares of my unit and the outraged ones of the suitors—both those who had been dismissed but lingered to see who would win her in the end as well as those still waiting for their chance to make their case.

I stopped in front of her table and swallowed hard. She smiled gently at me, her black eyes gleaming with kindness.

"Hello. Kayog tells me your name is Atlas?" she asked in a warm tone.

I nodded. "Yes, that is correct."

"My name is Venus, although I suspect you know that by now. Would you mind having a seat? Kayog thinks you would be a perfect candidate."

"I... I..."

By the Lights, I felt paralyzed, words failing me both from shock and growing panic. I fought the most vicious creatures on our homeworld without hesitation and without faltering. But this simple question had me burning with the urge to flee.

"What is the meaning of this?!" Ajustus exclaimed in a thunderous voice as he approached with furious steps.

Behind him, the crowd was also loudly expressing their outrage, not only that Venus would have me skip ahead of the line, but also that she even implied the possibility of me sitting in that chair.

"Razus, return to your post and remember your place!"

"Don't talk to him like that!" Venus snapped, jumping to her feet. "And the rest of you, cut it out!"

I gaped at her in disbelief as she glared at the Chancellor. She was fairly short by our standards—maybe 5'9 or 5'10—with the delicate bone structure typical of females. And yet, in that instant, the power of a thousand beasts seemed ready to surge from within her slender body.

There is strength beneath that fragile appearance.

"He's an Achromatic!" Ajustus exclaimed, the contempt in how he pronounced that last word making it clear it was all the explanation needed to support his stance.

"And?" Venus challenged before waving at herself. "In case you haven't noticed, I would also qualify as either Monochromatic or Achromatic, however your system works."

"You're human," Ajustus countered in a dismissive tone. "It doesn't count."

"Then it shouldn't count for him either," she countered in a harsh tone, which had the rest of the crowd riled up again.

Mortified, I decided to intervene to avoid things escalating further. I should have stopped the Temern before he got back to her.

"Prima Venus," I said in an appeasing tone, "I am extremely honored that you would consider one such as I. But there are others better suited than me."

"Better suited, how?" she asked with a hint of defiance.

I scratched my fur, my mind racing to find acceptable arguments that wouldn't sound like too much of a lie to my own ears.

"All of these people have wealth, status, connections, and the proper accommodations to receive both you and the Prism," I said carefully.

"But can they fight like you?" she argued.

I opened and closed my mouth a couple of times before shaking my head.

"Can they protect him like you could?" she insisted.

"Well, no but…"

"Who do you think Xarin would prefer?" she asked when my voice trailed off.

"All of that is irrelevant!" Aletros exclaimed from the middle of the crowd where he was still waiting for his turn. "The Razus is unfit and knows better than to even consider mating, though symbolic this union will be. Let us stop this nonsense and resume this process with proper candidates."

A majority of the people lining up cheered him on, a few of them addressing less-than-gentle comments my way.

"ENOUGH!" Venus shouted, startling everyone into silence. "You know, this is truly one of the most disgraceful displays I've ever witnessed. But thank you for showing your true faces," she continued in an icy tone. "All of you are going to be a hard pass for me. I'd rather jump into a pool of acid than marry anyone who thinks this kind of behavior is acceptable under any circumstances. It's not *your* choice to make, but *mine*. The Prism chose *me*, despite being an off-worlder, *and* a Monochromatic one at that. But after this spectacle, I can see why. Atlas has shown more class, decorum, and humility than the lot of you combined."

Emotion choked me. *I* was the one who defended others, never expecting recognition or gratitude for it. No one had ever defended me, least of all so fiercely. And fierce, that little human definitely was. Forcing myself out of the dazed awe her fiery speech got me under, I opened my mouth to tell her it was okay, but a haunting sound silenced me.

I jerked my head towards the chrysalis. My jaw dropped as luminous waves swirled over its surface. An irresistible melody beckoned me. With a will of their own, my feet took me to the hovering platform upon which the chrysalis rested. I realized I had reached for it when its soft heat warmed my palm. A gasp—echoed by multiple voices in the crowd—escaped me as a tingling sensation spread over my hand, up my arms, and throughout my body.

"Impossible," Ajustus whispered as a blissful sensation spread through my wings.

I glanced over my shoulders and stared in awe as the normally dull silver of my wings' eyespots seemed to light from within, making it shine with the brightness of a thousand suns. Power like I'd never felt before surged within me as if the floodgates of my stunted color channeling abilities had been flung wide open.

"See, Atlas, it appears the Prism approves of my choice," Venus said in a soft voice. "He also thinks your color doesn't matter."

CHAPTER 6
VENUS

I couldn't believe I just alienated the entire elite of Sylvar in less than one hour. And yet, I knew beyond the shadow of a doubt that this was the right course of action. Truth be told, I wanted to bitchslap most of them. I had seen self-righteous and entitled before, but these people were taking it to another level. And there was nothing I enjoyed more than knocking divas down a notch or two.

However, the intensity of the protectiveness I felt towards Atlas confused me. I didn't know him, but I recognized a person who had grown so numb to constant abuse they started to believe it was their normal lot in life. And that whipped my mama bear genes into a frenzy.

The look of wonder and the depth of emotions Atlas felt when the chrysalis called him seriously turned me upside down. I'd seen that same expression during some of my most gut-wrenching charity work when people who had lost all hope realized someone out there actually cared.

"This is an unsuitable pairing," Ajustus said, reclaiming everyone's attention. "An off-worlder and an Achromatic cannot possibly be our Prism's guardians."

Nothing could describe how much that male irritated the living hell out of me. I didn't know what he hid behind that loincloth of his, but my foot was itching something fierce to make its acquaintance.

"Once again, I remind you that the decision is mine to make. Xarin confirmed my choice. These are your laws. Are you challenging the will of the Prism to impose your own wishes?" I asked with a dare in my voice.

The fool had the decency of looking unnerved while the crowd muttered disapprovingly at him. For a reason I couldn't explain, the impressed glimmer in Atlas's eyes stroked my ego in the most pleasant fashion. Kayog, who had in a way initiated this whole mess, was standing by with this obnoxiously mischievous spark in his silver eyes.

To my shock, instead of begrudgingly conceding, the Chancellor doubled down.

"How can I not?" Ajustus replied with defiance. "Xarin was abducted. He spent at least two weeks under the control of ill-intentioned off-worlders. How do we know that *he* is the one speaking? How do we know that these strange and inexplicable choices aren't the result of external influences seeking to destroy us?"

As much as I hated to admit it, this wasn't an unreasonable concern. The way Atlas flinched, and judging by the troubled expressions that descended over the other people present, his comment struck a nerve.

I nodded in concession. "It's a fair question, Chancellor Ajustus. But I challenge it as being unfounded. Yes, the Prism was abducted, but his abductors *did not* want him found. Xarin calling me is the only reason they got arrested. And I can assure you that the sentence they will face will be horrendous. Violating the Prime Directive is a serious enough crime, but abduction and people trafficking—especially a minor—yields the most severe punishment permissible by law in the sector where the criminals were apprehended. They got caught in a sector ruled by the Obosians. There will be no mercy."

"Be that as it may, it doesn't mean they haven't damaged the Prism," Ajustus argued with a mulish expression. "We don't know what happened with them or during the time he was with you for that matter."

"You dare?!" Atlas exclaimed, taking a menacing step towards the Chancellor.

By the gasps his actions prompted, I suspected no one ever addressed Ajustus in that fashion, least of all an Achromatic. Strangely enough, while I was a big girl and loved fighting my own battles, seeing him surge to my defense that the Chancellor would dare imply I might have brainwashed Xarin in the short time he was with me tickled me pink.

"It's okay, Atlas," I said in a soothing tone before turning a cold gaze towards Ajustus. "I will let slide your underlying insult, Chancellor. This day has been fraught with emotions, and I understand how upset you are by things not going the way you thought they would. But remember that I'm not here by choice. I have a life, a career, friends, and family that this entire situation is tearing me away from. I thought I would be on my way home by now. But your Prism has chosen me, and I recognize that this is bigger than me and my little life."

I turned to look at the chrysalis. The shimmering waves that had faded after Atlas had removed his hand from its surface manifested themselves as if to acknowledge me. That further reinforced my determination as I glanced back at the Prometheans.

"When this whole mess began, I couldn't understand why he chose me, why I was being forced to put my life on hold for the next four months. Now I understand. I don't know any of you or your culture, but I know people and their motivations," I said, my tone hardening. "Xarin chose me as his Prima—the person sworn to look after his best interests—and that's what I will do."

I pointed an angry finger towards the chrysalis while making eye contact with as many of the suitors I had turned down as possible.

"In the past hour, *not a single one* of the potential candidates I spoke to expressed even once what you would do *for him*. You all bragged about yourselves, about the number of colors you can manipulate, and your influence. The most offensive part was that every last one of you concluded with an attempt to bribe me with what you could do for *me*. This isn't about you or me. It's about the Prism!"

While many of them looked offended to be thus called out, a surprisingly large number of others actually seemed embarrassed. It was all the more revealing that they appeared shocked to realize what disappointing behavior they displayed. It struck me then that they were so blinded by their culture of ostentation and bragging that they had lost themselves in it.

"Atlas didn't ask for anything that would benefit him or attempt to seize the opportunity to elevate himself. He only worried about Xarin's welfare. So of course I pick him over any other. Therefore, unless your laws somehow make him ineligible, then my choice is made. That is assuming Atlas consents..." I added, suddenly feeling a little less certain.

My innards twisted when Atlas hesitated. The prospect that he might reject me and the Prism had cold shivers running down my spine. I meant every word I just spoke and genuinely couldn't think of a single other candidate present in this room I could even tolerate the possibility of being married to for the next four months.

"It is not my place to reject the tremendous honor both you and the Prism are bestowing upon me," Atlas said carefully in a delightfully masculine voice laced with uncertainty. "However, I am merely a Black Guard. Despite being the High Commander, I reside in the barracks. Such accommodations are not suitable for an honored guest such as you, and even less for the blessed one."

The way his scales darkened and the embarrassed expression on his face made me want to give him a hug and tell him everything would be okay.

"See? He is unfit to shoulder such a responsibility," Ajustus immediately interjected.

It took every ounce of my willpower not to give him a roundhouse kick straight to the chest. In my entire life, I had never met someone I despised as much as that chancellor—and I had met my fair share of morons.

"His fitness is obviously not in question since your own Prism expressed his approval of him," Kayog intervened in a reasonable tone. "The accommodation issues seem like a very minor one that is easily resolved. After all, when the Shimli Survivors were returned home, my beloved Linsea had nothing but praises about the lovely guest house you put at her disposal during her short stay while ironing out diplomatic matters with your Senate. Surely you have another such dwelling that could be provided to the Prima, her mate, and the Prism for the four months until his hatching?" Kayog added, gesturing in turn at me, Atlas, and then the chrysalis.

"That sounds like a brilliant idea," I said, fighting the urge to laugh at the dismayed expression on the Chancellor's face.

"That is indeed a perfect solution," said the purple-winged male who had previously stated that I should simply become a Promethean when Ajustus challenged the fact that I was an offworlder.

"This is madness," Ajustus muttered, looking around the crowd in search of support.

"No, Ajustus," the purple male said, his tone and stare hardening. "It is the will of the Prism. Tread carefully my friend, your behavior is starting to sound treasonous."

The Chancellor visibly paled, especially in light of the condemnation visible in many eyes staring him down.

"I am merely trying to protect our savior," he argued feebly.

"Your arguments were heard and dismissed," the purple male said sternly. "Xarin has chosen his Prima, and she has chosen her mate. Let us end these proceedings before any of us commits the irreparable. Razus Atlas, do you have further concerns or hesitations regarding this union?"

"No, Senator Cassius. This addresses the only issue I foresaw in my ability to protect the Prima and the Prism," Atlas said in a firm and confident voice.

I liked that.

"Then it sounds like everything is settled!" Kayog said with enthusiasm, as if he was oblivious to the general dismay that reigned in the room.

The wretch finds all of this amusing.

I couldn't even be annoyed with him. Over the few times I met the Temern, I'd come to realize a real brat hid beneath that polished and respectable mature male exterior.

"As the UPO does not require a union between Venus and Atlas, you may simply proceed with your basic contractual wedding which, as I understand it, merely requires a signature from both parties," Kayog said.

"That is correct," replied the purple male Atlas referred to as Senator Cassius.

He gestured to someone. I realized the male approaching had been part of the attendants who had not sought to be one of my suitors. He was older, with orange wings. He placed a piece of parchment on the table in front of me. I glanced at it with a horrified expression.

While no advanced civilization used paper anymore, it didn't shock me that a primitive species would have physical contracts such as this one. But I had no clue what the words etched on it said.

"Ah yes!" Kayog intervened. "The Promethean alphabet has not yet been fully integrated in the translation device. The UPO's linguistics department is diligently working on it. It should only be a matter of days."

"I can translate it for you," Atlas offered.

I gave him a smile, suddenly feeling oddly timid at the thought he would be my husband, even though it would only be on paper—literally.

He quickly read through it for me, and it provided the answer to the various sections to be filled, namely my full name, age and place of birth, my parents name and all the usual stuff, which I wrote in Universal, and he translated into Promethean on the same line. We both signed—something I hadn't done in a long time as we usually just pressed our thumbs in the signature box of a digital contract.

For the strangest reason, my stomach fluttered when he put down the pen and straightened to look at me. I expected someone to say 'You may kiss the bride' and for him to proceed.

"There, it is done," Senator Cassius said. "The contract will be held in the Hall of Records until its dissolution at the time of your choosing. You may take your bride and the Prism to the Silver Mansion. Considering your chroma, it is fitting."

"Thank you, Senator," Atlas replied respectfully before turning towards me.

The depth of the disappointment that coursed through me left me speechless. I should be relieved I hadn't been forced to kiss a complete stranger, one that was part bug at that. And yet, my throat felt terribly constricted. I wanted to believe that it was sadness that my wedding should have been so expedited, transactional, and lackluster. Even Serena's symbolic human wedding to Szaro had been better than this.

"Do you need a moment to say your goodbyes to Kayog?" Atlas asked in a soft voice, his scales darkening with embarrassment.

Good God, he's adorable!

"Yes, please," I replied in a slightly nervous tone.

He nodded and smiled. "I'll be here when you're ready."

Atlas gestured for the two guards who had stayed closest to him during this entire proceeding, and they went to stand near the Prism while speaking in hushed tones. The other guards ushered the rest of the crowd out of the Great Hall.

"Well, I guess I should thank you," I said semi-begrudgingly to the Temern.

He smiled, his eyes gleaming with a paternal expression. "You're welcome, Venus."

"I wish Linsea could have stayed until the end of this mess. Please extend to her my warmest regards," I said, suddenly feeling overwhelmed at the thought I'd be here all alone, surrounded by people clearly unhappy about my presence.

"I will, my dear. I promise. Linsea would have loved to be here, but other urgent matters called her away," he said in a sympathetic voice.

"When isn't it the case?" I asked in a teasing fashion.

He snorted with a nod, then glanced at Atlas over my shoulder before turning his silver gaze back towards me with a serious expression.

"Atlas is a very good male, Venus. You can be each other's rock, shelter, and light in the darkness. Rely on him, and let him rely on you," he said with a disturbing intensity.

"I will," I said in a serious tone. "It's weird. I don't know him, but I feel deeply that I can trust him."

"Of course, you do."

I tore my gaze away from Atlas to glance inquisitively at Kayog, intrigued by the way he said that.

"Why 'of course?'" I asked.

The sound of thunderclap startled me. A short distance behind us, a black portal opened through which I could once more see the golden dragonkin.

"Because he's your perfect match," Kayog said, matter-of-factly. "And my ride home has arrived!"

I stiffened. "Perfect match? As in my soulmate?" I asked, shock and outrage audible in my voice.

"Yes, Venus. Atlas is your soulmate. Even when I don't try, I succeed," he said, shaking his head with a mix of amusement and disbelief. "It's something else being me."

"Wait, what? No!"

"Yes. And as you know, I'm never wrong," he said while patting my cheek affectionately. "Be happy, my dear. You deserve it."

Too stunned to react, I watched the Temern step through the portal, which collapsed behind him. I couldn't say how long I stood there, staring at the empty space before me. A dark shadow at the edge of my vision snapped me out of my daze. I turned to find Atlas towering over me. He was at least 6'4 and broad-shouldered, bigger than the average Promethean who tended to be on the lither side.

The commiserating expression on his face had my chest constricting.

"Do not be sad. I know this isn't the path or fate you wanted for yourself," he said in a gentle tone. "Know that you are not alone. On my honor, as Japhyr's Razus and as your mate, I swear to protect you and do everything in my power to keep you happy for the few months of your stay with us."

Another wave of emotion swelled within me, and I gave him a shaky smile. "Thank you, Atlas. I appreciate it."

"No, thank *you*, Prima, for the sacrifice you make for the welfare of my people. We are forever in your debt. Come, let's take you home."

I nodded. Side by side, the hovering platform of the Prism in tow, and his two Black Guards following, my *soulmate* and I exited the Great Hall on our way to what would be my new home for the foreseeable future.

CHAPTER 7
ATLAS

My head spun as we walked through the main street of the Legislative District. Of all the scenarios I envisioned as to how the events of the day would unfold once Ajustus informed us the Prism had been found, this never would have entered my mind.

I, a Black Achromatic, had a mate.

The look on my guards' faces would forever remain burnt in my very soul. It was the oddest mix of awe, shock, and hope that this could be the seed of a massive change that had always been deemed an impossible dream. Not only was one of us publicly and legally mated, but I had been blessed.

Every three generations, after he emerged from his chrysalis, the Prism would grant his blessing to a single person. He normally bestowed that honor upon the Primus or Prima, hence why Ajustus had been so eager to appropriate that title. Even now, the foreign power coursed through me, making me slightly dizzy, as if I had overindulged in alcoholic beverages.

The eyespots in my wings felt like gaping holes hungrily absorbing every color. For the first time, I got a glimpse of what it must be like to be an Achromatic White, with the energy of every color flooding your senses, demanding to be channeled into potent magic. And yet, what struck me as an immense upgrade was likely nothing but a trickle in comparison to what Polychromatics could achieve.

I would need to properly master this increased ability. Now, even more so than in my role as Razus of the Black Guard, every action I took going forward would be scrutinized and weaponized against other Achromatics.

A dense crowd lined the streets. We expected as much, as our people would want to bear witness to the Prism journeying through our city en route to what everyone assumed would have been Ajustus's mansion. But that crowd had grown exponentially as word of the unexpected turn of events quickly spread.

My Black Guards had already scattered along the path, keeping the people in check. Although I did not expect any attack or any form of upheaval, the Guards' presence would help prevent anyone rushing us as well as quiet down potential aggressive shouts.

Many faces displayed mesmerized expressions, bordering on religious fervor as they gazed upon the Prism on his floating platform. But a non-negligible number of other bystanders made no secret of their anger and outrage at seeing that one such as me and a Monochromatic off-worlder were chosen as the protectors of the divine Prism.

The one thing that seemed to somewhat appease them was the presence of Ajustus walking in front of us. Despite the humiliating way in which the Prism rejected him, the Chancellor wanted to claim some kind of ownership by taking the lead. It slightly annoyed me. But I still took a shamefully malicious pleasure knowing that I bested him—me, someone he deemed lower than dirt and so far beneath him.

Overhead, the master of keys was flying to go unlock the house. Normally, we would all be flying at only a couple of meters above ground. But as my mate didn't possess any wings

—another thing that made her appointment as Prima even more offensive to my people—we agreed to walk instead.

My mate...

I gave her a discreet sideways glance, and a maelstrom of emotions surged through me. Despite our obvious anatomical differences, Venus was very pretty... beautiful even. The way she put the elite in their places still left me reeling. My mate was fierce, strong, and not intimidated in the least by those people who so loved to throw their weight and influence around.

And she chose *me*. Venus freely picked *me*.

It's not a real marriage.

The searing pain that cut through my chest at that sad reminder took me aback. I didn't know this female. Yes, she chose me, but not out of love. I just turned out to be the less bad option in a pool of terrible ones. Our union would not be filled with the love, joy, and complicity that tied a true couple. There would be no offspring to embody that love. Anyway, there would be no future for me.

Still, for the next three to four months before my time came, I would get to be a husband. I would get to experience something my brothers could only ever dream about, even if only partially.

Apparently unfazed by the conflicting emotions expressed by the crowd, Venus was taking in the city with undisguised curiosity laced with a hefty dose of admiration. I immediately wondered what she thought of it, and how it compared to the cities of her homeworld as well as the countless others she visited when she traveled through the stars.

I still struggled with that concept despite having now inter-acted on a few occasions with other off-worlders and seeing their insane technology.

"We are in the Legislative District," I explained, breaking the otherwise comfortable silence between us.

Venus glanced at me, her curious and attentive expression

encouraging me to continue. For some silly reason, that made me feel warm inside.

"This is the Senate and seat of our government led by Ajustus," I said pointing at it. "Over there, you can see the courthouse. We have some minor courts scattered in other districts and neighborhoods of the city, but most of the major cases are adjudicated here. And these are respectively the Fiscal Administration Ministry, the Department of Education, and this other one houses Emergency Services."

"What about the Department of Defense?" Venus asked.

"The city only has the Black Guard Headquarters located a few blocks away from here," I replied, amused by her stunned expression. "It serves both as our barracks and command center. We're a peaceful species. There haven't been any wars between the major cities in centuries. We only ever deal with the standard crimes, and the occasional threat from roaming beasts in neighboring forests. Until recently, off-worlders never bothered us. Aside from speculations as to what could lurk beyond the stars, we didn't even know you existed."

"Wow," she whispered, visibly baffled. "So you and your guards ensure the protection of the entire city?"

I shook my head. "Civil Protectors handle the residential areas. They are mostly Gray, Blue, and Pink Monochromatics."

Her brow shot up with surprise. "Really? Why not Blacks?"

I smiled. For a reason I couldn't explain, her genuine curiosity stroked my ego. People usually didn't care much about protective services, except when they needed us.

"Because Blacks are more powerful when it comes to crime prevention as we nullify magic. Since Polychromatics mostly live in the Legislative District, other Monochromatics would struggle to counter potential attacks. Therefore, it is safer for them to deal with the commoners with lesser magic."

She frowned, not with displeasure, but the way one does when trying to solve a mystery.

"What about the Whites?" she asked.

I gave her an apologetic look. "They're outcasts. It's too dangerous to allow them to live within the city walls."

She recoiled and gave me a disbelieving look. "They're too dangerous, how?"

"They can channel every color. In a fit of anger, of panic, or of any other powerful emotional response, they could literally raze the city to the ground, whether intentionally or not."

"You say that as if it already happened before," she replied, her voice tense.

I nodded. "It has happened. Younglings are particularly dangerous where that is concerned. A tantrum by most other colors is fairly easily contained, but by Whites can be devastating."

She pursed her lips, then slowly nodded. "So they're not allowed to come into the city?"

I hesitated. "They're not forbidden to enter, but they're strongly encouraged to keep it to a strict minimum, and only when essential. Before they enter, they must wear a shawl over their wings. It is an occluding cloak that is locked by one of the Black Guards at the entrance of the city so that they cannot channel magic."

The displeased expression on her face shamed me, even though I had nothing to do with instating these laws. From the moment she arrived, Venus had not been exposed to the nicer sides of our culture. Before my time was up and she returned to her own people, I intended to show her that not everything and not everyone on Sylvar was as bad as she probably believed.

She suddenly pointed at a corner building as we reached another intersection.

"Is that a restaurant?"

"Yes," I eagerly replied, grateful for the change of topic.

"What do Prometheans normally eat?" she asked, her previous enthusiastic curiosity having returned.

"Meat, vegetables, and grains. From my understanding, our diet is fairly similar to yours. Except for fish and seafood. We do not consume those," I explained.

That took her aback. "No fish? Why is that?"

"Eating them often results in poisoning," I explained. "It's not all the time. It comes and goes, without any clear explanation. For certain periods of time, they will be entirely safe to consume. And then during others, they will have certain toxins that will prove lethal to us."

"That is strange. Are these periods always the same or on a predictable cycle?" she asked, looking troubled.

I shook my head. "It seems entirely random. For this reason, it was deemed safer to simply stop eating them rather than risking poisoning. Daily testing would be impossible to maintain in a viable fashion, especially for those who would make a living out of that industry. There's an environmental explanation, I'm sure. Unfortunately, our scientists have not figured it out yet."

"Yeah, I think you might be correct."

She opened her mouth to say something else likely on that topic, but her eyes widened as she noticed something to my left. Curious, I glanced in that direction to see what caught her attention.

"Is that a hair salon?!" Venus exclaimed, pointing at it.

"It's an aesthetician boutique," I gently corrected. "They offer hair care, shine scales, trim furs, groom antennae, and mend small tears and fraying in our wings."

The air of excitement on her face took me by surprise. Going to the aesthetician qualified as a chore, not something people normally were thrilled about.

"That's awesome! But what about mani-pedis?" she asked.

"Mani what?" I repeated, confused.

"Manicures and pedicures," Venus said, as if it was self-evident before showing me her hands. "You know, taking care of nails of both hands and feet."

"Oh!" I said with sudden understanding as we turned the corner into that final stretch towards our destination. "Yes, aestheticians provide grooming services for hand and feet claws."

"But do they paint them?" she insisted.

I recoiled. "No. We do not apply color to our claws."

Her shoulders slumped, and she gave me that wary look people had when asking something they feared would be denied or shot down.

"What about massages?" she asked.

I shook my head.

"Facials? Waxing? You don't have spas?" Venus asked back-to-back, with me apologetically shaking my head after each question. "Good grief!" she said, looking devastated before a horrified expression descended over her features. "Oh, my God, there's no way I will find my hair care products here!"

My eyes flicked towards the fascinating tight curls of her black hair, neatly plaited into two braids. "I'm not sure what products they are, and I suspect you are correct in that you won't find them here. But if you know the ingredients, I can ask one of our alchemists to try and reproduce it for you."

My heart sank at the defeated look she gave me. We'd barely been married for thirty minutes, and I was already failing my mate. Granted, no one could be reasonably expected to possess off-worlder products we'd never even heard of. But I was determined to fix it. However short our union would last, I intended to be the best husband she could have hoped for.

A few minutes later, we finally reached the Silver Mansion. I still couldn't believe that I would be setting foot inside, this time not as a Black Guard, but as the actual resident. It was one of the fanciest guest houses, reserved for the highest-ranking visiting officials to our city. The elite had to be seething at the thought that one such as I got to call this place home for the next three to four months.

A strange form of relief washed over me when we finally reached the mansion. Athalix, the Master of Keys, was already standing on the porch with the front door opened. I know the place well for having previously escorted esteemed guests here on various occasions. Judging by the begrudging fashion in which Athalix handed me the keys, he clearly struggled with the idea I would live here. Despite being a Polychromatic himself, he could never hope to sleep in this fancy residence. It had to sting in the worst way knowing that I would.

I'd never been the petty or malicious type. And yet, I couldn't repress a taunting smirk, which further infuriated the male. Venus had an unreadable expression on her face. And yet, at a visceral level, I believed she was also deriving some uncharitable pleasure at his discontent.

Ajustus stood stiffly on the porch next to us, while Pythus and Leodros went inside the house to make sure everything was secure within. It felt odd as I was normally the person leading such inspections. But under the circumstances, I technically qualified as one of the protected instead of the protector.

"This is a tremendous duty that has been bestowed upon you, Razus Atlas," Ajustus said in a pompous tone, projecting far more loudly than necessary.

But then, he always made a spectacle of everything. And in this instance, he was desperately trying to give the impression that he still had some form of control over the situation. Considering that the crowd gathered outside the house—and kept on the other side of the street by the Black Guards—couldn't hear our conversation, this display was even more ridiculous.

"The Senate will expect regular reports as to the welfare of the Prism, as well as regular access to him so that we can make sure all is well," he continued in a commanding tone.

"Reports will not be a problem," Venus interjected in my stead. "As for regular visits, the Prism will have to agree to those."

"Excuse me?!" Ajustus exclaimed, sounding outraged.

"Based on the tingling that appeared at the back of my head the moment you said that, it sounds like Xarin isn't too keen on hosting guests. I can only assume he needs to save his energy for his development," Venus said matter-of-factly. "Therefore, unless it is absolutely necessary or that the Prism himself requires it, I will severely limit random visits. If you need reassurance as to his welfare—beyond the confirmation by your highest-ranking public defender—then I'll be happy to have live conference calls with you to show you that he is fine. Your technology supports it."

By the Lights, there was something insanely sexy about watching my mate verbally slap that obnoxious male in the politest and most reasonable voice possible. Should I be ashamed to be this turned on to have her knock him down another notch or two and remind him that he wasn't in control?

However, as much as his dismay pleased me, I did not miss the spark of hatred in his eyes.

I didn't think he would do anything as reckless as an assassination attempt, but I didn't doubt he would find ways to make Venus's life impossible and undermine her authority at every opportunity.

The protective rage that surged within me left me reeling. The Chancellor would soon discover a far less gentle side of me if he tried to mess with her.

"As there has never been an issue with my reports in the past, I'm certain the Senate will have nothing to worry about," I said, holding the Chancellor's gaze unwaveringly, with a hint of dare in mine.

He pursed his lips and made a noncommittal grunt. "The only thing we care about is the welfare of the Prism."

"And we will ensure it," I retorted in a cool voice. "Now, as I believe my guards have completed their inspection of the mansion, it would be time to get Xarin properly situated and out of the sun. We wouldn't want the heat to dry his chrysalis more than necessary. Good day, Chancellor."

I nearly burst out laughing at Ajustus's expression. He looked like he had bitten into something foul to be summarily dismissed by an Achromatic.

Without waiting for his response, I waved a hand inviting my mate to enter. She gave me a smile, the amused spark in her eyes giving me a warm, fuzzy feeling.

We'd only met a few hours ago, and yet an undeniable type of complicity seemed to exist between us. A part of me felt like I'd known her forever. Granted, our similar dislike of the Chancellor and our sincere desire to protect the Prism were truly the bond that linked us. Still, I liked this inexplicable chemistry I felt with this fascinating female.

Pythus and Leodros, who were framing the wide doors into the greeting antechamber, stepped aside to let her in.

Ajustus utterly failed to hide his balefulness as he watched Xarin enter the mansion on his hovering platform. The fool didn't seem to realize that the Prism could perceive the negative energy emanating from him. He should know better.

He made a disgusted sound then walked down the entrance path towards the street. Once at the sidewalk, he spread his arms wide in a victorious gesture to the crowd, who shouted and acclaimed him. I clamped down on the urge to roll my eyes and turned to face the Master of Keys.

I wanted him to leave as well so that I could finally be alone with my mate. She and I needed to sort out how our lives had suddenly been turned upside down.

"As you know, Razus Atlas, the guests of the Silver Mansion are entitled to catering and decoration services. Will the Prima require them?" Athalix asked with constrained politeness.

Venus frowned while I clenched my teeth. With us now being married, he should have asked if both of us required those services. That he only asked if Venus wanted them was a not-so-subtle slight against me. A part of me wanted to call him out on it, but his bitterness wasn't worth my time or energy.

"Catering services would be good so that my mate can focus on adjusting to her new life among us," I said in a neutral tone. "For tonight's meal, please have a sampler platter prepared for her so that she can get a better sense of which dishes of our cuisine appeal the most to her, if any."

He pinched his lips, annoyed to no end to receive orders from me, but merely responded with a stiff nod. I then turned to Venus.

"Would you like to take advantage of the decoration services," I asked her in a gentle tone. "As you can see, the house is entirely white with silver accents, thus its name Silver Mansion. Normally, the decorator helps by adding furniture and other adornments matching the colors of the guests' wings, so that they can draft magic. But as you do not possess wings, do you still want to modify the decoration, or are you content with our surroundings as is?"

"I would definitely want the decorator," Venus said promptly. "This place is stunning but much too plain due to lack of color."

"Very well," I replied with a smile, before glancing at Athalix. "You've heard the Prima. We'll take both services."

He nodded stiffly before taking his leave. It couldn't have been too soon.

"The Prima's belongings have been set in the living area," Pythus explained. "Do you require a unit to guard the house?"

I shook my head. "The security system should suffice. But have a few of the night patrol add this street to their route. And disperse the crowd as soon as possible."

In the morning, I would go gather what meager belongings I had in the barracks.

"Understood, Razus."

He gave Venus a timid smile punctuated with a polite nod,

then cast a mesmerized glance at the Prism before taking his leave, shadowed by Leodros.

"Well, that was interesting," Venus said as soon as the door closed behind the guards.

"It certainly isn't how I expected this day to turn out," I said, slightly amused but also still pinching myself over it.

"Believe me, the last twenty-four hours still feel completely surreal to me. Landing here and being appointed as the Prima of a demigod did *not* feature in my schedule at all," she replied, looking a little overwhelmed.

She opened her mouth to say something else but suddenly blinked then shook her head, as if trying to dispel a wave of dizziness.

"What's wrong? Are you unwell?" I asked, instantly worried.

I unconsciously took a step closer to her, ready to catch her in case her knees wavered.

"What the heck?" Venus whispered, sounding confused. She blinked and shook her head some more.

"What's going on?" I asked, my worry cranking up another notch.

My antennae weren't picking up any airborne substances that could potentially affect her.

"I keep seeing a strange room flashing before me. It has a swirling back wall," Venus said while rubbing her temples.

"The boudoir!" I exclaimed.

"What?"

I smiled. "It appears that Xarin wants us to put him inside the boudoir."

In direct response to my comment, the surface of the Prism's cocoon shimmered with a soft glow.

"He sent me that image?!" Venus exclaimed while gaping at Xarin.

I nodded. "It is the common way the Prism communicates with his Primus, or in this case Prima. It might get tricky to interpret what he means at first, especially if he refers to specific locations. But I know this world well. If you describe to me what you see, I will help you decipher it."

"Oh, wow! That's actually kind of cool. But does that happen often? Does he have frequent conversations with people?" she asked, looking intrigued as she gazed upon the cocoon.

"Frequent, no. Based on history, interactions with the Prism are very minimal during his metamorphosis. It may occur a bit more frequently from time to time, but it's always only with the Prima," I explained while opening the secondary doors of the antechamber into the main living area.

Even though this wasn't a home I had personally acquired for her, seeing Venus's eyes light up as she took in the magnificence of the mansion awakened an irrational pride mixed with longing in my chest. Many a night, I fantasized about picking a home with my mate and decorating it based on her colors. I certainly had plenty of funds for it. After all, I had nothing to spend my wages on.

"Wow! This place is so incredibly luminous!" Venus whispered with awe as we walked past the spacious living area and headed down the wide corridor to the boudoir located on the right side of the house.

I nodded as I gazed at the large floor to ceiling windows covering a large part of the walls, not to mention the many light-wells on the ceiling.

"We need light to see colors and therefore to cast magic," I explained as I opened the door to the boudoir. "That's why most of our residences are single-story buildings with plenty of openings for the light to flood in regardless of the hour of the day. We also space the buildings far apart to avoid creating shadows on each other."

"Which explains those occluding shades for when you guys want to sleep," Venus said with understanding.

"Indeed. However, we do have pretty good night vision. But

it doesn't allow us to draft as our vision is then monochromatic," I replied.

We entered the room, and I guided Xarin's hovering platform directly in front of the large fireplace which sat below the feature wall of the room. Sculpted with lumen, the swirling pattern covering the entire wall attempted to replicate the shimmering lights of a magnetic storm. As soon as the platform reached its destination, the cocoon slightly glowed, expressing the Prism's approval.

Here, too, the large windows allowed for plenty of light and gave a stunning view of one of the mansion's three gardens. Two long benches and one large round pouf were laid out in a U-shape in front of the fireplace. All of them were white with silver cushions.

"This is insane," Venus whispered to herself as she stared at the wall.

"What is?" I asked in a soft tone. "The wall matching the image you saw?"

She nodded. "It's crazy how vivid it was. But how does he know what this wall looks like? Has he been here before? And right now, does he see us?"

I hesitated. "I cannot pretend to be an expert as to what powers the Prism possesses. From what we are taught, he cannot see the way you and I do. He hears everything within our normal hearing range, but he perceives things at a psychic and empathic level on a far wider range. It is said that he could communicate with his Primus or Prima even as far as the next city."

"Only the Primus or Prima? Could he contact you if you were in a different city?"

I shook my head. "He established a bond with you. Only you two share that connection."

She nodded slowly while studying the cocoon. "So what happens now? What else do we have to do for him?"

"Nothing," I replied with a smile. "If he requires anything

personally—which is unlikely—he will communicate with you with imagery. I suspect he will contact you, but not for himself. My intuition says he has plans for you that he will communicate in his own time."

"Plans like what?" Venus insisted.

I shrugged and gave her an apologetic look. "I'm just a Black Guard. I know nothing of the secrets of the gods."

"You're not just a Black Guard," she countered with an unreadable expression. "You, too, were chosen by the Prism and blessed. I suspect he has a plan for you as well, Atlas."

Her words troubled me, especially because they rang oddly true.

"Time will tell soon enough, I guess."

"It will," she replied in a mysterious tone.

"Come, let me give you the tour so that you can pick the room you wish to sleep in," I said, gesturing at the door.

She hesitated and cast an uncertain look at the chrysalis. "Is he safe here?"

The genuine worry emanating from her instantly had my chest filling with warmth. Once again, she was demonstrating why Xarin chose her. We were nothing to this off-worlder, and yet she expressed more concern for him than our own people had since his return.

"Yes, Venus. He is safe here. No one would dare attack him —not that he is helpless. But this house possesses a great security system, and I will have guards on rotation around the house, whenever I'm not here, and patrols when we sleep. And once again, if he needs anything, you will be the first person he will communicate with."

"Okay, then," Venus replied, looking relieved.

We walked around the house, visiting each of the four bedrooms, two of them large enough to qualify as master bedrooms. After she picked the one closest to the boudoir, I brought her meager possessions to the room.

A powerful sense of longing surged through me when she pointed where she wanted me to put them with an air of gratitude. The domestic feel of it all struck me hard. Even as I reminded myself that I should be grateful to spend the last months of my life playing husband in a true home, it still hurt that it wouldn't be real.

Although I couldn't deny that Venus possessed agreeable features, I wasn't attracted to her in the traditional sense. So why did I feel so sad that we would not be sharing a room like a normal couple?

Because you want to cuddle.

That, too, struck me like a boulder to the chest. Like all Achromatics, I never had a romantic partner. I didn't crave sex per se, but I longed for the affectionate closeness of a gentle embrace. The thought of falling asleep while holding someone special against me clawed at my heart.

Anyway, any weird fantasies I may entertain about her would go nowhere. As she was human, we were probably incompatible anatomically speaking. And even if we somehow were, we couldn't possibly have offspring. Our species were much too different for that.

To my shock, my overly fertile imagination started flashing countless images of what a child born of Venus and me could possibly look like. Dismayed, I even started wondering what it would feel like to hold my own child in my arms.

"I will leave you to settle in," I said, silencing these inappropriate thoughts before they drove me to distraction. "I will be in the other room at the back of the hallway if you need me."

"Okay. Thank you for everything," Venus replied, her dark gaze lingering on me with that strange expression again.

What I wouldn't give to know what thoughts were crossing her mind, and especially how she felt about being married to me.

Forcing a smile on my face, I turned around and left her room.

CHAPTER 8
VENUS

As I finished unpacking my far-too-few bags, I mentally made an inventory of all the things I needed for an extended stay here. Unfortunately, as much as I loved shopping, observing the crowd that lined the streets as we paraded our way here told me they likely didn't offer the type of outfits I needed.

Nobody wore any kind of top or shirt, not even the females. A few people had sashes, necklaces, braces, and arm bands, but that pretty much summed it up. Although their females appeared to have a smaller version of a human woman's breasts, the fur around their necks and chest did a good job hiding the nipples.

I had no problem letting it all hang out when relaxing on certain beaches or while visiting tribal species where females walked around bare chested. But I couldn't see myself emulating that here. In those other places, it helped me blend with the locals. Here, it would make me stand out more than actually wearing a shirt. The powerful sun also would do a number on my skin, which reminded me to add loads of solar cream to the list I would send to Linsea.

Dealing with these practical issues was merely a way for me to delay having to fully acknowledge the mess I had just landed in. While on the cruise ship, I contacted my parents to let them know what had happened. Right this minute, they would be freaking out over not having received an update. By now, I should be on my way back home. Saying they would go berserk once they found out the truth couldn't even begin to describe the shitstorm they would unleash. That definitely was one discussion I wasn't looking forward to.

They probably already know.

In fact, I was pretty certain they did. They undoubtedly harassed the Enforcers and the UPO all freaking day.

Fuck my life…

And wait until they hear about Atlas.

My stomach twisted painfully at that thought. How could he possibly be my soulmate? Since Kayog mentioned it before leaving, his words replayed in a loop in my head. A part of me wanted to believe he was just fucking with me since I'd been somewhat rude when he first got here. He knew I dreaded that he would attempt to matchmake me with a primitive alien. Considering what a mischievous personality he possessed, it would make sense for him to pull some type of prank.

He wouldn't joke about this.

And that was the crux of it. However playful the Temern could be, he took his role and reputation extremely seriously. When it came to finding the perfect match, Kayog was never wrong. He wouldn't tarnish his perfect streak just to pull a prank on me. Even had it been a joke, I believe he would have set the record straight within seconds.

I didn't know how to feel about any of it. A part of me wanted to feel excited about this. Finding one's soulmate was something to be celebrated. From what little I had observed about Atlas, he seemed like a good man.

Although some of his insectoid features creeped me out a little bit, he was rather hot. His lips looked particularly delicious. The gentle way he smiled at me felt like being wrapped in a freshly washed blanket, still warm from the dryer. There was an air of innocence and timidity that made me want to hug him. Simultaneously, an undeniable—and rather sexy—aura of authority and strength emanated from him. He was a lot more lithe than I preferred when it came to men, as I had a thing for big and brawny. But his well-defined muscles and firm body certainly qualified as droolworthy.

But I don't really want this.

That thought gave me pause. What exactly did I not want? Was my issue with Atlas himself? The prospect of marrying an alien? Or was it the fact that I might end up spending the rest of my life with this primitive species?

The strength with which that little voice at the back of my head screamed the latter actually sent an odd sense of relief flooding through me. Although I'd never pictured myself marrying anything but a human, seeing Serena's happiness proved that so long as you were with the person meant for you, the rest would fall into place. But I seriously didn't like what I had seen so far of the Prometheans.

Humanity went through similar phases. Based on our history, the Prometheans would require generations for their society to evolve to a place where everyone would be treated equally. Technologically speaking, they were centuries behind. From what I observed so far, their advancement compared to Earth circa year 2000. But socially and politically, it felt like they were barely coming out of the Victorian era.

Assuming things evolved the way Kayog implied they would, I couldn't see myself living on this planet permanently. Thankfully, this wasn't my focus for now. The upcoming weeks would provide ample opportunity for Atlas and me to figure out what—if anything—we wanted to do about this.

Did Kayog tell Atlas?

The almost instant panic I felt at that thought faded as quickly as it poked its head in. I highly doubted the Temern told him anything. Had he done so, I firmly believed that Atlas would have given it away in one form or another. For now, I intended to keep it to myself. A part of me wished Kayog had not told me. Then whatever blossomed between us would have occurred organically.

Or would it?

To my utter annoyance, I was forced to admit that, had he not warned me, I probably would have distanced myself from Atlas and erected defensive walls between us at the first sign of attraction. And then, I would have missed out on being with my soulmate.

That last thought made me flinch. I hated that my mind already accepted this as fact and was planning for us to be a long-term couple.

Heaving a sigh, I quickly freshened up in my en suite hygiene room, then exited my bedroom, and followed the hushed sounds of voices near the entrance. As I quietly approached, I noticed Atlas talking with one of his Black Guards, named Pythus, if I recalled correctly.

I walked slowly, giving myself a bit more time to secretly examine Atlas. He was indeed quite attractive, once you got over the otherworldliness of his features. I itched to touch his massive black wings. A thick horizontal stripe connected the silver eyespots adorning them. When the sun hit them just right, they almost sparkled like glitter. My fingers also ached to trace the pattern to feel their texture.

There was something noble in the way he stood straight, chin slightly lifted with an air of authority devoid of the slimy superiority displayed by the Chancellor. The deference displayed earlier by his men—and now by the one I presumed to be Pythus —spoke volumes about the type of leader he was. You couldn't buy or force the genuine respect they expressed towards him.

Not wanting to intrude on their conversation, as soon as I entered the living area, I made to head towards the kitchen, but both males turned to look at me. Atlas's warm smile did funny things to me. He gestured for me to approach, and I immediately complied.

"Venus, please meet Pythus, one of my senior officers and right hand," Atlas said, gesturing at his companion. "Pythus, this is Prima Venus."

For the most irrational reason, I felt somewhat slighted that he introduced me simply as the Prima and not his mate. But then, I never claimed that a woman's emotional responses always made sense, especially where their alleged soulmates were concerned. Furthermore, as he witnessed the entire mess that went down in their Great Hall earlier, Pythus already knew we were contractually married.

Pythus pressed his palm to his chest, fingers splayed over his solar plexus, right below the tip of his chest fur, then bowed his head.

"It is an honor to meet you, Prima," he said with great deference.

"The pleasure is mine, Pythus. But please, call me Venus," I replied with a smile.

He seemed taken aback by that request and gaped at me before casting an uncertain glance at his boss. Atlas was looking at me with an indefinable expression, but behind the softness in his eyes, I could swear I'd caught a glimmer of gratitude.

"You honor me... Venus," Pythus said at last, his scales slightly darkening when he pronounced my name.

It struck me then that he expected me to have a haughty behavior with him. I clamped down on the anger that instantly flared deep within. I hated that he—and others like him—had grown to expect to be mistreated and disrespected.

"When I'm not here, either Pythus or Leodros will be nearby to assist you should you require it," Atlas explained.

He then handed me a small device—antiquated by today's galactic standards—which I instantly recognized as some form of com system. I took it before glancing back at him questioningly.

"This is a caller Pythus set up for you. It will allow you to contact one of us if you are ever in need. I will explain its full function to you later today," he continued.

"Okay, thank you," I replied to Atlas before casting a grateful smile at Pythus.

The shyness on his face, and the way he shifted on his feet made me realize he was battling the urge to squirm. Fuck, it was stinking adorable. I bit the inside of my cheeks to keep myself from smiling.

"If there is nothing else, I will leave you now and return to my other duties," Pythus said, looking a little embarrassed.

"Thank you," Atlas replied. "We'll speak later."

After one last nod, Pythus left the house, looking like he was trying not to run away.

"He seems nice," I said when the door closed behind him.

"He is," Atlas concurred with conviction. "Pythus is a wonderful Guard and a good friend."

He appeared to want to say something more but changed his mind. This instantly piqued my curiosity, but I decided not to press him. He scratched his chest fur, right below his clavicle, and almost looked nervous, as if he didn't quite know what to say or do.

"Are you hungry? The caterer brought the sampler platter I requested so that you can test our food and see if there's anything you like."

"As a matter of fact, I'm quite hungry!" I said enthusiastically.

The broad smile that stretched his lips lit up his entire face. Damn, he was so incredibly handsome when he was happy.

"This way," he said, gesturing towards the kitchen.

We entered a spacious room that could have belonged on Earth. The Promethean architecture vaguely reminded me of a mix of elven design and Moroccan plaster on the decorated walls and soft edges of the furniture. Surprisingly, the long island of the gourmet kitchen didn't have any stools for people to sit at. Instead, they surrounded the long dining table on the left side of the dining space, next to tall patio doors that looked out onto the second courtyard of the mansion.

If not for the intricate carvings on the walls, the place would feel a little depressing and excessively sanitized with the white everywhere, from the off-white travertine-looking tiles on the floor to the ivory walls, and the just as pale furniture. The only splash of color, if it could even qualify as such, were the silver accents of the cushion and outlining some of the edges of the carvings on the walls.

He pointed at one of the comfortable-looking rectangular stools surrounding the table. The embroidery work on the cushion was spectacular.

"I guess you guys don't have chairs with backs," I mused aloud, as I settled on a stool on the left side of the table.

Obviously, it made sense for them not to have backrests as they would get in the way of their wings.

"No," Atlas said while bringing a few large trays of food to the table. "I will fix that for you. Just let me know what they should look like, and I will take care of it."

"Oh, no. Don't worry about it. This is fine, and it will force me to work on my posture," I said with a smile.

He frowned. "Are you certain? It is no trouble. You will be with us for a while. There's no reason you shouldn't have all the comforts you require when you need it."

"I'm sure," I reiterated. "If I change my mind, I'll let you know."

Although he nodded, the look on his face made it clear he wasn't convinced. With a certainty I couldn't explain, I believed he would try to get me a chair with a backrest regardless. It would indeed be smart to have one handy should I ever feel the urge for it. I didn't understand why I argued when he offered. Considering how Serena often called me a diva—which wasn't entirely false—I couldn't explain why I was acting so low maintenance all of a sudden.

Because you want him to like you.

That struck me hard. Could that be it? I'd never been the type to try and change myself to please a man. It made no sense that I would start doing that now, soulmate or not. In fact, if he truly was my soulmate, he would be entirely fine with my high maintenance self.

But the sight of the appetizing dishes he laid before me shifted my focus away. The delicious aroma of light spices wafted to me as I feasted my eyes on what could have almost passed for traditional Chinese cuisine, at least in appearance. My gaze flicked to roundish, stuffed dough that looked steamed. As a huge sucker for dumplings, my mouth immediately watered. I could only pray I wouldn't be traumatized by the taste of the stuffing because of unrealistic expectations.

Various sauteed and steamed vegetables, some of them mixed with meat—or at least what I assumed to be meat—sat next to bowls of roasted, barbecued, or braised meats. Another dish that drew my attention was some kind of whitish grain. From where I sat, I first thought it to be white rice, before realizing the grains were too short for that. It could have passed for cauliflower rice.

As soon as Atlas settled across the table from me, he gestured for me to dig in. I did not hesitate. Without being a health freak, I generally ate in a responsible fashion—which didn't prevent me from indulging in the occasional deep-fried decadence and sinfully sweet desserts. But this healthy and tasty food fully met my approval.

Granted, despite enjoying fancy restaurants, I wasn't a picky eater. Over the years working as an intergalactic lobbyist, I traveled to strange places and eaten even weirder stuff. I still struggled with anything that had a slimy texture or appearance. But I had eaten my fair share of bugs. Thankfully, they'd either been so transformed that you didn't recognize them for what they were, or they'd been buried deep enough in other things so that I wouldn't notice.

As we enjoyed the meal, we settled into a pleasant conversation, mostly with me inquiring about him and his species.

"Your wings look a lot thinner than the feathery ones Kayog and Linsea have," I said pensively. "Are they heavy?"

He shook his head, then paused as if reconsidering his answer. "In practice, no they're not. But technically, I would probably have to say yes. As we're born with our wings, our back muscles develop accordingly through regular use. However, if someone was unable to work those muscles for an extended period, they would struggle with them. That said, they get really heavy once they're wet."

I tilted my head with curiosity. "So flying in the rain is bad?"

He nodded. "It can be dangerous if the rain is heavy. It's definitely quite exhausting. So we'll normally look for shelter or fly under the canopy of a forest to avoid our wings getting weighed down."

I glanced at his wings. They were folded down behind him almost like a cape or the train of a wedding gown.

"How about when you sleep? Do they get in the way? Can they get damaged if you sleep on top of them?"

He chuckled. The way his eyes briefly went out of focus hinted that he had pictured something he found amusing or reminisced about a past incident.

"We can definitely sleep on them, but it can be really uncomfortable if they are folded as they create a bump beneath us. It also tends to cut off circulation in the veins. The tingling sensation when we finally move and blood rushes back in is quite unpleasant."

"Ugh, I know exactly what you mean. That pins and needles

sensation sucks, but I usually get it in my hands or in my feet," I replied.

He smiled with compassion. Once again, I couldn't help but notice how handsome he looked when he did.

"Personally, I tend to sleep on the side with my wings folded behind me. I think it stems from my training. When sleeping outdoors, it is easier to use them as blankets to keep me warm that way."

He no sooner spoke those words than I found myself trying to picture what he looked like asleep. To my dismay, the picture of him in a fetal position was quickly replaced by one where he and I were spooning, with his wings wrapped around us. I quickly cast it out of my mind and changed the topic.

"This food is excellent. I could get used to this," I said with a bit too much enthusiasm. "I also love good food, but I'm sadly not much of a cook."

Oblivious to the discomfort stirred by my wandering thoughts, Atlas beamed at me.

"I'm happy to hear you like it. I'm actually a good cook, although I rarely get to do it."

"Oh? Why is that?" I asked.

"I live in the barracks. As such, I normally eat with the Black Guards in the mess hall. We have dedicated cooks who prepare the meals for everyone."

"I see," I said before chewing my bottom lip while carefully choosing my words. "Is it compulsory for Black Guards to live in the barracks?"

He smiled, instantly understanding the real underlying question. "I'm not forced to live in the barracks. It is a choice we all naturally make. There is no point for us to acquire a house without a mate or offspring."

"You're still young," I argued.

He slightly frowned at me. "As you saw earlier, Achromatics like me do not marry. What happened today is a serious anomaly.

The only reason it was allowed was because the Prism himself confirmed that I should be your mate. Otherwise, we don't marry, and we don't have children."

"But that other senator confirmed that the law does not forbid it," I countered gently.

He nodded. "You are correct. But the backlash would be too great. You saw how upset many people were today. It would be a thousand times worse without the Prism involved to grant his blessing. But even if one of us decided to face the people's wrath, it would be cruel to doom our offspring to the same harsh life that we have."

It was my turn to frown. "As I have not studied Promethean genetics, I will not make any assumptions. However, for the majority of species, that is not how genetics works. The fact that you are an Achromatic doesn't necessarily mean that your children would be as well. Genetics are a lottery. You're never quite sure which traits from each parent you will inherit. In theory, Achromatics should be able to have Polychromatic children."

He nodded slowly. "Some of our scientists have expressed this as well. Their data also supports this, but mentalities are very slow to change. And without tangible proof, not just theories, people are even more reluctant to accept it. And none of us want to be the ones breaking the rules to provide that proof. The fallout would be too severe."

"So that means your parents were not Achromatic, correct?"

"Correct," he conceded. "Both of them are Polychromatics… as are my siblings."

"You have siblings?!" I exclaimed, surprised.

His face slightly closed off. "I'm the third child, with an older brother and sister. I don't know if my parents had more offspring after me. Somehow, I doubt they did."

"So you don't have any contact with your family?" I asked softly, wondering if I should move away from that topic in case it was still sore for him.

"None whatsoever," he replied, matter-of-factly before smiling. "It is normal here for parents to keep their Achromatic or Monochromatic offspring a secret. If we mingled, both my parents and siblings would be shamed by association. Worse still, it would significantly reduce the mating prospects of my siblings as potential partners would fear they would also produce one of us."

Judging by Atlas's expression, my face was loudly broadcasting the anger his statement awakened in me. A billion words burned my tongue. I wanted to tell him it was pure bullshit that anyone could imply an innocent child would be a shameful secret merely for the color of its wings. I wanted to tell him just how fucked up his society was. And it most certainly was. But I also knew that the type of radical changes his people needed wouldn't occur overnight with me making grand speeches about how they had it all wrong.

I also needed to tread carefully so as to not alienate him either. Although he was a victim of it all, Atlas was likely too deeply brainwashed for me to go all in challenging their culture. I could only pray my presence here, however short, would help stir them further onto the path of acceptance and mutual respect.

"How young were you when you last saw your parents and siblings?" I asked gently, relieved that my voice didn't contain any of the fury I felt deep within.

"A few minutes old," he replied teasingly. He chuckled when I gaped at him. "Achromatics and Monochromatics are left by their parents at the Birthing Hall with the caretakers, who then send us to the Asylum."

"To the what?!" I exclaimed—not to say shouted—completely flabbergasted.

My reaction clearly took him aback. "Infants like me are taken to the Asylum to be raised by others like us," he said cautiously.

"Define asylum for me," I said, my voice filled with tension.

"It is a shelter where the children are taken care of, fed, and educated in the various trades that will make them functional members of the society."

"So like an orphanage where they are raised and looked after?" I insisted, to be certain.

"Yes," Atlas answered, still looking confused. "Why did you react so strongly?"

I scrunched my face and shifted in my seat. "The word asylum triggered me. Although it also has the meaning of shelter and safe haven, we usually use that term to refer to the places where we lock up people with serious mental illness, the type that might hurt themselves or others," I explained sheepishly.

Atlas gaped at me for a few seconds before bursting out laughing. My cheeks heated that I should have automatically jumped to the worst possible conclusion.

"It definitely is not that type of asylum," Atlas said, still chuckling. "For what it's worth they are wonderful places. The Elders who run the Asylums are themselves Achromatic or Monochromatic, as are all the children. It is the safest place for us, growing up surrounded by others like us facing the same challenges we do. My time in the Asylum was probably the happiest years of my life."

I gave him a sympathetic look. "I'm glad those children have a safe and happy place to grow up. It's just unfortunate that they should be separated from their families over such misconceptions. Humans used to think less of each other based on color, country of origin, religion, language, and even gender. It took us centuries to finally realize we're all the same."

"Humans may be the same, but we're not," Atlas argued.

"You are the same, just with different talents. In the case of the Prometheans, your abilities are largely based on the color of your wings. But that doesn't make you lesser than someone else. Each of you have your own value and purpose."

To my surprise, Atlas seemed displeased by my words.

"You're making a lot of assumptions, Venus. You do not know us."

"You're right," I replied in an appeasing tone. "I don't know much about the Prometheans, but I know a lot about science. And I want to figure out what is causing… Torag?"

"Thaudras," he corrected. "You've heard of it?"

"Only what Linsea told me in the meeting room once the Prism decided he wanted me to stay," I said. "Is it true that people like you are sacrificed when Thaudras occurs?"

Atlas shifted his wings, an uneasy expression fleeting over his features. "Yes, sacrifices are required to end it."

Although I knew what his answer would be, my stomach nevertheless twisted to have it thus confirmed.

"Will *you* get sacrificed?" I asked carefully.

"Of course," he replied, matter-of-factly. "All Blacks and Whites are sacrificed first, and then the Monochromatics."

I slightly recoiled upon hearing those words. "Why are Blacks and Whites the first?" I asked, stunned.

"Because we appease the gods the most," he replied in a soft voice. "Without at least five Blacks and five Whites, the region affected by Thaudras will sustain massive devastation. Ideally, there should be ten of each."

That struck me as a vital piece of information.

"And what if only Monochromatics are sacrificed, no Blacks and no Whites at all?" I insisted.

"Then there will inevitably be massive devastation on a larger radius."

Which could only mean that the Blacks and Whites possessed a special trait required to help counter the magnetic surge. But what? This constituted the first lead I could follow to try and figure out what was happening.

"So how many people in total are sacrificed each time Thaudras occurs? You mentioned ten of each Blacks and Whites, for a total of twenty?" I asked.

He nodded. "And about another twenty Monochromatics usually suffices. However, each Black or White missing requires between five and ten Monochromatics in replacement."

"Ten Monos to replace a single Black or White?!" I exclaimed.

He nodded again. That, more than anything else, proved that the Blacks and Whites possessed a unique trait that was essential to containing the anomaly.

"So at least forty people are expected to be sacrificed in a few months," I mused aloud.

"Hmm, no, not exactly," Atlas said hesitantly. "That number would be accurate on average, but the impending Thaudras will be massive. The magnetic movements we have detected indicate it will be two to three times more devastating than any previous ones. We expect that at least one hundred and twenty of us will need to be sacrificed."

"Are you serious?!" I exclaimed.

He gave me a resigned smile.

"I'm not going to let you die, Atlas," I said in a tone that brooked no argument.

To my shock, his face instantly hardened. "It is my duty and that of every other Achromatic. Our sacrifice means the survival of our world and of our people. It is a death we go to willingly."

"Are you saying you want to die?!" I exclaimed, flabbergasted.

He hesitated then shook his head. "I do not wish to die, but I accept that I must for the greater good. There is no other way to save our world."

"What makes you so sure?" I asked, baffled.

He pushed back his empty plate and scratched the fur below his clavicle while his face took on a faraway expression.

"History makes me sure. Every three or four generations, the next Thaudras is announced by a sudden increase in births of Achromatic and Monochromatic children. By the time they reach between thirty and thirty-five years, Thaudras occurs." He refocused on me. "Our people thought the gods wanted to erase the stain that we were with this cataclysm. So they figured that if they preemptively hunted us, they could prevent it from occurring altogether."

I pressed a palm to my chest, horrified by my sudden understanding. "They killed all the Achromatics and Monochromatics?!"

He nodded with a grim expression. "All of them were killed at birth. But Thaudras still came. Except this time, there were none of us to be sacrificed. The burning light spread through Orist Valley, destroying the land, filling the air with toxic fumes, and poisoning the water."

"Oh, my God! It must have been terrifying."

"According to our history books, it was like the end days were upon them. In despair, the people asked for volunteers among the Bichromatics and Polychromatics. The Elders and the sick were first to be sacrificed."

"I guess that didn't help?"

"Not even in the slightest. They then sacrificed the young and healthy people. That also didn't help. When the devastation continued to spread and began threatening other cities, the people decided to track down the Pharoms."

"What are the Pharoms?" I asked, morbidly fascinated by his tale.

"They are the Monos and Achros who have left the cities and live in secret villages and clans," Atlas explained. "They were hunted down like animals and then sacrificed against their will. By all accounts, it was horrible for everyone involved. But it did end Thaudras. Some people claim it was the existence of the Pharoms that caused Thaudras. But our scientists argued that they were not at fault and that the cataclysm was simply inevitable."

"The scientist in me agrees with that assessment, even

though I still have much to learn about this entire phenomenon," I said carefully.

As much as my heart broke for those poor Pharoms, and as horrified as I felt by it all, it didn't truly shock me. Human history also had similar atrocities fueled by ignorance and bigotry.

"In the end, the population agreed that it was too risky not to have Achros and Monos in their midst. Therefore, they passed new edicts outlawing our executions at birth."

While this had been the right decision, it didn't dampen the fresh wave of anger that surged within me. They weren't forbidding the murder of these innocent children because they understood the error of their ways. They just wanted to keep them around as handy sacrificial lambs the minute things got heated.

"I would like to study this Thaudras phenomenon," I said cautiously. "I have some theories that could help solve the mystery as to why all of this is happening. Hopefully, we can stop it."

"Venus, sacrifices are inevitable," Atlas warned, his tone making it clear he thought I wanted to embark on a pointless crusade.

"Based on what you've just told me, it sounds like you indeed absolutely *have* to go in there. I just intend to find a way to make sure you come back out alive."

CHAPTER 9
VENUS

I woke up the next morning from a surprisingly pleasant sleep… under the circumstances. As bland as all the white was, the furniture screamed luxury. The mattress was sinfully soft. Normally, I leaned towards something a bit firmer, but this truly felt like lying down on a cloud. The silkiness of the blankets against my skin easily rivaled the gentle touch of a lover. My only complaint was how light it felt on top of me. I liked a heavy comforter weighing me down.

I stretched loudly before hopping out of bed. The occluding shades automatically reduced their opacity on a timer in the morning so that the room wouldn't be pitched in complete darkness. A single flick of a switch fully opened them, allowing daylight to flood in.

As I headed into the hygiene room for my morning routine, the recent events replayed in my mind. This entire situation still felt unreal to me, but as I loved a challenge, I bubbled with excitement at the prospect of tackling this issue.

I brushed my hair and rubbed some leave-in moisturizer in the tight locks before deciding to leave it natural instead of braiding it. For a split second, I considered going to check if

Atlas was already up and see if he wanted to share breakfast with me. A glance at my laptop sitting on the desk by the large arched window overlooking the garden reminded me of the chore I had already delayed for much too long. With a groan, I settled at the desk and connected to my messaging application.

Although the Prometheans achieved connectivity technology, it was still very basic and limited. The UPO allowed me to temporarily piggyback through their relay communication satellites. Sadly, with my current device, the connection remained much too slow and made live videos with an off-worlder impossible. Naturally, I would request an upgrade as part of the list of things I needed them to send me. But this minor setback actually played in my favor.

Very few things scared or intimidated me. I had no problem giving a tongue lashing to anyone acting like a smart ass to me. The only people who could make me squirm were my parents. Sending them a long offline message meant I didn't have to deal with their wrath in real time. I was fine with that making me a wuss.

Initially, I considered merely typing the message as it would transfer a lot faster, then thought better of it. Knowing them, if they couldn't see my face, they would immediately assume the worst, including that I was somehow being mistreated, or maybe even bruised and battered. My mother could be quite the drama queen. At the same time, a part of me loved their overprotectiveness. Dad turned into a real dragon whenever anyone threatened his baby girls, and my mom put to shame even the most rabid of mamma bears.

"Mom, Dad, just sending you a quick message to let you know that I'm fine and that everything is under control. I know you're currently making a major stink everywhere and harassing the hell out of everyone over me. Please stop it. As much as I didn't plan on landing here, I'm actually honored to have been chosen for this. This connection is too crappy for me to go into great details, but just know that this project is probably one of the most impactful for an entire species that I will ever be given a chance to partake in," I said.

I then proceeded to give them a short summary of what I encountered so far as well as request they get in touch with a couple of our contacts to start putting together a summary of the type of data and information I should gather. Despite my scientific background, I didn't know anything about nuclear physics. As we couldn't simply take things into our own hands, I needed to learn enough to be able to drop the proper types of hints so that the Prometheans themselves would be able to solve their problems.

After sending the message, I exited my room and stopped by the boudoir to check on the Prism. His chrysalis remained still on the hovering platform in front of the fireplace. Its soft color immediately translated to me as him being content and comfortable. It felt strange to be watching over a cocoon. A part of me wondered if I should spend time with him and talk to him. But Atlas said Xarin would call upon me when needed. Still, considering we'd met after he'd been kidnapped once, making sure he remained safe and sound seemed like the right thing to do.

Satisfied, I made my way to the kitchen to silence my growling stomach. As I crossed the living area, movement through the tall windows caught my eyes. I stopped dead in my tracks and stared in awe at Atlas performing some impressive battle moves in what had to be his morning training routine.

With a will of their own, my feet led me to the patio doors, and I slid them open, careful not to make any noise that would break his concentration.

Wearing nothing but the usual loincloth they called a tarp— which vaguely reminded me of an ancient gladiator skirt—Atlas was leaping and jumping, spinning on himself while thrusting a double-bladed staff at an invisible target. The way he would suddenly pull back with a single flap of his wings almost gave the illusion a powerful force had suddenly yanked him back. The control he displayed spoke of years of experience and true mastery.

I stood there drooling at the perfection of his body, each muscle lean and defined, bunching during a powerful attack, then relaxing and rolling beneath the shiny scales on his arms and legs. To my shame, I caught myself too many times feeling disappointed that, despite its shortness, his loincloth did a fantastic job of hiding the goods.

My jaw dropped when the eyespots in his wings began to glow at the same time he thrusted his hand forward, his palm raised in an arresting gesture. A gasp escaped me when half a dozen silver darts shot out of his palm to bury themselves into the ground with the piercing sound of a bullet.

Startled, Atlas spun around to face me, instinctively taking a defensive stance. Although it would be deemed menacing, I didn't feel threatened. With bone deep confidence, I knew he possessed enough self-control not to harm me in surprise. I raised my hands before me in a surrendering gesture, an air of wonder plastered on my face.

Atlas immediately straightened and took on a non-threatening posture with an air of guilt. I smiled and clapped while descending the few steps into the garden. He frowned at my hands with an air of confusion.

"What is that noise you are making?" he asked.

"We call it applause," I said, stopping a few steps in front of him. "It's how humans express admiration for someone's exceptional performance, or to congratulate them. Occasionally, it can be used in a sarcastic fashion to mock someone. For example, if they do something really stupid, you could clap your hands to say: way to mess up."

He seemed amused, his gaze locked on my hands as if he was picturing me clapping them again.

"So am I to understand you think I did something really stupid?" he asked.

I snorted. "If you are fishing for compliments, you're about to get served. I was definitely applauding because your performance was amazing."

The way his scales darkened made me instantly want to smoosh his face. I didn't think he had been trying to get me to compliment him. I suspected that behind his reserved exterior, Atlas had a pretty self-derisive sense of humor. But seeing him this embarrassed to be complimented made him even more adorable than he already was.

"Thank you," he said while scratching the fur below his clavicle.

It dawned on me that this gesture was some sort of nervous tick. But staring at his hand reminded me what had taken me aback during his performance.

"I didn't mean to break your concentration. But how did you fire those darts or needles from your hand?" I asked with genuine curiosity. "I thought Blacks didn't possess any magic?"

"We're not entirely deprived of magic," he conceded. "We have very little, and it is extremely weak compared to other colors. In our case, our wings' eyespots are the only color we're able to draft. Since the surface is very small, we cannot channel enough color to cast more powerful magic. The others can draft from the entirety of their colored wings."

"I see," I responded, fascinated. "But what you did was still really awesome. I'm impressed."

"You're too kind," he said with a boyish shyness that made me melt inside. "However, I am way more powerful today than I was yesterday, thanks to you."

My brow shot up. "Thanks to me?"

"By choosing me as your mate, you made the Prism bless me. It opened my wings' eyespots and expanded the spectrum of colors I can draft from. It used to only be silver and pale gray.

Now, my eyespots have a pure white inner ring that enables me to draft from any color. Too bad it is in such a limited quantity. But I'm still incredibly grateful."

I stared at his wings with wonder before glancing back at him. "I have no merit in you receiving that blessing. The Prism bestowed it upon you because of who you are. You made him want to bless you the same way you made me want to choose you. Do not underestimate what a powerful aura of honesty, reliability, and honor you project. Xarin sensed it the same way I did."

He shifted on his feet and scratched his fur again. The poor thing didn't seem to know what to do with himself, visibly unused to receiving such positive comments.

"Then I'm glad you and he felt that way," he mumbled, before glancing back at me.

Despite the absence of sclera or irises to make it clear where he was looking, I knew beyond the shadow of a doubt that he was examining my hair.

"Your hair is completely different from yesterday. It's quite beautiful," he said with an air of fascination.

I smiled and unconsciously ran a hand over it. "Yeah, I decided to leave it natural."

"I've never seen that texture before or such tight curls," Atlas said pensively.

"It certainly is different. Do you want to touch?" I surprised myself by offering.

He seemed just as taken aback. "You don't mind? That would be acceptable?"

The hopefulness in his voice made me smile. "It is entirely acceptable *if* the person offered for you to do so. It's also fine to ask for permission. But you should never touch someone's hair without asking first or receiving their consent."

He frowned. "That seems obvious."

I rolled my eyes. "You'd be surprised how often people have

done this to someone like me. And then they have the nerve to be upset when we reprimand them for just reaching out and touching our hair. The most infuriating part is that if they see someone walking around with their pet, they will ask the owner if it's okay to touch their animal. But they feel entitled to touch us without asking. It's quite offensive that they should show more deference to animals than to us."

My cheeks heated as he stared at me with a stunned expression, looking unsure how to respond.

"Sorry for going off on an impromptu rant," I said sheepishly. "It's just a sore spot for me. But yes, I'm happy for you to touch my hair."

He chuckled and approached his hand timidly. The powerful thrill of anticipation that surged through me took me aback.

"So incredibly soft," he whispered under his breath, looking mesmerized.

I almost chuckled when he gently pressed on it, only to see it bounce back when he released it, and then repeat the motion a few more times.

"So fluffy," he whispered again before sinking his fingers in my hair.

The part of me that wanted to shout at him not to mess it all up was instantly silenced by the other part that wanted to purr in reaction to the borderline intimate touch.

With much reluctance—and to my great chagrin—Atlas slowly removed his hand before looking at me with awe.

"Your hair is amazing. I have never seen or touched anything like it before. On Sylvar, everyone has hair like me. Even the humans I have seen so far all had hair like the male who accompanied you earlier, Tedrick."

"Human hair has a great variety of textures and colors," I conceded before gesturing at his chest with my chin. "But your fur looks just as fluffy."

He glanced down at himself. "It is indeed fluffy, but not as bouncy and light as your hair. You can touch, if you wish."

"Really?!" I asked in an overly eager tone that made him smile.

"Yes. So long as the person offered," he added with a glimmer of mischief in his obsidian eyes.

I snorted and made a face at him before reaching for his fur. I gently ran my palm over it and barely managed to repress a moan.

"Oh, wow! It's so incredibly soft! I thought it would be coarse."

His brow shot up. "Why would you think that?" Atlas asked, baffled.

"Because Prometheans physically share many similarities with the moths on Earth," I said sheepishly, hoping he wouldn't take offense at the comparison. Some of the tension in my shoulders faded when he merely nodded while waiting intently for me to continue. "On those creatures, what people think to be fur are actually spiky scales made of chitin."

"It's the same for us, but our spikes are softer," Atlas replied. "I suspect they serve the same purpose of thermal regulation to help us control the heat of our bodies in flight. Our fur also helps detect environmental changes like air current, temperature, and even the presence of a predator."

Atlas's voice deepened on the last words as I sank my fingers into the fur covering his chest. The deep vibration instantly turned me on. To my shock, the sensual expression that gradually settled on his face hinted that my touch was also arousing him.

That messed with my head in the most inappropriate fashion.

Forcing myself to behave, I reluctantly pulled my hand away from him and shifted my attention to the small scales covering his arms.

"Now those definitely look hard," I said.

He pursed his lips as if pondering how to respond. "Yes and no. It is difficult to explain. But you can touch them as well."

He didn't have to say it twice. Truth be told, I made that comment hoping he would offer.

The moment I ran my fingertips over the shiny scales, I immediately understood what he meant. The scales were indeed hard and yet pliable. Or rather, their small size allowed them to be flexible whereas one large chitin plate would have been unyielding. I traced the pattern of his scales with my index finger all the way down to his elbow before flattening my palm on his arm, and running it first in an upward caress, and then repeating the gesture downward. While the latter had been completely smooth, the former gently scraped my palm in a way that I found rather titillating.

"The texture is really cool," I said, giving his scales one last caress before dropping my hand.

"Cool?" he echoed, surprised.

I chuckled. "I didn't mean it in the literal sense. Humans sometimes use the word cool to mean something really interesting, pleasant, or appealing."

"I see."

I pressed my lips together to refrain from smiling when he cast a less-than-subtle look at my arms, left exposed by the sleeveless short summer dress I had donned.

"You can touch as well," I said, extending my arm towards him. "As you can see, humans are soft all over."

His smile confirmed he indeed hoped I would return the favor. He no sooner caressed the upper side of my forearm than a shiver coursed through me, and my skin erupted in goosebumps. Atlas recoiled, yanked his hand away, and stared at me with a panicked expression.

I laughed and raised my palm in an appeasing gesture.

"All is well, Atlas. This is a natural phenomenon. Human

skin does that sometimes. We call it having goosebumps," I explained.

His shoulders slumped with obvious relief although he continued to stare warily at my arm. "So you're not having an allergic reaction to my touch?"

"Oh, God no! Not at all!" I exclaimed, forcing myself not to laugh for fear he might be offended or think I was mocking him. "This normally happens in response to a powerful but pleasant emotion."

His eyes widened, and he stared at me for a second. I could see his wheels spinning as he digested my words. My stomach dropped when he slightly flicked his antennae. As I understood it, they behaved in a fashion somewhat similar to how snakes used their tongues to gather information about their environment and people near them. Serena's husband could deduce far too many intimate things about my sister simply by sticking his tongue out. Apparently, it could tell him with scientific accuracy just how aroused she was, when she was ovulating, or even if she was pregnant.

I flinched inwardly even as that thought crossed my mind. Serena took far too much pleasure making me cringe as she described these things to me. Nobody wanted to know about their sister's state of arousal.

But whatever Atlas's antennae revealed about me had the strangest expression fleeting over his handsome features—a mix of awe and confusion. He knew I was turned on. To my shock, I was fine with that.

"My touch doesn't displease you," he whispered as if to himself.

"It doesn't," I replied in a factual manner.

He stared at me for a few more seconds. I didn't know what I expected him to say or even what thoughts were coursing through his mind. How would he react if I told him that it was normal I should have positive reactions to his touch considering he was my soulmate? I was meant to crave intimate physical contact with him.

"I'm glad to hear it," Atlas finally said, with an unreadable expression that had a million questions firing off in my head.

Before I could respond, my stomach emitted the least discreet growl, broadcasting loudly that I was way past my breakfast time.

Atlas's scales turned almost as dark as his wings while a mortified expression descended over his features.

"Apologies, Venus!" he exclaimed. "I'm a terrible mate. Please, come. Let me feed you."

"It's okay," I said with amusement. "You did nothing wrong. I was on my way to get food when I spotted you training. It was such an amazing spectacle I couldn't resist but to come out and admire your skills."

He gave me that timid smile I was growing accustomed to and scratched his fur even as he gestured for me to proceed back inside.

Like last night, Atlas made me sit at the table while he brought various plates of food from the cooling unit. I could only assume the caterer dropped by while I was still sleeping. It was an impressive spread of cold cuts, fruits, dried breads, nuts, and cured meats that were part of their traditional breakfast.

All of it suited me just fine. However, to my chagrin, they didn't have an equivalent to coffee—another item I needed to add to the list I'd send to Linsea and the Enforcers.

"I'm free to be your guide today, if you wish," Atlas said after swallowing a mouthful of cured meats.

"Actually, now that Xarin no longer restricts my ability to move away from him since he knows I'm not going to abandon him, I was wondering if it would be possible to meet some of your scientists," I said carefully.

Atlas stiffened. Thankfully, it appeared to be out of surprise rather than outrage. "Our scientists? Why?"

"I want to get a better understanding of Thaudras. As I mentioned last night, our conversation gave me some leads I would like to pursue and validate with your experts," I explained. "Later tonight, I intend to send a list of things I require to Tedrick. Speaking with your scientists first would help me identify everything I will need."

"Things like what?" Atlas insisted, tilting his head to the side.

"Quite a few human research tools," I replied honestly. "But I also need personal care products for my hair, my nails, and my body in general," I added before casting a discouraged glance at my hands. "I can't believe I'm going to be stuck with a manicure bot."

"A manicure bot?" he repeated.

"A machine that can take care of my nails. It's nowhere near as good as a real esthetician, but under the circumstances, it will have to do," I said dejectedly.

"Is that something essential to your welfare?" Atlas asked with a concerned expression.

"If by essential you mean helping prevent me having an emotional breakdown, then yes, it is absolutely essential."

"What?!" Atlas exclaimed. "Then we must have Tedrick send this machine at once!"

I burst out laughing before giving him a guilty expression. "Relax, Atlas. All is well. I'm just being overly dramatic. I'm what humans call superficial or a high maintenance diva," I said with self-derision.

He looked confused. "Why do they call you that?"

"Because I can be borderline obsessive about personal care and having an impeccable appearance," I said sheepishly. "I hate dirty and broken nails. I normally get a mani-pedi every week and visit the hair salon every two weeks. My sister would laugh if she could see me right now."

He slightly frowned. "You do not get along with your sister?"

I smiled and shook my head. "No. I absolutely adore her. She just thinks I have all the wrong priorities on that front."

To my surprise, he gave me an intense and serious look. "There is nothing wrong with wanting to feel good about yourself and how you look. It's especially true if you actually have control over it. If you need your bot, then you should have it."

All of a sudden, I truly felt superficial. Although he spoke those words in a supportive and encouraging fashion, it didn't take a genius to realize his underlying meaning. Atlas didn't feel good about his appearance because his society made sure to let him know he was bad for being Achromatic. If he had any power to change it, if somebody allowed him to modify it, I believed he would have done so without hesitation.

Oblivious to my inner turmoil, Atlas smiled. "As for the scientist, I can take you to Kyrene. She is our greatest nuclear and optical physicist. She devoted most of her career to studying Thaudras. If anyone can provide you with the answers you seek, it is she."

CHAPTER 10
ATLAS

Although we didn't expect any trouble, and in spite of the great security system, I assigned Leodros to guard the Silver Mansion in our absence. I refused to give Ajustus any ground to find me lacking. Venus and I then walked to the principal research center out of the three located within the city walls.

We possessed vehicles, but they were rarely used, except to carry heavy items. Otherwise, people normally flew or walked to their destination. As she was still getting familiar with the city, Venus preferred to go on foot, which she also deemed a good way to get her steps in. That wording confused me until she explained it meant walking a certain distance daily for exercise.

Judging by the very appealing curves of her slender body, my mate was quite fit.

Once again, a wave of pride washed over me as Venus kept a completely stoic and unfazed expression despite the borderline rude way in which people were observing us as we walked past them. Her strength and dauntless attitude truly impressed me. From what Ambassador Linsea told us prior to Venus's arrival, my mate occupied a role in the upper spheres of politics, at a similar level to our senators, although in a different capacity. Based on our political representatives' behaviors, I expected her to have a demanding and superior attitude, with an overly fragile ego.

Being proven wrong pleased me beyond words.

As we entered the tall building, I stretched my neck to release the tension that had been discreetly building in my back the closer we got. My people could be very hostile when anyone questioned or challenged the origin and cause of Thaudras. Kyrene didn't worry me. She'd been studying the phenomenon her entire life and strongly promoted progressive laws and ideas. But I didn't know what welcome the rest of the staff would reserve for my mate.

Like every public building, and especially official or governmental ones, an abundance of white and light grays welcomed us. Here, as magic was not encouraged, very few windows allowed for natural light to come in. That didn't make the place dark or gloomy as plenty of artificial light sources compensated. But it always gave me a slight feeling of claustrophobia.

We didn't even have to introduce ourselves as we entered the reception area. Not surprising considering we were the talk of the town since the Prism chose us as his guardians. The receptionist merely indicated for us to proceed to a specific room, stating she would announce our arrival.

We followed the wide corridor in silence. Venus's eyes were flicking this way and that as she took in our surroundings. She couldn't read the signs and symbols on the walls as her translator couldn't yet handle Promethean letters. It still baffled me that the majority of off-worlders had a translation chip implanted at the back of their right ear at a young age.

That was yet another thing that made me fascinated by the incredible things other worlds had achieved and that their populations deemed normal. I would give anything to get to experience even just a small sample of the civilizations beyond the stars.

Our destination door swung open long before we reached it. Kyrene stood in the doorway with an excited expression that instantly wiped away any tension I felt. She beamed at us, her antennae flickering as she discreetly assessed the energy emanating from my mate, prompting me to do the same. Her scent was delicious, slightly sweet and spicy which screamed health. I didn't perceive any fear from her, but an eagerness similar to the one Kyrene was giving off.

To my delight, Venus responded to the older female's greeting with a similar warm smile.

"There you are! Come in! Come in!" Kyrene said, stepping outside the room to wave us in.

Even neatly folded behind her, Kyrene's long, dark-blue wings gave a glimpse of the other two beautiful colors adorning them: red veins and yellow eyespots. They made the scientist an incredibly powerful Polychromatic. As such, people often wondered why someone such as she would devote so much energy fighting for the rights of the Achros and Monos.

Like my parents, she had been forced to abandon her White Achromatic child—a secret I only knew of as the Razus of the Black Guard. She moved from her original city to the capital, supposedly for a new start. But she was a female on a mission, determined to enable a better future for her son and others like us. And above all, she was fighting a losing battle against time that would see him sacrificed with the rest of us.

We stepped inside an immense room with research equipment that I couldn't even begin to describe or understand the use of. Some large contraptions resembling the engine of some complex machinery or vehicle occupied the central area of the space. A few desks lined the right side of the room, with one longer table with a giant screen for meetings and discussions. On the opposite side, a massive counter with even more equipment covered most of the wall.

"Kyrene, please meet the Prima Venus," I said after she closed the door behind us. "Venus, this is Kyrene Veltis, Japhyr's most brilliant scientist."

"It's a pleasure to meet you, Prima," Kyrene said warmly. "And don't listen to him. There are far greater minds than me. But you will be hard pressed to find one more passionate about her work than I am."

"The pleasure is all mine. But please call me Venus. I'm quite informal," my mate replied with a smile.

"Only if you call me Kyrene."

"Deal!"

"Please, have a seat," Kyrene said, gesturing towards the meeting table at the back of the room. "Atlas said you wanted to discuss Thaudras with me?"

Venus nodded as we headed towards the table. "I'm quite curious to hear your theories on that phenomenon. As I'm not a nuclear physicist, I don't pretend to have the same type of technical knowledge you possess. However, I am a biomedical engineer, and this issue fascinates me."

By the way Kyrene's face lit up, my mate's words clearly pleased her.

"A fellow scientist! That is great news!" she said, her voice bubbling with excitement as we settled around the table. "Thaudras is truly a unique phenomenon. Maybe your off-worlder perspective can help us further understand what exactly is happening."

"I will gladly give what reasonable assistance I can offer… within the constraints of the Prime Directive," Venus replied cautiously.

"Naturally," Kyrene conceded, although I didn't miss the glimmer of disappointment that fleeted over her features.

I didn't fully comprehend the extent of the restrictions of the Prime Directive. Off-worlders already revealed themselves to us, and the UPO provided us with some advanced technology to allow us to communicate with them. Therefore, wasn't the damage already done? Why would Venus feel compelled to withhold some knowledge that could help my people?

"Generally speaking, Thaudras is like a miniature solar flare, but it occurs on Sylvar itself," Kyrene explained. "Essentially, intense magnetic fields in specific underground areas grow much too tangled and snap like a rubber band. This in turn releases a large amount of energy. If not contained, it creates a chain reaction that spreads throughout the land leaving devastation and high levels of radiation that makes the entire region unlivable until a Prism is able to cleanse it."

"But how do these magnetic fields arise? What creates them?" Venus asked.

"They're constantly active," Kyrene amended. "They are the power source that fuels all of Sylvar's energy systems through the various beacons. However, something causes specific areas to become unstable. There is no clear explanation as to what causes the surge. But once it begins, there is no stopping it. It grows exponentially until the explosion occurs."

Venus nodded slowly, a frown creasing her forehead. "But what about the radiation? Is it constantly present underground?"

"There normally is no radiation. The energy released by the beacons is totally clean. It's only once the tangled magnetic fields start to snap that radiation is generated. We can only speculate that something alters the otherwise clean energy. Unfortunately, our technology does not allow us to get close enough to the source to identify the cause."

"What do you mean by that?"

"Our equipment malfunctions before it can get deep enough," Kyrene replied.

"I see. So once the radiation starts spreading over the land, how does the Prism clean it?" Venus asked.

"He absorbs it," Kyrene answered, matter-of-factly. "Where all of us use our wings to draft color to create magic, he uses his in part to draw in the toxins poisoning the land."

"And what does he do with it," Venus asked, echoing the question popping in my head.

The general population didn't know much about how the Prism actually accomplished the things he did. We only knew that he used his power to realign the beacons and cleanse the land.

"He merely absorbs the radiation until it kills him," Kyrene replied.

Venus recoiled. "Seriously? Is that the fate that awaits Xarin?!"

Kyrene nodded. "Yes. That is the fate of every Prism."

Although I knew of his limited lifespan, my heart still constricted at the thought that this specific Prism—who had blessed me above all others—would only walk among us for a few weeks before vanishing for another three generations.

"But what if we find a way to stop Thaudras, or to at least prevent the radioactive emissions?" Venus argued.

Kyrene gave her an apologetic smile. "Unfortunately, that will not save him. Prisms have two cycles of life. The first after their birth as a normal infant lasts for about three weeks during which they do nothing but eat to stockpile their reserves. Once they form their chrysalis, the Prisms lose their digestive system during metamorphosis."

Venus's shoulders slumped. "So he's like a luna moth…"

"A what?" I asked, echoing the inquisitive look on Kyrene's face.

"Luna moths are insects found on Earth. They come out of their cocoons without a mouth or a digestive system and die within a week thereafter," Venus explained grimly.

"That's an apt enough comparison," Kyrene said. "The main difference is that the Prisms actually transform some of that radiation into energy to fuel their bodies even as it poisons them. So death is inevitable."

"What of Atlas and the other people to be sacrificed?" Venus asked.

A troubled expression fleeted over Kyrene's wizened face. "There is no question in my mind that they are the key to the mystery, but my people's bigoted views make it extremely hard to demonstrate why their mistreatment is wrong. And now they have some insane laws pending that will make things even worse."

I stiffened and gave the scientist a stern look. "These political issues are not Venus's concerns."

"They most certainly are," Kyrene snapped vehemently, startling both Venus and me. "She's the Prima, the voice of the Prism. She must know everything that is happening so that he can also express his stance on the matter."

"The Prism doesn't interfere in politics," I countered in a firm tone. "In our entire history, never once has he set foot on the floor of the Senate or voiced his opinion about the laws or the way our society behaves. It is not his role. If we want changes, it is for us, the people, to make our voices heard. It is unfair to want to lay this burden on the Prima."

"Xarin changed the rules the minute he brought Venus here," Kyrene argued stubbornly. "He chose an off-worlder and an Achromatic as guardians for a reason. He has already influenced our *informal* laws and societal structure by both endorsing the marriage of an Achromatic *and* granting you his blessing. The news has already spread through every city, and you know every Achro and Mono is currently thinking that maybe they, too, could have a life partner."

I shifted uneasily in my seat, unable to challenge any of her statements, especially since similar thoughts swirled through my mind since Xarin blessed me.

"Our world is potentially facing one of the most devastating Thaudras in our history," Kyrene continued passionately. "None of what is happening right now is a coincidence. We desperately need help. Until yesterday, I was all but losing hope. Now, we have a chance of thwarting Ajustus's mad plans and maybe saving all of you from certain death."

"What mad plan?" Venus asked in a worried voice. "What is the Chancellor up to?"

I heaved a sigh. "Ajustus wants the Senate to adopt a new law authorizing each city to create camps away from residential areas to round up every Achro and Mono."

"WHAT?! You cannot be serious?!" Venus exclaimed.

"Sadly, he *is* serious," Kyrene said grimly. "According to Ajustus, their presence in our cities is what triggered the return of Thaudras. And as the number of births of Achros and Monos has reached unprecedented levels this cycle, he believes there is a direct correlation with the bigger cataclysm forecasted to occur in the upcoming weeks. He hopes that by moving them far from us, Thaudras will happen closer to the camps, and thus spare the city."

My heart sank when instead of vehemently challenging that last statement, Venus pursed her lips and slowly nodded as if to express her agreement with it.

"I can see how he could draw that conclusion," she said pensively.

"So you concur?" I blurted out, the hurt I felt audible in my voice. "You think our presence is causing Thaudras?"

To my shock, Venus shook her head. "This is pure speculation on my part. I believe he's correct that there is a direct correlation, but not that you're the cause. I think you are the solution."

I recoiled, confused as to what would make her say that. "What do you mean?"

"The first thing I thought when you described what was happening was that this is a form of adaptation," Venus replied. "Thaudras always occurs after an average of thirty years following a surge in Achro and Mono births. It sounds to me that you are naturally preparing your defensive army. On many planets of the galactic alliance, there is a phenomenon called sequential hermaphroditism. It is when animals—mainly verte-brates—spontaneously change their gender. It mostly occurs for reproductive purposes, for example if there is a serious lack of one gender in the area, which could threaten the survival of the species."

Kyrene nodded with an excited expression. "We have similar occurrences with certain species here on Sylvar."

"But in the case of those animals you're talking about, their adaptation occurs because the scarcity is already ongoing," I challenged. "In our case, we are born three decades in advance. Therefore, the theory is that our continued presence in growing numbers is destabilizing the land."

"Time is a relative factor," Venus said softly. "Once again, this is pure speculation on my part, but based on what you've described, Thaudras can only be stopped mainly by Blacks and Whites. That means you have something that no one else does, which can counter whatever is causing that disruption. You are born early enough as soon as the first shifts in the magnetic fields occur so that you have time to reach maturity to face the challenge ahead."

"That seems farfetched," I argued. "Don't get me wrong, I would love nothing more than to discover that we are saviors instead of a curse to our people, but I don't see it."

"Venus actually makes some good points that we have also raised many times before, but failed to answer," Kyrene inter-jected. "We also believe that Blacks and Whites have something necessary to stop this disaster. The age of full magic maturity among Prometheans happens to be twenty-eight years old.

Therefore, that the surge of Achromatic births occurs thirty years before Thaudras supports your theory that those younglings arrive at the right time to be ready to face battle at the height of their power."

Although that struck a nerve, I couldn't help but argue further. "That could be the explanation, but it could also be that because we are at the height of our power, it also causes the land to be even more disturbed, triggering the cataclysm. Maybe the colors we are drafting are causing the disruption."

"Are you, though? You can nullify magic while the Whites can manipulate all colors. The combination of those two skills—as I cannot think of any other explanation—somehow stops nuclear fusion. The question is how, and what do those Achromatics do once they are sent into the affected region?"

"That's the question we've been asking in vain and are hoping you can help us elucidate," Kyrene said excitedly.

"We would need to look at all the data you have acquired over the years and see what new readings we can acquire in the region currently affected," Venus said, her eyes flicking from side to side as she reflected on the matter.

Human eyes still felt strange to me, with their white sclera and colored irises. But I loved how expressive they were, and how you never wondered what they were specifically staring at, which was trickier to assess with Prometheans as we all had entirely black eyes with no visible irises or pupils.

"The other question is have any of the sacrificed people ever come out of it alive by the time Thaudras ended?" Venus asked.

"No, never," I replied, my stomach knotting at the perspective of the fate that awaited me.

"Were any corpses recovered?"

"Yes," Kyrene said. "The remains of some of the last people to enter were found."

Venus instantly perked up. "Were any autopsies performed on them?" she asked with a sliver of hope.

I recoiled, instinctively shocked by that idea. To my dismay, Kyrene didn't display the outrage I expected from her, but simply shook her head in an apologetic fashion.

"Unfortunately not. Among our people, it is deemed sacrilegious and therefore forbidden," Kyrene explained.

"Your people never perform autopsies?!" Venus insisted, flabbergasted.

"Yes, we do. But not on the sacrifices. They are gifts to appease the gods," she specified.

Venus frowned. She opened and closed her mouth a couple of times, as if looking for the proper way to express the thoughts crossing her mind.

"I understand. But Thaudras could simply have a scientific explanation unrelated to your religious beliefs," she said carefully.

"I assure you, Venus, I do not believe for one second that our gods have anything to do with this. But mentalities are hard to change, especially when science isn't yet able to provide irrefutable proof of our assumptions. Therefore, we must pursue the work until we can finally provide those answers," Kyrene said.

I shifted my wings uneasily. A part of me struggled with accepting that the teachings we had been indoctrinated with since childhood could be wrong. The other hoped they would indeed be invalidated. Still, I was blown away to see how quickly my mate had reached similar assumptions as our wisest scholar about our situation. Her intelligence and scientific knowledge both awed and intimidated me.

But is she right? Could Achromatics like me be the solution and not the curse?

Her advanced off-worlder knowledge couldn't be dismissed. But our own history also couldn't be denied. The truth probably lay in a gray zone in between her scientific assumptions and our religious theories.

"If there's anything you can do to help, we welcome it," Kyrene said. "Well, within the boundaries of the Prime Directive," she quickly added.

Venus smiled then took on a pensive expression. "Give me any data you can share, any readings, theses, articles, and journals written on the topic."

"We have all of these. I will compile them for you," Kyrene said enthusiastically.

"I'm especially interested in Orist Valley," Venus said before glancing at me. "Is it possible for me to visit it?"

I hesitated, then looked questioningly at Kyrene. "Prometheans can go there for short periods of time. But I'm not sure that it would be safe for a human. There is a great deal of radiation lingering in that area."

Kyrene also frowned while examining my mate's soft skin. "Like Atlas, I'm not certain that it would be safe for you. Prometheans have slow cell division, which allows us to naturally repair any damage we sustain due to radiation, so long as the levels remain below a certain threshold."

"Then I will need a suit," Venus replied in a factual manner. "I will add it to my list."

"That's a good idea," Kyrene concurred. "Anyway, you will want to have one handy regardless as you will likely need to constantly wear it in the last days leading up to Thaudras."

"Why?" Venus asked.

"Some people near the area where the cataclysm will occur occasionally experience unexplained nausea, dizziness, bouts of extreme exhaustion, and even difficulty remembering things," I explained.

"This sounds like the side effects of a solar flare, which further supports your earlier comparison that Thaudras acts a bit like one," Venus said. "Thanks, this was extremely informative."

"It was my pleasure," Kyrene said, as we all got up from our seats. "I will prepare everything for you swiftly and send the first part to you before day's end, and the rest tomorrow or over the next two days."

"Thank you so much," Venus said with a warm smile. "I will keep you apprised of anything I uncover."

After a few more pleasantries, we exchanged our goodbyes and then left. We walked quietly out of the building, each of us lost in our own thoughts. As we stepped out onto the street, I glanced at my mate, surprised to find her also peering at me.

"You are so incredibly smart and knowledgeable," I blurted out, my scales instantly darkening as I barely stopped myself from adding that I felt unworthy to be her husband.

She shrugged, but I didn't miss the sliver of shyness behind the nonchalant gesture. "I'm a biomedical engineer. I'm just lucky to have studied in fields related to this issue. Had the cataclysm been related to something completely different, I would be utterly clueless."

I smiled, finding her humility rather endearing. Prometheans loved showing off and boasting about their qualities and achievements. Everything about my mate was refreshing.

"Still, the speed with which you have wrapped your head around this complex situation is impressive. Do you really think we are not the cause?" I added timidly.

Venus nodded firmly, the conviction in her eyes doing the most wondrous thing to me, even though she could not offer any certainty for the time being.

"I am convinced you are not a curse, and that this cataclysm isn't your fault. I do not believe your gods are punishing your people simply because you exist. I would bet my last credit that you are the solution, but I will need your help to prove it," Venus said.

"I struggle to accept that concept, but if there is even the slightest possibility that you are correct, then it is worth pursuing," I replied. "I do not wish to die, and neither do my guards. None of the Achros and Monos desire death. So whatever assistance you need from me, it is yours."

CHAPTER 11
ATLAS

Over the following week, Venus buried herself in work, studying every piece of data and documentation that Kyrene sent her. As much as it pleased me to see her dedication in trying to find a solution that could literally save countless lives—including mine—I couldn't help but feel discarded. Granted, we still shared our morning and evening meals, but little else.

To my shame, I had to admit it hurt.

It didn't make sense for me to have suddenly become so clingy and needy. And yet, I ached for her presence and especially her attention. My scales burned with embarrassment and longing as once again the memory of her fingers scratching my fur came back to the fore. No female had ever touched me like that. Worse still, Venus had almost looked attracted to me. Tasting her emotions through my antennae had been divine. I didn't know humans well enough to be certain, but I could have sworn that delicious aroma indicated her blossoming arousal.

I shouldn't be entertaining such thoughts. And yet, with each passing day, her face, her voice, and the way she smiled at me had become an obsession that filled every waking hour. My own fingers twitched with the need to caress the incredible softness of her scaleless skin. In the far too rare moments we now got to spend together, I would constantly battle the urge to draw her into my embrace and rub my face all over her. I didn't doubt it would feel like the most luxurious silk.

As I had never been with a female before and never allowed myself to think about one in romantic terms, I couldn't quite describe the nature of the emotions Venus stirred within me. Was it attraction? Infatuation? Something else? I had no idea. The only certainty was that I longed to be with her, to touch her and be touched by her. It didn't even need to be sexual. I just hungered for more of that gentle contact we shared in the garden as we discovered a bit more about our respective species' physical attributes.

By the Lights, what I wouldn't give to sink my fingers in that incredibly fluffy and bouncy hair of hers!

Stop it!

I indeed had to stop it. Even though she was technically my legally wedded mate, Venus would never truly be mine. Despite her best efforts, she likely wouldn't find a solution in time, and I would die in the upcoming weeks. But even if by some miracle, I survived this ordeal, Venus would leave me and return to the stars, and I would go back to my old life.

A searing pain lacerated my heart at that thought. My life had never been particularly joyful, but it also hadn't been bad. Compared to many other Achromatics, it would actually be deemed rather good. But since the day the Shimli survivors returned after being abducted by the Nazhral female for their Edocit leaf experiment, I started questioning my life. Meeting Venus only reinforced how unfulfilled—not to say trapped—I felt.

To my shame, the prospect of surviving Thaudras to only go back to my previous routine selfishly made me hope I wouldn't make it out alive. Our discussion with Kyrene, and the vehemence with which I had argued as to why our sacrifice was inevitable made me question myself. It forced me to acknowledge the distressing truth that over the past few years, I came to perceive Thaudras as my escape, my liberation from an otherwise meaningless life, where I was seen as no more than a pawn, chattel being bred and fattened as a sacrificial offering.

Venus rekindled my desire to live. But not here…

I wanted to travel to the stars, discover new civilizations, experience the wild things my mate sometimes alluded to during our conversations at mealtime. But I wanted to do it all with her by my side. If I survived, would she be willing to take me with her? Would she even be allowed based on the Prime Directive?

But won't I be a burden for her?

And that was the biggest issue. What did I have to offer to someone from such an advanced species that would make me valuable enough for her to want me to tag along? She was smarter, richer, better connected, and far more knowledgeable than I would ever be.

I can fight and protect her.

Would she even need it? The worlds she normally dwelled in all sounded extremely safe.

The beep of an incoming message from Pythus startled me. I glanced at it, relieved to find it was merely a status report. I spent the first couple of days pining after Venus while she remained locked up in her room working, then I went back to the Black Guard Headquarters and assigned Leodros to come stand watch here in my stead. Being physically away from Venus made it easier than constantly fighting the urge to go knock on her door under some lame excuse.

However, my guards had been bombarding me with questions both about Venus and the Prism. While I didn't mind talking about Xarin—not that there was much to say as he hardly interacted with us—I really didn't want to talk about my mate. Not only did it feel inappropriate, but I also feared I would give away the unseemly emotions she awakened in me. I couldn't even blame them for it. In their stead, I would also be dying with curiosity about an off-worlder, and what it felt like for one of us to be married—fake though that union was. Therefore, I elected to come back to the mansion and work from here instead.

Tomorrow, I would finally fly her to Orist Valley so that she could launch the probes Tedrick sent her. All that off-worlder technology was insane. I couldn't begin to imagine how many decades if not centuries it would take my people to achieve similar levels. The worst part of it all was knowing many of the things they sent us qualified as lower range to limit how much we would benefit from reverse engineering it.

Even now, I was semi-breaking the rules with the technology I secretly convinced Linsea Voln to send me. A part of me was ashamed to be spending my work hours playing with these tools instead of patrolling the city. Technically, I was doing my job to the extent that my presence ensured the protection of the Prima and the Prism. So long as I was nearby, alert, and ready to intervene at the first sign of trouble, I could pass time in any way I saw fit.

Since Venus spent the entire time in her room, I was doing the same in the separate room I set up as an office, where Leodros or Pythus could also stay whenever they shouldered the guard duty here.

Its size still boggled my mind. That office alone was much bigger than my personal quarters in the barracks. Not for the first time, I realized that I had enough wealth to purchase a house almost as big as this one. But I really wanted a mate to share it with, especially now that I had sampled what it felt like to live with a companion.

Still, this space provided me with the privacy necessary to focus on the holographic training device Linsea sent me. It wasn't what I originally requested. In truth, I abused my position by contacting her as my request had nothing to do with diplomatic or security matters. Then again, if one exaggerated a great deal, it could be said that ensuring the happiness of the Prima fell within my duty as her protector.

As asking Tedrick for the female care products my mate needed felt awkward, I reached out to the Ambassador. To my surprise, Linsea argued that merely sending me products for Venus wasn't the right way to go. Instead, she gave me this device at her husband's insistence. It seemed strange at first, but as his empathic abilities served me well the first time around, I didn't challenge the recommendation.

Going through the various training modules, I couldn't help but think how bizarre this whole thing was, although rather endearing. As I used to make and collect miniatures, I quickly took to this new technique. Even though this wasn't building miniatures, shaping, painting, and decorating nails shared many similarities.

Will she even appreciate my efforts on that front?

Venus had been so distraught finding out our aestheticians did not provide the services she needed, I wanted to believe she would welcome me stepping in to fill the gap. The great scores I was getting with each module steadily boosted my confidence. That didn't stop me from remaining super nervous about it. Maybe these classes weren't as advanced as the program claimed them to be. Maybe these were only beginner classes, and Venus would laugh at me when I finally built the courage to reveal to her what I had been up to in secret.

Just as I completed the twenty-third of twenty-five modules, a sudden knock on the door nearly made me jump out of my skin. As the Razus of the Black Guard, this lack of situational awareness was unacceptable. I'd been way too focused on this particularly challenging lesson.

I shot to my feet. In my panic, instead of shutting down the holographic screen floating before me, my fingers knocked something on the keyboard, blowing up the display instead, making it three times bigger. I cursed loudly and frantically tapped a few buttons, none of which reduced or closed the screen.

"Atlas? Are you okay?" Venus called out with a hint of worry in her voice.

To my dismay, she opened the door and poked her head in with a concerned look. Feeling mortified, I fumbled some more to close the screen but ended up activating the next module and cranking up the volume.

"Holy shit!" Venus whispered.

"I'm sorry! I'm sorry!" I repeated like an idiot. "The device is malfunctioning."

"Simulation, pause," Venus said while stepping inside the room.

My jaw dropped when the image froze, and the sound stopped. I wanted to flap my wings, blast through the thick windows, and fly away to another city where she would never see my stupid face again. My brain took a leave of absence, and words failed me.

"You're following a nail tutorial?" Venus asked with a stupefied expression.

My scales darkened, and my wretched hand went right back to scratch the fur below my clavicle. You'd think I would have overcome that nervous tick years ago.

"You said it was essential for you, but there are no spas here," I mumbled in a slightly defensive tone.

"So you decided to learn it?" she insisted with a disbelieving look.

"It is my duty as your mate to bring you happiness to the fullest extent of my capacities," I said in a firm tone. "I didn't know much about human nails, but I have been learning so that I may provide for you."

The strangest expression fleeted over her beautiful features. "But you're a warrior. This must be incredibly boring for you."

I shook my head. "It's unusual but rather entertaining. I like working with my hands, especially on small and delicate things. My main hobby is building and painting miniatures. So this has been fun and easy for me. In fact, I've been scoring quite well."

I turned back to the training device. Feeling less frazzled, My brain finally remembered how to operate it. I brought up the screen displaying all the modules of the program. The list detailed the name of the skill being taught, the completion percentage, and the score for those completed. It was silly, but I felt excessively proud at the impressed expression that settled on Venus's face.

"Oh, wow! Those are some truly awesome scores!" Venus exclaimed before turning to look at me.

Her air of wonder shifted into something I couldn't quite define but that moved me deeply.

"You did this for me?" she asked.

I nodded. "Yes, of course. It's a complete spa technician training program. I've only got two modules left for nail care. I've also completed the first eight hair modules—although I only focused on the classes devoted to your hair type. It covered washing, trimming, moisturizing, applying various treatments, and general care products. The one class that has been giving me a bit more challenge is braiding. But I'm confident I will get skillful at it with plenty of practice. But I have ways to go on that front. I also learned about facials, waxing, and massages. For the latter, I will need a bit more practice as well. I'm mostly focused on the nails since they seemed to be your main concern."

I shifted on my feet, feeling a bit embarrassed by the endless flow of words that tumbled out of me. Obviously, nervousness played a big role. But I really wanted her to be pleased with the work I secretly did over the past week, often quite late into the night, long after she went to bed.

"Are you serious?!" she asked.

"Yes, I am!" I said before my smile started fading, gradually replaced by worry at her shocked expression. "Unless you would rather I don't do that for you?"

I braced for her answer. Although the possibility of rejection lurked at the back of my mind from the moment I embarked on that project, the imminence of it becoming true hit me hard. It would cut me to the core.

Venus's face suddenly melted into a deeply emotional expression. "That's the sweetest thing anyone has ever done for me. I can't believe you went out of your way to learn all of that stuff just to make me happy."

A bolt of fire exploded in my chest, filling every cell in my body with the most delicious warmth.

"It's my duty, Venus. And it honors me to do so," I replied with the brightest smile. "Linsea sent me this training device. She also included all the tools and products to be able to perform the care in the real world instead of just virtually through the holographic program."

"Linsea sent you this?!" she exclaimed.

I nodded. "When I contacted her, I merely asked her for products for you. But according to her, Kayog suggested I follow this tutorial instead. It seemed like a good idea, so I accepted."

To my surprise, Venus slightly stiffened upon hearing those words. The strangest expression crossed her features, but she quickly wiped it off.

"Kayog suggested it? What else did he say?" she asked cautiously.

The way she said it took me aback. "He didn't say anything else, or at least Linsea didn't mention it. Why? Is there a problem?"

The eagerness with which Venus shook her head, and her obvious relief made me highly suspicious. I was missing something, but what?

"Since you're displaying such mastery, I wouldn't mind a

manicure," Venus said, wiggling her fingers in front of me with a hopeful expression.

She was clearly trying to change the topic. I considered prying further as to what else she thought Kayog might have said, but it didn't feel important enough to make a big deal out of it. So I let her get away with it.

"You want me to give you a manicure now?" I asked, feeling both scared and thrilled at that prospect.

"Yes. Why not?"

"What if I mess it all up?" I asked sheepishly.

Venus shrugged, seeming totally unbothered. "There's nail polish remover for that. Even if you totally mess up, it can't be worse than the state they're currently in. And you need real world practice."

I should be embarrassed by the silly grin that stretched my face, but I was just too happy. It shouldn't thrill me this much. However, I'd been dying to touch her again, even if it was only her hands. And now, this would allow me to do it for an extended period of time without seeming creepy for it. The tutorials also included some gentle massages of the hand and forearm as part of the process. I fully intended to spoil her—and myself—by doing it as well.

I eagerly grabbed the most comfortable stool for her and settled it in front of the narrower side of the L-shaped desk I had been working on.

"Please, have a seat while I go fetch my tools and equipment," I said in an overly enthusiastic voice.

My cheeks heated at the sight of the indulgent and slightly amused smile Venus cast my way. She was probably thinking me a bumbling idiot right now, instead of the fearsome Razus of the Black Guard that I was. That didn't bother me as much as it should. I would get to spend quite a bit of time with my mate, and she seemed happy about it.

I carefully placed my manicure kit and products on the desk, before sitting across the narrow edge from Venus. Feeling utterly nervous, I extended my open palms towards her. Without hesitation, my mate placed her hands on top of each. I almost moaned with delight at the soft warmth of her skin against mine. Bringing them closer to my face—not that I needed it—I studied her nails to assess the work required.

To my chagrin, her hands were nearly flawless, although some minor retouching would be welcome. No matter, I intended to go all out to show her how dedicated I had been in my studies to please her.

"Do you wish to maintain the same shape and color?" I asked, peering back at her face.

She nodded. "I like the square shape and that blood red color. They haven't grown too much, but I wouldn't mind having them filed a little bit."

"On it," I said with a confidence I didn't quite possess.

I took the nail polish remover and started cleaning the old one off her nails.

"By the way, was there something you wanted to ask me when you initially came knocking?" I asked.

"Oh, right!" she exclaimed. "I think Xarin is talking to me."

I paused what I was doing to give her a questioning look. "What makes you say that?"

"Over the past hour, I keep having flashes of a place I don't know. On top of that, I'm pretty sure I've been dreaming about it, too, but I can't swear to it," Venus said with a troubled expression.

"That doesn't sound unusual for a Prima," I said reassuringly. "What does the place look like?"

"Actually, I roughly sketched it out," she said enthusiastically. "Here, let me show you."

Using her left hand, which I had not started working on yet, she pulled a device that she called a com from her left pocket and placed it on top of the desk. She tapped twice on it before it projected a holographic image of a luscious valley.

Under different circumstances, I would once more marvel at this off-worlder technology, but I was too busy frowning at that landmark location.

"That's Keryth," I replied. "It's the valley near Japhyr where we've detected signs of the upcoming Thaudras."

"Perfect. Let's go there tomorrow instead of Orist," she said firmly. "There must be something Xarin wants me to see there."

I nodded, unsure if I felt more troubled than hopeful about exploring the site of my potential future demise.

"Very well," I replied.

"So, tell me about yourself," Venus said while observing the work I was doing on her nails.

Thankfully, her relaxed stance seemed to convey that, so far, my performance was adequate. Then again, it didn't take a genius to properly clean off nail polish.

"I don't think there is much left that I haven't already told you about myself. My life had been pretty uneventful before I met you," I said honestly.

"You never told me you were into miniatures," she countered teasingly.

I smiled. "Fair enough," I conceded. "But I honestly cannot think of anything else worth mentioning. I get up, train, eat, and go to work. There are very few serious crimes within the city walls. Outside work hours, when I'm not working on my miniatures, I will spend time with a few friends, either playing social games or competing in various sports or physical activities."

"No dates?" she asked in a strange tone.

"Dates?" I repeated, unsure what she meant. "Dates of what?"

She gave me a sheepish smile. "Humans don't only use that word to mark calendar days, but also to refer to activities you partake in with a romantic partner."

I recoiled. "No, of course not! Achromatics do not get romantically involved."

"But isn't it a little unrealistic to expect you not to develop feelings for someone else?" Venus asked softly. "I mean you grew up in a shelter surrounded by other people your age. Once you hit puberty, surely your curiosity was piqued."

I shrugged. "Once we reach the age of ten, they separate us by gender."

"Based on what that senator said in your gathering hall when I was trying to choose who I would marry, I understand that Prometheans also have same sex couples. Right?" she argued.

"You are correct, we do. For those cases, we have herbs and teas that help curb any temptation or sexual drive. If that doesn't suffice, the specific people feeling that attraction are separated," I explained.

"That's really sad," Venus said, looking genuinely sorry, but without condemnation or contempt.

"It is. The tea doesn't erase the loneliness we feel at times, but it makes our lives bearable. And yet, here I am now legally mated," I added in a teasing fashion to lighten the mood.

"That you are!" Venus said, returning my smile. "You are very charming."

My cheeks heated. "So are you," I replied clumsily with a timid smile.

Now done cleaning her nails, I carefully clipped them, validating the length with her as she didn't seem to have that much growth. Once done, I proceeded to filing and shaping them.

"What about you? Did this entire ordeal interfere with your dates?" I asked, relieved that the tension I felt at her possibly having a romantic partner pining away for her somewhere beyond the stars didn't show.

She snorted. "No dates here. According to my mother, I'm turning into a hopeless spinster. Most potential partners I've met were idiots. And the ones I actually would have considered to settle with were already taken."

My efforts to look sympathetic failed miserably. My heart was too busy rejoicing to know that no other male held hers.

"Both my mother and father are in politics. They occupy positions fairly similar to the one Ajustus does, but at a galactic level. More importantly, as demanding and insufferable as they can be sometimes, they're not assholes like him."

I burst out laughing. Prometheans had many terms to describe foul and despicable people. But this human expression referring to them as an anal orifice couldn't be more appropriate for one such as Ajustus. Especially considering every single word that came out of his mouth qualified as the foulest smelling feces.

She beamed at me. I'd come to realize that the same way I enjoyed making her happy, Venus liked seeing me smile, and above all hearing me laugh. Since her arrival, I had laughed more times than in the past five years combined.

As I started buffing her nails to smooth them down, I flicked my antennae. Her scent had slightly changed, taking on that spicy edge I loved so much. She was also displaying that soft expression I could never tire of.

"I have a younger sister named Serena. She's a hunter and dedicated to the protection of wildlife. During one of her hunts, she ended up getting married to an Ordosian who saved her life," Venus said wistfully. "In fact, it was Kayog that arranged that union as well."

My brow shot up. "Really?"

She nodded. "Here, let me show you her family."

She tapped on the interface of her com. Seconds later it projected the image of a pretty human who looked slightly like her, a massive male, and two younglings.

My jaw dropped. "He's a half snake?!"

Venus burst out laughing. "We generally refer to species like his as Nagas."

I gaped at the strange being and the miniature versions of him flanking the woman, before shifting my attention to her sister. I blinked and leaned forward to make sure my eyes weren't playing tricks on me.

"Are these scales on her shoulders?" I asked, baffled.

Venus nodded, and her smile broadened. "Yes, they are. It is an adaptation that she underwent after their union. Coupling changed her a bit so that she could bear his children. It freaked her out at first, but now she proudly flaunts them."

My eyes widened. "So the younglings truly are her offspring?! I didn't think two beings so different could be compatible for reproduction."

My mate snorted. "You'd be surprised how adaptable humans can be. In fact, we are the top race when it comes to reproducing with other species."

I stared at her in shock. To my dismay, the image of a mini version of Venus with my scales but tricolored wings with a dominance of gold flashed before my eyes. I immediately clamped down on it.

"And your sister is attracted to such a different species?" I asked carefully.

Venus chuckled. "Honestly, I'm not sure that Serena was drawn to him at first, or that he was drawn to her either. But now, they are both madly in love with each other. In truth, I also found him strange the first time I saw him. But now, I find him quite handsome, and their children are absolutely gorgeous."

My eyes flicked back towards the hologram, and I studied the unusual family with wonder.

"You would be surprised by the number of hybrid children that exist throughout the galaxy. So many people travel from one world to another and find love in the most unexpected places. True love transcends physical appearances and cultural barriers."

I glanced back at her, and my mouth ran away with me. "What about you, Venus? Could you marry and fall in love with someone with such a different anatomical appearance?"

The oddest expression crossed her features before taking a teasing edge. "I already did that first part, remember?"

I snorted, then nodded in concession. "You did."

"Like my sister with Szaro, I found you strange at first. But now I think you're very attractive," Venus continued pensively. "As far as the second part of the question goes, that's really on you, Atlas. Can you make me fall in love with you?"

My brain froze, and my scales felt on the verge of bursting into flames from embarrassment. I opened and closed my mouth a couple of times, unable to come up with an answer. The amusement in her eyes, and gently teasing smile only seemed to make my brain cooperate even less.

"Hang on, I will be right back," I finally mumbled before shooting out of my chair as if it, too, had been set on fire.

I ran to the kitchen to get a bowl of warm water and brought it back for her to soak her hands in. Having apparently taken pity on me, Venus didn't press me further on that question, and moved on to tell me some amusing anecdotes about her sister's life on Trangor with her Naga husband.

After a few minutes, I used a body scrub to exfoliate her hands. The purring sound that tumbled out of Venus's throat resonated directly in my groin. Blessed Lights! How could such an innocent sound have so powerful an effect on me?

Even the grainy texture of the scrub failed to mask the softness of her skin beneath. I took my sweet time, rubbing each digit, the palm and back of her hands, her wrists and even her forearms. The way my mate's gaze darkened and that her face took on a languid expression confirmed she appreciated my ministrations. I could have gone on for hours.

With much reluctance, I wiped off most of the scrub with a damp towel and let Venus go rinse thoroughly in the hygiene room. I went to empty the soaking bowl and returned to finish my task, pushing back any excess cuticles.

Venus proceeded to tell me about the fantastical worlds she visited, both in her capacity as a biomedical engineer and for her lobbying work. She only paused to moan some more when I rubbed a nourishing cream over her hands, giving them yet another mini-massage, and finishing it off with some cuticle oil.

Every word she spoke fueled my hunger to explore those foreign places I never could have imagined, and still struggled to fully grasp despite the vivid descriptions she gave me. Meanwhile, I applied the base coat, nail polish, and finished it all off with a topcoat to lock the color in place.

"If you don't mind, I would like to add an extra adornment on your middle finger," I said, both to delay the end of our little session, and because I was genuinely struck by a sudden inspiration.

"An adornment like what?" Venus asked with curiosity.

"Some of the tutorials showed extra little decorations like gems or other patterns on top of the nails. You didn't have any previously, but there is a very simple one I think would look pretty," I said nervously.

To my delight, Venus smiled then nodded, looking intrigued.

My stomach fluttered with nerves as she extended her hand palm down towards me, and I raised my right palm above it. A soft gasp escaped Venus when I drafted silver through my wings' eyespots, channeling it through my hand into small amounts of lumen to create a small dot at the base of her nail, a slightly bigger one in the middle, and an arc with a star in the middle at the top.

Once done, I glanced back at Venus, holding my breath as I waited for her reaction. She lifted her hand closer to her face to examine what I did. Her mesmerized expression filled my heart to bursting.

"That's beautiful. It shines almost like diamonds!"

"I don't know what diamonds are, but this is what silver lumen looks like," I said timidly. "This is the symbol of Kailu."

Her gaze flicked towards me questioningly. "Kailu?"

"It is our brightest constellation. Kailu is the blessed star that guides those who got lost in the darkness back into the light. Just like you…"

A powerful emotion crossed her beautiful face. Venus appeared on the verge of saying something before closing her mouth and simply smiling. Once again, I almost pressed her to say what she was holding back. She gave me her other hand so that I could repeat the pattern on the other middle finger.

"There," I said once done. "I hope it's not too terrible."

"Are you kidding? You did an amazing job. I can't believe you learned so quickly. Just know that from now on I will harass you on a regular basis for this type of pampering," she said with a huge smile.

"Harass me to your heart's content, Venus. It is my duty and my pleasure to do this for you."

"Now, let me return the favor," she said, extending a hand towards me.

I stiffened. "You want to paint my claws?!"

She burst out laughing. "No, silly goose. I'm not going to polish them. But those cuticles could use some love, and those hands are screaming for some moisturizing. You took care of me, it's only fair that I take care of you in return."

The strangest emotion filled my heart. I didn't know what it meant, but I embraced it. Without another word, I gave her my hand.

CHAPTER 12
ATLAS

The next morning, I skipped my usual training routine to stop at the local stables and retrieve one of the best trained Valrens available. To my relief, during one of our many conversations, Venus confirmed not suffering from any fear of heights. It would have made our journey to Keryth a bit more complicated.

I groomed and fed the creature, double checking that it was in top shape before leaving it attached in the garden. On my way back inside to have breakfast with my mate, I couldn't help another glance at my claws. A now familiar warmth spread through my chest as I reminisced about the events of the evening. I could almost still feel her touch on me as she manicured my hands.

It boggled my mind that she would have done what my people would deem service work for me. In all the ways that mattered, Venus treated me as an equal. As much as I loved it, a part of me feared I was developing an addiction that would send me into a spiraling withdrawal and depression once I lost what honestly should have been naturally granted to me.

Treating me like a person cost nothing.

Not wanting to let these somber thoughts taint the blissful memory of that wondrous evening together, I cast them out to focus on the positive. My mate loved how I handled her nails and not only looked forward to our next session, but was also eager to enjoy the other services I was training in. As much as it shamed me to admit it, for very selfish reasons, I would focus on completing the massage tutorials.

My fingers twitched with impatience at the prospect of touching and kneading every centimeter of her body, and of caressing the incredible softness of her scaleless skin.

To my delight, Venus was in a cheerful mood while we shared our first meal. I'd never been much of the talkative type, but with her, our conversations flowed easily. Well, except on the occasions where my brain froze over the silliest embarrassment.

As we readied to depart, Venus ran to her room and came back out with a relatively small bag with a long strap that she hung sideways across her chest.

"That's all you need?" I asked, pointing at the bag.

She glanced at it before looking back at me with a smile. "Yes. Today, I just want to send out a few probes to scan the area. Thankfully, technology has come a long way. The equipment is now sturdier, smaller, and especially a lot lighter."

"That's good to hear," I replied.

It still surprised me that she could carry equipment powerful enough to achieve readings that our own technology couldn't inside a container barely bigger than her head. Our devices would be at least four times larger, if not more.

"This way then. Your mount is waiting for you in the back," I said, gesturing towards the glass doors leading to the main garden.

"My mount?" Venus asked with curiosity. "We're not riding inside one of your vehicles?"

I shook my head. "There are a few crevices and chasms along the way that would prevent completing the journey by land. My people build very little infrastructure such as roads and bridges as between our wings and flying mounts, all of our needs are met."

"I see," Venus said, the same eager curiosity plastered on her face. "So what kind of flying mount is it? If you tell me a Pegasus, I'm going to squeal like a schoolgirl and rub it in my sister's face until the end of times."

"A Pega what?" I asked, amused by her mischievous enthusiasm.

"A Pegasus. It is a beautiful horse with massive bird wings in human mythology," Venus explained. "You can sit on its back to fly wherever you want."

"I have no idea what a horse is, so it's still not clear to me. But you also sit on the back of a Valren, and it flies you to whatever destination you wish. Let me show you," I said, excited to provide her with a new experience she would hopefully brag about for years to come to her sister.

I led Venus out into the garden and gestured for her to follow towards the pole where I had attached the Valren to. The large bush next to it hid most of its body. But the back of its long tail protruded, its golden and copper chitin scales Shining brightly under the early morning sun.

Venus's smile stiffened and gradually faded as we approached. A sense of unease washed over me when she cast a worried look my way.

"What's wrong?" I asked.

She bit her bottom lip, and her dark eyes flicked towards the location where the Valren waited. Having sensed our approach, it chirped with impatience. A powerful shiver coursed through Venus, and her skin erupted in the same tiny bumps she had the first time I touched her skin. This baffled me. That day, she explained goosebumps were a physiological response to a pleasurable trigger. But the look on her face expressed nothing even remotely agreeable.

My mate seemed scared.

That sent every single one of my protective instincts going into overdrive. What had sent her from playfully excited to visibly worried?

"What kind of creature is it?" Venus asked, stretching her neck to try and see past the bush.

"It's an inoffensive creature, fully trained, and entirely peaceful. I would never put you in danger, Venus. There's nothing to be afraid of," I said in a reassuring tone.

The Valren chirped again. It was a high-pitched rattling sound. Another shiver coursed through Venus. But this time, after stopping dead in her tracks, she even took a worried step backward.

"I… I have a bad feeling about this," Venus said in a shaky voice.

"It's okay, Venus. It is attached. You can safely approach to have a look first," I said in a soft voice.

Her eyes kept flicking between the tail of the Valren and me. After a few seconds, I extended a hand towards her. Venus hesitated, swallowed hard, then placed her trembling hand in mine. I hated seeing her this frightened. Why would the mere sight of a tail flip her mood around so radically?

I gently tugged on her hand to slowly resume walking towards the creature. However, the closer we got, the more Venus pulled me farther away. Realizing she truly wouldn't be comfortable approaching the creature until she had a better look at it, I led her on a wider radius around the bush, keeping a good twenty-meter distance between us and the creature. Although it lessened some of her tension, it did nothing to erode her blossoming panic.

In fact, the more of the creature she began seeing, the tighter she squeezed my hand.

"Oh, hell no!" Venus breathed out with a horrified expression as she took in the full majesty of the Valren.

She pressed herself against my side, her hand all but crushing mine while she gripped my upper arm with the other.

"There's no need to be afraid, my mate," I said reassuringly, baffled by her strong reaction.

"Fuck that! I'm not going anywhere near that thing!" she exclaimed, her eyes still locked on the Valren as if it was some abomination determined to devour her.

"But why?"

"It's a fucking bus-sized dragonfly with a moth's head, and shoulder horns!" she exclaimed, looking at me as if that description should make her reaction normal and obvious.

I didn't know what a dragonfly or bus were, but I had looked into moths after she'd compared me to one.

"And why is that problematic?" I asked carefully.

"I don't do bugs or any type of creepy crawlers," she said, the pitch of her voice slightly higher due to panic. "And that one's head is bigger than my entire upper body! That's going to be a hard pass for me!"

I stared at her, unsure how to react to this situation. The protector in me wanted to take her away and appease her. The rational male in me wanted to make her see that her fears were completely unjustified. But a third part of me was fighting the urge to chuckle at that reaction. Growing up, I witnessed people displaying all kinds of phobias. The irrational nature of some of those responses made them hilarious.

But what if her phobia is triggered by past trauma?

That thought sobered me for a split second. However, nothing in Venus's demeanor implied past trauma. Only a great deal if disgust.

"You know, in theory, I'm a bug, too," I deadpanned.

Venus jerked her head up to gape at me. I held her gaze unwaveringly, forcing a neutral expression on my face to hide my urge to laugh.

"I didn't mean you! I mean, yeah, you've got some insectoid traits, but you're not an actual insect!"

"Really? Technically, I'm a talking butterfly walking on two legs," I teased.

She shook her head. "No, you're more of a mothman."

"Aren't mothmen bad omens in human lore?" I challenged mockingly.

"Who told you that?" she asked, surprised.

I repressed a smile, glad that my ploy to distract her from her fear of the Valren appeared to be working.

"The Prometheans who had been abducted to Shimli said that one of their human captors told them stories about mythical beings that looked like us," I said.

Venus scrunched her face and shook her head again. "No, they're not bad omens."

"So that human lied?"

She pursed her lips. "Not exactly. It is true that some people interpret seeing a mothman as bad luck or the cause of an imminent disaster. Others say that they are a forewarning of impending doom."

"Which are both bad, confirming the statement of that human," I countered.

Venus shook her head again. "No. The second one is positive, in my opinion. If you are warned of an upcoming danger, you can try to mitigate it. And that's exactly what we're doing now. A mothman isn't a curse but an opportunity to act before it is too late."

I smiled at her, a tender emotion once more swelling through me. I loved how she always found a way to make me look at things in a more positive light, to make me feel like a force for good, like I had value.

"But I'm still not getting on that thing," she added glaring at the poor Valren.

This time, I couldn't help but laugh at her baleful expression.

"Don't you have shuttles we can use to fly there?" Venus asked, her voice filled with hope.

"I'm afraid not. Like I said, my people have not put much effort into developing transport technology as we have natural means of travel," I said in an apologetic tone. "We do have bigger creatures for mass transport. But I suspect you will like that one even less."

Her eyes widened in horror. "You mean you have an even bigger bug than that one?" she asked, pointing at the Valren.

I snorted. "No. It's not an insect, but a giant flying lizard about the same size as the mansion. It has a huge translucent pouch under its belly normally used for carrying their offspring. But we adapt it to travel inside instead, including cargo."

"Fuck. That!" Venus said in a way that had me bursting out laughing.

"Oh, Venus! You're beyond adorable."

"Thanks," she mumbled, grimacing. "But that doesn't solve our problem."

I peered up at the clear sky, its bluish color with stripes of purple indicating feeble winds and no risks of rain.

"Since we're going to Keryth, I can carry you, if you prefer," I offered.

Her right hand still clutching my upper arm loosened, and the strangest mix of surprise and hope settled on her beautiful face.

"You would carry me? Won't I be too heavy? Won't it tire you?" she asked sheepishly.

I chuckled. "I'm a lot stronger than you seemed to think."

Without waiting for her response, I picked her up, holding her sideways against my chest. She yelped, but swiftly slipped one arm around my neck, the other resting on my chest.

"By the Lights, you weigh ten times nothing!" I exclaimed, genuinely surprised by how light she felt in my arms.

Then again, she didn't have the added weight of wings and scales like our people did.

"That's good, I guess," she said timidly. "But I still feel a little abusive for making you carry me all the way there just because I'm a wimp."

I smiled. "I don't know what a wimp is, but I honestly do not mind carrying you. Keryth is nearby. Had our destination been Orist, I wouldn't have done it. But this is fine. If you are ready, hang on tightly, and off we go."

Without hesitation, Venus secured her bag on top of her stomach, tightened her hold around my neck, and further pressed herself against me. I would be lying by saying the feel of her body thus wrapped around mine didn't do a number on me. She felt as if she had been made to fit right there in my embrace.

To my utter delight, she had once more left her hair natural. It had a fresh, slightly citrusy scent that made me want to bury my face in it and inhale deeply. Naturally, I resisted the urge not to creep her out. But I felt no shame in discreetly enjoying the soft and bouncy feel of her tight locks against my cheek as I took flight.

By the Lights! I always loved the sense of freedom, weightlessness, and endless possibilities that flying procured me. The coolness of the wind whipping past me in a gentle caress, its resistance against my wings, and its mischievous attempts at flicking my hair in front of my eyes always gave me the illusion of companionship with an ethereal being as I soared through the sky. But my woman in my arms made this a whole new experience.

Granted, I had carried people while flying before, some in a similar fashion as I was holding my Venus right now. But they had been injured people or lost children that I was bringing back to safety in my capacity as a Black Guard. This was something else altogether.

This beautiful female was my wife. My lawfully wedded mate...

It no longer mattered that this wasn't a real marriage. Since

Venus entered my life, I had experienced the type of emotions and happiness I only ever dreamt of. Obviously, the physical contacts played a significant part in it. Even now, just holding her in my arms as we flew through the sky filled me with an incommensurable sense of well-being and fulfillment. But her mere presence, our conversations, the way she seemed genuinely interested in me as a person brightened my days in a way no words could describe. She was the last thought on my mind when I went to sleep and the first one when I woke. I didn't doubt she also haunted my every dream.

I intended to cherish every moment we had together, however banal.

We chatted amiably about the landscape, flora, and fauna as I flapped my wings at a leisurely pace. I could fly three times faster—more even in case of an emergency. However, the strong friction caused by wind resistance on her skin would inflict some serious discomfort to Venus. Our scales acted as natural protection to break the wind—her light shirt and skin-tight pants, not so much. While altruism mainly dictated that choice, I would lie by denying that selfish reasons also motivated me. After all, the slower we reached our destination, the longer I got to embrace my woman.

"What is that?!" Venus suddenly exclaimed, pointing straight ahead.

"It's the halo of a Sibris," I explained as I glanced at the multicolored shimmering lights that shot towards the sky in a continuous beam.

"The beacons?" Venus asked.

I nodded. "Yes, it is a close enough translation. It is the residual effects of the energy that powers our city. We call it halo because it is similar to our own magic halo."

"I thought your magic was lumen?" she asked with a slight frown.

I smiled. "Lumen is the physical manifestation of our magic, whereas our halo is pure energy that affects a target differently based on its color. I adorned your nails with lumen. It is a clay-like substance that we create by channeling colours. Very powerful drafters can make it clear, but most only create it in the color matching their wings. We use it for any construction and can shape it however we want before it stabilizes and solidifies, becoming as hard as stone. Our crafters and artists can create entire masterpieces with it. As we transform energy into physical matter, it is quickly tiring, especially if you're drafting colors that aren't dominant for you."

"Drafting? I've heard you say that a few times."

"Drafting is when we draw in and absorb a specific color through our wings to morph it into lumen or halo. I can only draft colors for casting through my eyespots, which are very small. So it wouldn't make sense for me to try to create big things without quickly wiping myself out. But small things like your nail adornments or the darts you saw me shooting during combat training are very easy to do."

"I see," Venus said with an air of fascination. "So if you could draft through the rest of your wings, you could do a lot more without tiring."

"Correct. That's why many Monochromatics and Bichromatics can acquire a great deal of fame for specialized services as they can draft large amounts of a specific lumen color for hours. As yellow, brown, and red are among the most common colors in that group, this is why you see a lot of statues and decorations in those shades."

"Oh, wow! I should have realized that sooner! That's awesome. But what of your halo? Do you have one?"

"Every Promethean does. It's magic energy that can destroy, be it shattering or sculpting, transform like melting or turning to ice, and create things like fire or a toxin, but not water—unless the caster uses their halo to gather the moisture from their environment. Where our lumen is the same for everyone—except for color—our halo vastly differs. In my case, before Xarin blessed me, I could only draft certain shades of gray and silver. My halo was therefore limited to kinetic impulses—like knocking or punching something with kinetic force from a distance—and electricity."

Venus gaped at me. "Electricity as in you could electrocute someone or jump start a dead battery?"

I chuckled before looking at her teasingly. "Yes, although I would avoid the former. But since the Prism blessed me, I can now draft very small amounts of white. Which means I can technically cast any possible magic for a Promethean. It's just very, very weak. Still, it is practical to now be able to perform anything including healing basic injuries or lighting a fire."

"Wow! That's super handy! So I'm guessing Reds are the fire masters?" Venus asked, her enthusiastic curiosity spurring me on.

"Hmmm, not exactly. They are the weakest fire mages, followed by Oranges, Yellows, and then Blues as the most potent ones."

Venus seemed taken aback at first, then her eyes widened with sudden understanding. "They can only cast a specific fire color. Which means Reds can only cast the lowest flame color, whereas Blues can cast the hottest one!"

"Exactly. But based on the environment and whatever they set ablaze, the flame will change accordingly, unless the caster sustains it with more of their halo."

"So what about Greens? Do they make plants grow?"

I snorted and shook my head. "Greens are the one group you really want to avoid making angry against you. Our flora has a lot more tints of blue. So Blues are both our botanists and scientists like Kyrene—especially those closer to Indigo. Greens are chemists with a propensity to cast toxins and poisons. They will work with botanists and farmers mostly to provide clean pesticides and as exterminators."

"Jees! So much for human lore about color magic."

I chuckled as I initiated my descent as soon as the tall trees below us gave way to Keryth Valley. It was a lush area that once teemed with life. Over the past few weeks, more and more of the fauna began migrating, a further sign of the impending doom. We held many large events such as fairs here. Considering it was barely a ten-minute flight under normal conditions—nearly twenty now because of the snail's pace I adopted—the cataclysm could quite literally wipe out the entire capital city of our planet.

The level of denial of our leaders still angered me. I submitted so many evacuation plans, including potential safe areas to relocate the population that will inevitably be displaced once the radiation occurs, but each of them were shot down. In light of the magnitude of the disaster forecasted by our scientists, it wasn't just unconscionable, but downright criminal not to take decisive action to protect our people. Once panic set in as the citizens attempted to flee the city, we'd likely sustain more casualties from the stampede and the dire conditions they would end up in than from Thaudras itself.

I landed effortlessly on the dark teal grass that stretched for nearly five hundred meters in front of us, and almost twice that distance sideways. Ahead, a wide rocky hill delineated the opening of the Sibris. I carefully put Venus back on her feet before taking in our surroundings.

Being in the presence of a Sibris' halo always gave my people a sense of comfort on top of a surge of energy. This halo was like pure magic we could draft from without requiring any transformation effort on our part. Now that I could draft white, it felt like a dam had broken and massive amounts of magic were trying to flow through me.

Oblivious to the thoughts swirling in my head, Venus removed a first device from her shoulder bag. Shaped like a disk large enough to cover her splayed hand, the device's narrow edges curved up towards the center, making it thicker in the middle. Little eyes on both faces appeared to serve as cameras or scanners. Although metallic, it looked too fragile to sustain the intense energy inside the chimney leading to the Sibris' core. Then again, off-worlder technology never ceased to amaze me. This delicate appearance was likely deceptive.

"Could you hold this for a second?" Venus asked, extending it to me.

I carefully held it between my two opened palms and observed with curiosity while Venus appeared to synchronize the large armband on her wrist with the device. My eyes widened when a holographic screen was projected from the armband, and Venus typed a few more instructions this time directly on the screen. The device in my hands suddenly came to life, startling me as it gently vibrated with a soft hum. A white light appeared around the narrow edges of the disk, as well as around the rims of the little camera eyes on its surface.

"Keep one hand underneath it, and please press the light at the top with the other hand once it starts pulsating," Venus said, her eyes still glued to the screen as she spoke.

Seconds later, the center of the elevated upper part of the disc lit up and started blinking. Following her instructions, I pressed it. To my shock, little blades jutted out of the edge—not the type that would cut and maim, but more like some type of propeller. As soon as I moved away my right hand—which had pressed the light—the device hovered off my left hand. It rose up a couple of meters before flying off at great speed towards the Sibris.

Venus immediately began preparing a second one. A million questions burned my tongue, but I kept quiet, not wanting to break her concentration. I didn't understand the countless symbols and graphs on her screen. Beyond the fact that they were in a language I didn't speak, I never had much of a scientific mind.

Not for the first time, the wonder my mate's intelligence awakened in me also clashed with how unworthy I felt of her.

She should find me boring. Yet, she always seemed genuinely interested and entertained by what I had to say.

After launching the second device, she pulled out a third one that had a completely different design. It was bullet-shaped and appeared made of a far sturdier metal. Glancing at the first two devices, I finally realized they weren't meant to go inside the chimney, but this one was. The disks were flying around the valley, hovering at varying heights over the ground, then moving closer to the Sibris.

This time, I didn't have to do anything with the giant 'bullet' other than to hold it while Venus did something on her armband. Moments later, the bullet shot straight up from my hands then flew directly to the opening of the beacon, then vanished within.

I glanced back at her with curiosity, still reluctant to speak so as not to distract her. The two disks continued to canvas the valley. However, their previous seemingly erratic movement radically changed. They were now hovering in parallel, following a specific path. Tons of data was scrolling on the holographic screen.

"Now, we only have to wait another fifteen minutes or so for these babies to work their magic," Venus said, looking back at me with a smile.

"What exactly are they doing?" I asked.

"The probe is gathering deep data that it's relaying to the scanners. It includes everything from depth, heat, gas, soil and mineral constitution, nuclear activity, energy and radiation levels, you name it. They are also creating a 3D map of what the probe is finding," Venus explained. "Hopefully, the probe will survive the journey below. If it does, it will bring back some samples that we can—"

Venus suddenly stopped talking and blinked, her gaze going blank. Surprised at first, I quickly realized the prism was likely communicating with her again. After all, he encouraged her to come here instead of Orist, as we initially planned.

She blinked again then refocused on me with a troubled expression. She opened her mouth as if to say something but looked towards the beacon instead, then around the valley as if she was searching for something.

"What is it? Did Xarin contact you?" I asked softly.

She nodded, her eyes surveying our environment for a few seconds longer before she glanced back at me.

"He sent me an image of you in front of the beacon with your wings spread wide and your eyespots glowing brightly. But it doesn't match. I don't see where you're supposed to stand to recreate that image."

"Describe the landscape of the image for me," I said, intrigued.

"The rock formation over there should be between you and the beacon. But that ridge is clearly behind it. On top of that, it is much too high. In the image, the Ridge is no higher than your calves."

"Oh! I think I know why that is. Let me fly over there to verify my assumption."

"Wait! I will go with you," she said.

My back stiffened, and I cast a worried look at her skin. She followed my gaze and then smiled.

"It's okay. The scanners detected no radiation whatsoever," she said reassuringly before pointing at the holographic screen. "You see these lights at the top right? They indicate the air quality, radiation levels, and heat levels. Green means everything is totally safe. Yellow means be careful, the levels are not dangerous but avoid lingering. Orange indicates danger and that there is radiation or toxins that can be lethal, requiring me to leave immediately and to take countering medication as soon as possible. Red means I am fucked. But as you can see, it's all green."

"Very well," I mumbled, feeling only partially reassured.

I picked her up and carefully flew closer to the Sibris. She chuckled when she caught me steadily checking that the little lights were remaining green. Instead of stopping in front of the well, I circled around it, and continued approximately twenty more meters away before the small ditch became apparent.

"Yes!" Venus exclaimed. "That's the spot!"

As I landed in the artificial recess, Venus frowned at the large pillars buried at regular intervals along the ditch.

"These are harvesters," I preemptively explained. "They gather the energy generated by the Sibris and transfer it to the city."

"How deep do these pillars go?"

"Not deep at all. They pretty much sit on the surface and gather energy from the halo. But they are not the cause," I said with conviction. "Thaudras regularly occurred long before we developed this technology. After we did, our scientists closely monitored their behavior as the cataclysms approached. There was no variation in how the harvesters behaved, no explosions or other malfunction that could have triggered it. However, Thaudras itself destroys them alongside everything else within the blast radius."

"I see," she said, eyeing them suspiciously for a few more seconds before refocusing on me. "Could you stand over here?" she asked, pointing at a location ten meters away.

I complied. To my surprise, the closer I got to that position, the more my eyespots tingled. By the time I reached it, they shone as brightly as a strong sun glare.

"Are you doing this voluntarily?" Venus asked, excitement in her voice as she glanced in turn at me and at her holographic monitor.

I shook my head. "The Sibris emits pure magic. My eyespots are itching to channel it."

"But you're not doing anything else?" she insisted.

"No. Like what?" I asked, intrigued. "What is your device saying?"

"The energy level emitted by the beacon has dropped by half a percent."

I nodded in sudden understanding. "Black wings naturally attempt to nullify magic. It is not surprising that they passively dampen some of the Sibris' halo."

"Can you try to deliberately nullify it?"

"Not all of this by myself," I said with a snort while glancing at the beam of dancing lights.

It had a twenty-meter radius, and the light beam faded into the sky.

"How much can you nullify?" she asked.

"I don't know. Let's try?"

She nodded eagerly. Wanting to impress her, I opened the floodgates, allowing my wings to greedily draw in the magic flux streaming behind me. Drafting magic as a Black Achromatic was generally a frustrating experience. Our wings lusted after the blissful sensation of channeling the magic coursing through it into something even more potent. But instead, they swallowed it, most of the energy vanishing into an endless pit, leaving us hollow. It was like a terrible hunger that could never be sated.

"Whoa!" Venus exclaimed, her eyes glued to her monitor. "It's dropping fast."

"How much?" I asked, her excitement fanning my own.

"It was three percent a few seconds ago but already jumped to four. Jees! And now five!"

It eventually plateaued at nine and a half percent.

"I believe I could absorb more, but I don't dare," I said in a slightly strained voice. "My eyespots are burning with the urge to channel the Sibris' halo."

"Don't hold back!" Venus exclaimed.

"No. You might get hurt!"

Her jaw dropped as she realized she was standing directly in front of me.

"Oopsie!" she said in the most adorable childish voice then ran a few meters to the side.

As soon as she was at a safe enough distance, I drew in even more magic through my wings, focusing on absorbing it. Simultaneously, a searing heat built in my eyespots. They felt overcharged and on the verge of bursting. The blissful sensation that coursed through me when I released it was akin to relieving an overflowing bladder after hours of trying to hold it in.

But I wasn't prepared for the two powerful lightning bolts that shot out of my upper wings' eyespots. We normally channeled magic through our hands for more precise targeting. They struck the hard stones of the rock formation in front of us with a powerful thunderclap, shattering a large section of it. Venus emitted a frightened scream and raised her palms in front of her face to protect herself from the showering rocks.

It had been an instinctive reaction as the debris fell too far away to even remotely stand a chance of harming her. Still, I ran to my mate in a panic.

"Venus! Are you hurt?!" I shouted, grabbing her by the shoulders to examine her from head to toe.

"No, no! I'm fine," she said distractedly.

Her fright already forgotten, she was staring at the shattered section of rock with an air of wonder.

"I thought Blacks only had weak magic?!" she said.

"We do! I've never cast anything this powerful. Then again, I've never channeled pure magic to this extent before," I said, just as blown away as she was. "It's the blessing, too. I can gather more power."

"We need to try this again," Venus said firmly.

I nodded, before frowning at the spot where I had been standing previously. "There's something else. I felt a greater surge of power when I was standing where Xarin showed you. I'm not feeling it here."

"Then we need to test that as well."

For the next hour, we experimented me nullifying and drafting magic in various positions around the valley and in the vicinity of the beacon. By the time we stopped, the probe had met its demise underground, but the scanners had gathered an insane amount of data that Venus believed would reveal key information.

As for me, this little test raised more questions than provided answers. My mate juggled with a billion different new theories, all of which supported her opinion that we were the solution. She made me promise to submit to a full scan in the medical pod the UPO sent her along with her other requests.

Considering Prometheans knew nothing of human medicine, it was a great relief to know this machine could heal most illnesses or injuries my mate could face during her stay on Sylvar. Worst case scenario, it would put her in stasis until she could be taken to a more advanced medical facility off world.

If it could help prevent Thaudras, I was all in.

By the time we flew back home, the only thing that mattered to me was the wondrous feel of my mate's body in my arms.

CHAPTER 13
ATLAS

The journey home quickly grew increasingly uncomfortable. Where the trip to Keryth had been an enjoyable experience, savoring the feel of my female in my arms, the flight back turned out to be pure torture. Something happened during our experiments in the valley. It was as if drawing so much pure magic into me also awakened all my senses, making me hyper aware, and overly sensitive to every touch, every sound, and every scent.

From the moment I picked up Venus, a pleasant heat sparked low in my belly. As I flapped my wings, the spicy aroma of her skin mixed with the citrusy scent of her hair product fanned that spark into an open flame. The caress of her skin against my scales turned it into a raging inferno.

To my dismay, I felt my rod gradually stiffen as blood rushed to my nether region. I tried to silently will it to soften again. Sadly, the more I fought it, and the harder I became. At thirty-four, I'd obviously experienced arousal before. But it never hit me with such intensity. A dull throbbing spread throughout my pelvic area, and my abdominal muscles contracted spasmodically.

Every time Venus shifted in my arms, whether to get a better view of something in the landscape below, or to turn back to look at me, the friction between our bodies sent electric tendrils coursing through each of my nerve endings. I felt hot and cold at the same time. A primal part of me wanted to shift her position so that she would straddle me instead, bury myself deep inside her, and wrap my claspers around her thighs to keep her locked in place as I unleashed my passion on her.

Such unbridled thoughts both shamed and distressed me. By all accounts, I was going into heat, and every cell in my being wanted me to claim my mate. This shouldn't be happening so abruptly. When Prometheans found a potential mate—which first manifested itself by a specific physiological response—a hormonal awakening occurred over a period of days. If their personalities also proved compatible, that awakening would pursue its course, and both partners would go into heat. But if an emotional bond didn't form, the hormonal shift would stall and then die down, leading each partner to go their separate ways.

Normally, once we started noticing the signs within us, Achros and Monos would start drinking myrdin tea to quell any chances of our sexual awakening growing any further. In my case, it very timidly started manifesting itself on the second day of Venus's arrival. I should have drunk the tea right then and there. But as the symptoms had been quite feeble and easily controllable, I chose to delay for as long as possible, and maybe even indefinitely if I managed to keep myself in check.

Myrdin tea dulled the senses. While it didn't make you apathetic, it dampened your emotional responses to external stimuli. Considering how little time I had with Venus, I wanted to enjoy the full spectrum of emotions and sensations she awakened in me. I wanted to continue delighting in the warmth of her skin against mine, the softness of her touch, the way her sultry voice sent delicious shivers down my spine when she whispered my name in that affectionately teasing fashion she sometimes used.

Never in a million years would I have imagined I could go from basic to maximum awakening. The Sibris' halo was the only explanation I could think of.

But whatever the cause, the burning hunger within me had me on the verge of going feral. If not from the discipline acquired over the years of training for, serving in, and then leading the Black Guard, the gods only knew how I might have lost control and ravaged my mate.

The thought that I could become so mindless as to hurt a female—my own wife—and force myself on her without consent horrified me. In a way, it struck me so hard it actually helped me rein myself in.

My claspers—which partially hung on each side of my rod— were aching to fully extrude. I fought it at first. But as my shaft grew increasingly erect, I allowed them to extend to their maximum length, recurving them in front of my rod to flatten it against my pelvis. Simultaneously, I slightly lifted the position I held Venus sideways against my chest to make sure she wouldn't get poked by the tip of my length.

Whereas I slowed the journey to the valley, in part to savor holding my female a while longer, this time, I flew as fast as I could without causing too much wind discomfort for Venus. Despite that, the twelve-minute flight back home wrecked me. I felt dizzy, almost drunk by the time I landed in the garden.

Leodros—who had taken over the guard duty for the Prism in our absence—came out to greet us. I groaned inwardly. The last thing I needed was for one of my warriors to bear witness to my weakness. By the way his eyes widened when he approached us, Leodros perceived the change in my scent. It was heavier, laden with a musk meant to attract a female. His antennae flicked, tasting my scent to confirm his suspicions.

My scales darkened with embarrassment. Thankfully, Venus

exchanging a few friendly pleasantries with Leodros took his attention away from me.

"If you have nothing to report that requires my immediate attention, I will hop in the shower," I said to him in a slightly gruff tone.

"Nothing, Razus," he replied.

"Excellent. You are relieved," I said, eager to go cool my blood.

Leodros nodded, smiled at Venus, then took flight.

"A shower sounds like a good idea," Venus replied. "I'll go take one as well."

I forced a smile on my face and willed myself to adopt a normal pace as I headed to my room. The whole time, I prayed the stiffness of my gait didn't reveal the discomfort in my groin that made me feel as if I was waddling.

I lingered under the shower for as long as was reasonably acceptable. To my dismay, the ice-cold water failed to douse the inferno raging in my loins. I was fully in heat. Release alone could lower the fever, but it would only be a temporary relief. The moment I found myself in Venus's presence again, my blood would boil with need.

The moment we hit puberty, our mentors taught us the theory of it all. The thought that people could be so weak to their physiological urges always struck me as amusing and as a sign of their lack of discipline and willpower. Now, my own reaction humbled me.

Still feeling on edge, I snuck out of my room, relieved to find Venus was still in hers. She was likely contacting her parents or forwarding the data she gathered to people better versed in that scientific field for analysis. I hurried to the kitchen and put some water to boil to prepare myself a large pot of myrdin tea. It saddened me beyond words that I would no longer enjoy the full range of emotions and sensations my mate stirred in me. But her safety superseded everything else. I couldn't bear her feeling scared in my presence because of a hormonal surge.

I was just starting to pour myself a cup when the discreet patter of Venus's step reached me from the hallway. Panicked, I put away one of the three jars containing the leaves the caterer had brought for me. Under different circumstances, it would have been deemed thoughtful. But in this instance, it had been his way to remind me that I was not a real husband to my mate and to remember my place.

"Something smells nice!" Venus said in a cheerful tone as she entered the kitchen. "Is that tea?" she asked, gesturing with her chin at it.

I nodded, feeling mightily uncomfortable.

"Sweet! Mind if I steal a cup?"

"No! That's not for you!" I instantly blurted out, my left hand pushing the pot further back onto the counter, away from her.

Venus stiffened and stared at me with a shocked expression.

"I'm sorry," I said, mortified. "I didn't mean to raise my voice. This is not regular tea. It is medicine."

Her instant worry should have warmed me to the bone that she should feel such concern for my welfare. Instead, it heightened the shame bubbling deep within.

"Medicine?! Are you sick? Was there radiation after all?"

"No, Venus. It's nothing like that," I said reassuringly.

"Then what is it? Why do you need medicine?" she insisted.

Another wave of panic swelled within me as my brain refused to cooperate and provide me with a convincing response to her question. I opened and closed my mouth, words failing me.

Venus narrowed her eyes at me, concern giving way to suspicion. "Atlas, what's going on? Why are you…?"

She froze, as if struck by a sudden realization. Her eyes flicked between the steaming cup and the full pot before slowly gliding back towards my face.

"Is it *that* tea? The one you said your people took to control their emotions?" she asked, her voice suddenly soft.

My scales darkened with shame. I shifted on my feet but caught myself right before my hand would start scratching my fur again.

"I'm sorry, Venus. I meant no disrespect. Please, do not fear me," I said, my voice taking on a pleading edge.

"I'm not afraid of you, Atlas. There's no reason for you to apologize," she said in a soothing yet assertive tone. "So I guess that means you're physically attracted to me?"

By the Lights, I wanted to hide my face and disappear from view.

"I'm sorry, Venus," I repeated, mortified beyond words. "I feel and want things that aren't meant for me, that I shouldn't covet. My mind knows better, but my body and my heart have a will of their own. You're so different, so beautiful, and so kind. In all my years, no one else's presence has felt as harmonious, appeasing, and right as yours. Being near you makes me happy."

The intensity with which she stared at me as I blurted out these words unnerved me. I couldn't tell what distressed me more between the fact that my words didn't seem to shock her as they should, or that she kept an unreadable expression as I spewed that inappropriate confession.

"But don't worry. I will not bother you with any unwanted advances. This will silence my aberrant behavior," I added quickly, showing her the cup filled with myrdin tea.

She frowned, showing her first sign of disapproval since figuring out the purpose of the tea.

"Your behavior is in no way aberrant," she said sternly. "There's nothing wrong with becoming attracted to someone you get along with. In fact, in our case, it's not only normal but expected."

I recoiled and gaped at her. "Normal and expected?!" I echoed in confusion.

She sighed and slowly nodded.

"Do you remember me asking you if Kayog told you anything after our union?" Venus asked.

I nodded, curious as to what that had to do with anything.

"You said no the previous time. Has that changed since?" she insisted. "Has he told you anything about you and me?"

"The only thing he told me in the Great Hall about you and me was that we were the best match. I have not spoken with him since that day. And in my few exchanges with Linsea, the only message from her mate was that I should learn to do the spa-related things for you instead of merely obtaining you a bot and products. Why do you ask? What do you think he should have told me about us?"

"We aren't the *best* match, but the *perfect* match," Venus said, her eyes flicking between mine with that same unnerving intensity.

"I don't understand what you're trying to say," I said, genuinely confused.

Venus heaved another sigh. She remained quiet for a couple of seconds before taking a deep breath and squaring her shoulders the way one does when they have settled on a course of action and decided to go for it.

"Before leaving through the portal, Kayog told me that you and I are soulmates."

"WHAT?!" I exclaimed, taking an involuntary step back from shock.

Venus scrunched her face. "Jees! Don't look so horrified. There are worse fates than being my soulmate."

Another wave of shame crashed over me. "I'm sorry! I didn't mean it like that, at all! It's just… I'm shocked."

She smiled. "Believe me, I was, too."

I silenced the part of me that wanted to latch on to this impossible revelation, to the folly that this wonderful female could be mine, that someone like me could be made for her.

"He must be mistaken. You and I are different species," I argued weakly.

Venus huffed and waved a dismissive hand. "So are my sister and Szaro."

"Right," I conceded, feeling a little stupid.

"You don't seem too thrilled at that prospect. My feelings are starting to get hurt," she said in a teasing fashion, although I could hear a sliver of unease in her voice.

"Oh no! Please do not interpret my reaction like that at all," I exclaimed sheepishly. "It's just that... good things don't really happen to people like me. Being chosen by you and receiving the Prism's blessing have already turned my world upside down. I keep waiting for all of this to come crashing down once you realize you've both made a terrible mistake. But instead of sending me away, you're telling me we're meant to be together."

The tender emotion that settled on her face moved me to the core.

"I get it. You haven't had an easy life, and this was certainly the last thing either of us expected. But Kayog is never wrong," she said in a sympathetic tone.

"So you believe it? You truly think we are soulmates?" I asked disbelievingly.

She nodded and held my gaze unwaveringly. "Yes, I do."

The wave of happiness that initially swelled within me quickly receded as I studied Venus's beautiful face. Although she seemed pleased to claim me as hers, there was also something akin to reluctance lurking in the depth of her obsidian eyes. Then another unpleasant thought wormed its way into my mind.

"You've known this for many days but only shared it with me now," I said pensively. "Does the fact that we are meant for each other upset you?"

My heart sank when she hesitated, and her face took on a troubled expression.

"No, it does not upset me. Initially, I didn't say anything

because I needed to digest the news. But then, I realized I wanted you to start liking me naturally, not because I said you should. However, I cannot deny that things are complicated."

"Complicated how? I'm not what you wanted? Or do *you* feel obligated to like me because Kayog said so?"

The firmness and conviction with which she shook her head soothed the lancing pain I didn't even realize had been piercing my heart.

"No. Kayog's words didn't force me to like you, they only made it easier for me to accept it. I never would have imagined my perfect mate would be a mothman, but I genuinely like you. There's no doubt in my mind that, in time, I will fall head over heels in love with you. The problem isn't you, it's me."

"Why do I not like the sound of that?" I said, my stomach knotting.

Venus leaned her hip against the counter and ran a nervous hand through the tight curls of her hair. She glanced around the room before gesturing at it.

"The problem is this. I don't think I can live the rest of my life on this world. Everything here is too different. And I'm not even talking about the freaky bug mounts," she added with self-derision, as if to lighten the mood. "Promethean technology is way too far behind compared to what I'm used to."

"You could help us with this," I countered as if it was self-evident. "With your assistance, Kyrene and our other scientists could take our civilization into a far more advanced era in record time."

"And that's *exactly* why my presence here would be a problem," she said apologetically. "This is the perfect example of why the Prime Directive is so important. Your people must evolve on their own. Yes, with my technological knowledge and my connections, I could easily help boost your technology by five hundred years or more. But your society is not ready for it."

"What do you mean?" I asked, confused.

"One of the greatest clashes faced by most societies deemed primitive is the conflict between science and religion," Venus explained. "Prometheans are facing it right now with people like your Senators and the Polychromatics in general deeming you sacrifices to appease the gods. And on the other side, you have those like Kyrene who believe that your gods have nothing to do with any of this as it is a scientifically explainable phenomenon."

"Exactly! And with your help, we can make that demonstration and save countless lives. Why is that a problem?" I argued, genuinely baffled.

"Because this belief has impacted your entire societal structure, your people's culture, politics, family unit, and everything else in between. Every revolutionary scientific discovery brings in major overhauls at many core levels of a society. Too many significant changes will spell disaster because the people aren't ready for it all. Revolutionary changes have to be introduced gradually so that the society can adapt and adjust before new things are brought in."

"If that is what you believe, then why did we go to Keryth today? Why are you gathering all that data and collaborating with Kyrene?" I challenged.

"Because I also believe that it wasn't a coincidence that Xarin found me and brought me here. Because I cannot sit by idly while another genocide is about to be committed," Venus said forcefully. "I'm treading very carefully. My goal is not to upend your culture and least of all to be your savior. I can help, but Prometheans have to save themselves. You have to want it for yourselves and take the steps to achieve it."

"That still doesn't explain what you're doing with this data," I insisted.

"I'm merely helping with the work your scientists are already doing. That first meeting with Kyrene was to assess just how far along they were in their understanding of the phenomenon. I genuinely believe she's on the right path, but your technology doesn't allow her to get the type of data and samples required to confirm her hypotheses. I can provide that, which is why I asked her for the list of things she needed. In some cases, I will toe the line by hinting at things she might want to investigate, but it still must come from all of you."

"I see," I said, my voice a little cooler than I intended it to be.

She smiled with an air that was both apologetic and commiserating. "You must think I'm cold and indifferent to your people's plight, but I promise you I'm not. My strong stance on respecting the Prime Directive is specifically because I *want* to see Prometheans achieve their golden era. It wasn't before year 2536 of Earth's calendar that humans finally became united as one people instead of discriminating against each other over ethnicity, gender, and religion. We'd been building towards it for centuries, but it took our first contact with aliens—what is now commonly referred to as off-worlders—for us to finally acknowledge that we are one people with slight differences."

"That's a very long time," I said grimly.

"It is. Prometheans have a loooong way to go. And I couldn't live here without wanting to change your people's culture and mentalities to be more in line with my own and current galactic standards," Venus said passionately.

"Would that really be a bad thing?" I asked.

"Yes, because it wouldn't be fair to any of you. Self-determination is vital. Your people should change because they *believe* it is the right path for themselves based on lived experiences, be they successes or failures. Then they'll embark on that journey and fight for it out of conviction, not because some stranger imposed their will on all of you."

My shoulders slumped. "I understand," I said, feeling crushed. "Well, you only have a couple of months to go before you can return to your own world."

A strange expression fleeted over her features. To my shock,

Venus closed the short distance between us and carefully placed her hands on each side of my waist, as if bracing for the possibility I might balk at the unexpected contact.

"You're right. I do. And when the time comes, you could come with me," she said with a nervous and almost shy voice.

I gasped. "Come with you?! You want me to leave Sylvar?!"

She nodded, her eyes flicking between mine. "Yes. You could join me on my crazy adventures throughout the galaxy. I work with a lot of primitive species, sometimes in dangerous areas. I could use a protector. We worked well together earlier. But you could also do something different altogether. After seeing you train every day, I know the Enforcers wouldn't mind adding you to their ranks. The possibilities are infinite. There's no rush though," she added quickly when I just stood there gaping at her. "Like you said, there are still a few months to go before it's time for me to leave. You can take your time to think about it."

"You really want me to go with you," I whispered, my voice filled with shock and wonder.

"I do, Atlas. We barely know each other now, but I already can't bear the thought of parting from you. By the time everything is settled here, there's no question I will want to keep you forever. You're mine, Atlas. And I am yours. Whatever the future holds, we will face it together."

"You and me together," I whispered.

An emotion I couldn't describe tightened my throat while the most wondrous warmth spread through my chest. Time appeared to stand still as I drowned in the dark depth of my woman's eyes. I didn't recall moving or seeing Venus move. But the softness of her lips pressing against mine lit a fire in the pit of my stomach. The rabid hunger that had gradually abated during our intense conversation came back with a vengeance.

With a will of its own, my right hand settled on her nape, as if I feared she would move away. My other arm wrapped around her waist, drawing her body against mine. A powerful shiver coursed through me when she came willingly and pressed herself against me. The possessiveness of her embrace nearly undid me.

Even though I'd never kissed anyone before, I wasn't clueless as to what took place between a male and a female. To my shame, I had once again abused my privileged access to a limited section of the UPO's network in my capacity of Razus of the Black Guard to learn more about humans. Due to the Prime Directive, they made sure the content available to species such as mine was severely restricted.

Despite my burning curiosity, I hadn't gone so far as to consult their explicit content. I browsed medical sites to learn more about human anatomy. In theory, it was to be able to provide emergency assistance in case Venus got injured away from home where we kept her medical module. In practice, it had been to assess just how compatible we were, even though I never dreamt the day would come when she and I would ever be intimate.

To my pleasant surprise, Prometheans and humans shared many anatomical similarities, especially in the reproductive department. We had three main differences with human males. Their rod looked smooth and rather plain, devoid of our ridges alongside the length and stimulation nubs at the tip. Their seed sacs hung outside their bodies in an insanely vulnerable position. And they didn't possess claspers on their pelvic bones to help latch on to their mate during coupling.

Although not insignificant, those disparities wouldn't interfere with a harmonious joining between us. The question was whether they would turn her off.

But Venus's hands boldly roaming over me cast out my wandering thoughts rife with insecurities. A moan escaped me when her blunt nails gently scraped the thin scales lining the crease between the base of my wings and my back. She broke the kiss and brushed her lips along my jawline and down my neck. Another shiver coursed through me, and a dull throbbing pulsated between my thighs as I hardened again.

By the Lights! Everywhere her hands and lips touched my skin felt like an open flame leaving a burning trail in its path. I should stop her, tell her this was not only wrong but forbidden to the likes of me, but I wanted… no, I *needed* more. Throwing all caution to the wind, I surrendered to my own urges to explore the softness of her body. I didn't yet feel bold enough to slip my hands under the short skirt of her dress, but I let them roam freely over the thin fabric as I caressed her.

Venus's soft moan triggered another surge of lust directly in my nether region. She rubbed her face against my fur moments before the hot wetness of her tongue licked my left nipple. A strangled cry escaped me, and my rod jerked against the thick leather of my tarp. My mate's startled gasp made me realize I had picked her up. She wrapped her legs around my waist and reclaimed my mouth in a hungry kiss as I carried her to my room.

CHAPTER 14
VENUS

I hadn't planned on getting frisky with Atlas any time soon. But as we spoke, something went off inside me, and I finally gave in to my urge to kiss those luscious lips of his. What I hadn't expected was for it to awaken the all-consuming desire now burning within me.

I didn't have enough hands to explore the perfection of his body. The clash of the hardness of his scales with the soft way they bent beneath my touch, and the gentle way they scraped my palms was the biggest turn on. Above all, Atlas's responses to my caresses were driving me insane with lust.

As soon as he picked me up, moisture pooled between my thighs, and my inner walls contracted with anticipation. Feeling his shaft hardening under his leather loincloth had me aching even more. Fuck, it felt massive!

A small voice at the back of my head was screaming that this was too fast, too soon. I'd never been the type to bang on a first date. Granted, he wasn't some random fling I picked up in a bar, but that also meant we should take extra caution handling this right as this would be the beginning of the rest of our lives.

It was also clear that Atlas was a virgin. He'd more or less stated as much when describing the restrictions people like him faced. I would lie by saying that the knowledge I'd be his first—and only—turned me on even more. Where his kisses and caresses felt a little clumsy, he more than made up for it with his passion. I didn't doubt once he fully unleashed it on me, my man would wreck me in the most wondrous ways, with or without experience.

Still, I would take great delight in teaching him everything I knew and exploring our sensuality together.

For now, I refused to set any boundaries and would let things follow their course to their natural conclusion.

My stomach fluttered when he pushed open the door to his room. He carried me straight to the imposing bed and carefully lay me down on it. It surprised me. Considering his lack of experience, and the fact he was showing signs of going into heat, I never expected him to display such self-control and restraint. In truth, I thought he'd toss me on the bed, yank off his tarp, rip my dress to shreds with his sharp claws, then fuck me senseless without proper foreplay or preparation.

He half lay on top of me, holding himself propped up on his palms framing me. The strained look on his face as he stared at me confirmed he was fighting to rein himself in. In that instant, I realized he was giving me a chance to back out and tell him to get off me. Even now, when many males would only pursue their own satisfaction, he was putting my welfare, needs, and safety first.

A powerful emotion swept through me. Yes, it was only a matter of time before I fell in love with that wonderful male.

I smiled, wrapped my arms around his neck and drew him to me. A deep growl vibrated through his chest as he crushed my mouth with a possessive kiss. Just like I previously did to him, Atlas then proceeded to brush his lips over my face, along my jawline, then down my neck. His hands glided over me, their touch both daring and tentative. I didn't want him to be hesitant or worried he might do this wrong.

The same way he strived to make me feel safe with him, I needed him to know he was also safe to freely explore his awakening sensuality with me. My body was his, and his was mine.

When his lips reached the curve of my right breast, he lifted his head as if waiting for my permission to proceed. To my surprise, instead of giving him the encouraging smile I initially intended, I found myself pushing on his shoulders. Stunned, he rolled to the side with a worried expression. But I followed the movement, continuing to push him onto his back before straddling him.

His worry turned to wonder when I grabbed the hem of the skirt of my dress and pulled it over my head. I tossed the garment onto the floor, and swiftly got rid of my bra. Leaning forward, I took his hands and placed them on my breasts. The lascivious look that descended over his features had me soaking wet in seconds. As he began to fondle my breasts, I kept my hands on the back of his.

Beneath my thighs, a hard length pressed against my core, making me ache for more. To my utter annoyance, the thick leather of his loincloth dampened the sensation. My palms glided down the sides of his muscular arms to his chest. As his fingers continued to tease and squeeze my nipples, I reciprocated, gently pinching and twisting his. He took a hissy breath, not due to pain but pleasure. The way his cock jerked against the apex of my thighs only had me throbbing more.

I bent down to claim his lips. Atlas immediately let go of my breasts to hold me close. A deep moan rose from me as the searing heat of his naked body wrapped around me. My man had held me a couple of times now when we flew to Keryth Valley. But this was the first time I got full skin-to-skin contact with him. Judging by the growling sound that rumbled through his chest, he also approved.

The heat emanating from him qualified as feverish levels. From what information I gathered in the data Kyrene forwarded me, it was a normal reaction for a Promethean male entering his mating frenzy. Too little research had been devoted to that aspect as Achros and Monos weren't supposed to indulge in their urges —a failure I intended to rectify. But right now, I wanted Atlas to do all the indulging in the world.

His calloused hands caressed my back, the right one sliding down to my rear end before giving my cheek a good squeeze. Poking my tongue out, I teased the seam of his mouth. To my delight, he parted his lips, welcoming the invasion. Considering his lack of experience, I had wondered if he was familiar with this way of kissing.

The silkiness of his tongue took me by surprise as it swirled around mine. For some reason, I thought it would have a rougher texture, almost like that of a cat. His sweet and tangy taste vaguely reminded me of honeyed lemon.

Once more deviating from my expectation, Atlas wasn't clumsy as we further deepened the kiss. He naturally adapted to me, first following my lead before gradually taking over, asserting himself.

That further turned me on.

I wasn't submissive, but not dominant either. In the bedroom, I enjoyed swapping roles based on our whim of the moment, and for my partner to be able to take charge and be open about his desires. This first glimpse of his underlying assertiveness pleased me tremendously.

As our tongues made each other's acquaintances, Atlas's hands were all over me, all restraint discarded. A delicious shiver coursed through me when his right hand snuck under the waist of my panties, around the curve of my bum, and started fingering my slit. His chest vibrated again with approval, undoubtedly at finding me wet for him.

From what I saw in the documents provided by Kyrene, their

females also shared quite a few similarities with us. Their slit generally resembled ours in size and placement, but they didn't have a clitoris or inner lips, and no pubic hair. I wanted to believe they had a nice big G-spot inside to compensate. But the single illustration I found didn't go that far. So it surprised me when Atlas didn't stop at teasing my vulva but continued until he reached my engorged little nub to give it some more than welcomed attention.

I moaned against his lips and my body shuddered under the sparks of pleasure that radiated through me. I ground on his hand for a little bit while devouring his mouth before breaking the kiss. As good as this felt, I needed to sate my curiosity about his body. When I started to kiss a path down his chest, Atlas initially attempted to resist, his hands gripping my upper arms to prevent me from moving down.

I lifted my head to stare at him sternly.

"Stay!" I hissed in a tone that brooked no argument.

He stiffened. The intense look on his face screamed loudly that he was seriously considering challenging me. His muscles swelled, and the predatory look in his eyes had my inner walls contracting and my breasts suddenly feeling heavy and achy. The dominant alpha lurking behind the sweet and sometimes timid virgin was rearing his head, and it was sexy as fuck.

After a few seconds that felt like a century, Atlas yielded, releasing his grip, but the rebellious glimmer lingered in his obsidian eyes. I couldn't decide if I was more turned on by this defiant concession or disappointed that he hadn't used his superior strength to flip me onto my back and show me who's boss.

Either way, I planned on making him extremely grateful he'd given in to my wishes.

I kissed a path down his chest, stopping for a second to rub my face all over his fur. I would never tire of its softness against my skin. In fact, I already anticipated the wondrous night I'd sleep in his arms with my head resting on that furry pillow.

Resuming my journey south, I lingered briefly at his nipples, licking, sucking, and nipping at them. Beneath my hands caressing his waist and chiseled stomach, his abdominal muscles contracted spasmodically.

The sound of his breath becoming labored as I kissed and nipped the skin around his navel sent a thrill down my spine. The fingers of his right hand sank through my curls when I detached the clasps holding his leather loincloth secure around his waist.

As soon as I tried to lower it, Atlas fisted his hand in my hair, giving it a good sting, but not in a painful way. I glanced up at him. The tension—almost fear—on his face threw me for a loop. For half a beat, I dreaded that his cultural indoctrination was taking over, pushing him to deny himself what his people deemed sacrilegious for someone like him. Then the sudden realization that he probably worried his anatomical differences might turn me off hit me.

"You're mine, Atlas. My husband. We were made for each other. I would see what's mine..."

He swallowed hard, his face revealing the inner battle raging within him. Although his tension didn't fade away, Atlas once more yielded to my wishes. He didn't release my hair but loosened his grip enough to make his meaning clear. I gave him a reassuring smile before tugging on the waist of his loincloth again. To my delight, despite his apprehensions, he lifted his behind to ease my task of ridding him of the garment.

Moments later, I feasted my eyes on his glorious nudity.

Although close enough to the real thing, the black and white illustration of a Promethean male's anatomy I had seen didn't do it justice. Generally shaped like a human cock, the entire length was covered in tight spiraling ridges that coiled from the base all the way to the tip. The head generally had the same shape as a man's glans, but a dozen little bumps covered it. Had I not seen the illustration showing it as being their default, I would have assumed they were subdermal implants. It had the same greige color as the rest of his skin.

My mouth watered, and my inner walls constricted in anticipation as my fertile imagination began to fantasize about how it would feel inside me.

And Atlas was massive…

But the two appendages on each side of his pelvic bone claimed my attention. They were telescopic claspers with the thickness of a pinky finger. In their currently collapsed length, they measured about eight centimeters. Once fully extended, I suspected they would reach nearly double that length.

Perfect to hook around my thighs and keep me in place while he has his way with me.

That, too, had my inner walls perking up, and my stomach fluttering. All of this should have freaked me out, but I couldn't feel more aroused.

I glanced back at Atlas. He was still tense, but his wariness dimmed, replaced by curiosity as he studied my reaction. The subtle movement of his antennae hinted he was tasting the air to help him assess my physiological response to his nudity.

"You're perfect," I whispered, my eyes locked with his. "Absolutely perfect… and mine."

This time, all tension bled out of him while a powerful emotion settled on his alien features.

"My mate…" he whispered, his voice filled with the same adoration burning in his eyes.

I smiled and boldly covered the base of his cock with my palm before gliding it upward until it closed around the head. Atlas's breath hitched. He closed his eyes, swallowed hard, then slowly reopened them. My man looked almost in pain as he stared at me with hooded eyes and clenched teeth.

It was my turn to study his reactions as I slowly began to stroke him, twisting my wrist as I did so to enhance the sensation and giving the head a good squeeze before moving back down.

In no time, he was breathing loudly, his hands fisting the bedsheet with such force I expected it to tear any minute. The head of his cock turned out to be quite sensitive. After squeezing it, I would flick my thumb over the little bumps. It clearly sent a jolt of pleasure through him. They weren't anywhere near as hard as they appeared to be visually—just hard enough to give a nice sensation, but pliable enough to easily glide in.

Unable to resist any longer, I leaned forward and gave his head a lick. Once again, he tasted like honeyed lemon, but this time with a hint of salt. Atlas emitted a strangled sound and jerked up in a half sitting position. Leaning on his forearm, he stared at me with an intensity that would have been intimidating if I wasn't so turned on. His breath grew even louder and came out in short bursts. After a couple more licks, I took him inside my mouth.

Atlas cried out. His hips jerked up in an involuntary movement, sending his cock deeper into my mouth. I yanked my head back just as the tip was hitting the back of my throat. Although my eyes slightly watered, I thankfully didn't go into a coughing fit, and dove right back in.

Loud, growly moans tumbled freely out of Atlas as I began to bob over him. His hand in my hair once more tightened its grip. Surprisingly, even as he was losing his battle to maintain control, he never fully lost it either. He didn't hurt me and didn't start thrusting upward, which could have spelled trouble for me. I didn't know how much of this was thanks to his Black Guard training and discipline. Whatever the cause, I was grateful for it.

As he was nearing the edge, I almost yelped in fear when his claspers jerked then suddenly hooked behind my shoulders. It didn't poke into my flesh and didn't hurt. However, the strength with which they kept me in place was quite impressive. That temporary scare slightly threw me off my game, but I got right back to it, determined to see him falling apart for me. His legs shaking, his stomach contracting, and his moans filling the room heralded his imminent climax.

Despite bracing for it, his orgasm still took me by surprise. Atlas's body seized, and a feral roar tore out of him. His skin had already been quite hot since he'd gone into heat. But seconds before his seed shot out, the base of his cock grew even hotter. Then the taste of honeyed lemons exploded on my taste buds. I nearly choked on the first powerful spurt, but quickly swallowed it, refusing to be defeated. My tongue, palate, and throat immediately tingled with a spicy sting as if a touch of ginger had been added to the mix.

But my focus remained on my man.

I glanced up at his beautiful face, even as I continued to bob over him. My hand moved in counterpoint to my mouth, stroking and squeezing him until he was fully spent.

Good God! He was magnificent!

Lips parted, eyes half-shut, his head slightly tilted back with an air of pure bliss, he was shaking while riding the waves of ecstasy. I felt incredibly powerful that I gave him so much pleasure.

I pursued my ministrations until his claspers finally released my shoulders, the telescopic part retracting into the lower half of the stem. After one last lick, I kissed a path back up his stomach and chest before lying on top of him. He instantly wrapped his arms around me in a possessive fashion, as if he feared I might vanish.

The tenderness, wonder, and something else I couldn't define in his eyes messed me up.

"My mate," he whispered, looking at me as if he didn't quite believe I was real.

Before I could answer, he crushed my lips in a searing kiss. I responded in kind. When our lips parted, I made to bury my face in his neck, ready to snuggle with my man. To my shock, the room spun, and I found myself on my back, with Atlas on top of me. He kissed me again, deeply, passionately.

His hands on me quickly made his intentions clear. As soon as he broke the kiss, I attempted to make a token protest. But the hardness in his eyes silenced me.

"Stay!" he ground through his teeth. "You're mine, Venus."

Hearing him echo my words in this slightly menacing fashion had my toes instantly curling. Eyes wide, I clamped my mouth shut while moisture all but gushed between my thighs. His antennae flicked again. And the subtle smirk that stretched his plush lips confirmed they told him how he was affecting me.

It should annoy me, but it was so fucking hot!

For the next eternity, he worshiped every inch of my body with his mouth and hands while ridding me of my panties. Like I had done with him, he tested my responses to his touch, lingering in all the places that triggered the strongest ones to confirm his suspicions, and coming back to them to make me moan for him.

When he settled between my thighs, I thought I would lose my mind. Atlas didn't play around, and immediately zeroed in on my clit. The burning heat of his mouth closed around it, and he began to suck on it with the avidity of a starving man. He sank two fingers inside me, moving them in and out at a frantic pace. In no time, he had me gyrating and chanting his name as pleasure swiftly built inside me.

I doubted Atlas knew about a woman's G-spot. However, thanks to his continued attentiveness to my reactions, it didn't take him long to realize at what angle he needed to thrust his fingers to trigger a strong response from me.

And then he went wild on it.

My climax didn't come as the slow rise of the tide but built with the strength and speed of a tidal wave, crashing into me with a violence that left me in ruins. My body jerked as I cried out in bliss. Atlas's left hand on my thighs tightened its grip, keeping me in place while he continued to feast on me. The prickling sensation of his claws only added to the whirlwind of sensations sweeping through me.

After a while, I vaguely felt him relent. But my clit continued to throb and pulsate, while my blood rushed in my ears in a roaring sound over the thundering of my heart. The searing heat of Atlas's body wrapping around me made me realize he was gathering me in his arms. Still dazed, I slipped my arms around him and pressed my body against his. I rested my head on the soft fur of his chest. Another shiver coursed through me when the soft, almost leathery texture of his wings settled over me like a blanket.

"My Venus, my mate… I will fight for you. I will fight to keep you forever. You are mine, and I am yours."

I smiled.

CHAPTER 15
VENUS

The next morning, I was disappointed to wake up in an empty bed. It shouldn't surprise me as Atlas displayed rigorous discipline with his daily routine. He got up with the birds, reviewed any report received overnight from the Black Guard, planned or revised assignments, as well as answered any other communication involving security details for officials, prominent visiting guests, or special large gatherings or events. He would squeeze in one hour of training before, after, or in between those tasks, depending on their urgency.

Still, I wouldn't have minded a bit more cuddling with him or even a good morning make out session.

My stomach fluttered as memories of last evening flooded my mind. I had not meant for our first kiss to take us this far—not that I had any regrets. I was more worried about pushing his boundaries too quickly. Although I wouldn't have minded going all the way with him last night—after all, we were soulmates—I was glad we had not. The more I thought about it, the more uneasy I grew about what had taken place between us.

His whole life, his society convinced him that coupling for someone like him was essentially a crime against the people and the gods themselves. Had I caused him harm by indulging in my own desires? Granted, Atlas had been a willing participant throughout the process. He even took charge a few times. So it wasn't like I coerced him into anything.

But he's in heat...

That thought twisted my insides. Atlas was indeed in heat. So much so that he'd felt compelled to drink that tea to dampen his libido. But I stopped him before he could. Therefore, had he truly been in the right mental and physical state to make that decision last night? Had I involuntarily taken advantage of him in a vulnerable moment? With him being a virgin and having had no prior hope of experiencing intimacy with a female, it just added to the list of external factors that could have influenced his choices.

The pleasant warmth I initially felt thinking about last night gave way to a queasy feeling. I needed to find Atlas at once to assess the extent of the damage I might have caused and grovel for his forgiveness. Fuck, I knew better! For someone who prided herself on being level-headed, calculated, and very analytical, I'd utterly failed in properly assessing the situation before acting on my impulses.

I jumped out of bed, slipped on my dress, and made a run for my room where I took a shower and changed. As expected, I didn't run into Atlas who was likely training in the garden. By the time I stepped out of my room, I'd rehearsed what I would say in a billion different ways. All of them felt weak to me.

As I approached the glass doors looking out onto the garden, I stared at Atlas. He had apparently completed his training and was doing a few final post workout stretches while cooling down. He was truly a stunning male. Any other day, I would be drooling. But guilt clouded the possessive pride I felt.

Taking a deep breath, I slid the door open and stepped out onto the patio. Alerted by the discreet sound, Atlas jerked his head up. His instant smile upon seeing me froze then faded, replaced by a guarded expression. He straightened and watched me approach quietly. I silently berated myself for allowing the look on my face or my body language to give away my inner turmoil. I had hoped to ease into it. However, his initial smile gave me hope that maybe I was overthinking things.

Or maybe it's wishful thinking because he's still too addled by his current state to fully think rationally.

"Good morning," I said, the smile I tried to give him feeling stiff on my face.

My heart sank when his wariness shifted into a cool and closed off expression. Man, I was seriously fucking this up.

"Good morning," he replied with the distant politeness one gave a stranger.

I licked my lips nervously, annoyed that the speech I previously rehearsed conveniently chose to fly right out of my brain.

"How are you feeling?" I asked, flinching inwardly that this was the best opening I could come up with.

He narrowed his eyes at me, and his posture further stiffened. It was subtle but undeniable.

"I'm feeling just fine," he replied matter-of-factly.

"That's good. I'm glad to hear it."

Fuck me sideways. Where the hell had snarky, smart ass, I-don't-put-up-with-anyone's-bullshit Venus gone to? I was acting totally brain dead right now. But then, I'd never been in such a situation.

This time, his face hardened, and a hint of anger sparked in his dark eyes.

"If there's something you want to tell me, Venus, just go ahead and say it," Atlas said in a clipped tone. "Is it about last night? Are you having regrets? If that's the case, just say so. I will not impose myself where I'm not wanted."

I recoiled and gaped at him in shock. "No! I don't regret what happened! Well, not exactly. Not really…"

I flinched and groaned inwardly at how fucking clumsy and

pathetic I was being. The deeply hurt look in his eyes, quickly hidden, stabbed at my heart. I couldn't handle this more poorly.

"I see," he said in a frigid tone.

"No, you don't," I said forcefully. "I don't regret what happened between us. You are my soulmate, and I want a future with you. I'm just worried it happened too soon, that you were not ready, and that I took advantage of you."

It was his turn to recoil. He blinked then stared at me with complete confusion.

"How did you take advantage of me?" he asked, baffled.

"You were in heat. I came on to you while you were under the influence of a hormonal imbalance. Had that not been the case, had you been clear-minded, would you have consented to this? It goes against everything your society dictates. And I didn't perform my due diligence last night to make sure you were in the right headspace before taking what I wanted."

"You're trying to protect me!" he whispered to himself, his voice filled with disbelief.

"Of course, I am!" I exclaimed with conviction. "I don't want you to regret anything or resent that it happened or how it happened."

He stared at me with the strangest expression, his antennae flicking, and his mind spinning. I held my breath, waiting for his response. To my surprise, he snorted, then shook his head as if he couldn't believe this situation.

"This is the first time anyone has ever cared what I wanted and deliberately put my wishes and welfare before their own desires," he mused aloud with an air of wonder and disbelief. "You didn't take advantage of me. You didn't trick me into anything. I want you, Venus. I've wanted you from the first day. Granted, it was weak at first, but it has steadily grown. Yes, I'm in heat, and it influences me. But only a female I feel physically, spiritually, and emotionally attuned to can trigger that response.

My entire being not only already consented, but it also longed for us."

The immense weight that had been crushing me since waking up suddenly lifted, and my shoulders slumped with relief.

I gave him a hesitant smile. "So… You're really okay with all of this? You're not having second thoughts?"

"Absolutely not! Last night was… the most wonderful day of my life. I want to be with you in every way… always. I chose you, just like you chose me. Yes, my society disapproves, but the past few days since your arrival has forced me to rethink and challenge many of the things I never agreed with but accepted as simply being our way. You are right that for our society to change, it has to come from us."

My heart soared, and a wave of emotions surged through me. He timidly extended his hands towards me. I willingly took them and let him draw me closer to him.

"But before I can push for global changes, I have to start with me. You made me realize that I deserve kindness and respect, that people cannot take from me and deny me basic rights and dignity unless I allow them to. Since birth, I've walked at the edge of life, content with the crumbs others deemed sufficient for me. No more. You are the most wonderful thing that's ever happened to me. With you, I've finally gotten a taste of what it's like to truly live. You have given me a reason to fight. And fight I will, for us, for the future I never thought possible. So long as you'll have me, I'm yours, Venus. By *choice*."

I'd never been the overly emotional type, but his words, the look in his eyes, the depth of feelings emanating from him almost like a physical entity wrecked me. Tears pricked my eyes, and a quivering smile settled on my face.

"Then you are mine forever," I said in a shaky voice.

He looked at me with an air of pure adoration before leaning down and kissing me. I melted against him, my arms closing possessively around his firm body. I gasped against his lips when he picked me up then wrapped his wings around us. I'd never felt so sheltered and wanted than in this instant.

Obviously, we weren't in love just yet, but this further confirmed that we were made for each other. Things could have gone so horribly wrong due to stupid misunderstandings. But that we managed to openly discuss our respective positions on the matter boded well for our future. With us coming from such different backgrounds ethnically, culturally, and technologically, honest communication would be vital.

Atlas broke the kiss then buried his face in my neck. We remained in each other's embrace for God only knew how long. I could have stayed like this forever. When he finally released me, Atlas gazed at me with a tenderness that made me warm and fuzzy inside.

"Let's go feed you, my mate. Then we can run the tests you wanted your medical device to perform on me," he said in a gentle voice.

I nodded and let him lead me to the kitchen. We made quick work of our morning meal, then Atlas hopped into the shower while I prepared the medical module. Overnight, I received some initial analysis reports from the Enforcers' research center, based on the data I collected in Keryth Valley. As I mentioned I would perform this full medical evaluation on Atlas, they sent a detailed list of parameters they wanted me to set in order to test specific things that the standard evaluation didn't normally include.

Apparently, the little experiment we performed based on the vision Xarin shared with me opened quite the can of worms—but in a positive fashion. While my own scientific background gave me a lot of hints as to what the preliminary data revealed, I didn't possess the expertise necessary to fully assess them, let alone derive accurate assumptions or even make potential connections that could lead to a solution.

But that had never been my role.

Granted, I used to build medical equipment. But my job was to create the functions required by the medical experts and design the interface and data processing that would allow them to achieve their goals. That did not make me a doctor, just like being an excellent car mechanic didn't make you an ace race car pilot.

When Atlas returned, I couldn't help but ogle him a little. Technically, he could have gotten inside the medical pod still wearing his tarp and sandals. I remained quiet when he removed the latter, but weakly said as much after he took off the former.

"Do you prefer I put it back on?" he asked in a provocative tone. "Do not lie."

I scrunched my face at him. The smug look that settled on his face should have pissed me off. Instead, it turned me on. I really loved the confident and assertive side of him that was steadily emerging. It told me he was genuinely starting to believe in us.

"I'll take that as a no then, my mate," he said teasingly before sitting at the edge of the module.

Shaped like a bullet, it had a clear glass dome that opened like the lid of a box but retracted into the right side. From a distance, it could easily be mistaken for a stasis chamber or escape pod. I tapped a button on the interface located at the foot of the module. A double-sided holographic display was immediately deployed above it, allowing both the patient and the operator to see the screen.

It took a moment to comfortably place Atlas's wings within the device. It didn't help that he became aroused during the process. Having no shame, I not only enjoyed the view but indulged in a wee bit of groping while at it—not that he seemed to mind. However, I eventually got back to a more serious stance, explaining once more the extent of the tests the module would perform, and the invasive information it would gather. Thankfully, by the time I was done, his erection had subsided.

"I trust you, Venus," Atlas said in a calm voice. "If you think this information can be useful, then I am happy to help provide it."

I smiled, leaned forward, and gently kissed him. I rubbed my nose against his, reveling in the gentle scraping of the small scales covering it, then straightened.

"You shouldn't feel any pain or discomfort. But if that happens, just tell me, and I'll stop it right away. Even with the dome closed, I will hear you normally," I explained.

He nodded. The trust in his eyes did funny things to me.

I launched the program. Atlas didn't flinch or stir, content to watch the multiple light beams of the various scanners run over him. He didn't balk when a few needles protruded from the sides of the module to prick different parts of his body for tissue and fluid samples. Simultaneously, the screen displayed a highly-detailed 3D model of Atlas, including skeleton, organs, nervous and circulatory systems.

Once done, I realized I had the most in-depth biological breakdown of a Black Promethean in the entire universe. The Prometheans who had been previously abducted had all been Polychromatics. As I opened the dome to let Atlas out, a sudden thought struck me.

"What's wrong?" Atlas asked when he saw me frowning. "Is there an issue with the tests?"

I shook my head. "No, but I was just thinking that your results alone are too limited a sample. Obviously, we're not doing an exhaustive study of the Promethean race. But it would be good to be able to compare your results with those of a few other Blacks to make sure we don't misinterpret things based on traits that might be unique to you, instead of shared by your people as a whole."

"That can be arranged," Atlas said without hesitation. "Many of my warriors would be happy to volunteer. And if your theory about us being the solution is correct, then you might want to test a few Whites as well."

"Oh, my God! You read the thoughts right out of my mind!" I exclaimed excitedly. "Any chance that could happen?"

He pursed his lips. "I can get a few Whites to come here, but it will stir a lot of discontent. Beyond the fact that the population doesn't like seeing them walking our streets, they will grumble even more finding out they are coming under the same roof as the Prism."

"Will they prevent them from coming?" I asked warily.

"So long as the whites are wearing a shawl, they cannot stop them from freely coming and going. But be prepared for Ajustus to try and create trouble over it as he keeps a close eye on what happens around this house," Atlas warned.

"Does that mean we should pass?"

"Absolutely not," he replied in a tone that brooked no argument. "Their bigotry and narrow-mindedness will not get in the way of this research. So long as no laws are broken, they can wail all they want."

"Excellent," I said, once again feeling turned on by this commanding side of him. "I will prepare the data and send it to the Enforcers' research lab and to Kyrene. Any chance we could go see her later today?"

"It shouldn't be a problem. I will inform her that we will drop by later on. Just let me know when you are ready to depart," Atlas said, making a show of putting his loincloth back on.

To my delight, once done, he drew me into his embrace and gave me an affectionate kiss. He lifted his head, studied my features with infinite tenderness, and caressed my cheek. Without another word, he dropped his hand, turned on his heel, and exited the room.

~

Kyrene greedily pored over the data I forwarded to her both yesterday and earlier this morning. In the back of the room, two of her assistants looked on the verge of having an orgasm as they also analyzed them. Their delight thrilled me as much as it did Atlas. He had come a long way since our first visit here where he expressed so much resistance to the concepts we discussed.

"How accurate is this data?" Kyrene asked, pointing at a printout of some of the readings I gave her.

It still boggled my mind to see them work with so many physical documents printed on actual paper—or rather their version of it.

"Extremely accurate," I said with confidence. "Why? What do you see?"

"If my interpretation is right, your probe is detecting a life form in this general area," Kyrene said excitedly. "Actually, more like multiple life forms."

I nodded. "I suspected as much but wasn't certain. Based on the latest readings, Their numbers have gone up, slightly, but unmistakably."

"Latest readings?" Kyrene asked.

"I left the probe underground," I admitted sheepishly. "Considering the harsh environment below, I initially thought it had been destroyed when the signal stopped. But then it resumed while we were flying back home. I don't know how much longer it will survive, but I'm saving all the data it continues to send."

"That's excellent news!" Kyrene said with a huge grin. "This could be the breakthrough we've been looking for. For decades, we suspected the presence of that life form, but our limited technology couldn't confirm it."

"You know what it is?" I asked, perking up.

"Maybe," Kyrene said hesitantly. "After the Thaudras that decimated Orist Valley, our people found a vast amount of large insects near the remains of the sacrificed who had not been completely incinerated. Unfortunately, those insects were dead and calcinated. The scientists at the time couldn't get anything out of them. All we have are a few sketches and their notes."

"You think they are related?" Atlas asked.

"We think they're the cause," Kyrene said with a conviction that left me reeling.

"The cause?" I asked with undisguised surprise.

She nodded. "We haven't encountered that species anywhere else on all of Sylvar. After Orist, the scientists specifically looked for these bugs at the end of the next Thaudras. Once again, a couple of them were found, in a similar burnt state. As it had been of much smaller scale and quickly stopped thanks to the sacrifices, we believe that's the reason so few of those insects were found."

"So their presence in Orist wasn't a fluke," Atlas said pensively. "But how could they cause such destruction?"

"Some form of disturbance destabilizes the magnetic fields below the Sibris. If Venus's readings are accurate, and the number of those insects indeed keeps growing, then whatever they're doing down there could be the triggering factor. Ideally, we would need to capture a few of them alive to see what they are doing exactly, and what the Blacks and Whites do to counter them."

The look she gave me made it clear she hoped I would offer to retrieve that sample for them. They didn't possess the technology to achieve it.

"I don't have the ability to capture those insects alive right now," I said carefully. "But I will relay your request to the Enforcers and see what can be done. As we speak, they are thoroughly analyzing the data I sent them."

"Thank you! Any help we get is a blessing!" Kyrene said with gratitude before taking an apologetic expression. "However, I'm baffled by this other data you sent regarding Atlas. Again, I do not want you to think I doubt the quality of your work, but I must ask how accurate those readings are. These numbers are off the charts."

"No need to apologize. We were quite floored as well," I said reassuringly.

Atlas and I then took turns recounting the vision Xarin sent me, which prompted us to test Atlas's casting abilities by the beacon.

"I'd never achieved such insane power before. The lightning bolt I cast rivaled that of a Polychromatic, and maybe even a White," Atlas said.

"Are you serious?!" Kyrene exclaimed. "You're still this powerful?"

He shook his head. "No. I felt it drain over time, although I remain a bit more powerful still than after receiving the Prism's blessing. I suspect that power will return if I try drafting again using the pure magic of the beacon's halo directly."

I couldn't repress a smile to hear him use the Universal translation of Sibris like I tended to do instead of its Promethean name.

"You need to test that again to confirm it," Kyrene said in a tone that brooked no argument.

"I agree. And I will ask a few of my warriors to perform the test as well," Atlas said.

My heart swelled with pride as I stared at my man. He underestimated himself so much, he didn't understand just how smart he actually was and what a great analytical mind he possessed.

"Excellent idea," I said, not mentioning that the same thought had surged in my mind.

"There's something else you should know," Atlas continued, a frown creasing his scaly brow. "Drafting from the Sibris sent me into heat."

Kyrene stiffened, as did I. It was a relevant admission for him to make. Every detail counted. But knowing his people's stance on the matter, I feared it would turn our only true ally here into an enemy. I braced for her to express disgust and outrage. But her shock soon gave way to the focused intensity of a scientist following a promising lead.

"What heat level are we talking about?" she asked carefully.

"Full heat. Not simply an awakening," Atlas replied in a factual fashion.

"By the Lights!" Kyrene whispered.

I didn't know how to interpret her expression or body language.

"Did you couple?" she asked.

I gasped, shocked she would ask something so personal, and mortified at the thought we needed to come clean about this for the sake of science.

Atlas turned his head to look at me, his expression unreadable. Then, to my surprise, he softly caressed my cheek with the back of his hand. Looking back at Kyrene, he held her gaze unwaveringly… unapologetically.

"We didn't couple, but we were intimate," he said in the same factual tone.

Of all the reactions Kyrene could have had, I never expected it would be this almost maternal approval.

"Have you noticed any change in you?" she asked.

I blinked, taken aback by the question, which seemed to confuse Atlas as well.

"No. I feel the same as before. Why?" he asked.

"In ancient folklore, there were tales of supernatural beings called Shadows. They were magicless and dark as night. But bigger and stronger than the commonfolk. On the days of Radiance, they would cast powerful magic through the Gift of Kiaris."

"What are the days of Radiance?" I asked with genuine curiosity. "And what is the Gift of Kiaris?"

"Radiance is a temporary event that occurs three or four

times a year," Atlas explained. "During a Radiance, the sky is covered in dancing lights and the halo of the Sibris nearly triples in size. It is beautiful to behold."

"Oh wow! I hope I'll get to witness it. But what of the gift?"

"I don't know," he said, casting an inquisitive look at Kyrene. "I never heard of it or of those Shadows."

"There are many tales that have fallen into obscurity. But I believe they hold invaluable information and lost knowledge." She turned to me before continuing. "Kiaris is the Goddess of Light, our principal deity. Her Gift is how our forebears used to call the Sibris."

My eyes widened in sudden understanding. "Magicless, dark Prometheans were able to cast powerful magic on the rare days the beacons were at their maximum output!"

"Exactly," Kyrene said. "The first time I stumbled on that tale, I actually tested that theory. But the Blacks who participated showed no particular increase in power. Could it be because the Prism blessed Atlas?"

"No," I said with a visceral certainty. "I mean, it's possible that it enhanced it, but Atlas felt a noticeable surge when he took position at the specific spot Xarin indicated in the vision he sent me. Your experiment probably failed because the subjects weren't standing at the right place."

"But now we know what to do," Atlas said with an excited smile.

"We do!" I replied with a grin.

CHAPTER 16
ATLAS

Over the following week, Venus examined fifteen Blacks and three Whites. We could have done it a little faster, but we wanted to pace the rhythm at which people were seen coming in and out of the house. Since we weren't committing any crime, we weren't actually hiding anything. However, we wanted to avoid unnecessarily stirring even more of the ire of our disgruntled neighbors. They still couldn't swallow the fact that I, a Black Guard, was both the Prism's protector and an official resident of the Silver Mansion.

Despite their discontent, they didn't make any noise about the Blacks. After all, as the Razus of the Black Guard, it made sense that my warriors would come to me to hand in their reports on sensitive matters or receive their orders. As some of them also took turns standing watch, especially when I needed to leave the mansion, that so many of them came and went over the course of that week only raised mild suspicions.

Things quickly turned ugly once the first White stepped through the front door. Their presence in town always unnerved the population who had been brainwashed into believing they were walking time bombs. In reality, and specifically because of their tremendous power, Whites were among the most disciplined and controlled casters among our people. From birth, they were taught rigorous techniques to keep themselves in check, regulate their emotions, and channel their anger into non-destructive responses.

Today, I had both Pythus and Leodros standing watch outside as a small crowd had gathered outside in protest when a fourth White showed up. The fact that it was Acamon only riled them up further. I ushered him in quickly and closed the door behind him, but not before exchanging a meaningful glance with Pythus. He nodded in understanding, ready to call back up if needed. We already had additional units patrolling nearby, and who would be able to help disperse the crowd should things escalate.

"It appears your neighbors do not approve of the guests you entertain," Acamon said mockingly, his voice dripping with sarcasm.

I snorted. "They certainly do not. Should I be ashamed to derive so much pleasure from their aggravation?"

He gave me an almost malicious grin. "By the Lights, Atlas, you've finally learned to express your true feelings rather than keeping them all bottled up. It appears marriage is doing wonders for you."

I playfully glared at him. "Marriage does agree with me," I replied in a non-committal fashion.

Although stated as a friendly tease, he was being both serious and accurate. My entire life, discipline, duty, propriety, and humility dictated my words and actions. As the Razus, I had to lead by example. Over the past couple of weeks, I realized that maybe I wasn't setting the right example. Maybe what I'd labeled discipline and decorum were in fact denial and submission.

We entered the guest room that Venus had turned into her office and where we'd also placed the medical pod. She was sitting behind her desk with an air of concentration while typing on her laptop. The minute she heard us enter, she jerked her head up to peer at us. She smiled broadly and jumped to her feet.

"Venus, this is Acamon. Acamon, meet my mate, Prima Venus," I said, unable to hide the pride in my voice.

"Prima Venus, it is an honor to meet you," Acamon said, pressing his palm to his chest.

The gesture had been polite and deferent. And yet, something about it instantly made me uncomfortable.

"The pleasure is all mine, Acamon. But please call me Venus. I'm really grateful you accepted to participate in this test."

"Of course, Venus. The work you are doing is important. It could save current and future generations," he replied politely.

She smiled, then went over the details of the procedure. Acamon listened intently and asked a few pointed questions about the medical module. Watching them discuss, speaking the same scientific language made me feel excluded. It was a completely irrational reaction as they weren't using terms any more complex than the ones Kyrene and Venus used during their two previous meetings.

But Kyrene isn't a stunning male in his prime.

I stole discreet glances at Acamon while unlocking the shawl one of my warriors had secured on him before he entered the city. Tall and extremely fit, Acamon was one of the rare true Whites. Most of the others had wings going from true white to an alabaster hue. Their eyespots could come in various colors, although they tended to be black, shades of gray, light blues, and pale browns. And their bodies usually had an off-white tinge.

Acamon was the purest white all over, including his long hair flowing down to the middle of his back. Even his eyespots boasted an ivory hue with a thin silver ring around them. Under the sun, his wings shimmered, giving him an almost blinding aura. The only other color on him were his black antennae and eyes.

His attractive features would have made him one of the hand-somest males in the region had he not been Achromatic. His intelligence, charisma, and strong leadership skills made him a force to be reckoned with. On top of being one of the most powerful casters on Sylvar—if not *the* most powerful—Acamon also happened to be a scientist like my mate, a medical doctor to be more specific.

A pang of jealousy surged through me upon seeing the air of wonder on my mate's face when I slid the shawl off Acamon's wings. They were truly a sight to behold, even without the direct reflection of the sunlight on them.

I immediately berated myself for my insecurities. Despite the clear admiration in her eyes, Venus wasn't casting covetous looks at him. Since our first kiss, she and I had been steadily growing closer, even though we had not gone all the way yet. Every night, we shared a bed, and not just to sleep. We were getting to know each other intimately, learning our preferences, and how best to please each other.

That I could perceive a White as competition testified to the fact that I had come a long way in revisiting my views as to our worth as individuals. That realization made me feel a bit better about my stupid reaction.

I helped Acamon get inside the module, setting his wings around him in the manner I found most comfortable and which we used with the previous candidates. Naturally, he kept his tarp on, as had everyone else. Venus then proceeded to run the tests with the same professionalism she displayed with the others. I hated that my knee jerk response stemmed from the fact I didn't believe I deserved her. It would take a long time for me to finally accept it. But that was fine.

Venus was mine, and I would fight to keep her.

Once the test was completed, I helped him out of the module. Even as he stepped out, his eyes remained glued to the holographic monitor on which Venus was finalizing the preparation of the data.

"Any chance you could share some of that technology with us?" Acamon asked nonchalantly.

Venus gave him an apologetic look. "I'm afraid that's not possible."

He smiled, having clearly expected that response. "Figures, but it was worth a try. How about the data?"

She nodded, although a strange glimmer flicked through her eyes. "We will share all the data that we have acquired for you to study and use as you see fit," she replied in a noncommittal fashion.

Acamon snorted before nodding in concession. He understood her underlying meaning. They would share the data but not the conclusions their advanced scientific knowledge would allow them to derive. As much as I respected their reasoning behind this approach, it also annoyed me to no end, especially in light of the dire situation my people were facing. That said, Venus had proven extremely clever in dropping the right hints when applicable to indicate to our scientists' what important information to further dig into.

"We appreciate it and intend to make the most of it," Acamon replied in a mysterious tone before turning his attention to me. "You've gotten yourself a fascinating mate, my friend. We all rejoice for you."

"Thank you," I said, touched by the sincerity of his words.

"No, thanks to the both of you," he said in a suddenly serious tone. "You have no idea the deep awakening your union has sparked. You are the symbol of hope. People are rallying and finally starting to question things they accepted for far too long."

Venus shifted uneasily on her feet. She was taking the Prime Directive very seriously. Although she supported the idea of an uprising of the Achromatics and Monochromatics, she didn't want to be dragged into it as one of the leaders of the movement.

In that, I agreed with her stance. We Prometheans had to spear-head those changes on our own.

"But please continue doing what you are doing. Well... except for one thing," he added with a taunting glimmer in his eyes.

"What thing is that?" I asked with the same curiosity reflected on my mate's face.

"You both need to couple more," he deadpanned.

Venus gasped, and I recoiled with shock and outrage.

"Excuse me?!" I hissed.

"You heard me," he said, this time his voice cooler and his stare hardening while his antennae flicked. "I can smell your scent on each other. There's no question you've been intimate. But for the time you've been married, it is still too weak."

"What we do is none of your business!" I snapped, taking a menacing step towards him.

I didn't know what had gotten into him. Acamon was never the rude or inappropriate type.

"As a physician and as an Achromatic, it is both my business and my duty," he retorted in a tone that brooked no argument. "Stop drinking that tea and stop holding back with your female. Myrdin tea is bad for us, especially for your kind. It stunts your endocrine system. Although subtle, you have started to grow bigger. Once you stop holding back it will be even more."

I froze upon hearing those words. Over the past couple of days, I noticed that my tarps felt a little tighter around the waist. I blamed it on the fancy meals provided by the catering service since my arrival here. Venus narrowed her eyes at him, her gaze intense as she waited for him to continue.

"Blacks aren't meant to be this lithe," Acamon explained while waving at me. "You are the largest breed amongst our people. What's holding you back from achieving your full development is a deficiency in steroid hormones. That tea directly impacts your adrenal cortex and testes. It keeps you from producing sufficient cortisol and testosterone."

"So it doesn't just kill their libido, but it also prevents the full development of their muscles, makes them weaker, and even causes depression," Venus said in sudden realization.

Acamon nodded firmly. "Exactly. What better way to keep the people you deem inferior in their place and compliant?"

That struck me hard. Once we hit puberty, they didn't ply us with myrdin tea, but almost. On average, male and female Achromatics and Monochromatics consumed the tea at least once a week, some more often, and a few almost daily.

He turned back to look at me. "Judging by your scent, you're in heat. Do not fight it, brother. Over the next two to three weeks, you will visibly gain body mass, and maybe even some height."

"Bigger like the Shadows?" I asked.

He blinked, confused. "Like what?"

"The Shadows," Venus repeated. "One of your scientists, Kyrene, told us about a folktale regarding magicless dark giants."

"Ah yes! The Shaydwin," Acamon said, his face lighting up with understanding. "Shadow is the modern name used in more recent versions of the tale before it fell into obscurity. I'm not surprised Mother would have told you of that tale. She was always quite fond of ancient texts."

"Mother?!" Venus exclaimed, stunned.

Acamon chuckled and flicked his pristine hair over his shoulder. "Yes. I am Kyrene's son."

Venus turned to look at me with a betrayed expression. "Oh wow! Why didn't you tell me?"

I held her gaze unwaveringly. "It is not my secret to tell," I replied factually.

She pursed her lips before giving me a stiff nod. "Fair enough."

"But yes, I believe Shaydwin was indeed the name given to Blacks in the olden days," Acamon continued. "Folk tales all have some elements of truth."

"Do you have the original text?" I asked, suddenly struck by an idea.

"We do, back in our library. If memory serves, we should have at least two of the four existing versions as the tale evolved over the centuries."

"I would like a copy of each, and of any other ancient folk tales you have lying around," I said.

Acamon lifted a scaly brow, intrigued by that request, but didn't challenge it. "Very well. I'll get that for you."

"You own a library?" Venus asked with genuine curiosity while placing the vials of samples from Acamon into some sort of temperature-controlled container.

"Not here in town," he replied. "I lead a Pharom."

Venus's eyes widened. "Oh! Is it a village with all White Achromatics?" she asked eagerly.

He shook his head. "We have both Achromatics and Mono-chromatics."

"Nice! Is it a big village?"

I flinched at the same time he stiffened. Venus took on a mortified expression when she saw him hesitate.

"My apologies. I didn't mean to pry. My curiosity got the best of me."

He smiled, the tension in his shoulders relaxing a bit. "No need to apologize. In your stead, I would be as well. Under the circumstances, we tend to be very careful and secretive to protect our people. But we are one of the bigger Pharoms. Our village counts a little over six hundred people. At least half are Whites, the rest are a mix of various Monochromatics, and only two Blacks."

She tilted her head to the side, looking fascinated. "Why so few?"

"Most of them joined the Black Guard," I responded in his stead. "We are heavily pushed in that direction almost from birth."

"You are forced to become Black Guards?" she asked with a frown.

I smiled. "No. It is a choice, but a wise one for us. Genetically, we're literally made for the role. It is also one of the better position an Achromatic or Monochromatic could aspire to in terms of wages, duties, and working conditions."

"Having them join the Black Guard greatly helps the Pharoms," Acamon explained. "They're our eyes and ears, help prevent abuse against us, and also help provide the things we aren't able to produce ourselves in our villages as they would require too big of an infrastructure for such a small population."

Venus nodded slowly. "But I'm curious about something. You say more than half your population are Whites. Isn't it difficult or dangerous to have so many gathered in a single place?"

Acamon and I snorted almost in unison.

"No, Venus. It is not dangerous, and we haven't had a single disaster," Acamon replied with a hint of sarcasm laced with the resentment he felt towards our leaders. "There are many ways to mitigate the risks, especially with younglings throwing tantrums. We've tried to present these solutions to the so-called elite. But they didn't want to hear it."

"They fear you," Venus said in a mysterious tone.

"They do, but not because of our alleged lack of control. What they dread is our power and the fact that *they* can't control *us*."

The approving smile Venus gave Acamon floored me. It struck me then that my mate had known for a while what kind of power plays occurred behind the scenes. It shouldn't surprise me. As my mate evolved in the highest spheres of politics on a galactic level, she learned to quickly recognize those signs.

"Understanding the motivations of your enemies is the most powerful weapon," Venus said, as if she read my mind.

"It is," Acamon concurred. "That said, would it be possible for me to see the Prism before I leave?"

I stiffened. This wasn't the type of request anyone made as it would be deemed highly inappropriate. People had specific times they could see the Prism: during the parade leading him to his place of residence during his incubation, and after he emerged from the chrysalis before his first flight.

However, as a White, Acamon would not have been welcomed in the streets of Japhyr during the parade, even with his shawl on. I silenced the instinctive refusal that burned my tongue and glanced at Venus. As the Prima, it was up to her to decide who could approach Xarin.

She tilted her head to the side and gave Acamon an assessing look.

"I personally do not have an issue with it," she said carefully, "but it is his decision to make. We can go ask him."

"I would greatly appreciate it," Acamon replied, failing to hide his surprise laced with hope.

Like me, he had expected to be automatically shut down if not chastised for even asking. Taking the lead, Venus gestured for us to follow her as she headed to the boudoir. My gaze flicked to Acamon's pristine white wings. I should demand he wear his shawl before standing in the presence of the Prism.

Why would I? No other color does.

As the prime protector of the city, and specifically of the Prism, I should be inflexible in the application of the law, both written and implied. However, this wasn't justice. Xarin represented the greatest hope for people like us. Acamon was not a threat to him. Even should some inexplicable madness take over him, I would be able to counter any attack Acamon might unleash.

Anyway, the Prism was many things but not helpless. With

his song alone, he could put the entire city under his thrall. That thought plagued me since his return, and especially after hearing how he lured Venus to his location in order to bind her to him. Why had he not used this ability to stop his abductors from taking him in the first place?

Because he wanted to be taken.

Had he known that he would find my mate in the stars? Had it been a gamble out of desperation knowing that an even greater cataclysm than the one that destroyed Orist would soon be upon us? I doubted that I would ever get the answer to that question, not that I would lose any sleep over it. All that mattered was that he brought my soulmate to me and stirred a wind of change that would sweep everything in its path in the upcoming weeks and months.

Although I trusted Acamon not to do anything stupid, I entered the room after Venus and turned to gesture for him to wait outside. However, he had already stopped, waiting respectfully to be invited in. I gave him a grateful smile that he returned in kind.

"Xarin, sorry to bother you, but there's someone here who would like to see you," Venus said in a soft voice. "Would that be acceptable?"

The surface of the cocoon lit up with soft shimmering colors that we had come to recognize as his way of expressing agreement or approval. I didn't know how to feel about the way my mate smiled. Like her, it pleased me that the Prism would acknowledge another Achromatic. But I couldn't help the ridiculous and unfounded insecurity that Acamon's presence continued to stir in me.

Venus turned sideways to gesture at Acamon to come in. My chest constricted upon seeing the vulnerable expression that descended over his handsome face. He was always so strong and dauntless, I had forgotten that his fierce exterior hid a soul that had been abused and battered even more than I had been by a society determined to make him feel less than a person.

He advanced with careful steps, as if he were walking on the thinnest ice. He stopped at a respectful distance from the cocoon. To my complete shock, he knelt down and draped his wings behind him like a long train. The shimmering on the chrysalis went up another notch.

"No words can express the depths of the wonder that currently fills my heart to be here before the Prism," Acamon said in a voice thick with emotion. "Your divine presence always brought peace to our people. But this time, you have given incommensurable hope to those who no longer had any. Thank you for allowing one such as me in your presence. Thank you for bringing this pure hearted off-worlder to us. And thank you for bestowing your blessing upon the finest among us. We will not waste these invaluable gifts. We will answer the call."

With each of his words, my throat tightened a bit more. Judging by the intensity of the gradually increasing shimmering on the cocoon, Xarin was also deeply moved by them. The delicate feel of Venus's hand slipping into mine startled me. I gave her a sideways glance only to find her staring at the stunning tableau of Acamon kneeling before the Prism. The soft glow emanating from the chrysalis reflected on the White's pristine scales, giving him an almost mythical halo.

As if in response to Acamon's last sentence, Xarin emitted a hypnotic song similar to the one with which he had beckoned me to him that first day in the Gathering Hall. But this time, it wasn't aimed at me. I held my breath when my friend rose to his feet and slowly approached the chrysalis as if in a trance. He reached a hand and placed it on top of its surface. An air of pure bliss settled on Acamon's face. It only lasted a few seconds before the melody stopped.

Acamon blinked, shock and wonder warring for dominance over his features once he realized he was touching the Prism. He carefully removed his hand, looking dazed as he pressed it to his chest.

"By the Lights," he whispered.

"Did he bless you, too?" Venus asked, looking mesmerized.

He shook his head. "No. Assuming he would have even wanted to, he couldn't. He can only give one blessing."

"He likes you. If he could have, there is no doubt in my mind he would have," Venus said softly.

My throat constricted at the powerful emotion that swept over Acamon's face, who struggled to hide it. As an Achromatic, learning to hide one's vulnerability was a matter of survival. But I understood all too well what he felt, for having been just as overwhelmed by wonder and gratitude to have been Xarin's chosen.

"He wants you to come with us to Keryth," Venus suddenly added.

We both stared at her questioningly.

"To Keryth? What for?"

"Now that Venus is done doing the medical evaluations, we're going to take a few of my warriors to Keryth to perform the same test I did, trying to block the Sibris' halo," I explained.

"But I'm not Black," Acamon countered, confused. "I can't block anything."

"I know. But Xarin showed me an image of you standing with Atlas by the beacon. Whatever the reason, I'm sure we'll figure it out."

CHAPTER 17
ATLAS

After dinner, Venus went back to her office to answer the countless messages she was receiving from both the Enforcers and Kyrene's team. Having quickly knocked out my own tasks—in no small part thanks to Pythus picking up most of the slack—I dove headfirst into the ancient folktales Acamon forwarded to me. It wasn't an exhaustive list, but he promised to continue digging for anything else he might find.

Some of those stories were truly fascinating, giving me a glimpse of what core values and philosophies were promoted at the time. Their evolution was evident in each iteration of a given tale. Where in the original someone might have been a good or gray character, they became a villain in a subsequent version, before turning into a hero in a third one. Each time, the story changed to the point where the original message was either completely lost, altered, or flat out reversed.

The challenge was that the original text in the old tongue was tricky to properly interpret. Some terms used back then had either become obsolete or held a completely different meaning at the time that I couldn't be certain I was translating appropriately.

I was so lost in my work that the sound of my office's door

opening startled me. I lifted my head to peer at Venus walking in. She was stretching her neck and rolling her shoulders.

"Tired?" I asked sympathetically as I rose to my feet to go greet her.

"Sore from spending so much time at my computer. My posture has really gone to hell lately," she said piteously.

"That's because you need a proper chair with a back rest," I grumbled severely while gently massaging her shoulders. "I'm going to make you one tomorrow regardless of your claims that you don't need it. I should have done it from the first day."

"You don't have to do that," she argued again, but this time with far less conviction than before.

"The matter is settled. You're getting one tomorrow," I said in a tone that brooked no argument. "You are wound up so tightly, your muscles feel like stone," I added disapprovingly. "Strip and go lie down in our bed. I'm going to give you a proper massage."

Although she made a face at me for what she called 'bossing her around' I didn't miss the excited glimmer in her eyes. This would be my second time giving her a massage. Truth be told, even though I was doing this for her, I'd lie by saying I didn't enjoy the experience as much as she did. Any excuse to touch my woman was a win.

"Fine, you bully," she mumbled with fake annoyance.

I smiled and watched her saunter out of my office.

In our bed…

It did wonderful things to me to be able to say that and for it to be reality. My mind still reeled at how my life completely changed overnight. I kept waiting for the moment it would blow up in my face. Sometimes, I woke up at night and touched Venus's hair or face for reassurance that I hadn't dreamt it all up, that this wasn't some wild fantasy that I would soon awaken from.

I closed my computer, did a quick round of the house,

locking things up, then grabbed the massage kit Linsea sent me. She had included a massage table with the oils. In fact, we used it the first time. However, now that our relationship had reached a different level, I preferred to do it in our bed. After all, it would be a lot more comfortable for the less than relaxing way I intended to finish off our little session.

A delicious flame lit up in the pit of my stomach as I eagerly made my way to my bedroom, which she now shared with me. As soon as I opened the door, a bolt of lust exploded at the apex of my thighs when I took in the view that greeted me.

Fully naked, her curly hair splayed around her beautiful face, my mate lay on her back with her legs slightly tilted to the side, one hand on her stomach, and the other playing with a lock of hair near her nape. My mouth watered as I stared at the dark areolas of her breasts and the perky little buds begging to be licked and nipped.

Promethean females didn't have prominent breasts like humans. Although theirs were also rounded, they were barely bigger than a male's. Like us, our females didn't wear shirts or upper clothes. Breasts were not considered sexual body parts here. They were merely another part of our anatomy with its functions.

It had felt odd the first time Venus removed her dress and underwear. According to her, they were of average size by human standards. To me, they were massive. Seeing how she responded to me fondling them had taken me aback. Initially, I gave them plenty of attention merely to please her. But now, I'd grown quite addicted. Their softness, the way they perfectly fit inside my palms, and how the nipples hardened beneath my touch prove to be quite the turn on. And their texture on my tongue…

Blood instantly rushed to my rod. I silently willed it to behave. There would be time later for it to get the attention it craved. For now, I wanted my hands all over my woman, to feel the silkiness of her skin, watch it cover itself in those ridiculous little bumps as she shivered with delight, and hear those sweet moans and voluptuous sighs that drove me insane with desire.

Her body was pure perfection. It still boggled my mind that I had not found her attractive the first time I laid eyes on her. The absence of scales, fur, antennae, and obviously wings had skewed my expectations as to the definition of beauty. But in spite of our anatomical differences, everything about my Venus was harmonious and titillating. From her endless, slender legs, to the scrumptious flaring of her hips, narrow waist and generous breasts, every part of her demanded to be caressed and worshiped. Even her dainty toes made me want to nip at them—which I might have done once or twice while polishing them for her.

But it was her face that mesmerized me the most. Those lovely pitch-black eyes, so expressive and framed by the longest natural eyelashes I'd ever seen hypnotized me. That cute scale-less nose of hers always had my index finger itching to playfully tap it. But it was its softness whenever Venus affectionately rubbed it against mine that had me melting from the inside out. And that mouth… those plump and juicy lips that I couldn't stop devouring were a real drug for me. Thinking of how greedily she used them on me had me nearly come undone. The inferno of her mouth swallowing me was an addiction I never wanted to recover from.

A sinfully sensuous smile settled on her face, and the pink tip of her tongue peeked out to lick the center of her upper lip. My rod jerked in response behind my tarp. She shifted in the bed as she turned onto her stomach, undulating her body in a less-than-innocent fashion. Naturally, my gaze zeroed in on the plump globes of her behind. They were round, soft, and just the right amount of firm. She wiggled them briefly, pretending to adjust her position. But one glance at her face confirmed she was looking at me over her shoulder, spying on my reaction.

The wretched female was trying to turn me on and succeeding spectacularly.

My palms twitched with the urge to reach for her behind. I simply couldn't decide if it was to give her a good spanking or to give each cheek a proper squeeze. Then again, they were begging to be bitten.

But when it came to temptation, two could play that game. I wasn't the Razus of the Black Guard for nothing. When it came to self-control, I had her beat. And soon, I would have her begging for the release only I could give her.

Standing by the side of the bed, I opened the bottle of massage oil. Its fresh scent wafted to me. Not too fruity, not too spicy, it was bright and faintly citrusy with a hint of vanilla. It was subtle enough not to mask Venus's natural delectable scent. It quickly absorbed into the skin, helping relax the muscles, leaving the skin smooth instead of sticky or tacky. But the best part? The oil was edible. This meant we could peacefully transition from the massage into something spicier without worry.

I knelt on the bed next to her, poured some oil in my hand, and rubbed it between my palms to warm it. As soon as I began to massage her trapezius and shoulders, Venus emitted a grateful sigh that instantly put a smile on my face. I loved her pleasure in all its forms, and especially when I was the one giving it to her.

Despite the provocative pose she'd initially taken, Venus was genuinely all knotted up with tension. All naughty thoughts flew out of my mind as I worked each muscle until it relaxed. I moved down her back, massaged the muscles of her behind with clinical professionalism, then pursued my way along her legs, ending with a full-on foot massage then finished off with kneading her arms. By the time I was done, my mate's body was languid. She looked a little groggy when I turned her onto her back.

By the Lights, she was so beautiful… And all mine.

This time, I started with her face and head, making her even groggier. My mate loved getting her scalp massaged and scratched. I lingered there longer than planned to enjoy the purring sound she made while her eyes fluttered.

When I finally moved down to her neck, Venus's relaxed stance gradually shifted. While I continued to give her a proper massage, I made sure to give extra attention to all her erogenous zones, like that sensitive spot below her right ear. She looked at me with hooded eyes when my hands ventured towards her chest.

Where I had shown restraints massaging her behind, I did no such thing when I reached her breasts. There was nothing clinical in the way I fondled them. My mate's lips parted as I cupped each breast and flicked my thumb over the nipples until they hardened. Eyes locked with hers, I traced the dark circles of her areolas multiple times with my thumbs.

Only once my antennae picked up the scent of her arousal did I relent and proceeded with giving her stomach—and in particular her ticklish belly button—some attention. She called it an outie, because it poked outside instead of being recessed. This time, I didn't resist temptation. Leaning forward, I gave it a little nip. Venus chuckled and her entire body jerked in response.

I lifted my head to peer at her with a mischievous smile.

Our gazes connected, and a powerful silent communication passed between us. In that instant, I realized that I was slowly but surely falling in love with my woman. And despite the insecurities that continued to plague me, I believed she, too, was developing deep feelings for me.

Giving up all pretenses of pursuing the massage, I lowered my head and began to kiss and caress her stomach. My movements were slow and tender as I aimed to express the powerful emotions and endless affection she stirred in me. My hands and mouth freely roamed over upper body. Not a centimeter of skin escaped my attentions.

By the gods, I would never tire of the delicious shivers that coursed through her whenever I touched her just so, the voluptuous sound of her sighs in my ears, and the sweet saltiness of her skin that even the massage oil couldn't mask.

And that musk…

The scent of my mate's arousal was the most intoxicating aphrodisiac. It made my mouth water, my skin burn with the fever of heat, and my rod throb with unfulfilled desire. With a will of its own, my right hand slipped between her thighs even as my tongue was busy teasing her nipple.

Finding my mate soaking wet for me sent a bolt of lust exploding in my loins. By the Lights, how I wanted her! I sank two fingers inside her, while my thumb settled on her little nub. Venus's breath hitched, and she involuntarily arched her back.

Once again, I lifted my head to look at her. Blood rushed to my groin at the sight of the lascivious expression on her face. Eyes hooded, the tip of her tongue peeking out, Venus was staring at me as if she wanted me to ravage her.

How I wanted to do just that.

She lifted her pelvis in counterpoint to the movement of my fingers dipping in and out of her. By the way she ground her sex on my hand, my female needed more to push her over the edge. Naturally, I was more than happy to give her just that.

I kissed a path down her flat stomach. Her abdominal muscles quivered in anticipation, and her breath came out in short, shaky bursts. She didn't resist when I spread her legs wider to settle between them. The scent of her musk was driving me insane with lust. My rod throbbed painfully, and my claspers twitched, willing me to climb on top of her instead and make her mine while they kept her in place.

Clamping down on my selfish desires, I gave her clitoris one last rub with my thumb, then closed my mouth around it. Venus cried out, and her right hand slipped into my hair, fisting it. Once more, she gyrated against my face as I sucked on her little nub. The tartness of her essence exploded on my taste buds and set my loins on fire. The sound of her moans as I made love to her with my fingers and my mouth further fanned the flames.

I closed my free hand around the base of my rod and squeezed it almost painfully to silence the throbbing—not that it helped in the least. The fever of heat came back with a vengeance, demanding that I take my mate, fill her with my seed, and mark her with my scent so that no other would dare approach what was mine.

The human body was a wonder. Everything about it was soft. Her pelvic area was not only devoid of the scales Prometheans possessed, but it was also hairless. As the few illustrations I had dared look at on biology websites displayed pubic hair for both human genders, I expected to find between her thighs a smattering of the same soft curls on her head. It saddened me to discover she had them removed by laser. Still, it didn't lessen my enjoyment of her silky folds glistening with her essence.

Her inner walls—just as smooth, wet, and warm—were greedily clenching around my fingers moving in and out of her at increasing speeds. I couldn't help but wonder how they would feel around my rod as I lost myself inside her. For days now since our first kiss, I ached to fully be one with my mate. We had done everything else since, and our bodies had very few mysteries left for us. More than once, I felt as if she wanted me to go all the way, but then lost some of her boldness. I couldn't tell if it was because she wasn't ready to cross that line, or because she wanted me to request we do.

Tonight, I intended to do just that.

As Venus's moans grew louder and her gyrations intensified, heralding the imminence of her climax, I crooked my fingers inside her to rub the little bundle of nerves that systematically had her screaming my name in no time.

And in no time, she did.

I couldn't wait to see what the nubs covering the tip of my rod would do to that sensitive spot once we coupled.

Venus threw her head back and cried out while a violent spasm rocked her body. Her hand in my hair tightened almost savagely. The powerful sting resonated directly in my rod. I clenched my teeth, not out of pain, but to rein myself in. The urge to jump on top of her and ram myself in clawed at me with a fierceness that left me reeling.

Refusing to lose that battle, I focused on my woman's pleasure, keeping her flying high with my hand and mouth on her sex. I only relented after her grip on my hair loosened and her body's trembling ebbed.

I lifted my head to peer at her. The way she gazed upon me destroyed me. Venus wasn't in love, but that glimmer in her eyes was a first taste of how she would look at me once she was. There was nothing I wouldn't do for that day to come sooner than later.

She tugged on my arms to make me get on top of her. I complied, then claimed her lips in a tender kiss. As our tongues mingled, Venus caressed my back on each side of my wings. Instead of moving back up, her palms continued their downward journey before settling on my behind. To my shock, she pressed me down against her and lifted her pelvis to rub it against mine.

I froze. My head jerked up, breaking the kiss, and I locked eyes with her.

"Make me yours," she whispered against my lips.

I stared at her while the fire burning in the pit of my stomach spread throughout my body, like liquid flames coursing through my veins.

"You accept me, Venus? All of me?" I whispered, my throat constricted by emotion, and my voice made deeper by the burning desire consuming me from within.

"Yes, Atlas. I want all of you. I want to be one with you," she replied with fervor, her eyes flicking between mine.

"You are mine, Venus. Now and forever," I said before crushing her lips in a possessive kiss.

She responded in kind, her arms tightening their embrace around me. Of their own free will, my claspers extruded and circled around her thighs. Venus gasped against my mouth but didn't balk. They didn't tighten their grip just yet. Until I was fully sheathed, they would simply remain at the ready.

I rubbed my length against her slit, coating it with some of her essence, then broke the kiss. My entire body shook with desire, but my need to protect her superseded everything else. As much as the past few days of intimacy with Venus had helped me rein in my urges when interacting with her, I dreaded my inexperience and current heat would get the best of me.

With infinite care, I started pushing myself inside my woman. Barely a couple of centimeters in, her body began to resist my invasion. I clenched my teeth and buried my face in her neck. My skin burned with the fever of heat. My claws extruded, and I sank them in the soft mattress to avoid hurting my mate. I focused on my breathing and on the soothing feel of Venus's hands caressing my back. Words weren't necessary for my woman to understand what inner battle was raging within me. I should be the one reassuring her, making her feel safe, instead of her helping me shackle the feral beast inside me.

In that instant, I realized that had we gone all the way before, I likely would have lost this battle. And Venus had known...

By Kiaris's Light, my woman truly was perfection. In such a short time, she'd learn to know me better than anyone else, probably more even than I knew myself.

With controlled and shallow movements, I gradually inserted myself in her searing warmth. My loins were ablaze. Each careful thrust threatened to make me come undone. And then her body yielded to me.

A bestial growl tore out of me as I suddenly found myself fully sheathed. Venus gasped, and her blunt nails dug into the small of my back, sending another lightning bolt in my groin. I remained still, fighting to silence the volcano threatening to erupt deep within. After a while, my mate's inner walls contracted greedily around my length, demanding I begin to move, which further battered my already frayed control.

I finally realized that forbidding myself from moving wasn't helping but only increasing the torture. Bracing, I started slowly rocking in and out of my woman. I nearly spilled my seed at the first stroke. By the Lights! I would die with pleasure. Each thrust felt like a lightning bolt striking my nether region then sending electric tendrils outwards that lit up each of my nerve endings.

The endless string of moans tumbling out of me sounded like feral growls to my own ears. Venus's voluptuous sighs mingled with mine as she writhed beneath me. Her grip tightened on my behind, and she lifted her pelvis to meet me thrust for thrust. Her enthusiastic response spurred me into increasing the pace.

And yet, I needed more… much more.

Slipping my left arm under her knee, I lifted her leg to open her wider. My left clasper loosened its grip, while the right one tightened its hold around her other thigh. I ground my pelvis against hers. By the way her body jerked and the strangled cry that escaped her, the motion had perfectly stimulated her clitoris, sending a jolt of pleasure through her. I started taking her deeper, harder, faster. In no time, I was pounding into her.

The thin coat of perspiration covering her dark skin glistened under the soft light of the room. I covered her neck and face with kisses as the inferno within threatened to make me burst into combustion.

I was lost in a sea of ecstasy, pleasure too much to bear driving me to the edge of madness. I couldn't seem to get close enough to my woman. The harder I took her, the hungrier I became for her. My mouth, hands, and every centimeter of my skin didn't suffice to feel all of her. Judging by the sound of her voluptuous moans, the almost desperate way she touched and kissed me, Venus seemed as overwhelmed by sensations as I was.

She spoke words I didn't understand, not that it mattered. Her tone told me all I needed to know. I could only assume bliss was overriding her translation implant, making her speak in her native language or Universal instead of Sylvan, the Promethean language, as she normally did with the loveliest accent.

Venus suddenly arching her back and emitting a shout halfway between pleasure and pain, cast such musings right out of my mind. I hadn't seen her orgasm sneak up on her. Eyes tightly closed, lips parted, my mate was clawing at my back as she flew on the wings of bliss. I cried out and felt myself spill a few drops. Something broke inside of me, and I abandoned all caution.

My claspers extended fully, wrapped halfway around my woman's thighs, and locked her into position. Unless she tore them right off me, Venus wasn't going anywhere. Lost in a world of sensations, I unleashed my passion on her. The tight grip of her inner walls caressing me with each stroke wrested one blissful moan after the other out of me—although rabid grunts would likely be more accurate. The slapping sound of flesh meeting flesh mingled with my growls and my mate's drawn-out moans.

She felt so incredibly good, I never wanted this to end. Liquid lava swirled in my loins, begging for release. Although she just came down from her second orgasm, I could sense Venus cresting again. As much as I wanted to wreck her all night long, I wouldn't be able to last much longer. But I refused to fall apart without taking her along for the ride. I shifted the angle of my thrusts until a violent spasm jerked her body, confirming I'd struck her sweet spot. A strangled cry rose from her throat, and she once more dug her nails into my back in that way I loved so much.

After a few more powerful strokes, Venus shouted my name, swept away by rapture. Her inner walls clamped down almost painfully around my length, and I roared my own climax. I clasped my hands on her hips in a bruising hold as my seed erupted deep inside her. A blinding white light exploded before my eyes. The room spun around me as I continued to pump in and out of my woman, my movements erratic as a devastating orgasm engulfed me.

The eyespots of my wings felt ablaze. I vaguely realized I had deployed my wings and unconsciously drafted an impressive amount of magical energy, ready to be blasted out. I dispelled it, distraught by the thought of the damage I might have caused had I fired lightning in the throes of passion.

I claimed Venus's lips in a hungry kiss, our labored breath intermingling as my seed shot out of me in a blissful flow until the last drop was spent. I collapsed on top of her before rolling onto my back while simultaneously pulling her on top of me. Anyway, she had no choice but to follow as my claspers kept her tightly attached to me.

Although my rod gradually softened, I remained buried deep inside my woman. She laid her head on top of my fur, listening to the thundering of my heart and holding me with a possessiveness that rivaled my own.

"I'm keeping you, Atlas. You're mine, now and always," she whispered against my chest.

My left arm tightened around her, and my right hand caressed her hair while a powerful emotion I didn't dare name yet filled my chest with warmth.

"As long as I draw breath, I am yours, my Venus."

CHAPTER 18
VENUS

The next morning, I was walking on a cloud. Despite the countless times we'd gotten frisky together, last night took our relationship to another level. Emotionally, I was fully invested. That he and I would spend the rest of our lives together was no longer a hypothetical based on Kayog's assertion that we were soulmates. The bond that formed between us was entirely of our own doing.

I wanted a future with that man. And the only way to guarantee it required beating this damn cataclysm.

That determination allowed me not to feel so bummed out that we had to socialize. In these early days of our relationship, the selfish part of me wanted for us to remain isolated, basking in each other's presence, and strengthening the bond uniting us.

As I loved a good mystery, especially one that would result in saving countless lives once resolved, I didn't balk at the task laid before me.

Today again, Atlas carried me in his arms as we flew to Keryth Valley. Obviously, I didn't want to ride that nightmarish giant bug they called a Valren. However, I had to admit that, even without my bug phobia, I would have still chosen to be carried by my man instead. A lifetime wouldn't suffice for me to tire of his gentle embrace, the unusual feel of his scales against my skin, and his delectable scent.

Atlas made me feel protected and cherished.

As we began our descent in the valley, I spotted the dark silhouettes of two more guards in the distance flying towards the beacon. Throughout the day, we intended to perform the magic absorption test on at least eight guards, and another seven tomorrow, based on the results we got during this first round. A mix of hope and worry battled in equal measure within me.

Finding a solution to Thaudras was no longer just a matter of avoiding a genocide. The future I was hoping to build with Atlas depended on it. I refused to be widowed any time soon. But what if what happened with Atlas was a fluke? No, that wasn't the right word. What if his situation couldn't be replicated because the Prism's blessing gave him a special edge?

I doubted this was the case. After all, Xarin gave me that vision with Acamon standing next to Atlas right here by the Sibris. It meant he also had a role to play. I just couldn't wait to figure out what it was. Unfortunately, Acamon couldn't be here today due to prior engagements. Despite my impatience, I welcomed the delay. The surest way to fail was to have too many irons in the fire at the same time. Figuring out the situation with the Blacks first constituted a significant enough undertaking that would require my full attention.

As soon as we landed, I whipped out my scanner freshly calibrated with new parameters provided by the Enforcers' nuclear engineering team. It would hopefully help me detect other anomalies like the one Xarin pointed us to the first time, allowing Atlas to achieve such a high magic casting performance.

Focusing on my task, I activated the device. In seconds, four different spots appeared on the interface. They surrounded the beacon, but not at an equal distance and without any obvious pattern justifying their position.

I glanced up in the direction of the closest one. To my shock, Atlas was already heading straight for it. He'd spread his wings wide instead of neatly folded like a cape behind him as he usually kept them. The eyespots glowed, not as intensely as when he drafted pure magic the last time, but enough to hint he was either trying to channel the pure magic emanating from the nearby beacon, or the magic itself was latching on to him, eager to be used.

Fascinated, I observed him quietly as he continued to advance towards the first spot. His antennae oscillated as he looked ahead with an air of deep concentration. The closer he got to the location marked on my scanner, the brighter his eyespots glowed.

Oh God! He can sense it!

Last time, he hadn't been aware of the presence of an anomaly until I made him stand right on top of it. Now, I couldn't tell if he felt it as soon as we landed, or if he actively tried to detect it on his own. He stopped right in the middle of the location on my scanner, then turned to look at me with an air of wonder.

"This area is similar to the one I stood on during our last visit," he said.

I nodded. "It is. I was just about to tell you to go there, but you found it on your own."

He shook his head. "It called to me, like a giant magnet drawing me in."

My jaw dropped, even as a wave of excitement bubbled within me. "That didn't happen before, right?"

He shook his head again. "No. I've never felt this pull before. I can sense at least two more not too far from here," he added, pointing in the direction of two of the remaining three spots detected by my scanner.

The one he didn't seem to perceive sat the farthest away from our position.

"I wonder what triggered that response," I mused aloud.

So many things occurred over the past few weeks, changing him in a way that would be impossible to fully replicate in a clinical setting. Atlas had stopped drinking myrdin tea for twelve days now. He'd been fully embracing his sexuality, which was clearly reflected in the hormonal levels of his latest blood works. Xarin's blessing made him more receptive to magic. And he'd already interacted with the pure magic of the beacons. Maybe his muscle memory was kicking in, or maybe he'd developed new muscles or affinities since our first experiment.

"I don't know," he replied absent-mindedly before heading towards the second closest spot.

He reached it seconds before Pythus landed near us. We exchanged the usual greetings and updated him as to what was happening.

"Do you feel anything?" I asked Pythus. "Some kind of pull towards the location where Atlas is standing?"

He shook his head. "No. I feel nothing."

"Come stand here," Atlas commanded, gesturing for him to approach.

Pythus complied. No sooner did he enter the affected area than his eyes widened. His eyespots—a darker shade of gray than Atlas's had been before the Prism's blessing—started to glow.

"Whoa! That's different," Pythus whispered with an air of wonder.

Leodros joined us just at that moment. Unlike the other two males, Leodros had brown eyespots. From my observations of the other guards since my arrival on Sylvar, shades of grays—from very light to very dark—were most common for the Blacks' eyespots. But a few of them had also displayed shades of beige to brown, and variations of reds—the latter being the rarest. Therefore, while Atlas and Pythus could invoke lightning, Leodros could reshape the ground and petrify living objects.

Atlas and I explained in detail the experiment we previously performed and repeated it with both of his guards standing in the same area. Although neither male displayed the same level of power Atlas did—likely because of the blessing—they significantly weakened the flow of pure magic coming out of the beacon, as well as displayed nearly triple their normal power when casting spells.

Individually, none of them could dampen the magic of the beacon by more than ten percent. But when used simultaneously, their combined abilities reduced it by thirty-five percent. The compounded effect couldn't be denied. Atlas's words came back to mind regarding the fact that without at least five Blacks and five Whites, the region affected by Thaudras would suffer major damage, but that ten of each would be the ideal scenario.

With five Blacks, the magic of the beacon would drop by at least fifty percent. With ten, it would fully stop it.

But that magic is clean. There's no radiation.

And that confirmed we still didn't have the full picture. Nevertheless, this undeniably constituted one of the keys to unlocking this mystery. I just couldn't figure out what role the Monochromatics and Whites played in it.

We repeated the test with the other candidates as they arrived. To avoid drawing too much attention to what we were doing, we had people trickle in at different times. A crowd of Achromatics by the beacon after days of many of them visiting the very house sheltering the Prism would stir even more grumbling.

Frankly, I expected Ajustus to come barging in with self-righteous anger that we dared defile the home of the Prism with the unwashed masses of inferior beings. Considering the number of people who loudly and belligerently gathered outside the mansion during those visits, there was no way the news hadn't reached the Chancellor. So why did he remain quiet?

He's plotting something.

And that scared me more than I would ever admit. I'd take the enemy I can see any day over the threat that lurked in the shadows, ready to strike when you least expected it.

After the last guard departed, I launched a new probe, modified according to the Enforcers' specifications to turn it into an extractor—a sample collection device. Contrary to my initial assessment, it wasn't intense heat messing with the first probe I sent, but the strange magnetic field that powered the entire planet. That also answered some of my questions as to how the 'sacrificed' managed to linger in the bowels of Thaudras long enough to stop it.

I launched the extractor inside the crater of the beacon. Within thirty minutes, it returned with its belly full of the bugs hiding underground. Although no warnings went off on the interface of my bracer controlling the extractor, I still placed a deployable biohazard container on the ground. I moved to a safe distance and directed the extractor to settle inside before remotely sealing it.

You could never be too careful with this stuff.

On our way home, we made a detour by Kyrene's research lab. I seriously hesitated about bringing the container straight to her. This technology was far too advanced to be left in their hands. But at this point, I'd stepped over the line of the Prime Directive so many times this constituted a truly minor offense. Anyway, as I would reclaim it in the morning before heading back to Keryth, they wouldn't have enough time to attempt to properly reverse engineer it.

That said, I suspected Kyrene would be far more interested in the contents of the extractor than in the container itself. She would be the first Promethean in history to hold one of these bugs still alive.

The next morning, her assistant didn't make a fuss handing me back the extractor. When I expressed my surprise at not seeing Kyrene, she explained the scientist worked through the night, and the team all but dragged her kicking and screaming to bed. They needed her focused and functional if they were to win this race against the clock.

Back in Keryth Valley, we resumed the process with more of Atlas's Black Guards. By then, it was mostly to assess how the Blacks with different colored eyespots reacted. In all cases, his warriors benefited from the same boost in power.

However, I was stunned when three of them turned out to be females. It shamed me to have automatically assumed that, since Prometheans were a primitive species, their elite protection forces would have been exclusively male—a very narrow-minded misconception on my part. It was all the more embarrassing that Linsea reassured me on the role of females in the Promethean society. After all, here the potency of your magic defined your power, not your physical strength.

And then Acamon came.

I felt a little guilty to be this excited about it. Nothing so far gave us any hint as to what the role of the Whites could be. But that Xarin specifically requested his presence told me that we were about to get another juicy piece of the puzzle. I wished he could simply tell me what we were looking for. Then again, a part of me wondered if maybe he also didn't know, and only strongly felt there was some sort of connection.

I stood mesmerized as Acamon flew down towards us. If not for his butterfly wings instead of bird wings, he would have truly resembled an angel descending from the heavens. They shone under the bright rays of the sun at its zenith, giving him a divine halo. There was something beautiful, mysterious, but also dangerous about that male that would have many ovaries exploding in his mere presence. His aura of authority and the barely contained power that seemed to exude out of his every pore made him even more attractive.

Was I not falling head over heels for my Atlas, I could have seen myself falling for this male.

The other two Whites who came to our house to be tested had contrasted their ivory complexion with a colorful tarp where the color matching their eyespots dominated. Unlike them, Acamon stuck to entirely white outfits, like the rest of him. He was so pale compared to the others that a part of me wondered if he had a form of albinism. However, the molecular genetic tests the medical module performed on him didn't indicate it. I couldn't tell if it was because he truly didn't have albinism or because our limited knowledge of Promethean biology failed to identify such markers.

He landed gracefully near Atlas.

We exchanged a few pleasantries then asked him the same questions as the others, whether he felt the presence of the anomalies. The depth of the disappointment that struck me when he said no took me aback. For some reason, I'd expected him to have some kind of a sixth sense that would have made everything fall into place.

Atlas led him to one of the special areas. Like the previous candidates, he immediately felt a shift the moment he entered that zone. His lips parted in shock and a small gasp escaped him. To my surprise, he jerked his head left and right, as if looking for something or someone.

"What's wrong? What are you looking for?" Atlas asked, echoing the questions that popped into my own mind.

"Did you have other Whites here before me?" Acamon asked instead of responding.

Atlas frowned with a confusion that reflected mine. "No. You're the first we've asked to join us here. Why do you ask?"

"This is a vortex," he said, waving at the area beneath him. "We teach young Whites how to create them to help focus their magic for long and complex tasks. But we also use it to boost the output of the low-level Monos who live among us."

"Oh, my God! You *create* these?!" I exclaimed, excitement bubbling inside me.

He glanced at me with a sliver of amusement at my enthusiasm. "We do, although not as massive as this one," he added with a slight frown as he glanced around us. "Such a large focus radius would take a long time to implement—at least twenty minutes. But it also wouldn't last more than a couple of hours unless it was steadily fed. If you say these have been here for days, then there is something maintaining it."

"The bugs?" Atlas asked.

I nodded pensively. "I guess it could be a possibility. But why only in these specific areas and not over the entire valley? They also seem to only have a positive impact. So are they related in any way to Thaudras? I just wish there had been more recordings of this phenomenon for us to be able to establish any pattern about their appearance in relation to Thaudras."

Acamon's frown deepened as he seemed lost in thought for a moment. "Polychromatics would have felt it but likely not made particular note of it. Standing in the presence of the Sibris naturally heightens our magic casting abilities. As Polychromatics are always widely open to drafting colors, their enhanced ability to channel pure magic here wouldn't strike them as odd. But for Monos and Achros, whose drafting powers are quite limited, the difference is extremely notable."

Atlas nodded. "As our presence here isn't legally banned but strongly frowned upon, we avoid these areas. This would explain why there are likely no actual records of it. The Black Guards are pretty much the only Achromatics who come here for security during large events. But we always remain on the outskirts, as discreet as possible."

I pinched my lips in anger at this ridiculous treatment they received. And yet, I couldn't hate the Polychromatics for it as we'd had a similar shameful history on ancient Earth.

"So you say that making such a large vortex would take about twenty minutes," I mused aloud, forcing myself to refocus on more constructive topics. "But if multiple Whites—say five of them—combined their efforts on a single area, could you reduce that time accordingly?"

Atlas's eyes widened with sudden understanding. "Like combining the Blacks' powers quickly dampens the output of the Sibris!"

I smiled at him with approval that he was quickly reading between the lines. If it came to that, I would break the Prime Directive rules to help them find a solution. But so long as I could simply drop hints and let them figure it out, I would continue to toe the line. Secretly, though, I was steadily growing more and more impressed with Atlas's analytical skills. It boggled my mind how much he underestimated himself—no doubt due to a lifetime of being told he was less than. But my man was super smart. I would make sure to point it out to him until he finally acknowledged just how awesome he was.

Acamon first narrowed his eyes, then a slow smile stretched his lips. "Yes, with five high-level Whites, we could create an area of this radius in a couple of minutes. Five Blacks would need to stand within that radius to benefit from it. But that wouldn't be quite effective in the long run if the goal was to counter something within the Thaudras well."

"Why is that?" I asked, my shoulders slouching a bit.

"Because the cataclysm spreads over a vast area," Atlas responded in his stead. "We would need to be able to move around to deal with it. Considering the speed at which it spreads —at least based on the lore on this topic—having to wait for the Whites to create a new vortex every few meters for us to move to would be impractical. How long would these vortices even last?"

"Built this way, barely a couple of minutes," Acamon said with a dismissive gesture. "It would be a bad idea. But for something like that, it would be better to pair one White with one Black and cast focused pure magic directly on them."

Atlas and I both froze.

"We can generate a halo of pure magic like the Sibris,"

Acamon said with a sheepish expression. "Obviously, not to this magnitude, and it's not something we do too often. We normally keep it to very specific situations to punctually boost a Monochromatic. But as we have to remain next to them the whole time, it is simpler to just create a vortex so they can do their work at their own pace, and we can go about our business in the meantime."

"Why did none of us know about this?" Atlas asked, stunned.

"We avoid speaking of our abilities to others," Acamon said in a slightly defensive tone. "People fear us enough as is. It would be stupid for us to give them even more reasons to do so."

"Right," Atlas conceded, though he still seemed a bit troubled by it.

I couldn't blame him. As the head of security of an entire city, it had to be unnerving to realize he knew far less about the extent of a possible threat's power than he thought.

Acamon's face hardened. "We are *not* a threat, Atlas," he said in an icy tone, as if he'd read the thoughts crossing my mind.

Atlas recoiled. His shock appeared to instantly mollify Acamon.

"I know, my friend," Atlas said in an appeasing tone. "I'm just shocked and ashamed to realize just how little I know of our own people. Considering I grew up alongside Whites, I should know this."

Acamon's stance relaxed, and he smiled. "There's no reason to be ashamed. We've made it a point to limit how many people know. It just confirms we've been doing it right."

"So it seems," Atlas replied teasingly before taking on a serious expression. "Would you use this ability on me?"

"Certainly," Acamon replied.

He immediately raised his palms, and the silver eyespots of his wings began glowing. But Atlas lifted his hand in an arresting gesture.

"No. Not here. I don't want this current vortex to affect the result," he said.

Another wave of pride surged within me. Once again, my man was showing an analytical mind that I doubted he even realized he possessed. Acamon nodded and followed him out of the affected area. I merely smiled, content to tag along while they sorted it out themselves.

Once at a far enough distance, Atlas signaled for him to proceed. At first, Acamon moving behind Atlas surprised me, but then his reason became apparent. As Prometheans drafted color and magic through their wings, standing behind him gave him access to a broader surface not blocked by his body.

I watched, mesmerized, as Acamon started summoning pure magic. The eyespots in his wings pulsated with a bright glow while the rest of his wings seemed to be lit up from within. His entire being seemed to be illuminated by the light emitted by his wings. In that instant, he truly resembled a divine apparition. And then his halo—the magic harvested by his wings—shot out of his palms like a white beam aimed straight at Atlas.

It was as if the beam struck a wall the moment it entered in contact with his dark wings. They absorbed it greedily, and their own eyespots began to glow. Whatever fear I might have held at the prospect this could harm Atlas instantly vanished. The look of wonder—not to say of bliss—on his face had my excitement cranking up another notch.

And then Atlas raised his palms and launched a lightning bolt so powerful it sounded like a bomb had gone off. Large chunks of rocks and dirt flew up at least four meters in the air before raining back down. Had he not targeted such a large distance from us, the debris undoubtedly would have hurt us.

Both men gasped and stopped what they were doing before staring in disbelief at what their combined powers achieved. Atlas stared at his hands in shock before glancing over his shoulder at his friend with rounded eyes. The same shock and awe were plastered all over Acamon's face.

"Am I to understand boosting another person has never yielded such a powerful response?" I asked carefully.

Acamon shook his head, his eyes still glued to my man. "No, never. Then again we never used it with a Black. There was no reason since they nullify magic. We need to try this again!"

"Definitely," Atlas said, a savage grin settling on his sensuous lips.

The two of them spent the next hour using their combined abilities. Thanks to the blessing Xarin gave him, Atlas wasn't limited to casting gray magic—which mainly revolved around electricity and lightning—but any magic thanks to the now white rims of his eyespots.

It was like watching two kids in a toy store as they went on experimenting with him casting everything from earth, fire, water, and even life magic. They did it while moving around at varying speeds and even in crouching positions. By the time we called it a day, we knew we had found the key weapon to help us win the incoming war.

"We must pair all the mature Whites available with my Black Guards," Atlas said in a commanding tone. "We must take advantage of the next few weeks we have left for this to become second nature for each team."

"Agreed," Acamon said in just as decisive a tone. "I will draft the list and talk to my people. We should be able to begin training in the next couple of days."

"Perfect. We're going to beat this thing, brother. I can feel it in my bones," Atlas said.

"We're going to beat it, for this generation and all the others to come," Acamon replied.

My throat tightened when the two men clasped each other's forearm in a 'handshake' reminiscent of the way ancient Romans used to greet each other. What wrecked me was the glimmer of genuine hope in their eyes. These two exceptional beings spent their entire lives being reminded they would be sacrificed before they reached their thirty-fifth birthday. But today, there was a real chance they would get to live to an old age.

The deep gratitude visible on Acamon's face when he glanced back my way to bid his goodbyes turned me upside down. While I helped get us to this point, the merit mostly rested on their shoulders and on the Prism for pointing us in the right direction. I was merely the messenger.

I could only wonder why he had not communicated this to his previous Prima or Primus. Had these anomalies not occurred back then? Had the person supposed to speak for him ignored or misinterpreted his request? Had they followed it but failed to solve the riddle?

Chances were that those questions would never be answered. It didn't matter. We were on the right path. We would find the solution. Like Atlas, I could feel it in my bones.

CHAPTER 19
ATLAS

The discovery of the vortices—and by extension of the Whites' ability to feed pure magic to us—was revolutionary. Combined, our powers made us nearly unkillable. Over the ten days following that first experiment, we trained in earnest. My mate rigorously recorded our progress, measuring our output levels, as well as monitoring any physiological changes this triggered.

And the changes were undeniable.

All of us Blacks showed clear signs of muscular growth, proportional to our higher hormone levels. I benefited from the greatest gain. We assumed the fact that I was the only one sexually active explained that discrepancy. But the most important factor was a significant increase in our resistance to radiation. As these traits had been steadily growing since the beginning of our training, we believed they would continue to do so if we pursued it.

We were building an invincible army.

What I wouldn't have given to speak to our forebears who had been sacrificed. It broke my heart to think each lost generation died by figuring out too late what to do, and how their joint abilities would have shielded them through that ordeal. By the time they did, they had sustained too much radiation that even our slower cell division couldn't help overcoming.

I glanced up from the plates I was dressing for breakfast to stare at my beautiful mate entering the kitchen. The wretched female wore a see-through pink nightgown she called a negligee. The purpose was clearly to entice rather than cover anything. The way her dark nipples pressed against the flimsy fabric drew attention to them even more than had they been left bare.

Venus smiled and came to stand behind me. She wrapped her arms around my waist and rubbed her face against the fur on my nape. My own smile stretched my lips as a wave of affection surged through me. I turned my head to look at her over my shoulder. Pushing up on her tiptoes, she lifted her face towards mine to kiss the corner of my jaw.

By the divine lights, I was crazy for this woman.

We didn't speak. It often wasn't necessary between us. We were often content simply being together. I turned back to finish fixing the plates. Venus's left hand lazily caressed my bare stomach while the right one fiddled with the strands of my fur on my chest.

After breakfast, we would go back to see Kyrene for an update on the research she was performing. As much as Venus kept repeating that we owned all these discoveries, there was no question she deserved a great deal of the credit, especially where the live bugs were concerned.

Kyrene was all but burning herself out working around the clock studying the little creatures. The previous scientists named them Zuras when they were first recovered after the cataclysm of Orist. Venus said the bugs could have passed for a dark-red version of Earth's silverfish. How that oval-shaped bug with eight legs, a pointy tail, and two antennae could be compared to a fish initially baffled me. But she explained the name came from the wiggling way the insect moved, which resembled the movements of a fish.

But unlike the silverfish, the Zura had three eyespots: one on its head, the second on its back, and the third near the tail.

All three allowed it to draft colors and cast magic through its antennae.

The trouble was that they produced the pure and clean magic that shot out of the Sibris and powered our cities through our energy harvesters. So what was causing Thaudras? We were still missing something.

Venus's fingers abandoning my fur to start teasing my right nipple refocused my wandering thoughts on her. A purr vibrated through my chest, making her chuckle with a smugness I found incredibly sexy. I turned around to face her. Before I could say a single word, the heat of her mouth closed over my left nipple, and she wantonly explored the rest of me with her hands.

By Kiaris, how I loved the way my woman claimed me. I never wanted to belong to anyone as much as I did with her. The possessiveness of her touch, in her eyes when she looked at me, in her kisses as our tongues mingled filled me with an emotion that was steadily growing stronger in my heart.

Seeing how often we made love, I feared my Venus would have tired of my attentions by now. To my delight, her libido rivaled mine. She initiated as often as I did and had no inhibitions when it came to exploring our sensuality together. As I'd never been with a female before—let alone a human—it could have been a true disaster. But my mate made me feel safe from the start to freely express my wishes and fantasies, never once shaming me for my initial clumsiness.

Obviously, I was no sex god—just yet—but I had gained a great deal of confidence. A part of me was annoyed that she was taking the lead. Whenever she did, Venus insisted on pleasuring me all the way before she allowed me to reciprocate. My female should climax first. But fine. I'd make sure to make her scream my name multiple times afterward.

While her tongue continued to draw wet circles around my areola, Venus gently raked her blunt nails over my abdominal muscles, sending a delicious shiver down my body.

"Breakfast is ready," I protested weakly, even as my fingers sank into her curly hair.

She gave my nipple a good nip, the sting resonating straight in my loins, then lifted her head to peer at me.

"Is it?" she asked in a lascivious tone.

My mate stopped raking her nails on my stomach and caressed a path down between my thighs. My breath hitched when her palm settled on my rod over my tarp, and I instantly hardened. She rubbed it a couple of times before giving me an approving smirk.

"You're right. Breakfast *is* ready!"

Venus detached the clasps holding my tarp in place while kissing her way down my body. She didn't waste any time with elaborate foreplay and immediately took me in her mouth. A rumbling moan vibrated in my throat.

Nothing should ever feel this good.

I threw my head back and took a hissing breath as my woman took me deep in her throat. My legs felt wobbly, like they'd give up under me any minute. I leaned against the counter, my free hand resting on the edge for extra support. It took me a moment to realize the weird sound in my ears emanated from my claws raking the polished stone surface of the counter.

Venus bobbed before me with her legendary greed. You'd think she was indulging in a royal feast after nearly dying of famine. In all the ways she touched me, my mate always made me feel like the most desirable male in the universe, like she couldn't get enough of me.

My abdominal muscles contracted almost painfully while an

inferno raged in my loins. Venus knew exactly how to drive me to the brink of madness. Every time she grazed her teeth over the spiraling ridges of my length had me shivering with pleasure. Her hand squeezing the base of my shaft and stroking me with a twist of her wrist sent fiery tendrils radiating from my nether region throughout my body. But it was the way she sucked my head and rubbed her tongue all over its nubs that wrecked me. Each time, I felt struck by micro-lightning bolts electrifying the tip of my cock and then spreading to every cell and every limb.

Our nubs' purpose wasn't just to provide extra sensations to our females. For the males, each one also acted in a fashion similar to a human woman's clitoris. And Venus knew exactly how to stimulate them to make me fall apart in no time.

My legs beginning to tremble tipped her off about my imminent climax. She swallowed me deep and hummed. I cried out as a bolt of fire exploded in my loins in response to the vibration on my sensitive nubs. In an involuntary response, I yanked Venus's head back by the hair I still held in my right hand. It had been strong enough to give her a more solid sting than I intended, but not enough to actually hurt her.

Venus yelped and looked at me with a mix of shock and confusion. Before she could ask what was going on, I slipped my hands under her armpits and effortlessly lifted her up. She yelped again—the sound instantly muffled by my lips crushing hers— and hung on to my shoulders with both hands. I straightened from the counter I'd been leaning against, and with three powerful flaps of my wings, I crossed the short distance to a bare section of wall near the glass doors leading to the patio.

I slammed Venus's back against the wall. She moaned against my lips and wrapped her legs around me. The scent of her musk wafted to me, making my rod more painfully hard than she'd already made it. Over the past few weeks, I discovered that my mate enjoyed a bit of rough play. It worried me at first, but I soon started enjoying the power exchange, made easier and safer by her clear communication as to her likes and limits.

And right now, even though I was taking over, she didn't fully yield to me. Hanging on to my shoulder with one hand, she snuck the other one between us to yank aside the nearly non-existent piece of fabric she called a thong. The stronger scent of her musk made my mouth water even as my pelvic muscles contracted with need.

Under different circumstances, I would have hoisted her onto my shoulders, buried my face between her thighs, and feasted on her glorious essence with the same greed she had devoured me. But I gave in to her implicit demand and rammed myself in with one powerful thrust.

She cried out against my lips, and I grunted under the exquisite burn. I didn't pause to let her fully adjust to me and immediately set a punishing pace. By the way she moaned, caressed me, and ground her pelvis against mine, my Venus fully approved.

Kiaris smite me! I could literally die with pleasure. I lost myself in her as she gave herself to me. There was something incredibly thrilling to have my woman helpless but to take everything I gave her, trapped as she was between the wall and my body. But her voluntary submission made it even more powerful.

Our moans mingle with the slapping sound of our flesh colliding and of the thumping of her body against the wall. Thin though the fabric of her negligee was, I wanted to rip it to shreds to feel her naked skin against mine. When it came to my woman, I hated the humans' need to wear clothes. Without slowing the speed and force with which I was taking her, I slipped one hand under the open front panel of her top to caress her.

I shifted my angle until Venus emitted that strangled cry I loved so much, confirming I nailed that sweet, sweet spot of hers. I drank in the voluptuous sounds of her pleasure as we both drowned in the same all-consuming passion. Too lost in the delicious sensation of her burning heat stroking me with its tight grip, I didn't see her climax swooping in on her. Venus shouted as bliss swept her away. Her nails dug into my flesh, and her inner walls clamped down on my cock, wresting my own orgasm from me.

My back seized, and I rammed myself deep with a savage roar as my seed shot out into my woman. Every drop was like liquid ecstasy pouring out of me. I continued to rock in and out of her until I was fully spent. Breathing heavily, I buried my face in her neck. Venus sank her fingers in my hair and rested her cheek against the top of my head.

We remained quietly in each other's tender embrace as our hearts settled. I couldn't say how long we stayed like this. I eventually lifted my head to look at my mate.

"I'm falling in love with you, Venus," I blurted out in a whispered voice.

The words no sooner crossed my lips than I stiffened. I hadn't meant to speak those words so soon, honest though they were. But the powerful emotion laced with an undeniable joy on her face wiped out my blossoming tension.

"Good. Because I'm falling in love with you, too, Atlas," she whispered, her eyes filled with affection.

I kissed her again, pouring into it the depth of the tenderness that warmed my chest.

"You are the light of my life," I said while admiring her beautiful face before brushing aside a lock of her curly hair off her slightly damp forehead. "Until I met you, I didn't know what happiness and truly living meant. I am sorry that I cannot give you the proper courting you deserve, take you out on fancy outings, nights of entertainment, or sightseeing around the land. But I promise to make it up to you."

"Hush, you silly male!" Venus said in a gently chastising tone. "I may be a high-maintenance diva, but you have nothing to make up for. All the things you mentioned sound wonderful, but there's no time for that right now. Anyway, I wouldn't be able to enjoy them while worrying about the threat hanging over your head. Saving you and the others is our only priority. We'll have a lifetime for you to show me your world, and for me to show you the galaxy."

Another wave of adoration surged through me as I caressed the cheek of my mate.

"I hear you, Venus. I just wish I could be a better husband to you," I said sheepishly.

She snorted. "Are you kidding? You're the best husband ever! Unlike me, none of my friends can brag about their spouses giving them at home mani-pedis, facials, hair treatment, and full body massages... with benefits," Venus said, wiggling her eyebrows in a lurid fashion on the last two words, making me snort. "And you personally serve me catered food at every meal!"

"I don't prepare it," I argued feebly.

"So what? It doesn't matter where it comes from," Venus countered as if it was self-evident. "In the end, you're still pampering me and providing for all my needs. Even under these difficult circumstances, you make me smile and make me feel safe. You're so smart, strong, honorable, and hardworking, it fills my heart with pride to call you mine. Every night, I go to bed looking forward to the morning just because I will get to see you and be with you again. You are *not* failing me, Atlas. I couldn't have wished for a more perfect partner than you."

I opened my mouth to respond, but emotion constricted my throat and words failed me. Just as I was about to lean forward and kiss her instead, my spine stiffened. I jerked my head up and strained my ears to listen to an ultrasonic clicking sound. Its strength indicated the sender was about five minutes away.

"Atlas? What's wrong?" Venus asked with a sliver of worry in her voice.

Too focused on the message, I activated my tymbal muscles

to respond. Venus gasped and instinctively pushed away from me, pressing her back against the wall as she stared worriedly at my chest.

"What was that? Why did your chest do that?"

I blinked and refocused on her. "It's just my tymbal. It allows me to send ultrasonic sounds over a large distance," I replied absent-mindedly while pulling out of my mate and putting her back down on her feet. "I was just responding to Pythus. Something serious is happening, but I don't know what yet. Get ready. He will be here any minute."

Venus nodded and hurried to the hygiene room. I hated the look of worry on her face, and the fact that my words caused it. As her husband, my role was to appease her, not scare her. After picking up my tarp discarded on the floor by the counter, I went into another of the countless hygiene rooms of the mansion to get myself sorted out. In the couple of minutes it took me, Pythus was already landing in the garden.

I went outside to greet him. Before I could say a single word, his antennae flicked, and his scales darkened. My cheeks heated in sudden understanding at the sight of his mortified expression. The strength of Venus's scent all over me told him what he'd interrupted with his sudden call.

By now, my warriors knew—or at least strongly suspected—that Venus and I were intimate. We hadn't discussed it. A part of me felt I should as the Black Guards followed my lead in all things and held me as their role model. Based on our societal standards, my actions would be deemed highly inappropriate, if not immoral. But another part felt that my private life was nobody's business, and that I didn't owe anyone any explanation for loving my wife.

His embarrassment suddenly faded, and a strange expression settled on his face.

"Your happiness is a wonderful thing to see, Razus," Pythus said in greeting, as if he'd read the thoughts crossing my mind.

"Thank you," I said, taken aback by the unexpected shift.

"You were always the best of us. And now, you're the embodiment of hope for two entire breeds."

I shifted my wings with embarrassment. "I'm just one piece of the larger puzzle."

"The core piece," Pythus said in a tone that brooked no argument. "You have brought a massive wind of change. You're a Black blessed by the Prism, married to an off-worlder, and living as equal amidst the Elite."

"Equal is a strong word. But I see what you mean," I said cautiously. "Is this what you wanted to talk about?"

"It's part of it. The word is spreading that Venus and you are trying to save us from being sacrificed."

"That's old news," I replied, confused.

"Yes, but Ajustus is angry about it."

I stiffened. "Angry about *it*? Not just the fact that he doesn't control the Prism?"

He shook his head. "We've been monitoring the level of discontent among the citizens following the tests Venus performed on us right here in her medical pod. People were furious that Achromatics, especially Whites were allowed anywhere near the Prism. But our training in Keryth Valley has also been discovered. The Polychromatics fear that Venus is trying to convince us to refuse to be sacrificed."

"WHAT?! That's not at all what she's doing!" I exclaimed needlessly. Obviously, he knew that.

"But they convinced themselves of it. Worse still, after spying on our training in Keryth, they started spreading the rumor that she's building an army to take over control of Japhyr. They think the off-worlders are invading us from within. Kidnapping Xarin was the first step in their nefarious plans. They believe he's been brainwashed, and that she's controlling him."

With each of his words, I felt my blood drain from my face a bit more.

"It's all lies! Where did you hear this?"

"In the Senate," Pythus replied grimly. "Ajustus is calling an emergency session to be held in two hours from now. He wants an immediate vote on his Egress Law."

Cold fury surged through my veins. It had only been a matter of time. Frankly, it surprised me it took him this long. But he'd likely been waiting for Venus and me to give him more ammunition about how unfit and dangerous we were. What better way to get people to do his bidding than by manipulating their fears?

Venus walked out of the house at that instant and joined us. We quickly updated her as to what was happening. The same anger I felt shone bright on her beautiful face.

"That son of a bitch!" she hissed. "Of course, he'd try to use me as the villain to advance his agenda."

"We must attend the session," I said in an imperious tone. "Let's feed you, my mate. In two hours, we'll answer his false accusations."

CHAPTER 20
VENUS

A massive crowd had already gathered outside the Senate. Many more people also filled the public gallery within the chamber. It felt like we had entered an ancient Roman amphitheater but with arched windows and the same type of elaborate plaster carvings on the walls one would find in Marrakesh.

The Chancellor throned on an elevated dais in the center of the back wall of the floor. On each side, the Senators sat on their chairs shaped like semi-circular bleachers divided into two halves by a large section for supplicants to sit on the limited number of benches available or to stand. Above them, on the opposite end of the Chancellor's chair, a huge balcony allowed hundreds of people to bear witness to the proceedings. Giant screens framed the throne on the back wall, and similar ones also hung outside the building so that the people who couldn't make it inside wouldn't miss what was happening.

The entire city appeared to have shut down so that everyone could attend.

The heavy tension filling the air almost felt like a living entity. An insane number of Black Guards lined the entrance stairs and the temporary fences set up in front of the building.

Even more of them stood in watch, scattered among the crowd on the balconies. But it was the number of them, alongside multiple Monochromatics and Whites that held my attention.

If not for my status as the Prima and as the Razus' wife, I might not have had the opportunity to stand on the main floor with the other people present to challenge the new law being proposed for a vote.

My eyes widened when I recognized Acamon standing next to a handful of other Whites, three of whom I'd never met before. As the leader of one of the largest Pharoms, he wasn't officially a citizen of Japhyr. Furthermore, as Whites weren't allowed to live within the city walls, it surprised me they were granted any say in the establishment of the laws. But his presence pleased me tremendously. He was playing a huge role in our efforts to solve Thaudras. His voice could help tip the scale.

As soon as my gaze met the Chancellor's, the hatred in his eyes felt like a physical slap in the face. This male was out for blood. Considering how quiet he'd been for more than a month since my arrival, I didn't understand what was fueling his reaction. I hadn't messed with him or challenged his authority in any way. Saving Japhyr from the impending cataclysm would ensure he maintained his current lifestyle. So what the hell had crawled up his ass that he'd resent me so much?

One glance at the other Senators indicated many of them seemed to share his hatred of me. Had they all been gorging on the venom Ajustus was spewing about me? However, a handful simply looked at me with a guarded expression, except for Senator Cassius—the Purple who had silenced Ajustus when he tried to challenge my choice of Atlas as my husband. His face was unreadable, but his intensity hinted he had strong opinions about what would or should happen.

Atlas led me to an empty spot in one of the front benches of the supplicants' waiting area. It appeared to have been specifically saved for me. On our way there, I spotted Kyrene, who gave me a stiff nod. That, too, gave me hope for a positive outcome. I would just need to remind myself to keep my mouth shut as this wasn't my battle to fight, except if he tried calling me out or slandering me.

It took another twenty minutes before everyone finally settled down and the proceeding began. The Chancelor rose from his throne in a pompous fashion and strutted his way down the four steps of his dais to come stand before a podium with a microphone. As soon as he was in position, Ajustus's obnoxious face appeared magnified on the giant screen as he began to address both the Senate and the citizens.

"Dear Senators and esteemed citizens of Japhyr, I have called this emergency session to settle a matter that has lingered for far too long and that must be handled for the safety of our city and of our children."

I barely repressed the urge to roll my eyes. God, how I hated when politicians used the welfare of children as an emotional weapon to draw sympathy to their cause. He didn't give a shit about any child. He just wanted to pull at people's heartstrings.

"As you all know, Thaudras will soon be upon us," Ajustus continued in that grandiloquent tone he erroneously seemed to think made him sound more refined and princely. "The signs show an acceleration of the instability in Keryth Valley. An acceleration which suspiciously matched an increased activity and presence of Achros and Monos in that very region."

The disbelieving gasp that escaped me and the other Achros and Monos present with me in the supplicants' area was buried by the angry mutterings of the rest of the attendees. Their indignation infuriated me as it wasn't aimed at Ajustus for the horrible thing he was implying, but in support of his statement.

"For decades, we have put the needs of the majority at serious risk for the benefit of a dangerous minority. As a result, they now constitute nearly a quarter of our population—an all-time historical record," Ajustus said, the volume of his voice cranking up a notch to underline the importance of his words. "Once again, it suspiciously matches the record size of the cataclysm bearing down on us. These are not coincidences."

He paused to let the malicious implication sink in as his gaze roamed over the attendees to gauge their response. Apparently pleased with what he saw, he rested both hands on the edges of the podium and leaned forward, his gaze intense as he continued to spew his venom.

"Of all the cities on Sylvar, ours counts by far the largest number of Achromatics and Monochromatics. By this I mean five times more than the city in the second position on that front. Looking at these numbers and the fact that *we* are under threat of annihilation, the reality cannot be denied. *Science* cannot be denied. These breeds' excessive presence within our walls is directly responsible for our city's imminent destruction. The gods are angry!"

A deafening roar rose from everyone in the crowd, including the Senators. I sat there in disbelief as the Black Guards burst into action, forcing people to quiet down and resume their seats. A couple of Polychromatics who didn't seem to want to behave ended up getting zapped with a low-level electric discharge by some of the Black Guards with gray eyespots before getting escorted out.

As with every governmental building, the walls were all white or gray, depriving the masses of Polychromatics of sufficient color to draft from.

Fury burned in my gut that the Chancellor of the city should hold such incendiary rhetoric at a time when his people already lived in fear of a natural disaster they had no real way of defeating.

Or so they believed...

"Please! Please!" Ajustus said, raising a palm in an appeasing gesture once the crowd mostly settled down. "There is no need for violence."

Oh, fuck you!

That ass wipe deliberately needled the crowd into this specific reaction. I didn't miss the triumphant glimmer in his eyes when the people went berserk. He was enjoying this.

"While Achromatics and Monochromatics are a threat to the survival of Japhyr, it is not their fault they were born the way they are," he said with false empathy. "They have genuinely tried to contribute to the prosperity of our beloved city, but once gangrene sets in, the only way to stop it from spreading and save the host, is by severing the infected limb."

"Are you fucking kidding me?!" I whispered under my breath.

I glanced at Atlas, who had returned by my side once the ruckus subsided. Despite his clenched teeth, he was staring at the Chancellor with a surprisingly controlled expression. It dawned on me then that this wasn't the first time he'd had to stoically take verbal abuse from Ajustus and others of his ilk.

"As Thaudras clearly occurs wherever the largest population of Achros and Monos is located—as demonstrated by historical records—I submit the text of the Egress Law for immediate vote and adoption in order to save our beloved city," Ajustus said, lifting his chin with a hint of defiance, as if to dare anyone to challenge him. "Its provisions would instate a city-wide ban of all members of these two breeds. They will be moved to a temporary settlement at a safe distance from our city, with all the amenities necessary for their comfort. Relocation to this settlement will be mandatory for all of them."

The uproar that greeted his words was even louder than the previous one. I jumped to my feet, genuinely scared for the first time. Atlas gestured for me to stay put, glanced over my shoulder, and nodded at someone behind me before turning away. I yelped and instinctively tried to fight back when a muscular arm wrapped around me.

"Peace, Venus," Acamon's voice said next to my ear.

Only then did my brain register the white skin and ivory scales of the arm holding me. That was who Atlas had nodded to. All tension bled out of me, and I let Acamon push me behind him for protection. I didn't miss the convenient absence of a lock on his shawl, and how it was already loosened, ready to come off should he need to use magic in self-defense.

Every Black Guard spread their wings wide open as a number of Polychromatics and Monochromatics raised their hands, their palms glowing from the weak halo of their magic. None of them could draft enough magic as the hue they could channel was available in too small quantities on the wings of other Prometheans. When their magic fizzled like so many snuffed candles thanks to the intervention of the Black Guards, a few actual physical fights broke out.

The ease with which the Blacks restrained them was frightening in and of itself. They didn't even use magic, just their advanced hand-to-hand combat skills. If there ever was a revolt, the Polychromatics would never stand a chance. No wonder they kept dousing the Achros and Monos with that tea to keep them depressed and submissive.

Once they got everything under control again, Ajustus took the pinched expression of a disappointed parent as he resumed talking.

"I understand this is a distressing topic for all sides of the conflict. But you need to control yourselves and act like the civilized people that we Prometheans are," the Chancellor said in a haughty tone. "If you cannot behave, we will be forced to evacuate the Senate, and only the handful of representatives present on the floor will be allowed to remain—if at all—so that we may complete these proceedings."

"If you want people to act civilized, then stop vomiting your barbaric rhetoric!" Kyrene exclaimed.

A general gasp greeted her comment and a deadly silence settled over the assembly as every eye turned towards the scientist. She took a few steps towards the open center of the floor to stand by the microphone meant for the supplicants.

"I have not yet opened the floor," Ajustus said in an icy voice.

"I deem it open," Kyrene snapped. "How dare you speak of science when you can hardly perform accurate basic mathematical calculations? There is nothing scientific about the speculations on which you base your conspiracies and baseless theories."

"It is a fact that Thaudras systematically occurs near cities that have the greatest number of Monos and Achros," Ajustus argued forcefully. "It is also a fact that the magnitude of the cataclysm is proportional to the population of those breeds in the affected region. Will you dare deny it?"

"I do not. But they are not the cause. They are the cure," Kyrene snarled. "You cannot simply pick and choose the parts of history that suit your narrative and dismiss the rest. The greatest devastation our people faced occurred near a city that had slaughtered every single one of their Monos and Achros at birth. That didn't stop Thaudras. Our ancestors had to hunt down the Pharoms throughout the planet to gather enough to end the cataclysm. Had *they* been the cause, Thaudras would have occurred where they were located. But it didn't, it occurred in the midst of the largest Polychromatic population. If we were to follow your logic, Chancellor, then this would mean that *we* Polychromatics are the cause, not *them*."

My heart swelled with pride as shocked murmurs greeted her harsh words. Ajustus looked on the verge of choking on his own tongue as he stared at the older woman in disbelief, outrage, and a hint of fear. In that instant, I realized that thought had already crossed his mind many times.

"Are you calling us a curse to our own city?" Ajustus finally blurted out.

"No, I'm merely showing how illogical your reasoning is,

when clearly the facts show they are not the cause but the cure," Kyrene said sternly before glancing around at the Senators and then the crowd. "Most of you know who I am, and the fact that I have devoted my life to finding a solution to Thaudras. Over the past few months, we have progressed by leaps and bounds. We are so close, I can almost touch it. This Egress Law will do nothing but further alienate the very people who can not only save our city and our way of life, but also end Thaudras."

"As is their duty!" Ajustus interjected.

"It is *not*!" Acamon suddenly said, eliciting even more gasps.

The silent fascination with which the people had been listening to his mother quickly shifted to a more hostile edge.

"You have no say in these proceedings, *White*!" Ajustus said, putting as much contempt as he could in the way he stated Acamon's color. "You're not even a citizen of Japhyr."

"I and all others like me have a say when your kind expect us to lay down our lives to protect yours," Acamon replied with equal contempt as he came to stand next to his mother. "Your so-called settlements are nothing more than open air prisons where you want to corral us so that you can more easily offer us in sacrifice once Thaudras inevitably still happens right here in Keryth Valley. Remember well that the lives of hundreds of Polychromatics didn't appease the 'gods' who you claim unleash their wrath. It was people like me and the Black Guards who stopped it. Once you've exiled us to a safe distance from Keryth Valley and Japhyr, you may find us a lot less willing to help you with *your* problem."

I flinched inwardly. Although his words were both accurate and warranted, that last sentence would set fire to an already volatile situation.

"You're threatening us?!" Ajustus whispered in disbelief. He then pointed an accusing finger at Acamon before looking at the crowd with an air of self-righteous indignation. "*This* is but one of the many threats this law is attempting to thwart! He's been conspiring against us and poisoning the minds of our people. We caught him and other Whites training an army in Keryth Valley to turn on us!"

"That's a lie!" Kyrene shouted.

"It is not! We have proof!" Ajustus replied with a malicious glee that proved he'd been waiting for the opportunity to spring this up.

He gestured at the clerk of the Senate. Seconds later, his face on the giant screen was replaced by what looked like a bird's eye view of the valley captured by a drone camera. My heart sank at the sight of two dozen Black Guards and as many Monochromatics of various hues paired with Whites as they cast focused magic, bringing down lightning and blowing shit up. In a perfectly orchestrated script, the camera zoomed in to capture me clapping with a huge grin on my face. Then the image froze on the specific frame that made me look evil instead of bubbly like I'd been that day.

It looked *really* bad.

"Under the supervision of the off-worlder, the Whites have been infiltrating our city, corrupting the Black Guard, and are now building a vicious army!" Ajustus shouted. "You bore witness and even held a protest outside the Silver Mansion where the so-called Prima received these dangerous pariahs in the home of the divine Prism! We must expel them from our city before irreparable damage is done!"

"YOU DARE!" Atlas shouted before I could express my own outrage.

I had never seen him so angry. With his muscles bunched up as he marched towards the center of the floor, it suddenly struck me just how much body mass he'd gained over the past weeks. The change had been so gradual that I'd barely noticed it, like when you gain weight, and it just creeps up on you until one day it slaps you in the face when old clothes no longer fit.

A glance around the room showed all the other Blacks had

also increased their muscle mass, though none anywhere near as much as my man. By the look on the attendees' faces, they were realizing it, too.

"The only corrupted person here is *you!*" Atlas hissed. "You've spent your entire career ostracizing and belittling us, defunding any scientific research that could help end these disasters, fueling hate and fear against us, and spreading disinformation. Why? Because you fear us. As you should."

My jaw dropped. Ajustus visibly paled while the rest of the crowd showed the first signs of genuine fear.

"You, too, Razus? The off-worlder turned you against us?" Ajustus whispered in complete shock.

"The *off-worlder* has done more for us in a few weeks than this entire Senate in generations!" Atlas snapped. He turned to look directly at the audience on the balconies and pointed an angry finger at the giant screens that still displayed my face with an evil expression. "The footage he showed you is real. We are indeed building an army. Not to fight Polychromatics, but to protect all of us."

"And we're just supposed to believe this?" Ajustus spat.

"What you believe is irrelevant, Chancellor," Atlas said with disdain, looking at him over his shoulder before turning back to the crowd. "Below the Sibris, there are parasites growing in insane numbers who cause the catastrophic disturbances. Venus helped us confirm the nature of those creatures that our primitive technology prevented our scientists from fully understanding for decades. What that camera captured on Keryth Valley, is Achros and Monos training to defeat that threat."

He turned to the clerk and signaled for him to replay the video. The clerk hesitated and cast a nervous glance towards Ajustus. The Chancellor's glare clearly said for him not to comply. The clerk swallowed hard.

"Replay the footage," Senator Cassius ordered in an imperious tone.

The clerk jumped in surprise, then replayed the footage.

"This isn't off-worlders manipulating us to invade our world," Atlas said. "It is us reclaiming our ancient heritage. Venus has nothing to do with this. The Prism sent us to the valley, setting us on this path of discovery. Kyrene's mentioning old folklore about the magicless shadows prompted me to dig deeper into tales of old. Acamon pointed out that in the old language, Shadows was actually Shaydwin—the giant magicless Blacks—who would cast powerful magic through the Gift of Kiaris on the days of Radiance."

"What do old folk tales have to do with anything?" Ajustus grunted.

"Silence!" Senator Cassius said in an icy tone, leaving the Chancellor speechless. "We will hear what the Razus has to say."

Atlas nodded at the Senator before continuing.

"But just like Shaydwin had changed to Shadows over the years, I found out the original script did not refer to the gift of *Kiaris*, but the gift of the *Wirkanis*—the luminous Whites. Radiance was the old name for a halo of pure magic. The tale was never about some mythical dark beings receiving a blessing from the Goddess of Light on the rare days where dancing lights filled the sky. It was about how the Whites can enhance the Blacks by focusing their pure magic halos on us. *That's* what we are training for."

A heavy silence crushed the room as the same troubled expression settled on every face.

"But if you want us to leave, go ahead, and pass the stupid law that will have absolutely no impact on preventing Thaudras from occurring in Keryth. Just be warned that we will not be herded and confined in that *settlement*," Atlas said, pouring all the contempt he could muster in that last word.

"It is a mandatory provision of the law!" Ajustus argued.

The dark look Atlas cast his way gave me chills.

"And how do you intend to enforce it, Chancellor? Who

among you can coerce a Black Guard into following your bidding?" he said in an evilly sweet tone. "Do not confuse our disciplined upholding of our duty for weakness, despite the constant abuse you subjected us to."

"And where will you go if the ban is instated?" Senator Cassius challenged.

"In the shelter the Black Guards and Monochromatics of Japhyr have been secretly building with our personal resources at a safe distance from the city," Atlas replied matter-of-factly.

"What?! You were planning on deserting?!" Ajustus exclaimed.

"No. We were performing the duties you and the Senate deliberately shirked," Atlas replied with disdain. "For the past six years, I have pleaded with you to build a safe haven to evacuate the population to when Thaudras comes in case it takes too long to stop it. Once the radioactive fallout occurs, and once panic sets in, many innocents will die, become injured, or end up homeless. You have systematically refused with one pathetic excuse after another. You don't care about the people. All that matters to you is power and your personal comfort. Denial is about to slap you in the face."

"That shelter was built for us!" Ajustus shouted.

"No, Chancellor. *We* built it for ourselves. We might have considered granting asylum to the rest of you. Now, I'm not so sure anymore."

I didn't know how I felt about this entire situation. A part of me was turned on as hell by this ruthless side of Atlas. The other worried that he was burning bridges at a time where their people needed to rally and come together as one. And a third one felt those harsh words needed to be spoken, the abscess pierced, and for all of those entitled fools to finally get their long overdue rude awakening.

"You would leave us to die?" Senator Cassius demanded.

"According to all of you, our departure will magically

prevent Thaudras. So you have nothing to worry about, right?" Atlas said tauntingly.

"Ajustus promotes that nonsense. The rest of us know better," Cassius said in a dismissive fashion that had the Chancellor's scales darken with fury. But he ignored him. "And what does the Prima say to all this?"

Although used to speaking in front of large audiences, I felt intimidated when every eye turned towards me. Lifting my chin proudly, I walked to the microphone next to Atlas with an assurance I didn't quite feel.

"The Prima has no say in the matter," I said in a neutral tone.

Atlas recoiled, as did Acamon and his mother. The shock and air of betrayal on their faces stung, but I kept a stoic expression as I further explained.

"As the Chancellor pointed out, I am an off-worlder. As per the Prime Directive, it is not my place to interfere with the path your people want to set for yourselves, socially, politically, or technologically. Right now, I'm merely an observer in these proceedings, despite what some people try to insinuate," I added, casting a pointed look at Ajustus.

"But you *have* interfered in our affairs. You were seen many times in Keryth with the Achromatic army," he challenged.

"I was there as an observer, as an assistant to my husband, and as a voluntary aid to your top scientist," I replied casually. "Kyrene asked for a specific set of data that your technology couldn't gather. I gladly performed the scans and sent them to her for analysis. It is no different than me using our technology to bring a heavy piece of refined marble to a sculptor for them to shape into a masterpiece. And no different than us using our advanced technology to bring the Prism back to your people after his abduction. I see no crime or interference in any of this."

He pinched his lips in annoyance. "So you will not try to get in the way of the Egress Law?" he insisted.

"Like I said, I have no say in this matter. Prometheans will make their decision on that topic, and I will react accordingly," I said with a shrug.

"Meaning?" Senator Cassius asked.

"Atlas is my husband. If he is banned from the city or chooses to leave it, I will follow him wherever he goes, as is my duty," I said with a cold smile.

"As is your duty," Ajustus concurred with a satisfied, predatory grin.

"And what of the Prism?" Cassius insisted, a frown creasing his brow.

"What of him?" I asked with false innocence.

"You would abandon him to follow the male you're only temporarily mated to?" he asked with a sliver of annoyance.

"Of course not!" I retorted with the least genuine surprise. "I am the Prima, and Atlas is Xarin's chosen Blessed Guardian. Wherever we go, he goes."

Right on cue, bewildered voices erupted all over the room, while Atlas gazed at me with a glimmer of proud approval in his eyes, reflected on Acamon's and Kyrene's faces. It took every bit of my willpower to suppress a smug smile.

"SILENCE!" Cassius shouted at the crowd as he shot to his feet.

"See?! She's plotting against us!" Ajustus exclaimed.

"Oh, cut it out already!" I snapped, no longer making any effort to hide my exasperation. "I'm tired of your insinuations and slander. Let me remind you that I didn't choose to come here. Xarin chose me, not once, but twice. Yes, he chose *me* over *you*, and he also publicly chose *Atlas* over *you*. Get over it! This isn't about you and your petty ego."

I shouldn't have said that, but frankly, I was past the point of caring.

"And this isn't about some nefarious plot for us to invade Sylvar. If that had been our plan, your planet would have already fallen to us. If the UPO or the Enforcers wanted control over the

Prism, we simply wouldn't have returned him after capturing his abductor. We travel the galaxy, for fuck's sake! We came here through a freaking portal that connects worlds lightyears away. Your people who got abducted by that Nazhral female before the Enforcers rescued them told you about the technological wonders of other worlds. Do you really think we need some elaborate scheme to infiltrate your society if that was our goal?"

I ran my hand in frustration through my hair. With so much at stake, my patience with this nonsense was seriously running thin.

"I stand before you as the chosen voice of the Prism," I said in a tired voice. "What you've seen on that recording was initiated by his will. *He* wants the Achromatics to work together, which allowed them to rediscover long-lost powers. His guidance has helped your most brilliant scientist get within reach of a solution to your people's greatest threat. Isn't that all that should matter? Instead of chasing conspiracy theories, listen to what they have to say. And I will continue to follow Xarin's wishes. And so far, he wishes for me to stand by his Blessed Guardian, the Razus of Japhyr. Wherever he goes, we'll go."

Atlas and I locked gazes. The love on his face melted me from the inside out. The loud voices arguing all around us faded into white noise and I drowned in the dark depths of his obsidian eyes.

Yes, wherever he goes, I'll go.

CHAPTER 21
ATLAS

The Chancellor's plans backfired spectacularly. It boggled my mind that, as a seasoned politician, he should have made such a dire mistake as to present that video. Sure, he presented it in a way to make us look like a major threat. What he achieved was to make everyone—including us—realize that we were the true power of our people.

As the debate unfolded, all the pieces of the puzzle I'd gathered during my research in our old folklore finally fell into place. Achromatics used to be the dominant breeds of the Prometheans, with Blacks and Whites balancing and enhancing each other.

Based on those ancient texts, we'd been honored, even revered. I couldn't say what triggered the change, but the written lore gradually shifted, with the names of Whites and Blacks getting gradually removed or changed in subtle ways, until the lore no longer referred to us at all. The tone of the writings about us also grew increasingly negative and disdainful, like an insidious lethal disease spreading among our people. And before we knew it, the 'lesser' breeds had climbed to the top, and we had become pariahs.

For generations, they kept us docile with myrdin tea, drilled into our minds that we were a scourge and burden on a daily basis, that our sole purpose was to offer our lives to appease the gods when the time came in repayment for the hardships we brought upon our people.

And we believed it.

They lied to us, rewrote our history, banned the books that could have enlightened us about the truth of our nature, and used religion and fear of the wrath of the gods to keep us under their thumb.

No more.

I hadn't meant to make the statements I did and yet regretted nothing. For the first time, the Polychromatics understood they had pushed us too far, and that it finally dawned on us that we owed them nothing, least of all our lives. More importantly, they realized they didn't have the power to coerce us into doing their bidding. Between that intimidating video and the ease with which we stopped the brawling, even though they outnumbered us ten to one, they could no longer deny the tide had turned. It also dawned on them at long last that once we left, chaos would ensue with no one to rein it in.

That idiot Ajustus had convinced himself he could exile us but that essential workers would return during the day to keep the city running like good little lackeys, not to say slaves. Teaching him the error of his ways had been orgasmic. As much as they feared us, the citizens of Japhyr needed us more.

It was both exhilarating and terrifying. The well of bitterness within each of us after a lifetime of abuse ran deep. The next few weeks would be critical to make sure Achros and Monos didn't seek retribution or start treating the Polychromatics the way they previously treated us. Vengeance would serve nothing and only start another vicious cycle.

This was our chance at a new beginning, a prosperous and safe future, and above all at peace and equality for everyone.

After Venus's speech, Senator Cassius essentially took over

the proceedings, chastising Ajustus every time he interjected. Soon, even the attendees booed him into silence. On top of watching his law failing, the Chancellor lost standing and status in both the chamber and with the public. Cassius shifted the discussion to the research Kyrene had been performing. She was more than happy to provide extensive details about her findings, Venus's help in acquiring advanced data on top of the live Zuras, and the role of the Achromatic pairings.

By the time she completed her presentation, it wasn't just a wind of change that swept through the Senate and every corner of our city, but also one of hope. The dissenting voices drowned beneath the overwhelming support we received.

After centuries of helpless resignation, we had something tangible to fight back with.

We devoted every waking hour to training and further studying the changes in Keryth Valley. With Senator Cassius pretty much taking over the leadership of the city, all non-essential Monos and Achros were relieved of duty so that they could join us in our preparation efforts.

Three days after the Senate showdown, the Prism went completely quiet. Venus felt uneasy about it. Not only had she grown used to the small tingling at the back of her nape indicating his psychic presence at various times of the day, but the dull color his chrysalis had taken worried her. I reassured my mate that he had entered the final stage of his metamorphosis. Xarin was now growing in size at an exponential rate. Venus said his cocoon's new shape reminded her of a sarcophagus. Once she showed me an image of one, I had to concur with her comparison.

Over the following four weeks, the bond between my wife and me further deepened. I was irrevocably in love with her. Thanks to the changes occurring within our society, Polychromatics were showing more tolerance towards us, enabling me to take my mate on a few outings and even attend a few shows held in our great theater. Many of them still displayed some unease, but we were no longer getting kicked out. You didn't change an entire society overnight.

Although Venus enjoyed those moments of semi-normalcy, they failed to achieve my purpose. With each passing day, she was becoming increasingly tense. Despite her best effort to hide it, I knew her too well now. Too often, I caught the worried glances she cast in my direction when she thought I wasn't looking. The way she kissed and hugged me reeked of despair.

My wife was afraid she'd lose me.

I didn't want to die, but above all, I didn't want to leave her alone. Try hard as we may, we still didn't know what destabilized the Sibris to trigger the cataclysm. Extensive study of the Zuras revealed nothing to enlighten us. All their responses to the various stimuli Kyrene exposed them to yielded beneficial results. The Zuras weren't parasites.

So what in the divine Lights were we supposed to do with our newfound powers?

On the fifth week, the ground began to shift, and Venus's probes detected the first signs of radiation. Although the levels were extremely low, she immediately donned a radiation suit—a course of action I fully approved of. I hated how it hid her beauty from me. But at least, it would keep her safe.

The wisdom of that choice quickly became apparent. Within hours, small lightning-shaped fractures streaked the landscape of the valley. Their random position gave no clue as to what was causing them. Although we'd set the temporary command center at a safe distance from the fractures, I seriously contemplated moving it farther to keep my mate safe. If things turned ugly, she didn't have wings to instantly escape. Granted, Kyrene and at least one Black Guard were always by her side, but it still unnerved me.

Then the Sibris split wide open, the north edge of the flat crater rising vertically as if pushed from below. It transformed the beacon into a gaping mouth, screaming at the sky at a forty-five-degree angle. The steady beam of light streaming out of it dwindled to a trickle while pure light started shooting out of the fissures throughout the valley.

Thaudras had begun.

The first twenty-four to forty-eight hours would be relatively uneventful, with the fissures spreading their tendrils wider. Radiation levels would grow exponentially, then the ground would quake, splitting into even bigger craters that would spit out toxic energy, killing all life in the vicinity.

"Atlas! You're needed!" Pythus suddenly shouted, waving for me to come to the command center.

I'd been flying near the cave-like opening that the Sibris had turned into, trying to get a better sense of the dangerous place I would soon be forced to enter. Worried by the urgency of his voice, I flew past the hundred and twenty Achros and Monos gathered around the field, ready to face the fate that awaited us. Thankfully, our natural Promethean resistance to radiation had been enhanced since we stopped messing with our hormonal balance by no longer drinking myrdin tea. It wouldn't start harming us for at least two to three days, until its concentration levels passed a certain threshold. The gods willing, we would end this before we got to that point.

As soon as I landed in front of the tent, the look on Kyrene's and my mate's faces had my anxiety going up another notch. It was an odd mix of wonder, fear, and disbelief.

"What is it?" I asked as I rushed to their side.

As I closed the distance with them, my gaze shifted to the giant holographic screen projected by Venus's laptop. The previously grayscale images my mate's probe used to capture from the belly of the Sibris was in color. The countless fissures now allowed enough light below that the camera of the probe no longer relied on night vision.

For some reason, I expected the ground and walls of the

subterranean cave the Zuras dwelled in to have a dominance of ochre, blacks, reds, and dark browns. But everything looked gray and white, with tiny veins of various shades, like a multicolored marble.

No wonder Polychromatics got decimated in Orist.

There weren't enough colors for them to draft from. It didn't answer why Monochromatics fared better, but it made obvious why Achromatics were quintessential.

Hundreds of thousands—if not millions—of Zuras crawled all over the place. They were stacked one upon the other in a thick blanket, their dark gray and rust chitin scales contrasting sharply with their pale environment. The creatures moved almost in sync, the slow movement akin to gentle waves at high seas.

Although my mind registered all this information in seconds, something far more troubling retained my attention. Just like the valley above had begun to heave before splitting and fracturing, the ground of the cave also seemed to be fighting a losing battle against some intense pressure from below. Whatever was causing it was massive.

Then I spotted the two gigantic legs that had pierced through it.

"There's another life form down there," Venus said, excitement and worry filling her voice in equal measure. "It's below the Zuras' cave and trying to climb up. From what I'm seeing so far, this thing is humongous, at least three to four times the size of your Valrens. I believe the depth and the magnetic fields prevented my probe and scanners from detecting it."

"Is it the source of the disturbance?" I asked, a thrill coursing through me.

"I think so!" Venus said before glancing at Kyrene for confirmation.

She nodded with the same excitement my woman displayed. "These readings are fantastic. The radiation levels peak around where the large creature is emerging. But look, some of the Zuras appear to be fleeing it while others are flocking to it."

I frowned and narrowed my eyes at the screen while studying the contradictory behavior of the Zuras. Then it hit me.

"They're not flocking to it. They're trying to help it climb out," I said, confused.

"What makes you say that?" Venus asked, surprised.

I pointed at the Zuras surrounding the hole the creature was piercing to escape. "Judging by the grayish color of the halo emanating from their antennae, the Zuras are casting kinetic magic to help collapse the edge."

As if to confirm that statement, more little bugs joined the others, their kinetic halo pulsating with greater intensity as they continued to expand the opening.

"Why would they help it?" I mused aloud. "If that creature is causing the radiation, shouldn't they want to kill it?"

"They would," Acamon concurred. "Our research confirms the Zuras are negatively affected by radiation, like we are. Either they're unaware that the creature is emitting those particles, or they believe that killing it right there would be more damaging to them."

"Because the remains will continue poisoning the air within their lair!" Kyrene exclaimed with sudden understanding. "But our ancestors never found the remains of one of those giant creatures before. Did it just move, leaving destruction in its path until it burrowed deep somewhere else?"

"Maybe the Achromatics obliterated it," Venus interjected pensively before turning to look in turn at Acamon and me. "We've all seen how powerful your combined magic is. If you'd been one of your ancestors, entered the rift, and ended up face to face with that creature. What would you instinctively do?"

"Destroy it," I said without hesitation.

"Burn it to cinders," Acamon concurred.

"Should you go kill it right away then, before the radiation levels go up?" Kyrene asked hesitantly.

I caught myself glancing inquisitively at my mate. Our companions emulated me, and she uncomfortably shifted on her feet.

"My survival instincts scream for you to slaughter it immediately," Venus said carefully.

"But?" I insisted.

She pursed her lips and studied the video on the holographic screen still displaying the creature painstakingly trying to come out. We couldn't even see its head.

"We don't know what we're dealing with just yet. I want to run some more scans to try and get a better sense of just how big that creature is, what it is exactly, and if there is more than one."

I smiled, relieved to hear her echo my instinctive thoughts.

"We still have forty-eight hours before things become critical," I said. "We should take at a minimum half a day more to gather additional intelligence about this creature, understand why the Zuras are helping it, and settle on a plan of attack. At least we know exactly where it is located. We can use the various fissures to enter the subterranean cave and attack it from multiple angles."

"Which will allow us to take it down faster," Acamon said approvingly.

"Then let's get to work," I said in a commanding tone.

For the next couple of hours, Venus and Kyrene dissected the information the probes and scanners gathered while also studying the behavior of the Zuras and the unknown giant creature. In the meantime, with the aid of the Whites and Brown Monochromatics, we reshaped the openings of strategically located fissures in the valley. With their earth magic, they shifted the ground to create a smooth ramp down into the belly of the cave beneath the Sibris. It was large enough to allow three

Blacks to lead the charge side-by-side with their wings fully deployed in order to more effectively block or draft magic.

We assigned Blue Monochromatics to erect an energy field to seal their entrances to prevent the Zuras from scuttering out to the surface. Halfway through dividing our forces equally around each access point, my mate called Acamon and me back in the tent.

My stomach dropped at the sight of the spectacle that awaited us. Saying the creature was massive would be quite the understatement. Its oval head with multiple eyes of varying shapes protruded from the hole, crowned with two long antennae with drop-shaped tips. The creature was clearly casting magic through them as the rounded ends glowed with a familiar halo. Two smaller spindly legs jutted out between its neck and the edge of its shoulders, where the bigger front legs still struggled for purchase at the edge of the hole it was trying to climb out of.

However, it was the network of circular craters on the visible part of its upper back that retained my attention. It was as if someone had scooped round chunks of flesh out of it, or that it suffered some terrible disease that left those circular pockmarks on its back.

"What in the divine Lights is that?" I whispered, horrified.

"It's their Queen," Venus said in an ominous tone.

"WHAT?" Acamon and I exclaimed simultaneously.

"The bio scans I've performed indicate that this thing is the same species as the small Zuras," Venus explained grimly. "It's not uncommon among insects for their queens to be significantly larger than the rest of the hive or for the female to be bigger than the male. I just never imagined such a huge difference."

"But what makes you assume it's their Queen? It could simply be a mutation or a related species," Acamon challenged.

Venus pointed at the holes in the back of the creature.

"You see those holes? They used to be fertilized eggs that she carried on her back. On Earth, the Surinam toad behaves in a similar fashion. I assume that like the toad, this creature grows a thick layer of skin for the eggs to sink into and which protects them during gestation. Once the offspring hatch, they leave behind those recessed scars," she explained. "I wish we could get some blood and tissue samples from it to better understand what is going on with her."

"From the part of her we can see so far, it doesn't seem like she has any eggs left to hatch," I said pensively. "Could she be coming out to mate again?"

"Doubtful," Venus said with a frown. "Again, I'm just speculating based on the Surinam toad, but once her younglings hatched, she should have shed that extra skin the eggs were embedded in. Based on the scan readings, her leftover skin is old, and it seems diseased."

"She's dying," Acamon said as if struck by an idea. "She served her purpose, grew too old, or became ill."

"The dying theory makes sense," Kyrene said excitedly. "The Zuras you captured were of different ages, based on the number of rings of their bodies. The simulations we ran implied that the oldest captured would be close to eighteen-years. With such a small sample, we have reason to think some of them might be much older. If the Queen dying causes Thaudras, then her life-span would be between seventy-five and one hundred years."

"No, that doesn't add up," Acamon countered. "If it occurred every time a Queen died, then Thaudras would occur at every Sibris, assuming each one is actually the entrance to a Zuras hive. But it only happens near a single city every three generation."

"Fair point," Kyrene said pensively. "Maybe the new Queen travels to a different hive? Maybe it's a recessive gene that randomly kicks in for one of the Queens. But that it occurs every three generations is too much of a coincidence to be one. And I can't think of anything our people actually do that could have the type of environmental impact that would cause this mutation or trigger that illness—assuming our speculations are accurate."

"Traveling to a new hive makes the most sense to me," Acamon said. "It's common for colonial insects to send off young queens to create their own nests."

I froze then jerked my head towards my mate. "The Zuras that were moving away from the giant Queen, could there have been a young Queen among them leaving the nest?"

"Shit!" Venus hissed under her breath. "I didn't think of that and didn't track where they went. The exodus ended a few hours ago. So your guess is as good as mine. I just… What the fuck?!"

Startled by my mate's sudden expletive, I followed her gaze back to the holographic screen. The tiny Zuras were climbing on top of the Queen. At first, I thought they were attacking her or maybe even trying to eat her. But then I realized they were casting lumen—the solid form of our magic—and filling the holes left by the empty eggs on her back.

"They're sealing them up," Kyrene mused out loud, her creased forehead showing how intensely she was analyzing the situation. "Venus, can you bring up that radiation map?"

My mate's eyes widened, as if in sudden understanding of what the scientist was after. Her fingers flew over the keyboard of the laptop controlling the two probes below. The image zoomed in as the probe providing this main feed descended closer to the Queen. It was equipped with what Venus called a stealth shield, making it invisible to the creatures. Although it emitted a soft hum, it was buried by the wooshing sound emitted by the Sibris' beam of pure magic and the clicking noises of the countless Zuras crawling below.

A line chart appeared as an overlay at the bottom of the screen.

"Fuck me!" Venus whispered with excited disbelief. "The radiation emissions have dipped where they sealed the empty creases. She's leaking!"

Moments later, the Queen began thrashing, trying even more aggressively to wiggle through the still narrow opening. At first, I thought it was so that her young could seal more of the holes in her back, but she quickly proved me wrong. The round tips of her antennae glowed with a blue halo, and then the Zuras closest to them burst into flames.

"By the Lights!" Kyrene whispered.

"Shit!" Venus exclaimed.

Complete chaos erupted. The Queen was acting like a rabid, trapped animal, trying to obliterate her colony. They were fighting back but only seemed to use defensive tactics, shielding themselves with kinetic walls to counter her magic while they continued to rush towards the holes in her back. She crawled out a bit more, revealing a greater number of the empty shells along her spine. A thick, murky yellow liquid oozed out of them, like radioactive pus.

"They can't kill her," I said with sudden understanding. "The radiation is inside her!"

"Judging by these readings, she's a walking nuclear bomb about to burst," Kyrene said. "Radiation cannot be neutralized, other than by the Prism. We must contain her."

"We have to go in at once," I said firmly, glancing at Acamon. "We need the Whites and Gray Monos to keep the Queen trapped in the ground and only gradually push her up while we seal the sores on her back."

"And then encase her in the thickest lumen shell you can," Kyrene said.

"Agreed," Acamon replied. "Is there any way we can grant her a gentler death than asphyxia inside a lumen casing?"

"Based on the scans, her chitin scales are very thick. The force required for a dart to punch through it might shatter a large segment of it. We don't know yet where the radiation stems from. If it's in her blood, those of you in the front line may get exposed to a lethal dose," Kyrene cautioned.

"Is there some kind of cryogenic canister you could trap inside the lumen casing you will build?" Venus suggested. "If you put a remote detonator on it to set it off when ready, it could keep the Queen from thrashing or suffering. Once Xarin removes the radiation, you would have a perfectly preserved specimen to study."

"Ah, my dear Venus, how I wish we did," Kyrene said in an apologetic tone.

"Hmmm, we could use sleeping gas or a potent anesthetic," Acamon said pensively.

"Let's do it," I said in a decisive tone before turning to Kyrene. "If we don't have it here, request someone bring what we need at once from the hospital."

"Yes, Atlas."

CHAPTER 22
ATLAS

Over the twenty minutes that followed, we briefed our units as to what was about to take place. Pride swelled in my heart seeing the determination on every face. In many ways, the tough life we led prepared us for this challenge. It also didn't hurt that the Black Guards were our people's finest warriors and hunters, therefore undaunted by what awaited us. The Monochromatics who would join us below were also seasoned fighters as we retained those who served as Civil Protectors in the residential areas.

The anesthetic canisters arrived five minutes before we finished the briefing. We agreed to give them to the Whites—three in total—as their greater magic would more easily allow them to unravel a small section of the lumen shell we would craft and use kinetic magic to slip it inside.

Pythus, Leodros, and I would each lead the three main units of ten—five Whites paired with five Blacks—that would attack the Queen. Their teams would flank her, while mine would perform the frontal assault. Between us, at three and nine o'clock, the remaining two teams would protect a dozen Monochromatics each responsible for controlling the giant creature. A similar set of backup teams would await at the surface to take over if things went sideways for us.

"My brothers and sisters, today we hold in our hands the fate of not just our city and the citizens we have sworn to protect, but the future and peace of the entire Promethean race and of our very planet," I said in a solemn tone, projecting loudly so that all could hear me. "For the first time, we do not go in blind, fighting an unknown enemy at the cost of our own lives. We have a plan, a clear target, and weeks of intensive training during which every single one of you shone like our brightest star. It is with great honor that I go to battle by your side this day. Together, we will make history. And tonight, we will recount the tale of how we prevailed, of how we survived. The blessing of the Lights upon you!"

The warriors echoed that last sentence in a warlike cry.

At that instant, movement at the edge of my vision drew my attention. I jerked my head up to see a drone flying overhead. Its primitive design compared to the devices Venus had been using betrayed it as belonging to my people. Either our media or our Senate were observing—not to say spying on—our efforts.

Despite the resentment I felt towards our leadership—and to a certain extent our population in general—we set up an evacuation plan that would allow everyone to seek refuge in the escape settlement we secretly built should things go awry. I simply prayed it wouldn't come to that.

Dismissing the drone from my thoughts, I turned to look at the gaping hole of the cave entrance the Sibris had turned into since the terrain shifted.

"Atlas!" Venus's voice called out, startling me.

I turned around to see my mate running towards me. I frowned upon seeing she had not put her helmet back on before coming closer to this area. Granted, the radiation levels on the surface were still too negligible to present any type of a threat for a human. But anything that even remotely threatened my mate set my nerves on edge.

Apparently oblivious to the nearly one hundred and twenty people surrounding us, not to mention the drone filming us from above, Venus ran to me and threw herself into my arms. I caught her effortlessly and didn't resist when she drew my face towards hers to crush my lips in a kiss that screamed of desperation.

I tightened my embrace, slightly lifting her off the ground as I returned the kiss, pouring into it the depth of the emotions I felt for her. When our lips parted, she pressed her forehead against mine, and we silently savored the tender moment for a few seconds. She eventually moved her head back to lock gazes with me. The look in her eyes nearly had me come undone.

"You go in there, kick that thing's ass, and come right back to me. Do you hear me, Atlas?" Venus said in a commanding tone that failed to hide the worry gnawing at her.

"I hear you, my mate," I replied tenderly. "My body, heart, and soul are yours, my Venus. I love you and intend to spend the rest of my life with you. Nothing, not even that radioactive Queen will keep me from coming back to you. Anyway, you owe me a guided tour of the galaxy. Don't think I'll give you an excuse not to make good on that promise."

She snorted, love and sadness warring for dominance on her beautiful face. "I love you, too, Atlas. And you'll find out that the best way to piss off a human woman is to ruin her travel plans by being a no show. So get your butt back here, or I'll come get you myself. Deal?"

"Deal," I replied softly before reclaiming her lips for one last passionate kiss.

With much reluctance, I put her back on her feet. To my shock, the soft hum of hundreds of wings clicking saluted us as every member of our units gathered in the wrecked valley gazed upon us with a glimmer of hope and approval. My mate and I had truly become a symbol of the fundamental changes that were finally sweeping through our society. This first public display of affection between us only cemented it.

And after today, once we were victorious—and we *would* be —my brothers and sisters would undoubtedly start reclaiming their right to love, to family, and to a future filled with dreams and opportunities.

To my surprise, I realized Kyrene had also come out of the tent and was embracing Acamon with undeniable maternal affection. She devoted her entire life keeping this a secret to avoid undermining her credibility as the top scientist in her discipline. The shocked expressions on every face followed by a powerful air of awe and longing underlined just how deep their hurt ran to have been discarded by their families and denied parental love and acknowledgement.

This, too, I hoped would sow even more seeds of change.

After one last caress on my woman's cheek, I marched to the entrance of the Sibris, gesturing for my unit to follow. Acamon fell into step with me, although he remained a couple of steps behind, a distance that would increase slightly once we entered the cave.

I took a deep breath then used my tymbals to produce ultrasonic clicks informing every unit that I was in position, ready to go in. Each unit leader responded in a similar fashion. Although we possessed long-range communication systems, this method was the safest as we couldn't be certain how the magnetic fields below might negatively affect our much weaker technology. But the ultrasonic sounds we could naturally emit traveled far and wide enough that we could more easily coordinate our efforts without risk of losing contact.

Once I received all the confirmations, I signaled for the Blue Monochromatics to drop the kinetic fields they had set up at each entrance to prevent the Zuras from crawling out. Surprisingly, as soon as the path was opened, the crawlers remained inside. But then, based on the camera feed from the probes we'd been watching, the Zuras who hadn't fled were busy attacking the Queen.

Heart pounding, I spread my wings wide as I stepped down the artificially created incline into the cave. The other four Black Guards of my unit flanked me, their wings similarly deployed as we walked side by side, forming a protective wall. Seconds later, a pleasant heat washed over my back as Acamon started sending low-level waves of pure magic at me. From the corner of my eyes, I noticed the eyespots of my Guards starting to glow as the White they'd respectively been paired with did the same for them.

I didn't know what I expected upon entering this underground lair. Granted, I'd seen its appearance through the camera, but it didn't deliver on the suffocating air and excessive heat my mind instinctively attributed to such an environment. Far from being warm, the temperature leaned on the cooler side. Obviously, the air wouldn't qualify as pleasantly fragrant, but it didn't reek. The smell of wet soil covered in damp leaves came to mind. However, the ground was definitely not damp.

The hard surface almost felt like polished stone, but I recognized it as residual lumen. Channeling magic always created small physical particles that almost looked like dust. During normal usage, the quantity was too negligible to even be noticed. On construction sites where casters heavily channeled to erect buildings out of lumen, large amounts of it would accumulate throughout the day and needed to be cleaned off to avoid it condensing into this solid, almost marble-like material.

The ceiling of the cave hung far lower than I would have liked, with barely a spare meter over our heads. As it was uneven, it dipped down in certain places, some lower than our height, forcing Leodros's team to bend as they approached from our left. Straight ahead, another similar dip made it impossible to get a full view of what awaited us. From this angle, we could simply see the front legs of the Queen, clawing at the ground for purchase while the swarm of Zuras scurried around, some of them climbing on her.

But the loud screech ahead followed by an angry rattling sound had my blood turning to ice. I braced for the Zuras to attack us. To my pleasant surprise, although a few of them hovered around us as if to assess how much of a threat we represented, they all turned away from us to refocus on their mother.

I'd just begun bending down to pass the lowered ceiling section when a blinding yellow light rushed in our direction. Without hesitation, I dropped to my knees, wings spread wide, and cast a kinetic wall before us. To my relief, my companions reacted in a similar fashion. The yellow lights turned out to be a still forming fire blast. Part flames, part yellow magic, it crashed against the invisible kinetic wall, as if stopped by a glass panel. Our black wings greedily absorbed the lingering magic, while the Whites dispelled the flames.

Considering the size of the fire blast, the little Zuras couldn't have cast it, which only left the Queen. That she would launch such an attack with half the magic unused indicated that she was a novice caster. She possessed great power that she hadn't mastered. This made her incredibly unpredictable, just like untrained young Whites. They could cast every type of spell, but you never knew if they would use the full power of the magic drafted or only part of it, like the Queen just did. Had she not wasted half the magic, her fire blast could have generated sufficient heat to seriously injure us.

She threw a few more fire blasts in quick succession. Judging by the locations where the explosions of light went off, the Queen was shooting randomly, like a panicked animal lashing out. In the time it took us to cross the five meters of lower ceiling, we deflected six more blasts from her, one of them inexplicably made of ice shards instead of fire.

My jaw dropped as the cave opened up, giving us an unimpeded view of the creature. By the Lights, this thing was much bigger than the camera let on! Its head alone was a little taller than my entire body and exceeded my width, even including my wings fully deployed. Its antennae were at least a meter long each and thicker than my arms, with a spiked sphere at the tips.

They glowed with an intense halo, followed by a flash of bright light before they fired off their spell. Judging by the way she wildly waved her antennae and frantically fought to free herself from the hole she was still steadily carving, the Queen was enraged. A part of me believed she was actually rabid or had gone feral as a result of whatever illness turned her insides radioactive.

Four of her giant front legs—two on each side—were now out of the hole, exposing what I believed to be her torso. Wide flaps connected them on the sides, giving the impression that if airborne the Queen would have been able to glide on air currents. Were those the vestiges of fuller wings that had allowed her to fly to this location to repopulate this nest?

From this frontal angle, I could see two large eyes on each side of her face, and three smaller ones directly in front, where I would have expected to find a mouth or nose. Only when it reared its head back in another effort to wiggle free of the rocks and hard dirt preventing it from climbing out did I notice the massive vertical slit where its neck and chest would be. It split sideways, giving a glimpse of a sea of sharp teeth before releasing that ear-piercing shriek again.

As disturbing as it looked, the real source of concern was how her struggle to free herself was scraping the flesh off her back, causing the hollow parts to bleed with toxic pus. Hundreds of dead Zuras surrounded her body as she continued to fire at them.

"Monos, trap her front legs!" I shouted as my unit advanced directly towards her.

I immediately repeated the command with ultrasonic clicks.

Although the ground was mostly light-gray due to the

condensed lumen residue covering it, the hole created by the Queen had exposed the ochre dirt beneath it. In seconds, the latter began shifting around the Queen's legs, like a volcano rising from the ground. Even as dirt ensnared her legs, the Brown Monochromatics invoked thick vines, which they wrapped around her shoulders, further trapping her.

Palms raised before me, I gathered as much halo as I could from the steady flow of pure magic Acamon was feeding me, then started firing it as an uninterrupted stream of kinetic force at her antennae to keep them from aiming towards our Monos. Leodros on the left side of the cave and Pythus on the right both emulated me, trapping her antennae in a triangle that would only allow her to cast upward.

Enraged, the Queen fought even harder to free herself, but failed miserably and ended up nearly immobilized.

While the Browns maintained her restraints, the Grays and their paired Whites shifted their attention to the exposed sores on the Queen's back. With tons of pure gray lumen residue covering the walls and floors of the cave, the Gray Monochromatics had plenty to draft from, allowing their paired Whites to cast their own magic directly at the Queen as well, accelerating the process.

I stared in awe at the tiny Zuras joining their efforts to ours, their lumen the same marbled hue as the one covering the ground as it filled the holes in their mother's back.

While Pythus, Leodros, and I continued to imprison the Queen's antennae, our Black companions moved closer to her to nullify any magic she might cast. The combined power of their wings snuffed out the Queen's halo even as it began to form around her antennae. But they had to shift a few times until they found the best strategic position so that their magic absorption wouldn't interfere with the spells of our units restraining the Queen and sealing her back.

The benefits of the past weeks spent training together shone through. Each team worked efficiently with few words required for their members to understand what was needed. In minutes, the exposed section of the Queen's back had been completely covered in lumen. Before we even finished, the little Zuras began moving the dirt around the hole trapping their mother to expose more of her as she remained all but paralyzed by the Monochromatics' snare.

In that instant, I realized we were truly going to make it.

"Monochromatics, try to lift another segment of the Queen without releasing her," I ordered both vocally and with ultrasonic clicks.

The two units moved slightly ahead of us to the side. Using earth magic, the Browns shifted the dirt behind the Queen, opening it by a couple of meters. She immediately attempted to raise the lower half of her body through that opening. To my shock, a narrower segmented section appeared with a series of shorter legs vaguely reminiscent of those of a centipede. The way it curved in at the end hinted that she possessed an even longer tail than we imagined.

More disturbingly, right below those legs, the translucent skin of her swollen underbelly gave a glimpse of a huge concentration of that same yellowish pus oozing out of her back. I couldn't tell if something had happened to her in the depths where she previously dwelled, or if she had always been like this. But there was no question her insides overflowed with that radioactive waste. If we pierced her belly, the ecological disaster that would ensue would be devastating.

And none of us would survive.

I spread the warning, and once again, the Browns shackled this new section of the Queen's body with thick vines. The little Zuras gave up their efforts to dig up their mother and assisted the Grays and Whites in sealing her back.

My heart soared as we progressed just as efficiently. In less than ten minutes, we were readying to move on to what I hoped would be the final segment. Then would come the challenge of rolling her onto her back to lay down a thick coat of lumen on her belly to avoid any potential leaks before we finalize the cocoon that would completely contain her.

The same excitement was on full display on every face as I gave the order to lift more of her body. As with the previous round, the Browns and Grays moved forward to open a two-meter-long rectangular hole behind her.

They never finished it.

As soon as the ground loosened behind her, the Queen whipped up her tail. It quickly got stuck, indicating there was an even longer segment remaining. However, in her growing distress, the Queen continued to whip her tail upward. The ground behind her swelled from the pressure below. It undulated, as the surface had done before the fissures appeared.

A sense of dread washed over me seconds before complete chaos erupted. A thundering sound resonated in the back, and large chunks of dirt and rocks exploded upward before raining down on us. Startled shouts filled the room as the units backed away.

But it was the six-meter-long giant tail with a two-pronged fork at the tip that turned my blood to ice. With that same terrifying screech, the Queen swiped her now liberated tail up, slapping the low ceiling with such force that it sent large sections of dirt flying out, piercing right to the surface. She then whipped it sideways, nearly squashing the nearby warriors and sending a few of them flying back.

My heart skipped a beat seeing some of them crash against the side walls and others get buried under chunks of the collapsing parts of the ceiling. Flying debris rushing our way forced my unit and me to cover our faces even as we shifted our kinetic magic towards it. In the few seconds that took, the Queen seized this brief release of her antennae to bombard the room with magic. The Blacks having temporarily scattered due to the sudden mayhem, our anti-magic protection radius collapsed. The Monos and Whites barely had time to dodge while casting kinetic walls to avoid getting burnt to cinders. The Blacks closest to the Queen dove and flew out of range, barely escaping getting squashed or speared by her tail.

Her savage movements as she wiggled in every direction quickly loosened the dirt trapping her body. When the first vines snapped around the middle segment, I realized it was just a matter of seconds before she completely freed herself. Worse still, her struggles violently rubbed her underbelly on the sharp edges of the hole, and the bulging section behind her middle legs appeared frayed. I couldn't say for certain due to her erratic movements, but radioactive yellow pus seemed to be trickling out of it.

"Whites, control her tail!" I shouted, forcing back the rising panic trying to rob me of rational thoughts. "Blacks, to me!"

Despite the cramped vertical space, I flew the short distance to the Queen's head and all but stood on her left shoulder, wings spread wide to snuff out the halo of her antennae. Pythus and Leodros joined me, one standing on the opposite shoulder and the other on her nape. Despite her thrashing, her upper body still bound by the thick vines made it a more stable place to stand than the ground, which was shaking worse than during an earthquake.

Struck by an idea, I began to cast lumen around her antennae, binding them together. Without hesitation, my two lieutenants and the rest of the Black Guards joined in that effort. I berated myself for not thinking of it sooner.

Following my lead, the Whites who had been forcing the tail down through kinetic magic so that it could be bound to the ground with vines shifted to wrapping a large enough quantity of lumen around the tip. Not only did it eliminate the threat of the sharp forked tail, but it also made it too heavy for the Queen to easily wave it around.

She still attempted to push herself up and break free of her shackles. But by then, we had sufficiently regained control of the situation to thwart her efforts. The Monos jumped right back into action. This time, instead of shackling her with dirt and vines, they cast lumen around her limbs, like a thick plaster cast, blocking any future movement she might want to perform.

To my shock, I noticed a pile of withered Zuras on the right side of the Queen's body, near the area of her underbelly I suspected was leaking.

"Acamon, with me!" I yelled, gliding down to that section but not standing too close.

Even from that short distance, I could clearly see the leak as the Zuras in the back tried to seal it. In an impressive display of power, Acamon sent pure magic to my wings with his right hand while casting lumen directly at the Queen's wounded side with the other. Only a true master could simultaneously perform two different types of magic.

Now that her antennae were fully wrapped in lumen, we assigned a single White to maintain its integrity as the Queen vainly continued to try shattering it with magic. With her entire body exposed and mostly restrained, I ordered the Monochromatics to finish sealing the holes in her back—which extended over her midsection and the upper half of her tail—and shifted everyone else's focus to building the lumen cocoon around her.

Thanks to their greater magic, the Whites created a casing for her head, in which they placed the first anesthetic canister and sealed it around her shoulders. Acamon set off the remote trigger, releasing its content within the casing. Moments later, the Queen went still. My heart ached for the creature. Up close, I could see how sick she had become. Even her chitin scales looked diseased, the edges frayed as if eaten by rust.

The myriads of holes in her back testified to the fact that she had given birth to hundreds of young, but nowhere near the number currently filling this cave. Had she coupled again over the years? The gods only knew how long her health had deteriorated while she continued to fulfill her duty. I could only speculate as to what could have turned her insides into this radioactive substance. Could whatever she ate down there be the cause?

With much care and coordinated efforts, we turned the Queen onto her back with a mix of kinetic and earth magic so that we could complete the casing under her, but not before allowing Venus's probe to get a close scan of her distended belly. Considering the massive size of the queen, at least four meters wide, and twelve to fifteen meters long, it took an insane amount of time to complete our task. Even with the Whites feeding us pure magic, the Monos quickly burnt out as creating lumen—a physical transformation of magic—was significantly more taxing than creating a halo magic like for kinetic pulses, fire blasts, or lightning bolts.

Thanks to our Shaydwin enhancements, the Black Guard trudged on aided by the Whites. I couldn't tell how many hours it took. By the time we finished, a sense of surrealism settled over us.

"It's done," Pythus whispered in disbelief, breaking the deafening silence that had settled over the room, only disturbed by the scuttering of the Zuras. "We did it. We survived."

"We did it," I echoed, my throat tightening.

Tears pricked my eyes as our new reality sank in for all of us. The same powerful emotion I felt could be seen on every face. Then as one, the males and females of the Black Guard and Civic Protection started embracing each other, cheering and crying all at once.

Despite our determination to beat the odds, we came here prepared to die. But now, a single thought replayed in a loop in my mind.

I'm coming back to you, my Venus.

CHAPTER 23
VENUS

The battle with the Zuras Queen lasted exactly four hours and twenty-four minutes. To me, it felt like forty years had been shaved off my life. When she whipped out her tail and started knocking the Prometheans around like ragdolls, I thought my heart would stop. On the surface, her tail knocking the ceiling of the cave made the ground look as if it was waving or bubbling. Greater cracks had zigzagged the valley and caused some terrain collapses.

More than once, I fought the urge to run down there and discharge my blaster on the Queen. But obviously, that would have been the dumbest thing possible. By the time it ended, I could have wept with relief. In fact, both Kyrene and I did, clinging to each other like two drowning women.

Getting the gigantic lumen cocoon containing the Queen out of the underground lair would have been an impossible task for most primitive species. But the Prometheans once again blew me away. With the Monochromatics being completely exhausted, and the Blacks' magic being too weak in comparison, the Whites took charge with Acamon in the lead.

Forming a circle on the surface, right above the location of the cocoon below, they shifted the ground with earth magic, creating a ramp next to her. Then, using a combination of air and kinetic magic, they gently pushed her up the slope until she rested horizontally in the valley. They roughly resealed the opening, as well as the other fissures on the surface to protect the small Zuras below and prevent anyone from tripping or getting hurt up top. Over the course of the following week, Brown and Blue Monochromatics—who were the most gifted when it came to gardening and landscaping related magic—would come to mend the valley, returning it to its former flawless glory.

While the warriors battled below—but only after they had regained control of the Queen—Kyrene and I extensively discussed what to do with her. Obviously, coming here this morning, we never expected things would turn out this way. The Queen was much too dangerous to bring to the city. There were too many questions and too few answers. Although my scans indicated that the lumen casing they built around her was effectively containing all the radiation emanating from her, we couldn't be certain how long it would last.

We also couldn't leave her below as she would kill the otherwise highly beneficial Zuras if the leak occurred in their lair. Therefore, we concluded that the best approach would be to leave her right here in the valley and to erect a temporary structure around her that could contain the radiation should the lumen casing falter. Once Xarin emerged from his cocoon, instead of a large, devastated area to handle, he would have her neatly packaged inside a safe container.

My heart constricted once again thinking of the Prism. Deep down, I couldn't help the feeling that I was somehow failing him for not figuring out a way to save him as well.

However, the Zuras helped distract me from these somber thoughts. Their peaceful behavior towards the Prometheans utterly baffled me. During the battle against the Queen, it had made sense as she represented the greater threat. But when it ended, they didn't turn on the intruders to cast them out, but instead turned their attention to repairing the extensive damage to their lair, as well as fixing the twisted crater of the Sibris.

As much as my inquisitive scientific mind burned with the desire to enter the cave to explore it in person, my phobia of insects totally forbade it. The only way anyone would get me in a confined space filled with millions of creepy crawlers was if they dragged my dead body inside.

Thankfully, my faithful probe allowed me to roam around every little corner alongside the Black Guards. During the battle, the Queen's tail shattered a large section of wall which revealed a secret room. To our shock, millions of alveoli filled with eggs covered the entire walls and ceiling. They were similar to the ones that had covered the Queen's back, but significantly smaller, and the fleshy substance keeping them in place looked visibly newer and healthy.

A series of tube-like ramps in the ground led to the lower level from whence the Queen had attempted to escape. We realized then why the egg holes on her back were so much older than her offspring population. Before she left her original nest—probably after mating—the males had likely placed the fertilized eggs on her. She reached her new home here in Keryth carrying the first members of her colony on her back. After they hatched, she burrowed deep to a birthing chamber, laying eggs that her hive moved to the hatchery. It would explain why the holes in her back didn't account for the massive population of the colony.

Judging by the scans my probe performed, only a fraction of the eggs were currently maturing. The others appeared to be in the form of stasis. We could only presume that the Zuras activated their maturation as needed to maintain a healthy population. This would explain why a Sibris without a Queen could continue to thrive for centuries.

A part of me envied Kyrene and the rest of the Promethean scientific community. Studying this fascinating species would revolutionize their world on a societal, political, and religious level. After much debate, a part of me decided I would conveniently 'forget' one of my probes here to help Kyrene pursue her research with more ease.

Yes, it violated the Prime Directive. But at this point, I was well past merely toeing the line. It was for a good cause and wouldn't give them the type of unfair edge that this guideline sought to avoid.

Naturally, when Atlas finally emerged from the cave, I all but crushed him in my arms while wearing my protective suit. I hated not being able to touch his skin or kiss him, but the risk of radiation poisoning was too real.

Each member of the unit underwent some thorough decontamination, not that they truly needed it. Their natural resistance was mind boggling. But more importantly, they intervened early enough to nip it in the bud before it could reach dangerous levels.

However, this experience explained why none of the sacrificed people ever survived before. There was no question in my mind they all entered and joined forces to kill the dying Queen, causing her to spill the radioactive substance inside her even as she destroyed everything and everyone within. Extensive study would be needed to understand what caused the nuclear explosion during prior Thaudras. I suspected as the Queen further spiraled out of control, a glitch in her attempts at casting magic caused a chemical imbalance which set off the type of chain reaction needed to trigger a nuclear explosion. But this would be for people better versed in nuclear physics to sort out.

Between the footage captured by the Promethean media drones on the surface and by my probes' cameras underground, the population in every city bore witness to the heroism of those they had belittled for generations. Although they were hailed as heroes upon their return to town, it took an entire week before the reality that Thaudras had been averted finally sank in.

The top scientists around the planet flocked to Keryth Valley to run their own tests to confirm the magnetic and radiation levels in the region had fully returned to normal. On the seventh day, the halo of pure magic of Keryth Valley resumed shooting out of the repaired Sibris.

An hour later, Xarin's chrysalis hatched.

The pressure at the back of my head, which I hadn't felt in weeks, returned that morning, warning me of his imminent awakening. When I entered the boudoir, I observed eight luminous lines appear on top of the chrysalis, shaped like an eight-point star. After this long silence, Xarin sent me an image of Japhyr's Great Hall. In minutes, Atlas warned the Chancellor, and the Black Guard came to escort us through the streets of the Legislative District. Walking hand in hand, Atlas and I led the march to the Hall, Xarin's chrysalis behind us on his hover platform, with guards flanking us.

Despite the last-minute warning, the streets quickly filled with people eager to bear witness to his passage. Instead of simply standing there and observing, they followed in our wake, turning this into a procession with soft chants accompanying us. A fairly subdued Ajustus greeted us at the entrance of the Great Hall. He seemed to have aged ten years over the few weeks since his disastrous attempt at pushing through his Egress Law. His authority completely plummeted. While he retained the title of Chancellor, he no longer had the power that came with it. Everyone knew he wouldn't be reelected at the end of his current term.

We led the hover platform to the dais at the front of the Hall. The crowd rapidly congregated within. Unlike my first time here when I chose Atlas as my husband, an equal number of Achros, Monos, and Polys had been allowed inside. Their population still had a long way to go before each breed received full acceptance, but they were undeniably on the right path. The rest of the people gathered outside.

Like on the day of the Egress Law vote at the Senate, the Prometheans installed giant screens outside the Great Hall so all could bear witness to what would soon happen. As I didn't know when Xarin would make his appearance, I stood with Atlas near the chrysalis, the rest of the onlookers standing at least ten meters behind us with a wall of Black Guards in front of them.

The wait lasted barely thirty minutes.

The surface of the chrysalis began to glow in a rainbow of colors. Then the top slowly opened up like the petals of a blooming flower. A blinding light—similar to the pure magic beam of the Sibris—radiated from within the cocoon. I blinked repeatedly, my eyes watering. Through blurred vision, I watched in awe as the Prism lifted his torso into a sitting position, folded his knees against his chest, and then pushed up onto his feet. He turned to face us, his body looking like a luminous silhouette glowing from within.

He spread out his wings. They differed from the other Prometheans, their shape similar to those of the Luna moth with the longer strand at the tips of the lower wings. My chest constricted at this visual reminder that, like those moths, Xarin didn't have a digestive system. This magical moment of his birth also began the timer of his imminent death.

The blinding light surrounding him faded, as if absorbed within his body. Only then was I able to make out his features. When I first saw Acamon flying down into Keryth Valley, I remembered thinking he resembled an angel descending from above. Xarin looked like an ancient god coming to pass judgment upon mortals.

His skin was translucent. A galaxy of opalescent colors appeared to be trapped beneath. His face was breathtaking, with slightly oversized eyes that glowed white and devoid of any irises or pupils. A very delicate bump indicated the location of his nose, as if it had stopped halfway through development—at least by human standards. Although on the thin side, his lips had a very sensual curve to them, and somewhat quirked into a mysterious smile. He didn't have any hair on his head. However, it was covered in the same scales smattering his forehead and the bridge of his nose, similar to those boasted by other Prometheans. And his antennae, a pristine silver white, were much longer than average, recurving slightly behind his head.

My eyes flicked to his broad and toned chest. He was muscular but with the slender body of a dancer. Instead of the fluffy fur his people possessed at that location, scales forming an intricate pattern adorned his pectorals and descended over his stomach where a human man might have a happy trail of hair. For the rest, the same type of scales covered the sides of his arms and legs. But his crotch was smooth and empty like a child's doll.

He slowly flapped his wings behind him, the motion almost hypnotic. I instinctively understood that he was drying them, although they barely looked humid. Without a word, he hopped down the hovering platform his chrysalis had been sitting on and gracefully landed on the elevated dais of the Great Hall.

Behind me, a soft humming sound rose from the crowd. I didn't need to look over my shoulder to know they were clapping their wings in a sign of deference. At the corner of my eyes, I saw a few Senators get down on their knees behind the Black Guards. By the look on the faces of the latter, they appeared to internally debate whether they should kneel as well. My brain was telling me I should, but I was too transfixed to move as the Prism slowly advanced towards me.

His graceful gait gave the impression he was gliding more than walking. When he was barely a meter from us, Atlas—who was standing on my left—made as if to kneel. Xarin flicked his right wrist, the silver halo around his palm vanishing half a second later. I felt the kinetic force which tapped against my husband, preventing him from kneeling.

The Prism didn't speak a word or even spare him a glance.

Even without irises to clearly indicate what he was looking at, I knew beyond any doubt that he was staring at me. My breath caught in my throat when he stopped barely a foot in front of me. I tilted my head back to look at his face, although his glowing white eyes hypnotized me.

A shiver coursed through me, and my skin erupted in goosebumps when he cupped my cheeks with both hands. My skin tingled under his touch as if a weak electric current emanated from his palms. Simultaneously, a strange warmth radiated from them, spreading through every cell of my body. Xarin leaned forward. For an insane second, I thought he was going to kiss me, but his face stopped barely inches from mine as he studied my features.

I remained there paralyzed, and time appeared to freeze.

"My beautiful Prima," Xarin said at last.

A violent shiver coursed through me at the sound of his voice. It was breathy and androgynous, but also sounded as if dual voices overlapped.

"For centuries, I longed for the one who would finally help my people open their eyes to what always lay before them. For generations, I searched for you. The moment I touched your soul on that star vessel, I knew I found the one."

"Did you know?" I breathed out, my voice barely audible to my own ears.

I couldn't believe those were the first words I'd spoken to him. Since my arrival on Sylvar, I speculated about the thousand different things I wanted to ask him once I finally got to meet him face to face. And yet, my stupid mind went directly to the one question that plagued me since this entire adventure began. Did he know that a sick and dying queen was the cause? And if so, why not simply communicate it to his Primus or Prima? Was it one of those weird trials heroes had to go through in order to earn the right to live or receive the great prize they were chasing after?

He smiled, and his eyes glowed.

"No, my Venus. I didn't know what the solution was, only that you would help bring it to light. You had the right mindset to understand the messages I sent you and the proper tools to take them to the next level. Thank you for saving my people, for exceeding all the expectations I had set on you, and for being the greatest blessing I could have ever given this generation and the future ones to come."

"I only helped to the extent I could," I said in a voice filled with emotion. "Your people saved themselves with your help and mine. I just wish I could help save you, too."

He chuckled, his face taking on an air of incredulous amusement. He gently caressed my right cheek and the side of my hair.

"My Prima, I do not need to be saved," Xarin said as if it was self-evident. "I am here to serve a specific purpose. Thanks to all of you, my work is already half done. For the first time in centuries, instead of leaving with the feeling I barely did enough for this world, I will leave peaceful and excited at the prospect of returning. I cannot wait to see how my people will have achieved greater harmony when next I return. Do not be sad, my Venus. I am happy."

Something settled in my chest as I heard the sincerity in his voice. I didn't quite understand what he was or how any of this worked. For humans, as with many advanced species, religion had taken a significant back seat. While I personally didn't follow any organized religion, I believed in the existence of a greater power above and of people's immortal souls. I had traveled enough strange worlds to acknowledge that certain things couldn't be explained other than by faith.

In this instant, I believed with bone deep conviction that the being standing before me was of the divine.

He leaned forward and pressed his lips to my forehead with a tenderness that brought tears to my eyes. A moment later, his wings wrapped around me, filling me with the same electric warmth that his palms sent through my cheeks. My entire body tingled. The electric sparks seeped into my flesh, into my bones, and coursed through my veins. My knees wobbled, and a thousand icy needles pricked my spine from my lower back all the way to my nape and into my skull. I gasped, the odd sensation neither painful nor pleasurable.

It only lasted seconds before the Prism released me. I stared at him in shock while he smiled at me with a mysterious expression. At a visceral level, I knew he had done something to me, but I had no idea what. Before I could question him about it, he turned to look at Atlas, who was staring at him with a mesmerized expression.

"Atlas, my Blessed, my Shaydwin," Xarin said with a voice filled with so much affection it turned me upside down.

Judging by the expression on my husband's face, he was even more deeply affected to be thus acknowledged by a being his people deemed a god.

"Thank you for taking on the heavy burden I laid on your shoulders and leading the charge in our time of need. The purity of your soul called to me as strongly as your mate's. Your strength, honor, determination, and selflessness made you the perfect champion to lead our people out of the darkness they were losing themselves in and back into the light," Xarin said in a gentle voice filled with gratitude.

Like he had done with me, he cupped Atlas's face between his hands. I thought my man was going to cry so powerful was the emotion on his face. It wouldn't have been tears of sorrow, but of a joy too much to bear.

"You have honored and blessed me beyond anything I should have even been entitled to," Atlas said in a shaky voice. "You have made my life more meaningful than I ever could have dreamt of. You have given hope to people who had none left."

"No, my Atlas. *You* did that. While your peers may not have recognized your worth, I did, as did my Prima. We all have a role to play during our journey in the mortal realm. You have gone above and beyond. And for this, I thank you."

Once again, as he did with me, Xarin pressed his lips to Atlas's forehead before drawing him into his embrace and closing his wings around him. I stared in awe as his eyespots glowed with rainbow colors, electric tendrils appearing to crawl all over their diaphanous surface. He released him less than ten seconds later.

A general gasp escaped everyone upon seeing Atlas's wings. Even from where I stood, and despite them being folded like a cape behind him, it was plain to see that the white rims around his previously silver eyespots had expanded to engulf their entirety. Atlas would now be able to cast powerful magic of every color.

"Impossible!" Ajustus whispered in angry disbelief. "There can only be one blessing!"

By all accounts, the Prism could only grant a blessing once, which he had done on the day of our wedding. But was this truly a second blessing or merely the second-half of an initial partial blessing? Whatever the case, a single hard glare from Xarin to Ajustus sufficed to silence him and have him bow his head in shame.

Dismissing the disgraced Chancellor, Xarin returned his attention to Atlas. To my surprise, he took my left hand and placed Atlas's right one on top of mine.

"I entrust my Prima to you, Shaydwin. Take good care of her for me. Honor, protect, and love her," Xarin said before turning to me. "I give you my Blessed, Venus. Cherish, guide, and love him. Together, you will bring hope, peace, and relief to many other worlds as you have done for us. Remember us fondly during your journey."

I looked at Atlas. Our gazes locked, and something magical that transcended anything I ever felt before passed between us. I drowned in the dark depths of his eyes and barely realized he was drawing me into his embrace. As he leaned down to kiss me, I vaguely perceived Xarin moving away from us and heading towards Acamon and Kyrene.

But the world around us ceased to exist. All that mattered, all I could see, was the man I loved.

EPILOGUE
VENUS

That day, an even deeper change occurred within the Promethean society. By all accounts, the Prism rarely addressed the citizens once he emerged, aside from his Prima or Primus. After blessing me then Atlas—for a second time—Xarin took a moment to publicly thank Kyrene, Acamon, the Black Guards and many of the Monochromatics standing inside the Hall.

Historically, the Prism was heavily apolitical. While he did not make any speeches, his blatant embrace and gentle respect towards those deemed lesser sent a powerful message that none could ignore.

I watched him fly away with conflicting emotions. It was odd as for the three months spent among them, I somewhat thought of Xarin as a child in my care, almost a son. Seeing and speaking to the ancient god he turned out to be flipped all of that on its head. And yet, I couldn't deny the sense of loss that I felt knowing what fate awaited him.

To my great chagrin, we were not allowed to follow him or even bear witness to what he did in Keryth Valley. Apparently, the use of his powers not only destroyed any technology in range, but it could also prove hazardous to the health of any person in his vicinity. He spent a week in the valley with the remains of the Queen before heading back to Orist Valley to pursue his cleansing of the most devastated area of their world. According to Kyrene, it would likely take him at least two more rebirths before Xarin completed that task as the size of the territory affected during that cataclysm had been extensive.

Atlas and I remained on Sylvar for four more weeks after Xarin came out of his chrysalis. I'd been ready to get out of there almost the same day, but as the Razus of the Black Guard, Atlas had a lot to manage in order to do a smooth transition of power. Thankfully, aside from a few of the warriors getting seriously banged up when facing the Queen, we suffered no casualties. Therefore, no major reshuffling was necessary among the Black Guard or the Civic Protectors.

Unsurprisingly, Pythus was elevated as the new Razus. To my delight, he openly began courting a beautiful Gray Monochromatic of the Civic Protectors who had fought during Thaudras. It stirred some mumbling, but not the outcry and indignation that such a behavior would have triggered in the past.

The greatest surprise was that after Kyrene publicly claimed Acamon as her son—although that secret had been outed when she embraced him moments before he went into battle—more parents started trying to establish a line of communication with their estranged Achromatic and Monochromatic offspring.

Atlas's family did not.

As they lived in a different city, the sweeping changes occurring in Japhyr were occurring at a much slower pace in other areas, the difference more significant the farther they were located.

To my relief, Atlas was not crushed by this indifference. They were strangers to him. As he was planning on leaving this planet forever, he failed to see the point in attempting to establish a relationship with them now. It still boggled my mind that they wouldn't eagerly seek to be associated by blood to one of the main heroes of this entire saga.

Another great surprise was finding out that Senator Cassius presented a motion to open two new seats in the Senate, one reserved exclusively for an Achromatic and the other for a Monochromatic. Obviously, Ajustus attempted to challenge it. The motion barely passed, with a single vote majority. But all that mattered was that it did. Acamon was chosen by unanimous vote for the Achromatics. A few people tried to challenge that appointment as he wasn't an official resident of Japhyr.

As he remained the leader of his Pharom, and the people living in his village had no desire—at least in the short-term—to move to the main city, the challenge to his role as a Senator had merit. That said, as Whites still weren't allowed to live within the city walls, the locals had no choice but to grant this deroga-tion to allow fair representation.

A long and arduous path lay before them, but it was also an exciting one full of promises and possibilities. I just hoped they would tread carefully and not go to the other extreme. After being deprived of rights for so long, the sudden realization of how much more powerful they in fact were could lead to retalia-tion or some people even seeking to reverse their roles. Instead of leading them to a brighter future, it risked throwing them into an endless vicious cycle that would ultimately benefit no one.

But that was their journey to embark on. All I could do was drop a handful of hints about potential pitfalls to avoid.

Leaving Sylvar was bittersweet. Many of the Achromatics and Monochromatics perceived Atlas's departure as a form of abandonment in a time where one of the leading figures of their 'revolution' would be needed to help further their cause. Others saw this as further proof of the endless possibilities that this life had to offer. So long as you kept fighting and pushing forward, good things however improbable would eventually come to you.

It especially saddened me to part with Kyrene. After so many weeks working alongside her, she had become a friend. Because of the Prime Directive, communications with her and the rest of her people would be extremely limited if not completely nil.

That reality finally hit Atlas on the second day of our journey back to Earth. On a few occasions, he expressed concerns about how he would fit in my world, in my life, and what his purpose would be. He felt particularly distraught about the fact that the comfortable wealth he acquired on his homeworld was useless on the galactic scene. He didn't want to be a burden to me or to have no way of contributing to the household.

Granted, he knew that my family was rich and that I owned considerable personal wealth as well. Although credits were not an issue, I understood very well where he was coming from. In his shoes, I also wouldn't be comfortable at the prospect of relying entirely on my partner for my financial security and independence.

Initially, I hinted at him potentially joining the Enforcers. As the Razus of his people, he more than qualified to become an agent. Obviously, he would need to undergo some training regarding intergalactic laws and rules of engagement, but that would benefit him either way. While that piqued his curiosity, he surprised me by wanting a role that also included more intellectual involvement.

Over the course of the months leading to us defeating Thaudras, Atlas developed a great passion for studying the ancient lore of his people and deciphering the hidden messages within. In truth, his analytical skills played a huge role in turning the tide for us.

A contribution that didn't go unnoticed by both the UPO and the Enforcers.

As the Prometheans remained a major mystery to us, Atlas became an invaluable asset and a bridge between the intergalactic alliance and his people. Unbeknownst to us, the

UPO—through Linsea—had opened diplomatic discussions with the Promethean Senate.

As I guessed during my first conversation with the Temern Ambassador, the UPO was highly interested in the unusual power source that fueled the cities of their home world. But they also wanted to learn more about their species as a whole.

When the Enforcers first approached Atlas about helping them build a library or database about the Prometheans, I instinctively went into overprotective mama bear mode. But Atlas quickly had me take a backseat. My man didn't need me to babysit him on that front. As the head of security of the capital city of his planet, he knew better than to blindly divulge sensitive information that could jeopardize national security.

That said, considering how primitive Prometheans were in comparison, there weren't too many secrets Atlas could keep that would have any significant impact should the UPO and the Enforcers go rogue and try to invade them.

Still, with the approval of the Promethean Senate, Atlas began to collaborate with the Enforcers, not only to help them build their archives on his species, but also to fix many of the inaccuracies gathered over the years. All that data was naturally fully shared with the Prometheans. The generous compensation my mate received for this work was just the icing on the cake.

On top of this, Atlas discovered a new passion for combat simulations in the holodeck. Such a technology blew his mind. The first thing he did was work alongside a technician to recreate the Zuras Queen as realistically as possible, and then run through countless scenarios on how to more efficiently defeat her. This expanded into him developing extensive combat and training tutorials for his people. Thanks to the second blessing Xarin gave him, Atlas effortlessly cast every possible spell, like a White, just without the full extent of their power.

Speaking of blessings, it turned out the Prism's hug hadn't been all that innocent. In the week that followed the unusual embrace Xarin gave me, my eyes itched, pricked, and watered to the point I thought I was developing some kind of seasonal allergy. On the seventh day, it stopped. One look in the mirror revealed my irises now possessed an extra white ring at the outer edge.

Yes, ladies and gentlemen, I could now cast magic.

It was super weak. Nothing that would represent a real threat to anyone. But it was enough to perform basic healing, like fully mending a small cut, reheating the tea in my cup, or closing a door left ajar with a kinetic blast.

And above all, it was a major bragging right.

Even my sister Serena—with her pretty scales and enhanced strengths following her marriage to Szaro—was drooling with envy over my new abilities.

I never expected that visiting her would turn my world around the way it did, but I couldn't have been more grateful. I was happy and madly in love.

Three months and four days after emerging from his chrysalis, Xarin died.

That morning, the familiar tingling at the back of my nape took me aback. How could he reach me halfway across the galaxy and all the way to Earth? The tingling gave way to a wondrous sense of well-being, pure joy, and endless love that surged through me, wrapping around me like a warm blanket. It faded away after a few seconds. I sat there frozen, unsure how to react. I instinctively knew it had been Xarin saying goodbye. My mind shouted to me I should cry, but my heart felt at peace.

A discreet knock resounded on my office door moments before Atlas walked in. The look on his face told me everything I needed to know.

"You felt him, too," I said in a factual manner.

He nodded and smiled in a way that said everything would be okay.

I rose to my feet and went to him. He pulled me into his embrace, and I rested my head on the soft fur of his chest.

"Prisms cannot feel physical pain. Xarin didn't suffer. He was happy, at peace, and full of love," Atlas whispered in my hair in an appeasing tone.

I nodded against his chest before lifting my head to look at him. "He was. You know, we're both young enough that we might still be around the next time he returns. Maybe we'll get to see him again," I said, only half-teasing.

He snorted. "Now that my entire generation has survived Thaudras, I no longer doubt anything is possible. So let's add that to our list of long-term goals."

I chuckled. "Deal!"

"Deal," he echoed before kissing my lips.

~

ATLAS

I fought the urge to squirm while all but standing at attention as my father-in-law critically examined me. He didn't quite approve of the fact that my people never wore shirts or upper body clothes. But he seemed satisfied by the ornate white leather loincloth I was wearing for my traditional human wedding to his daughter. It had been designed by an up-and-coming human fashion designer called Farah Toussaint. Apparently, she was a close friend to Belle, the artist who would paint a portrait of Venus and me.

My mate's parents were both the rather intimidating sort. They constantly looked grumpy, like they always found some fault with you or were bracing for your flaws to suddenly jump at them when they least expected it. And yet, whenever they spoke to others about their daughters or sons-in-law, their pride shone brightly. More than once, I caught myself smiling as he boasted about the heroic deeds of both of his daughters saving countless innocents' lives.

"This will do," Mr. Bello said with begrudging approval as he finished examining my attire, down to the matching white leather sandals on my feet. "I trust you remember what to do?"

"Yes, Sir," I replied in a subdued tone.

"Good. Do not be late," he grumbled.

He cast a warning glance at Szaro, who was 'sitting' on top of his folded tail a little to our left, then exited the dressing room with determined steps. I turned towards my brother-in-law with a slightly traumatized expression. He chuckled, then his lips parted in a grin, showing the tips of his fangs, as he straightened into a 'standing' position.

Even a month after leaving Sylvar, I still struggled with the insane diversity of sentient species in the galaxy. Venus had shown me images of Szaro before. And yet, meeting him in person a few days ago still blew my mind. The male truly was impressive. His broad shoulders and muscular torso could have belonged to a Promethean, except for the fins on the side of his arms and the different type and pattern of his scales. But his lower body shaped like a long snake's tail fascinated me. The things he could do with the rattle at the tip, from appeasing or paralyzing, to enhancing the potency of the venom he injected into his prey left me reeling.

His face was also a source of wonder. Like my people, he had scales on his forehead and the bridge of his nose. But the vertical slits of his golden eyes disconcerted me. More than once, I found myself itching to touch the strange bumps that lined the inner side of the wide cobra hood on his head.

Szaro flicked his forked tongue at me. I immediately flicked my antennae, tasting the air as he was for any information it might reveal about his current state of mind.

His smile broadened.

"Do not be distraught by his demeanor," Szaro said in an amused tone. "Father Daniel totally approves of you."

"He sure has an odd way of showing it," I mumbled.

Szaro snorted. "He does. Considering the circumstances of my marriage to his younger daughter, believe me, he was far less charming with me than he currently is with you."

He burst out laughing at the horrified look I gave him.

"Do not fret, brother. He will soften in time, once he stops feeling like he must have his guard up," Szaro said reassuringly. "Daniel Bello merely needs to project the image of a strong patriarch worthy of his daughters. If he didn't deem you worthy of Venus, he would never walk her down the aisle and give her away to you. It takes a very special male to win the heart of Venus Bello. She waited a long time to find her soulmate. There's a reason you are the Blessed of Sylvar."

It was my turn to snort, although his words deeply touched me. I still struggled with accepting my own worth after a lifetime of being told I was less than.

"Thank you, Szaro," I said with sincere gratitude.

"Do not mention it," he said with a nonchalant wave of his hand. "Now, come on. Let's go get you married. I will try not to make a mess of this whole best man thing."

"By all means, do," I said teasingly. "Your blunders will hide my own."

He laughed and shook his head at me. "Neither of us shall make any blunder. We do not want to face the wrath of Venus's mother."

I shuddered, making him chuckle further, then let him lead the way into the garden where the wedding would take place. It was beautiful, set on the Bello estate, with a large body of water in front of an impressive mountain range in the backdrop. On the left, they'd erected a huge tent where the meal would be served, and people would dance. On the right, rows of benches and beautiful floral arrangements led to a small dais in front of the water. A group of musicians sat to the left of the dais.

Szaro gracefully slithered next to me as we proceeded down the makeshift aisle to the front where a female cleric awaited us. The throngs of relatives and friends of my mate filled the benches. My stomach fluttered with nerves as we took our positions on the dais. Having no doubt noticed my nervousness, Szaro flicked his tongue at me, then gently started shaking the rattle at the tip of his tail. A sense of peace immediately washed over me. I gave him a grateful sideways glance, and he winked at me.

I just really didn't want to mess things up.

An eternity later—which meant between five and ten minutes —the musicians started playing a soothing, slow paced instrumental music. My heart leapt in my chest. I straightened my shoulders, and my eyes widened as the bridal party exited the mansion.

Walking in male-female pairs down the aisle, three Black Guard couples opened the march, followed by three Brown Monos, then three Gray Monos, and finally four Whites, forming an almost perfect gradient from darkest to palest.

Tears pricked my eyes, and my throat constricted. As Venus wanted a traditional human wedding, she insisted on me allowing her to plan it according to her fairy tale vision. As I knew nothing of it, I'd been more than happy to yield to her in that. She told me what the general plan was, but never mentioned she would pull some serious strings to get a few of my people— my closest friends—to attend.

Prometheans didn't have the capacity to travel off-world.

The powerful emotion I felt was reflected on the faces of Pythus and Leodros, as well as Acamon closing the march. I swallowed and blinked rapidly to stem the tears pricking my eyes. Szaro placed a hand on my shoulder, giving it a gentle squeeze.

When they reached the front of the aisle, the bridal party split in half, the females going left and the males going right. They formed a V on each side of the dais, but standing in a way that wouldn't block the attendees' view of the proceedings.

The music shifted to something a bit more playful. Then the most adorable couple walked down the aisle: a Pink Polychromatic flower girl, and a Blue Polychromatic ringbearer. As they reached the front, the music once more changed, this time into the nuptial march.

A wave of emotion surged through me as I stared in awe at my mate. She was wearing a sleeveless, formfitting white dress with golden embroidery embedded with shiny stones. The skirt widened in ruffles below the knees all the way to the ground. Her face wasn't hidden behind a veil as was sometime the case for human brides. An intricate round headdress sat on top of her head like an oversized tiara. Behind it a long, diaphanous veil cascaded down her back and shoulders, turning into a long train held by two human females: her sister Serena and her friend Belle.

My mate was looking at me, bright-eyed and with a huge smile on her face, while hanging on to her father's arm as he led her down the aisle.

The world around us ceased to exist as she closed the distance between us. I vaguely heard her father say something as he placed Venus's hand in mine. I believed I replied something but couldn't swear to it. My brain couldn't process anything that wasn't her.

"My Venus," I whispered. "You're so beautiful. I love you so much."

She blinked away the tears welling in her eyes and gave me a trembling smile. "I love you, too, Atlas. More than life itself."

Overwhelmed by emotions, I leaned forward to kiss her. But seconds before our lips would touch, I heard Szaro clear his throat, and his right hand landed on my shoulder, pulling me back.

"We're not at that part yet," he whispered, his voice filled with amusement.

I stiffened, and my scales darkened while discreet chuckles rose from the attendees. Venus giggled and gave me a guilty look before looking sheepishly at the cleric. Far from offended, the priestess gazed upon us with amused approval.

The entire ceremony flew by in a daze. I barely recalled answering the priestess or even speaking my vows. I only remember her telling me I could kiss the bride. When our lips touched, the air crackled with magic energy as my fellow Prometheans cast dancing lights all around us, emulating the rare day of Radiance on our homeworld, while the guests cheered and applauded.

But all that mattered to me was the beautiful woman in my arms, my impossible dream, my soulmate, my love.

THE END

ACAMON

ZURAS QUEEN

VALREN

ALSO BY REGINE ABEL

THE VEREDIAN CHRONICLES
Escaping Fate
Blind Fate
Raising Amalia
Twist of Fate
Hands of Fate
Defying Fate
Imperial Fate

BRAXIANS
Anton's Grace
Ravik's Mercy
Krygor's Hope
Keran's Dawn

XIAN WARRIORS
Doom
Legion
Raven
Bane
Chaos
Varnog
Reaper
Wrath
Xenon
Nevrik
Rogue

PRIME MATING AGENCY
I Married A Lizardman

OTHER
True As Steel
Alien Awakening
Heart of Stone

337

ABOUT REGINE

USA Today bestselling author Regine Abel is a fantasy, paranormal and sci-fi junkie. Anything with a bit of magic, a touch of the unusual, and a lot of romance will have her jumping for joy. She loves creating hot alien warriors and no-nonsense, kick-ass heroines that evolve in fantastic new worlds while embarking on action-packed adventures filled with mystery and the twists you never saw coming.

Before devoting herself as a full-time writer, Regine had surrendered to her other passions: music and video games! After a decade working as a Sound Engineer in movie dubbing and live concerts, Regine became a professional Game Designer and Creative Director, a career that has led her from her home in Canada to the US and various countries in Europe and Asia.

Facebook
https://www.facebook.com/regine.abel.author/

Website
https://regineabel.com

Regine's Rebels Reader Group

https://www.facebook.com/groups/ReginesRebels/

Newsletter

http://smarturl.it/RA_Newsletter

Goodreads

http://smarturl.it/RA_Goodreads

Bookbub

https://www.bookbub.com/profile/regine-abel

Amazon

http://smarturl.it/AuthorAMS

www.ingramcontent.com/pod-product-compliance
Lightning Source LLC
Chambersburg PA
CBHW070340010826
48976CB00017B/354